BY CAROLINE PECKHAM

THE RISE OF ISAAC SERIES

CREEPING SHADOW

BLEEDING SNOW

Find the latest information on upcoming releases and more at:

http://www.carolinepeckham.com

For my sister, Susanne,
Without whom this book may never have seen daylight

ACKNOWLEDGEMENTS

A heartfelt thank you to:

My sister, Susanne, for the many hours spent reading, re-reading and re-re-reading Creeping Shadow to get it where it is today, for the late night book conversations with one foot out the door, and for her undying belief in my writing when I myself was in doubt.

My parents, Pauline and Steve, for all the years of support and love, for always taking the time to read to me until I was old enough to take the books from your hands, and for believing that I can succeed in any area of life that I set my heart on.

My close friend and flatmate Kirsty for taking the time to read my work and make it better than it was before and for putting up with my madness daily.

My dear friend Kathleen for being one of the first to read Creeping Shadow as a finished piece and for her contagious enthusiasm for life which never fails to inspire me.

My darling friend Vicky who, although has been almost ten thousand miles away for the past two years has supported me every step of the way and has been by my side since we first met all those years ago in junior school.

And for all my followers on Wordpress who share the passion and love for stories that I do.

CREEPING SHADOW

CAROLINE PECKHAM

CONTENTS

PROLOGUE

The Girl in the Road

Alison gripped the steering wheel tightly, her wedding band pinching her skin as it caught on the leather.

A stream of headlights briefly illuminated the beaded droplets hitting the windscreen and the view beyond was momentarily distorted before a squeal of wiper blades cleared the glass.

Heavy clouds curtained the sky, casting the world into dismal tones of blue and grey. The traffic trundled along at a painfully slow rate, the glaring red of brake lights intermittently punctuating the gloom.

Alison leant her cheek against the window to see how far she was from the turning.

Thump.

She ignored the noise and squinted in an attempt to improve her vision.

Thump.

Alison gritted her teeth in concentration and slowed to a halt as the car in front of her stopped dead.

Thump.

"Oliver, that's *enough*," she said, resting a hand firmly on her son's knee as his dirty wellington boot kicked out towards the glove compartment once more.

He grinned and she raised an eyebrow at him before releasing his leg.

Alison turned her attention back to the road, digging her nails into the soft material of the steering wheel. Sirens cut through the monotonous hum of idling engines and flashing red and blue lights caught her eye in the rear-view mirror.

A fire engine blared its horn as it passed on their left and Oliver sat bolt upright in his seat, watching it go by. An ambulance followed it closely and stopped a few hundred feet up ahead of them.

Alison edged forward as the traffic began to move once more. She spotted the turning and keenly pressed her foot down on the accelerator.

The car in front swerved onto the other side of the road, revealing a chaotic scene beyond it. An overturned vehicle lay in the middle of the tarmac surrounded by the emergency services. A police officer was guiding the traffic around the devastation.

"What happened to that car Mummy?" Oliver asked quietly.

"Someone's had an accident," Alison said softly, catching a glimpse of a man on a stretcher.

A sick feeling stirred inside her stomach as she indicated and quickly turned the car down a narrow lane.

Trees crowded over the road, casting the lane in darkness but the car's headlights banished the shadows as they moved. They drifted along the winding lane until the sound of sirens faded into the distance, leaving the main road far behind.

The rain suddenly gave way to a heavy fog and Alison braked, causing the wheels to skid on the mess of dead leaves that littered the ground.

Her heart fluttered and she took a shaky breath to calm herself.

"You okay?" she asked, glancing at Oliver but he was distracted by something ahead of them.

"There's someone out there," he whispered, leaning forward in his seat and narrowing his eyes.

Alison snapped her head back to face the front. She watched as the fog lifted, revealing a solitary figure beneath the bowing trees that encaged the road. The woodland swayed and leaned from a blustery wind but the person remained perfectly still, watching, waiting.

"Who'd be out in this weather?" she mumbled as she manoeuvred the car away from the roadside to give them a wide berth.

The mist descended once more so that a swirling cloud of white swallowed the road and the figure disappeared behind it.

"I think he's waiting for us," Oliver said in a quiet voice.

Alison went to respond but was silenced by a flash of purple light. It radiated throughout the mist, momentarily illuminating curling tendrils of fog as they moved across the road.

She slowed the car to a halt with a low squeal of the brakes, thumbing her wedding ring instinctively. She swallowed in an attempt to dislodge the lump that had risen in her throat.

"Mum, what is it?" Oliver asked in a hushed voice, a look of fright registering in his eyes.

Alison chewed her bottom lip and didn't answer.

"Perhaps we should go back," she whispered after a moment, not removing her gaze from the road.

Just as she pressed her foot to the clutch, the fog swirled and the figure emerged. The man strode toward them; he was tall, dark and shrouded by shadow. The headlights cast an eerie glow in the mist around him but his face remained obscured beneath a hood. He raised his hands towards the car and purple fire ignited within his palms, flaring at them threateningly.

A breath caught in Alison's throat and she lifted a trembling hand to her mouth, her fingers brushing her parted lips. The man closed his right hand, extinguishing the flames that flickered in his palm, and beckoned for her to exit the car.

Alison tentatively reached for the door handle.

"Where are you going?" Oliver asked in alarm.

"Just lock the car when I get out," Alison said, her voice shaking as she undid her seatbelt.

Every fibre in her body advised against it, but she was drawn toward the man with a desperate and hopeful longing that she couldn't ignore.

She fumbled to tuck her long, blonde hair into the hood of her raincoat and exited the vehicle.

"Mummy don't leave me!" Oliver cried, scrambling after her across the driver's seat.

Alison shut the door firmly and pressed the button on her key before he could follow. A *click* sounded as the car locked and she stowed the keys in her pocket, feeling a pang of guilt.

The mist clung to her skin as she turned towards the road and a gust of wind flung her hood back so that her hair whipped around her face in a flutter of strands. The rain drummed against the tarmac and the trees creaked and groaned as the wind bent them to their limits.

Alison blinked out into the darkness, her eyes falling on the figure. The man turned and walked away, causing the mist to snake around his body as he cut a path through it.

"*Wait!*" she called urgently, hurrying forwards.

She glanced back, not wanting to stray far from Oliver but the man's presence drew her onwards. He stopped at the side of the road and waited, his stance hauntingly familiar.

Her heart hammered as she approached him. "William?" she asked quietly, her bottom lip quivering.

She could sense the man's gaze on hers, though his features were still concealed beneath the shadow of his hood. He turned abruptly and strode into the trees, pressing his palms together to smother the last of the flames so he was instantly swallowed by darkness.

"No," Alison breathed then bolted after him.

She stumbled as her foot caught on something and, as she looked down, a gasp escaped her throat.

It was a child. She must have been around six years old, the same age as her son.

Alison dropped to her knees beside the girl and pushed a mop of blonde hair away from her pale face. Her eyes were heavy with dark circles and her lips were a worrying shade of blue. She wore only a thin, summer dress that was soaked through to the skin.

Alison pressed two fingers to the girl's neck and found the steady beat of a pulse. She glanced back to the road, hoping to see the pinpricks of headlights heading towards them. She cursed when she saw none and rummaged in her pocket for her phone. It was dead, though she was certain it had been fully charged.

"Dammit," she hissed, staring at the girl as she decided what to do.

Alison gritted her teeth and lifted the child into her arms, sparing a last, hopeful glance back toward the trees as she turned to her car.

She hurried over, awkwardly retrieving the keys from her pocket and opening it with a *click*. She wrenched the back door open and laid the girl across the seat. The child groaned and Alison relaxed marginally. She was still alive.

Oliver was craning over the passenger seat to look at her. "Is she okay?" he asked, his eyes wide in alarm.

"I think so, but we need to get her to a hospital," Alison said, keeping her voice as calm and level as she could manage.

Alison shut the back door and returned to the driver's seat. Oliver was still looking around at the girl.

"Get your seatbelt back on," she instructed, pulling him around to face the front.

He strapped himself in and she accelerated down the road.

* * *

Alison sped into the hospital car park and stopped outside Accident and Emergency, throwing Oliver a reassuring smile.

"Here we are. Let's go. Put your raincoat on," she said.

Alison scooped the girl off of the back seat and rushed towards the entrance whilst Oliver splashed his way across puddles behind her. She sprinted through the hospital doors, nudging people aside as she went. She skidded to a halt at the front desk, her wet shoes squeaking on the floor.

The receptionist sprang to her feet and pressed a button on the console in front of her. "What happened?" she asked as a shrill buzzing sounded in the ward behind her.

"I found her in the road. I don't know if she was hit by a car o-or," she stuttered, thinking of the man who had led her to the child. "She's unconscious!" Alison blurted, adjusting her hold on the girl.

The woman gave a sharp nod and turned expectantly at the sound of a squeaking wheel. A short man appeared, hurrying towards them with a hospital trolley.

"Lay her down here," the man instructed.

Alison gently placed the girl on the mattress. She leant over her, brushing wet strands of hair out of the girl's face. She stepped aside as the man pushed the trolley back into the ward.

Alison gripped Oliver's shoulder firmly and gave him a half smile. She felt tears spring to her eyes and wiped them away with the back of her damp sleeve.

"Are you alright, Mummy?" Oliver looked up at her.

"I'm fine, Olly." She sniffed then lifted Oliver into her arms, kissing his cold, wet cheek. "Where can we wait?" she asked the receptionist.

"Down the hall and to the left." She gave them a sympathetic smile as Alison nodded and walked away.

* * *

It hadn't been long before the police had shown up to question Alison. At first they seemed suspicious but, once she had taken a breathalyser test and answered their questions, their attitude had softened towards her.

She had neglected to mention the figure in the road. In hindsight, she wasn't sure whether it was right to protect a man on the assumption that he was her husband.

Just over an hour had passed and they had heard nothing.

She was unable to keep Oliver occupied any longer and his boredom was beginning to show. His damp clothes were sticking to him which was only further contributing to his already aggravated state.

"*Muuum*, when are they going to let us see her?" he moaned.

"Not much longer, Olly," she said with a sigh, running her fingers through his dark, brown hair.

"We've been waiting for *hours*."

"Don't exaggerate. I'm sure we'll hear something soon," she said. "Why don't you draw a nice picture for her?"

"Mmm, okay!" he said with renewed enthusiasm and returned to the table in front of him, reaching for a pencil.

Alison sat back in her chair and anxiously picked at the pink nail varnish on her fingernails. The once-busy waiting room had diminished to a sparse few people who were slowly called away until only one remained. She picked the last stubborn flake of varnish from the tip of her index finger and absentmindedly brushed the remnants from her knees.

"Would you like to see her now?" a voice spoke.

Alison looked up to see the receptionist smiling at her kindly.

"Yes," she said, jumping to her feet.

"She's doing well. The doctor wants to keep an eye on her overnight but he's satisfied there's nothing wrong with her," the receptionist said.

Oliver grabbed his picture and hurried to keep up as the receptionist led them down a corridor.

As Alison opened the door she spotted the girl lying in bed. Her eyes flickered open as they entered the room and Alison's gaze locked with the child's bright green irises. Something instinctive stirred inside her and she sensed an attachment to the girl that she couldn't explain.

"Hello, sweetie. I'm Alison, how are you feeling?" she asked.

She moved to the chair beside the bed and took the girl's small hand in her own. She blinked at Alison but didn't answer.

Oliver climbed up onto the bed, knelt next to the girl, and offered her the picture he had drawn. She sat up, reached for it and unfolded the page then a smile pulled at the corner of her mouth. Alison stifled a laugh as she caught sight of the drawing: a pink unicorn with a machine gun for a horn.

"I'm Oliver. What's your name?" her son asked the girl.

"May," she said quietly.

"Is that your name? May?" Oliver asked excitedly.

"May," she repeated, looking up at Alison with a wide-eyed gaze. She smiled and the little girl smiled shyly back at her.

"What else do you remember?" Alison asked gently.

May shook her head. "Nothing."

"What about your parents?" Alison tried.

May shook her head, tears gathering in her eyes.

"That's okay." Alison squeezed her hand.

"Where's your family?" Oliver asked.

"I don't know," May whispered. "I can't remember anything."

1

Gone

Ten Years Later

Oliver hurried out of the school gates, rounding the corner to find his sister waiting for him on the curb. Her uniform was tucked in and buttoned up neatly whereas Oliver's shirt hung messily over his trousers and his tie was undone, pointlessly strung around his neck. The traffic had eased to a slow trickle, just a few parents arriving to pick up kids who were attending extracurricular activities.

May shook her head at him in mock disappointment and he laughed, glad she had received his text about waiting for him. Whenever Oliver had to leave school late she was always there to walk home with him because of all the clubs she attended. They were polar opposites in that sense, though Oliver never begrudged her the constant A grades or the way the teachers favoured her. He just had no interest in school even though, when he actually tried, he did pretty well.

Oliver grinned and jogged the last few steps over to May. "Sorry," he said.

"Save it for Mum. That's the second detention this week, you know?"

"How do you know I had detention? Maybe I decided to stay on to finish my homework," Oliver said, fighting a smile.

May gave him a look that said she knew better and he laughed.

"Was it Mrs Robertson again?" she asked, grimacing at the woman's name.

He nodded and they started walking down the road, heading home. "She has it in for me. It was only some stupid essay on career choices I was supposed to do."

"Yeah but if you just sucked it up and *did* your homework she wouldn't be able to give you detention."

"She'd just find something else," Oliver said with a shrug.

"I guess, but at least mum wouldn't get so angry," May said, walking around a puddle to avoid getting her shoes wet.

Oliver ran a hand through his dark hair and knew his mum would want to cut it again soon. As a hairdresser, she rarely let either of them have a split-end for more than a day.

They approached the local shops and Oliver nudged May towards them, reaching into his pocket. He retrieved the list his mum had given him that morning and picked up a basket as he entered the shop. May trailed behind him, tapping out texts on her phone as he dropped milk, bread and cheese into the basket.

He paid and they exited the shop, discovering that it had started raining. May retrieved an umbrella from her bag and opened it. Because he was taller, Oliver took it and held it above their heads, the raindrops drumming on the canvas as the shower became a downpour.

They quickened their pace to a jog and turned down the narrow lane that led home. The arching trees provided some cover as they hurried along and eventually turned onto their road, moving past the row of houses until they reached number seven.

They skirted their mum's car on the driveway and Oliver retrieved the keys from his pocket. He jiggled the key in the lock in the usual way until it turned then held the door open for May, collapsing the umbrella before entering himself.

The small porch was a mess of shoes and one wall was laden with coats hanging on hooks. They kicked off their shoes and went through the next door that gave access to the house.

Oliver mentally prepared himself for the conflict he was about to face. "Mum?" he called.

There was no answer so they moved into the small living room where family photos gazed at them from every wall.

May dropped down into an armchair and switched the television on. "Maybe she's with a client," she suggested.

Oliver nodded and exited the room, moving past the cream-carpeted staircase towards the kitchen. There was a conservatory at the back of the house where their mum cut people's hair. He glanced into it, confirming it was empty before returning to the kitchen.

Oliver placed the food he had bought in the fridge. As he shut the door he spotted a chopping board and recipe book laid out with a series of ingredients atop the mottled, blue worktop. The book was open on a recipe for a casserole.

He grabbed the house phone on the counter and dialled his mum's mobile number. It started to ring and he turned abruptly at the sound of a song playing in the kitchen, hanging up as he spotted her phone which was making the noise. It lay on the dining table which was tucked into a corner beneath a noticeboard; it was crammed full of important letters, bills, events and cards.

He checked the calendar pinned up on one corner, noticing she had only had two appointments that morning. He picked up her phone and tried to unlock it but couldn't guess the passcode.

Oliver exited the kitchen and went upstairs, checking the bathroom before entering his own room. He changed out of his damp uniform into jeans and a t-shirt then pulled on a hoody, zipping it up against the cold.

His room was small and simple with white walls and navy sheets on the bed. He had a desk below a window for his laptop and a shelf beside his bed for books composed mainly of thrillers, mysteries and detective stories.

He opened his laptop and found it still switched on from the previous night. The webpage he had been browsing was still up, describing the ideal candidate for the British security service. He hadn't fitted the profile, especially in terms of his grades though it was the only career he could ever imagine himself in. He had deleted his essay on career choices after realising that.

"Olly?" May called from the hallway.

He shut the laptop with a sigh and hurried out, spotting May across the hall looking into their mum's room.

"What is it?" Oliver asked.

She turned to him, looking pale and frightened.

He blinked in surprise, feeling his gut constrict. "What's wrong?"

"We need to call the police," May said, her eyes wide with fear.

Oliver hurried across the hall and pushed past her into his mum's room.

He gasped in shock.

It had been ripped apart as if someone had taken a chainsaw to her possessions. The curtains and sheets lay in tatters, feathers were strewn everywhere from the torn pillows and the bed was chopped clean in half.

"MUM?" May shouted, her voice shaking.

There was no response.

Oliver's heartbeat thundered in his ears. "She's not here," he breathed.

May reached into her pocket and retrieved her mobile. Oliver gazed at her numbly as she phoned the police, feeling as if he was going into shock.

* * *

Oliver and May sat in the living room while they waited for the police to arrive. They were given the advice to ring their mum's friends incase she was with someone. They were still dialling people when the doorbell made them jump.

Oliver sprinted to answer the door with May hot on his heels. He wrenched it open and found a young policeman standing there. He had blonde hair that was swept back over his head and gelled perfectly into place.

"Good evening, I'm Officer Hawking. I hear your mother has gone missing, is that correct?"

"Yeah, come inside," Oliver said, stepping aside to allow the man access.

Hawking stood in the hallway, gazing around it as if he could sense something they couldn't. "How long do you suspect she's been missing?" he asked.

"I'm not sure. We were home from school by four thirty so anytime before then," Oliver said.

"She was here this morning," May added.

Hawking nodded slowly.

"Her room's been ripped apart," Oliver said frantically, gesturing to the stairs.

"What if she's been hurt?" May said, her eyebrows knitting together.

Hawking didn't respond but instead began climbing the stairs so they hurried after him. "Which room is your mother's?"

Oliver led him along the corridor and gestured to the door on the right. He gulped, feeling his mouth go dry as he caught sight of the devastation beyond the doorway.

Hawking moved ahead of them and glanced into the room, nodding as he took in the scene. "Okay. Perhaps you'll leave me a moment to do a sweep of the room?"

Oliver gazed at him in surprise. "Don't you want to take a statement? O-or ask us about places she might be or enemies she might have?" he stuttered, overwhelmed with worry.

Hawking raised a single eyebrow at him. "*Does* she have any enemies?"

"Of course not," May snapped.

"Well then," Hawking said. "We'll get to the questions once I have completed my investigation. Thank you." He dismissed them, disappearing into the room.

Oliver moved to follow the man but May pressed a hand to his shoulder and shook her head. He gritted his teeth and let out a sharp breath of frustration through his nose, letting her lead him back downstairs.

As they descended to the hallway, the doorbell sounded once more.

Oliver ran towards it, desperately hoping he would find his mum standing outside waiting to explain everything. He flung open the door to find a policewoman there and his stomach dropped with disappointment.

"Hello, I'm Officer Welling I've come about a report of a missing person. Can I come in?" She had sharp, angular features and dark hair that was tied in a knot at the back of her head.

"What?" Oliver frowned in confusion. "There's already an officer here."

"There is?" Welling asked, furrowing her brow.

The officer lifted her radio and pressed a button, making a short jingle of noise. She spoke into the receiver and waited for an answer.

"*You're the first to respond. No other officer on the scene. Over.*"

"There's a guy upstairs," May insisted.

Welling nodded. "Show me where he is. Perhaps there's been some confusion."

They led her upstairs and Oliver gestured to his mother's room. "Mum's stuff's been destroyed. The other guy is investigating it."

Welling nodded and walked ahead of them, disappearing into the room.

She exited a moment later. "There's no one in there. And what items were destroyed exactly?"

Oliver sprinted past her and stopped dead as he gazed into the bedroom.

It was in perfect condition as if the room had never been ransacked and there was no sign of Officer Hawking anywhere.

May appeared beside them and gasped. "What's happened? How has it all been put back together?"

"What's going on here? You kids aren't winding me up are you? It's an offence to waste police time."

"We're *not*," May said in a panic, turning to her. "Our mum's missing."

Welling frowned. "When did you last see her?"

"This morning before school," May said.

"Her car's in the drive and I tried ringing her but her phone's in the kitchen. She never goes anywhere without it," Oliver said.

"Okay guys. Well everything looks pretty normal here, there's no sign of a break-in so I'm sure you don't need to be alarmed. No doubt she's got held up somewhere or she's just popped round to a neighbours' house," Welling said calmly.

"No. She wouldn't. Why would she be out this late and not ring? And her room was destroyed! That guy must have fixed it somehow," Oliver said, becoming breathless with his anger.

"You need to take a deep breath and calm down. Can you ask a relative to come and stay with you?" Welling asked.

"We don't have any relatives," May said, shaking her head.

"A friend then or perhaps a neighbour?" Welling suggested.

"We don't need to ring anyone. We need to be looking for our mum," Oliver snapped.

"A person cannot be reported as officially missing until they've been gone for more than twenty four hours. If she hasn't turned up by tomorrow-"

"No! You're not listening. Her room was destroyed, what if she's been attacked? That guy must have something do with it. He must have been pretending to be a policeman!" Oliver said wildly.

Welling eyed him suspiciously. "Have you taken any illegal substances tonight?"

"*What*?" Oliver asked in disbelief.

"Alcohol? Drugs?" Welling pressed.

The insinuation set his blood boiling and he went to retort but May touched his arm. She filled her gaze with warning then turned back to the officer. "He's not had anything. He's just upset."

Oliver shrugged his arm out of her grip but bit his tongue before he said anything more.

Welling frowned. "I want you to call a friend or neighbour to take care of you tonight. If your mother hasn't turned up by tomorrow you can file a missing person's report down at the station and we'll start an investigation into her whereabouts."

"Fine," Oliver said through gritted teeth, anxious for the woman to leave so he could get out looking for his mum.

"I'll be waiting here until this is all organised, you understand?" Welling said, watching him closely.

"We don't need a guardian, we're sixteen," Oliver said, trying to keep his tone level.

"By law, you are only allowed to be left alone overnight if you are at no risk of harming yourselves. As I'm quite aware that you are both going to charge out the front door the second I leave, I'm deeming it more appropriate that you're under adult supervision tonight."

Oliver nodded, trying to keep his anger contained as he walked off down the corridor to retrieve the phonebook.

He couldn't understand how Hawking had done it but knew, if it was worth covering up, his mum must be in serious trouble.

2

The Family Tree

Oliver sat next to his sister in the back of a BMW that smelt of leather and lemons, suggesting it had recently been valeted. The car wound through narrow lanes surrounded by trees that arched over the road, the tips of their leaves tickling each other in the wind.

Their social worker, Mr Greene, leant around to talk to them from the passenger seat. May continued to stare out of the window, her eyes glassy and her jaw set.

"I know this is going to be difficult but your grandfather is very excited for you to come and live with him," Mr Greene said.

"We've never even met him," Oliver replied, folding his arms.

"No, but that doesn't change the fact that he's family and he'll take very good care of you both."

"I just want to go home," May muttered.

"We shouldn't be moving so far away. I want to help the police look for her," Oliver snapped.

"She's only been missing a week and we're already being relocated," May agreed.

Mr Greene gave them a sympathetic look. "The police know what they're doing. It's best if you leave them to it. I can let you know if there's any news on your mother's whereabouts."

"We should be helping. No one knows her as well as we do," Oliver said stubbornly, resenting the man's pity.

"You'll feel better when you get there. Wait 'til you see the place. You guys are gonna love it," Mr Greene said, turning back to face the front and closing the subject.

"I don't care how nice it is. It isn't our home," Oliver said, catching a look of frustration from May.

He sighed and leant against the window, balling his fists. He had to bite his tongue more than he normally would of late, knowing that his actions could affect the both of them. His quick temper had already caused him problems with the police during the investigation.

May had warned him not to mention Hawking again and even they had barely spoken of it since. He couldn't understand how the man had managed it and fear raked at his heart when he considered the notion that Hawking had something to do with his mum's absence. Since that night, he was left in a state of anxiety and found himself plagued by vivid dreams that brought his fears to life.

After a week of searching, the police had looked for his mum's will. It had stated that her father was to be given full custody of her children in the event of her death. Oliver knew next to nothing about his grandfather who lived miles away in the countryside. It was only now that he truly appreciated how odd that was.

* * *

The car entered a quaint village, winding up a hill past a small school. Locals were meandering up the street looking happy and content with their lives and Oliver stared out at them bitterly, wishing he was back in his own home.

The car approached a steep hill covered in trees on the outskirts of the village. At its base sat a wide gateway with an ornate sign upon it that announced their arrival at Oakway Manor. The driver indicated, turned off of the road, and drove through it.

The track wound higher and higher up the hill, the trees so dense that they blotted out the sunlight. Oliver peered into the gloom and May pressed her face gently against the window.

"Are we nearly there?" she asked.

"Yes, this is your grandfather's estate," Mr Greene said.

"What? He owns all of this?" Oliver asked, distracted for the first time.

"Uhuh, great isn't it?" Mr Greene said enthusiastically.

"I guess," Oliver said, his eyes flicking from tree to tree as the car moved through the woodland.

They emerged in a clearing and caught their first glimpse of their grandfather's home. Oliver sat forward in his seat, taking in the grand building.

It looked as though it had once been a fine, manor house but now the grey stone was cracked and aged; thick vines wrapped around the walls which seemed to be holding parts of the building together.

A colossal tree appeared to have grown straight through the heart of it, creating a gaping hole where it burst through the rafters. The canopy hung over the house in a display of brightly coloured leaves, splashes of yellow and orange signalling the start of Autumn. Branches reached out through the top windows and their boughs were bent where they had grown skyward in search of sunlight.

"May, are you seeing this?" Oliver glanced at her.

"I see it. Why's there a tree growing out of it?" she asked, looking stunned.

"There you are. What do you make of that then?" Mr Greene asked smugly, as if unveiling a grand prize.

"Are we actually going to be living here?" Oliver looked at the man disbelievingly, unable to truly accept how much his life was changing.

"Yep," he said, smiling at them.

Oliver felt an irrational surge of anger towards the man though he knew Mr Greene wasn't to blame for their situation.

The driver revved the car's engine as it laboured up the steepest part of the hill, coming to a stop with a jolt as he pulled the handbrake. Mr Greene exited the vehicle and opened the door for May. Oliver climbed out slowly and looked up at the building, wondering who would choose to live in such a strange house.

An enormous, wooden door creaked as it opened beneath a twisted, stone porch. A tiny man appeared in the doorway wearing a suede coat and a fancy neckerchief. He had a thick head of dark hair accompanied by a short beard.

Their grandfather was much younger-looking than Oliver expected and would have assumed the man was in his forties if he hadn't known it was impossible. He had a round nose and large, round eyes to match which bulged as they landed on Oliver.

In his haste, the man half ran, half fell down the crumbling, stone steps. He grabbed Oliver's hand and shook it vigorously.

"Oliver, great to finally meet you. Just wonderful. Don't you look like your mother? You can see she got all the looks in the family, eh? Good for you, good for you."

Oliver nodded vaguely, feeling bemused. "Thank you, er, sir."

"Oh good heavens, you can forget about calling me *sir*. We're family after all, aren't we? Just call me Ely. Bit odd after all these years to call me Grandpa, I'd expect."

Oliver opened his mouth to answer but his grandfather dove towards May before he had a chance.

"And this must be May. Aren't you a beauty? At least those parents of yours left you something, eh? Whoever they were."

Oliver noticed May's cheeks touch with the familiar hint of crimson that often appeared in front of strangers.

"Thank you," she said quietly, shaking Ely's outstretched hand. "You don't look old enough to be our grandfather."

Ely chuckled, running a hand through his hair and Oliver suddenly noticed there were, in fact, flecks of grey in it. "You're very kind but I can assure you I'm quite ancient." He rubbed his eyes as if he were weary and when he took his hand away Oliver noticed heavy creases around them.

Oliver frowned, wondering why he had ever thought the man looked so young.

Their grandfather's expression became grave as he surveyed them. "But of course you must both be feeling quite distraught about your mother. I'm sure she'll turn up soon, no doubt there's a perfectly reasonable explanation for her disappearance."

Oliver nodded stiffly, thinking of Hawking once more and May mumbled her assent.

Mr Greene moved in front of them and offered his own palm in greeting. "Good to see you again, Mr Fox. We've had a long trip from London, would you mind if we went inside?"

"Not at all, not at all. Follow me," Ely said, spinning on his heel and traipsing back into the house.

They followed him and arrived in an impressive hallway where the wooden floorboards creaked beneath their feet. The trunk of the tree grew up through the centre of the room, almost six feet wide with a carved, circular door hanging open on silver hinges. Inside, an alluring staircase of polished wood spiralled upwards out of sight.

"What do you think, guys?" Mr Greene asked excitedly.

"It's, different," Oliver said slowly.

"Yeah, great," May said uncertainly, tucking a strand of hair behind her ear.

A *tip-tapping* noise came down the stairs. It grew louder and louder until a large, long-bodied black cat appeared at the bottom wearing a fancy bow tie around its neck. Its eyes were circular and fiery orange in colour. The animal sat and trilled a loud meow.

Ely lifted the creature into the air and the cat snuggled into his arms, looking back at them curiously. "This is Humphrey," Ely announced.

May stepped forward and petted him, making the cat purr loudly.

"Is there somewhere we could talk privately, Mr Fox? There are a few final things we need to go over," Mr Greene said.

Ely nodded and placed Humphrey on the floor where the cat began weaving in between his legs.

"Of course, not a problem." Ely turned to Oliver and May. "Why don't you go and get your things in from the car? Then I can show you two to your rooms," he said, dismissing them and ushering Mr Greene through a door to their left.

Oliver went back to the car and the driver popped the boot. He swung his bag onto his back and chucked May's to her before walking back up to the house.

"I can't believe this is happening," May said, fiddling with the strap of her bag.

"We'll just be here 'til they find her. This place isn't that bad," he said.

"Yeah, but it's not home," she said, almost accusingly.

"I didn't say it was," Oliver said with a frown.

They returned to the hallway where Mr Greene was shaking Ely's hand as they said their goodbyes. Mr Greene turned to them as they entered.

"If you have any problems you can always give me a ring," he said in a serious tone, passing them each a card with his contact details on. "I'll let you know if there's any news on your mother's whereabouts. Just sit tight."

Mr Greene clapped Oliver on the shoulder and walked through the front door, leaving him feeling thoroughly abandoned.

"Wonderful. Cheery-bye," Ely said, shutting the large, wooden door with a *bang* that echoed up through the house. He turned to Oliver and May. "Follow me."

Ely disappeared into the tree trunk as he ascended the staircase with Humphrey trotting merrily after him. Oliver placed a foot on the first step and looked up to see the stairway spiralling out of sight above him.

As they climbed, he caught glimpses of corridors that led away from the staircase. Some were dark and uninviting whilst others bright and intriguing. They reached the higher levels where tree branches curved along the ceiling and stretched out into the sunlight through crumbling holes in the walls.

Ely led them down a wide corridor where vines were splayed across the wallpaper resembling long, spindly fingers. They reached two doors on either side of a vast, amber-tinted window which caused a warm light to be cast across the mahogany floor.

"This is your room, May." Ely gestured to the room on the right. "It was your mother's when she was growing up," he said with a sad smile.

Oliver instantly burned with curiosity.

"And, Oliver, you'll be staying in my son's old room. Your uncle Pilford was a bit of a neat-freak but you can be as messy or as tidy as you like." He smiled.

Oliver started at the news that he had an uncle and felt a pang of fury at his mother for never telling him. He buried the feeling as guilt writhed inside his stomach like a worm. He didn't want to be angry at her until she had returned safe and sound.

Oliver stepped up to the tall door, turned the intricate handle at its centre with a *squeak* of metal then moved into the room.

The ceiling was high but the bedroom felt cosy. It was swathed in rose-tinted, evening sunlight that bled into the room from a glass-paned door which led onto a balcony. A small fireplace crackled quietly on one side and a bed was tucked in a corner next to it.

There was a worn, red armchair in front of the fire and a teak bookcase sat beside it. Oliver approached it and found the shelves empty. Dust marked the edges where books had sat, suggesting they had recently been removed. He frowned, wondering why they hadn't been left in place.

Oliver turned and went through the glass door, gazing out from the balcony. It overlooked a steep garden that ran down to a mass of trees, beyond which, were fields and farmland as far as the eye could see. Magenta-coloured clouds hung in the sky which was painted in pastel shades of pink, orange and purple. It was so unlike the city townhouse he was used to but he couldn't deny that the setting was beautiful.

Looking up, Oliver saw the large canopy of the tree that grew through the house, swaying in the wind. Withered, brown leaves came floating down in a sudden breeze that caused the hairs on his arms to rise.

He noticed that the balcony allowed him to enter May's room so he moved across the platform, slid the other door open and joined his sister and Ely.

Oliver recognised his mother's style in the decoration of the large room. Soft, pink cushions were piled on the bed and silk curtains hung around the balcony door. There was an oak wardrobe on one side of the room and an exquisite dressing table which held trinkets he itched to examine. With a flutter of fear he recalled her devastated room back at their old house but forced the image away.

"What do you think of your room?" Ely asked him.

"It's great. Thank you," Oliver said, a little overwhelmed.

"No need to thank me. I'm more than happy to have you here. It really is marvellous to meet you both finally."

"Why *haven't* we met you before?" May asked, turning to face him.

"I'm sure your mother had her reasons," he said vaguely.

"What about our uncle? Where's he?" Oliver asked curiously.

"Pilford? He works for a university," Ely said.

"Can we meet him?" Oliver asked hopefully.

Ely opened and closed his mouth before answering. "Perhaps, one day." He began backing towards the door. "I'll leave you to get settled in."

Ely exited the room before they could ask any more questions.

May eyed the room and ran a finger across a silken throw on the end of the double bed. "I can't believe Mum used to live in this place and she never brought us here," she said, sounding hurt.

She sat down on the edge of the bed as Oliver walked over to the dressing table. There was a selection of necklaces hanging on a knob by the mirror. He picked one up and let it run through his fingers, the small crystal on one end glistening as it caught the light.

May sighed. "Is this it then? Mum's really gone?"

Oliver frowned and turned back towards her. "Just until they find her."

"But where is she? What if something awful's happened to her?" May's eyes watered but she didn't cry. "That Hawking guy, her room - what if we told Ely? Maybe he'd be able to convince the police?"

Oliver picked at the gem hanging on the chain in his hand, avoiding her eye. "Why would he believe us? All the evidence is gone."

"But we could *try*," May implored.

Oliver dropped the necklace back onto the surface and looked up at her. "He'll just think we're making it up, like everyone else does."

She sighed in resignation and Oliver began rummaging through the drawers in the dressing table, curious to see more of his mother's possessions.

"We don't have to start school right away, do we? I can't bear facing people just yet," May said, sounding exasperated.

"At least you make friends easy. I think it took me about four years to make friends at our old school," he exaggerated.

May laughed. "That's because I actually *attend* school though," she said with a grin.

Oliver shut the final drawer, letting out a breath of frustration. "They're all empty."

"I guess Ely must've cleared out Mum's stuff to make room for ours," May said with a shrug.

"I'd like to see her things though," Oliver said, a mischievous glint entering his eye. "I wonder where he put them."

May raised her eyebrows at him. "Maybe he'll show us."

"Or we could just have a look around ourselves?" he suggested.

"I don't know if he'd be very happy with us snooping around," May said doubtfully.

Oliver walked purposefully towards the door. "Well if he has nothing to hide he won't mind us exploring, will he?"

3

Hidden in the Dark

There were two other doors in the corridor so Oliver tried the first one, just along from his mother's old room. He turned the handle but it was locked.

Oliver moved to the room opposite and, with a surge of excitement, found it open. He peered inside, finding a gloomy bedroom with heavy curtains drawn across the window and a thick, musty smell in the air.

Oliver ran his fingers across the wall, feeling the grooves of textured wallpaper beneath his touch. He discovered a light switch and flicked it, illuminating stacks of boxes piled on the floor and atop a bed.

"Should we go in?" May asked, peeking under his arm.

Oliver nodded and crept into the room. He brushed his fingers across a box on the bed and found a layer of dust deposited on it. A tingle ran up his spine as he got the distinct feeling that the room was somehow sacred, perhaps having remained untouched for years.

He pushed his fingers under the lip of the closed box and lifted it but the cardboard resisted, unmoving. He frowned and tugged at it harder but the box wouldn't open.

"That's weird," he muttered.

"What is?" May asked, hovering by the doorway.

"I can't open it." He tried the box beside it but was met with the same problem.

He lifted one onto the floor and knelt down beside it. Despite pulling hard, the cardboard didn't even tear.

"Leave it," May insisted through gritted teeth.

He turned to find her looking at him anxiously. "Aren't you curious?"

She nodded and tucked a long strand of hair behind her ear. "Yes, but it doesn't look like Ely wants us going through this stuff. He's glued the boxes shut."

"If it were glue I could rip it," Oliver muttered thoughtfully.

"Olly, *come on*," May said with a slight edge to her voice.

He rolled his eyes and exited the room. "Do you reckon we might have another uncle or aunt we don't know about?"

"Maybe," May replied, sounding hopeful. "We should ask Ely."

They descended to the floor below and tiptoed down a corridor that ended in a single, large door. Oliver turned the handle and pushed it open, wincing as the hinges creaked. May clapped a hand to her mouth as she started giggling and Oliver grinned.

He peeped inside and found an enormous bedroom with a fourposter bed draped in grey material at one end. At the other, was a colossal desk made from dark wood engraved with symbols and patterns around the edges. It ran the length of an entire wall and had a hollow space beneath it where a four-wheeled stool was located. Piled atop the desk was a mountain of papers and books.

"This must be Ely's room. Maybe we shouldn't go in?" May said, but Oliver was already crossing the hardwood floor to investigate the desk.

A leather-bound book lay open at its centre portraying a diagram of a hand, facing palm up in the middle of the page. Arrows pointed to various lines on the image with strange words annotating it.

Oliver turned the page to find a more detailed diagram that displayed various fingers and different angles of the hand. A floorboard creaked behind him as May crept up to the desk.

"Do you reckon he's into palmistry?" Oliver asked.

"What? Like fortune telling?" May asked, looking doubtful.

"Yeah, look at these." He showed her the diagrams.

"My friend was into all that stuff. This doesn't look like that, though." May frowned and her forehead filled with tiny creases. They vanished as she picked up a piece of paper that caught her attention. "What do you think this is?"

Oliver cast his eyes over the drawing of a spiral that was interspersed with circles at random intervals.

"No idea," he said.

He glanced around the desk and spotted a pile of books that had been haphazardly placed on a wad of papers. They wobbled precariously as he lifted the top book and the one beneath it slid forward, shooting towards the floor.

Oliver winced as it hit the wood with a loud *thud* and they stood in tense silence, waiting to see if Ely had been alerted by the noise.

Oliver sighed with relief a moment later and stooped down, crawling under the desk to retrieve it. As he lifted the book a small scrap of paper was disturbed from beneath it. He reached for it, grasping the piece between two fingers.

"DINNER'S READY!" Ely's voice boomed up the stairs.

Oliver jerked upwards in shock, hitting his head on the underside of the desk with a loud *crack.*

"Argh," he groaned, pulling in a sharp breath of air between his teeth.

"Quick, get *up*," May said in a panic.

"Don't worry about me it's not like I smacked my head or anything," Oliver said, crawling out from underneath the desk.

He stood, placing the book back on the desk and stuffed the piece of paper into his back pocket before rubbing his head to ease the pain.

They snuck out of the room and Oliver shut the door quietly, feeling a rush of adrenalin pump through his veins. He turned to find May grinning at him and he shoved her playfully in the arm before leading the way back to the staircase, tiptoeing as they went.

As they descended, the sound of talking carried up to them from below. They reached the entrance hall and Oliver looked around, uncertain of where to go.

"Ely?" he called out but received no response.

They followed the voices through to a large kitchen where several people were gathered around a breakfast bar that was topped with black, grey-streaked marble.

The group looked young, perhaps in their early twenties; the men were dressed in smart suits and the women in party dresses. They laughed and chatted amongst themselves seemingly unaware of Oliver and May's presence.

"Um, excuse me?" May said but none of the strangers reacted.

The two of them lingered awkwardly in the doorway for a moment then Oliver stepped further into the room and the group turned to face them, looking surprised.

A woman broke apart from her companions, flicking a long strand of white-blonde hair out of her eyes. She glanced back towards the others with a meaningful glare and they fell silent, eyeing Oliver and May curiously.

"Can I help you?" Her voice was smooth and velvety and her smile revealed a set of brilliant, white teeth.

"We're looking for Ely," Oliver said, watching the strangers over her shoulder who were beginning to whisper amongst themselves.

"Oh, you must be his grandchildren. He's been telling us all about you. I believe he's in the dining room." She gestured to a doorway behind her.

"Thanks," Oliver said vaguely, retracting his gaze from the group.

They walked through the doorway and pushed past a trio of older men who were dressed in business suits. There were others gathered around a long dining table, piled high with food. The lighting was dim but not dark enough to hide the strange looks they received as they crossed the room.

Ely was sat on a red, chintzy sofa with a plate of food on his lap. He spotted them just before they sat down next to him.

"You must be hungry. Grab a plate and have whatever you want. The broccoli quiche is delicious," he said, gesturing to the buffet.

Oliver's stomach rumbled but he was too curious to eat just yet. "Ely, who are all these people?" he asked in a low voice.

Ely smiled. "They're just some friends and acquaintances." He stuffed a cocktail sausage into his mouth with a shrug. "Lots of people come visiting here. Grab a plate." He gestured to the food again.

Oliver frowned and gazed around at the party. He stood and heard May follow him as he approached the table, picked up a plate and filled it. As he returned to his seat a thought occurred to him.

"Are any of these people related to us?" he asked his grandfather curiously.

Ely shook his head and Oliver felt dejected.

"Will we get a chance to meet any other family?" May asked him eagerly as she swallowed a mouthful.

"Um, probably not. No," Ely said in a high pitched voice then cleared his throat and continued to eat.

"Why not?" Oliver asked in frustration.

"Well, my children live quite far away, you see? I rarely get to see them myself." He sipped at a glass of red wine as he spoke, avoiding eye contact with them.

"Wait, how many children do you *have*?" May asked.

"Four," Ely said airily.

"*Four?* We have three aunts and uncles we've never even *heard* of?" Oliver asked incredulously.

"Yes. There's your uncle Pilford, who I mentioned earlier, then your uncle Eugene. And, um, well, your mum's twin sister, Laura." Ely downed the remainder of his wine.

"*What?*" Oliver blurted, sharing a shocked look with May.

Ely continued to stuff food into his mouth so there was little opportunity for him to respond. Oliver narrowed his eyes at him. "Did Mum fall out with the family, then?" he pressed.

"Something like that," Ely said, getting to his feet. "I better just see how everyone's getting along," he muttered as he walked away.

Oliver raised his eyebrows at May.

"Mum has a *twin*," she said disbelievingly.

Oliver nodded, feeling dazed. He looked closer at the people standing around the room. The group they had bumped into in the kitchen were chatting animatedly at one end near the men in business suits, a cluster of teenagers were whispering together in one corner and a pale-faced lady was standing alone, hovering by the buffet.

One of the teenagers noticed him watching them. She had long, black hair which she curled around a finger as she spoke to the red-haired girl beside her. They both glanced at Oliver and May then burst into a fit of giggles. The two of them moved away from their group and started talking excitedly.

"We should speak to those girls," Oliver said suddenly.

"Why? They were laughing at us," May said, gazing stubbornly away from them.

He nudged her. "Which is exactly why we should talk to them. Find out what's so damn funny."

May grinned and raised her eyebrows at him in challenge. "Okay, after you."

Oliver placed his plate beside him on the sofa, stood up and walked over to the girls.

They started as they spotted him approaching and he felt a distinct feeling of satisfaction at riling them.

"Hi, I'm Oliver, this is my sister May," he said with an overly friendly smile.

May stepped to his side and he almost wanted to laugh at the look of surprise on their faces.

The girls shared a look then the one with long, black hair spoke. "I'm Dawn, this is Zara."

Up close, Oliver noticed that Zara's hair was more copper than red. She had an upturned nose which gave her a permanently snooty expression. She smiled but didn't say anything.

"So, what are you guys doing here?" Oliver asked, aiming his question at Dawn who seemed more approachable.

"Oh, you know. Just visiting," Dawn said, throwing Zara another look.

"Where are you guys from?" May pressed.

The girls burst out laughing and Zara even snorted.

Oliver scowled at them. "What's so funny?"

"Nothing, nothing at all," Dawn said airily, trying to suppress her laughter.

"Aww, it's like watching animals at the zoo," Zara said in a baby voice, making Dawn shriek with laughter.

"What's that supposed to mean?" May snapped.

"Well an animal bred in captivity doesn't know there's anything beyond its cage does it?" Zara continued, looking at them with feigned pity.

"What's your point?" Oliver said, straining to understand her insult.

"Don't bother Zara. I'm not sure their little brains could understand even if we *did* explain," Dawn said, her mouth curving up into a cruel smile.

Oliver grimaced and turned away from the girls, anger bubbling under his skin.

"What the hell was their problem?" he snapped as they walked away.

"I dunno. Let's try talking to someone else," May suggested, glaring back at the girls.

As they moved through the room, it seemed that everyone at the party was actively avoiding them. Backs turned as they walked and the odd glance they did receive was quickly withdrawn as Oliver tried to engage the onlooker.

"I'm sick of this. Let's go upstairs," Oliver said eventually and May nodded, looking disgruntled.

They returned to the entrance hall and climbed the staircase, heading for their rooms. When they reached the turning, Oliver was suddenly filled with the urge to do something defiant and decided to keep climbing.

"Where are you going?" May asked as she hurried to keep pace with him.

He didn't answer but continued to ascend the stairs, passing corridors where the walls were barely visible beneath masses of tangled vines. They reached the top and exited the stairwell.

The room was a dark attic full of branches that fanned across the ceiling and escaped through holes in the roof. A window rattled loudly at one end as a cold wind whistled through the gaps; it let in a slither of moonlight, casting a silver sheen across the floor.

There were wooden chests everywhere and papers that had been scattered chaotically around the room. Oliver reached down and picked one up, finding a more detailed spiral diagram than the one they had discovered in Ely's room.

At the top of the spiral was the only word he recognised: *Earth*. Descending down it, at varying intervals, were the words: *Aleva, Glacio, Brinatin, Theald, Arideen*, and *Vale*. Beside each word were symbols and more diagrams that he couldn't make sense of.

"What is this?" Oliver asked, holding it out to May in a frustrated gesture.

She took it and squinted at the writing in the gloom, the moonlight making her pale skin gleam.

"I don't know. Is that referring to *planet* Earth?" May asked, looking confounded.

Oliver shrugged.

May passed back the paper then started rummaging through a chest filled with various objects. As she extracted a wooden box, something small hit the floor, bounced twice then rolled towards Oliver's foot.

He used his toe to stop it and picked it up between his finger and thumb. It was a pea-sized ball that was translucent and glistening as if it were emitting a tiny amount of light.

"May, come and look at this," he said but she didn't answer. "May?"

Oliver looked up.

She had the small box in her hands and was staring down at the contents in puzzlement.

"What's wrong?" Oliver asked.

He tucked the tiny ball into his pocket and felt the scrap of paper there with a jolt as he realised he had forgotten about it.

May took what appeared to be two large medallions from the box and hung them from her finger by their chains. They were shaped like a heptagon and made from a faded, silver metal with a hole on each point that had tiny clasps. Next to each hole, running around in a circle clockwise, were the words from the diagram: *Earth, Aleva, Glacio, Brinatin, Theald, Arideen* and *Vale*.

One of the objects spun on its chain, caught by a sudden draft blowing through the attic so Oliver could see the back of it. There were four words engraved upon it in swirling, silver writing that made his heart jump up into his throat.

Property of Oliver Knight

4

Deception

"**W**hat the hell are these things?" Oliver gasped and took the pendant from her, staring at his name. May twisted the other one around to reveal her own name and confusion crossed her features.

"I don't know. Maybe we should put them back?" she said uncertainly.

Oliver frowned, turning the pendant over to look at the front. "What do those words mean? They're on the diagram too."

A noise from downstairs made them jump.

"Put them back. I want to get out of here," May whispered in a panic.

He passed the pendant back to her and she returned them both to the box.

They ran downstairs and paused in the corridor outside their rooms. The wind buffeted the floor-length window beside them, the darkness outside causing their reflections to show up on the pane.

"Maybe they're gifts from Ely?" May suggested.

Oliver shrugged. "Could be, or they could just be another one of Ely's secrets." He let out a weary sigh. "I'm gonna go to bed."

May nodded then rubbed her arms, shivering from the cool air in the corridor. "Okay, see you in the morning," she said.

Oliver nodded and entered his room, feeling the welcome warmth of the fire wash over him. He stoked it with an iron poker and added a fresh log to encourage the embers back to life.

He pulled the curtains across the balcony door and readied himself for bed, getting under the thick quilt and sinking into the soft mattress. Sleep tugged at him and, just before drifting off, he watched the scrap of paper fall out of his jeans that were draped over the back of the armchair.

* * *

Oliver awoke early the next morning to find the fire had died in the night so the air in the room was icy. He recalled the scrap of paper and threw his covers back, jumping out of bed and crossing the room in a few paces.

He snatched the paper up from the floor and cast his eyes over the handwritten words upon it. He realised it was the torn edge of a letter and the blood drained from his face as he read it, forgetting about the cold in an instant.

forget, that discretion is my middle name.
situations are to be handled.
Hawking.

Oliver exited his room and crossed the hallway to May's door, feeling a wave of adrenalin surge through him. He knocked lightly, assuming she would still be asleep but was surprised to hear her answer promptly.

"Come in."

Oliver hurried inside and found May fully dressed sitting cross-legged on her bed with a book in her lap.

"What's wrong?" May asked, frowning at the sight of him.

Oliver dropped the torn piece of paper in front of her and anxiously ran a hand through his messy hair as he watched her read it.

She looked up at him, her bright eyes widening to their furthest extent. "What is this?"

"I found it in Ely's room. It looks like part of a letter." Oliver pointed at it accusingly.

"Do you think Ely's been in contact with that Hawking guy?" May asked incredulously.

Oliver nodded. "What else could it mean?" he stated rhetorically.

She nodded and eyed the piece of paper in her hand like it was a bomb she had to diffuse.

"We need to find the rest of it," Oliver said.

May looked up at him. "What? You mean go back into his room?"

"Yeah, why not? We need to see all of this letter."

May nodded slowly. "Okay, we'll have to wait until he goes out. I don't wanna risk him finding us."

"But May-"

"*No*. I'm serious. If he's involved with that guy..." she trailed off and Oliver fell still.

"You're right. He could be in on the whole thing," he said in a hushed voice as if Ely might be listening at the door. "We'll wait 'til he's out then search his room."

* * *

Weeks went by and Autumn was fully upon them. Most of the leaves had fallen from the enormous tree that grew through the house, leaving its branches bare.

They had soon discovered that Ely neither seemed to work nor leave the house at all. Deliveries arrived at the door every so often, bringing supplies to the manor. Oliver wondered if their grandfather wasn't leaving them unattended on purpose.

They had eventually faced starting at a new school in the village. The other children were welcoming but Oliver found it hard to bond with anyone. He still clung in hope to his old life and a small part of him expected to return to it one day soon.

Oliver breathed heavily as he and May walked up through the estate to Oakway Manor on their way home from school on a Friday afternoon.

"Does this place have to be on top of such a ridiculously huge hill?" May said, panting.

Oliver laughed through deep breaths.

They approached the porch and leaves crunched under their feet on the steps. Oliver reached for the door but it opened before he touched it. A tall man in snow boots and a thick, fur-lined coat bumped into them.

"'Scuse me," he said, avoiding their eyes.

He was halfway down the hill before they even considered trying to talk to him. They had become so accustomed to the many faces that came and went from the house that they rarely tried to engage anyone in conversation any more. And, if they did, they were only met with evasive answers.

"I want to know why there's always strangers here," May said, leading the way inside.

"Maybe Ely's more sociable than he seems?" Oliver said bitterly, shutting the cold out with a loud *clunk* as the door closed. "How long are we gonna be living here before he decides to be honest with us?" He kicked off his wet shoes in frustration.

"There's more chance of Mum turning up than that ever happening," May said stoically, taking off her navy coat.

Oliver felt his stomach constrict at the mention of their mum. They had avoided talking about her, neither of them wanting to upset the other. He decided not to dwell on it. "Yeah, you're probably right. Maybe we should phone Mr Greene?"

"And say what? Our grandfather has lots of friends, please help." She cocked an eyebrow.

Oliver laughed. "Maybe not."

Mr Greene had only checked in on them once and brought no news of their mum's whereabouts. The little he did have to say was that the police were still looking for her but were exploring other options. Oliver had fretted about what that really meant ever since.

They climbed the stairs and spent the rest of the afternoon discussing their options in Oliver's bedroom.

"I think we'll have to go in Ely's room while he's still here. We managed before," Oliver said, getting up off his bed and pacing around the room.

"But if he catches us-"

"So what? I'll confront him and he'll have to explain everything," Oliver snapped.

"And blow our chances of ever finding out the truth," May said, rolling her eyes.

"Fine. Then what's the alternative?" Oliver asked.

May breathed in deeply and released it through her nose. She glanced out of the window beside the door and raised her eyebrows as something peaked her interest.

Oliver followed her line of sight and blinked as he spotted snowflakes floating down outside in a lazy descent. They began to form a thin sheet of white on the balcony railing as they started to fall in a flurry.

"Maybe all we need is a distraction," May said thoughtfully.

"Like what?"

May turned her attention to him. "We could try and convince Ely to come on a walk with us so we can see the grounds."

"Then what?" Oliver asked.

"Then you say you need to go back to the house for something?" she suggested. "And search his room."

Oliver nodded and hope ignited in his chest. "That could actually work."

May grinned. "I know."

* * *

The next morning they walked into the kitchen where Ely was busying about. Oliver cleared his throat as he stepped into the room and their grandfather swung around. He was in the middle of preparing them breakfast, scrambling eggs in a frying pan.

"Ah!" he said brightly as they entered. "I was about to call you two. Take a seat."

Oliver perched on a stool beside May at the breakfast bar as Ely dished them out eggs and toast. His stomach grumbled loudly in response and Ely chuckled lightly.

As they ate, Oliver kicked May under the table to prompt her.

She took a sip of juice before speaking. "Um, Ely?" she said innocently.

Ely looked up from his food with a pleasant smile. "Yes, my dear?"

"I was wondering if you'd give us a tour of the grounds? It's so pretty here and we haven't spent much time in the countryside before, especially in the snow." May gave him her puppy-dog eyes which Oliver knew had worked on their mum a thousand times.

Ely's shoulders straightened a little. "Yes, of course. I'd be happy to show you around. Perhaps after breakfast?"

"That'd be great," Oliver said, giving him a warm smile.

The snow had fallen heavily in the night, carpeting the world in a thick layer of white. They followed Ely out of the front door, down the aged steps and onto the steep driveway that disappeared into the woodland ahead. The snow sat atop the leaves like a dusting of sugar.

Ely turned on his heel and led them away from the drive around the back of the house towards an expansive snow-covered garden which was glaringly bright beneath the grey sky.

"There used to be stables on the grounds but they were demolished by my great grandfather almost a century ago. It's a shame really," Ely said, pointing towards a flat area beyond a large pond. "I have drawings of them that a stableboy did. I keep them in the library."

"There's a library here?" May asked curiously.

Oliver glanced back at the house as they descended the hill towards the pond. Snow sat in the water, turning to an icy slush on the surface.

Ely continued to describe the history of the house and grounds but Oliver grew increasingly preoccupied with getting back to the manor.

"Um, Ely?" he interrupted.

Ely raised his eyebrows at him.

"Sorry, I just need the bathroom. I'll meet you back here," Oliver said, hurrying back towards the house before Ely could answer.

Showers of snow were kicked up by the toes of his shoes as he ran. He glanced back as he headed around a corner of the house and relaxed as he spotted Ely and May still standing by the pond several hundred yards away.

Oliver ran up the stone steps and pushed through the door into the entrance hall. He kicked off his wet boots and charged across the hallway to the stairs where his socks slipped on the polished floor. He hurried up the spiral staircase, feeling a flood of adrenalin fuelling his muscles as he ran down the corridor towards Ely's room.

He reached for the handle and turned it, praying it wasn't locked. He let out a breath of relief as the door opened then crept across the floor toward the desk. It had been tidied since his last visit so he pulled open drawers one at a time, checking the contents. He was careful to leave everything where he found it.

Oliver felt the minutes ticking by and his heartbeat began to increase.

After searching every nook and cranny of the desk he stood back away from it, gazing around the room in frustration.

He spotted a wastepaper basket tucked beneath the desk to one side, concealed in the shadows. He felt a swoop of excitement and dove toward it but, just as he grabbed hold of the wicker bin, the *ker-clack* of the front door shutting sounded.

He cursed internally and started hurriedly checking through the contents. He could hear someone on the stairs and tipped the bin up in a panic, his hands spreading through the screwed up balls of paper as they flew across the floor.

There amongst them was a handful of torn pieces. He grabbed them, stuffing the bits into his pockets then scooped the rest of the rubbish back into the bin.

He pushed the basket back into place and tiptoed across the room, exiting it and shutting the door as quietly as possible. He let out a slow breath to calm himself.

A shadow danced in the stairway as someone ascended them and he pressed his back against the wall, waiting.

When they passed, he fled down the corridor and descended to the entrance hall.

"Oh, there you are," Ely said from across the room then frowned in confusion. "May went to look for you, didn't you pass her on the stairs?"

"Er, yeah," Oliver lied quickly. "She just went back to her room."

Ely nodded. "We were waiting for you but it got a bit too cold."

"Sorry I, er, got a phone call from a friend," Oliver said, trying to keep his demeanour as casual as possible.

"Not to worry," Ely said with a smile, heading toward the kitchen.

Oliver sprinted up to May's room and entered, finding her sitting on the bed.

"Did you find it?" she asked excitedly as he shut the door.

Oliver nodded, retrieving the pieces from his back pocket. "I think so."

He laid them out on the bed and they started fixing the letter together like a jigsaw, sitting crosslegged opposite one another.

"I think that's it," May said, laying the final piece in place. "Read it out."

Oliver cast his eyes over the words as he read them aloud. "Dear Mr Fox, further to your enquiry, the situation has been dealt with efficiently as per my usual professionalism. Mrs Knight's children were present but no doubt, being minors, their account of my presence will be dismissed by the authorities. Your cooperation has been most helpful but, perhaps you forget, that discretion is my middle name. I'm in no need of reminding of how these situations are to be handled. Yours sincerely, Orion Hawking."

Oliver looked up at May, seeing the same dawning apprehension in her eyes that he felt himself.

"It's a coverup," May whispered.

"Ely's involved in Mum's disappearance. We have to call Mr Greene," Oliver said in a panic.

May grabbed her phone from the bedside table, pressed several buttons then held it to her ear. She chewed her lip anxiously as she waited for Mr Greene to answer.

"Oh, hi Mr Greene, it's May Knight-" She paused as he responded. "Yes well, actually everything's not alright, we came across a letter that suggests Ely's involved in covering up our mum's disappearance." She paused once more and Oliver waited anxiously. "Yes, it is about Hawking, how did you know-"

Oliver raised his eyebrows in surprise and signalled for her to put the phone on speaker.

She pressed a button and Mr Greene's voice burst into the room. "Yes, your grandfather told us he's been in touch with a private investigator named Hawking who's looking for your mother."

"But that's not what this letter suggests at all," May implored.

"It's all under control," Mr Greene said dismissively. "I'll give you a call in another couple of weeks."

"Wait-" May tried but Mr Greene said his goodbyes and the line went dead.

"Ely's covered his tracks. We have to confront him," Oliver said, standing up.

"What?" May said, sounding alarmed. "No, we should call the police or something."

"The police won't do anything! You saw what that Hawking guy managed to do, Mum's room was destroyed one second and the next it wasn't. How do you explain that?"

May shook her head. "I don't know." She got to her feet, looking at him anxiously. "What are you gonna do?"

"What do you think?" he said, snatching up the pieces of the letter in his fist then marching purposefully from the room.

Oliver's footfalls thundered loudly throughout the house as he hurried down the staircase. He heard the quieter steps of May jogging along behind him, trying to keep up.

Humphrey poked his head out of a corridor then hightailed it back the way he had come as he spotted them barrelling past.

"What's all that racket?" Ely called from a corridor to their right and Oliver veered down it in response.

He strode towards a door which was left ajar; a narrow strip of light stretched towards them across the floor. Oliver took a calming breath and pushed the door lightly so it swung open on creaky hinges.

He couldn't help but be distracted by the vast room that lay ahead of him. It was a library of a thousand books all organised in the most unusual way. The floor was made of crystal-clear glass that looked down upon hundreds of books which were perfectly arranged into a spiral beneath the pane. The walls were similar, rising several floors high in a circle of glass as if they were inside a tunnel of books.

Oliver opened and shut his mouth as he spotted Ely beside a glass podium in the centre of the room.

Ely smiled at them as they entered. "A little elaborate, I know, but this library is state of the art. I had it fitted last year. You can type in the book you'd like to read on this screen and it'll retrieve it for you. And if you don't know what you want you can browse the entire library right here, it's all at your fingertips."

Oliver felt the pieces of the letter in his hand and was reminded of the reason he had been looking for his grandfather. His anger had diminished slightly which, he thought, was probably a good thing. "Ely we need to talk to you about something."

Ely raised his eyebrows in surprise. "Oh? And what might that be?"

Oliver lifted his hand and opened his palm so some of the pieces of paper fell to the floor.

Ely paused, eyeing it with a fearful look. "What's that?" he asked.

"It's a letter from a man called Hawking, addressed to you." Oliver kept his voice steady, gauging his grandfather's reaction carefully.

May looked between the two of them nervously.

"Oh, is it now? And where did you find that then?" Ely asked, walking towards him slowly.

"In your room," Oliver admitted, jutting up his chin.

Ely's nostrils flared. "You went in my room?" His voice was a little too high for Oliver to be fooled by his calm tone.

"Yes," Oliver said.

"We just wanted to know more about you. You haven't told us anything," May tried to explain.

"That letter is private," Ely said.

Oliver stiffened and tried to bite back his anger but it burst from his lips anyway. "You're involved with covering up Mum's disappearance. You know what happened to her, don't you? Where is she?!"

Ely's face contorted angrily. "How dare you? I've done no such thing!"

"That Hawking guy hid what happened to her room. It was ripped to pieces and no one believed us!" Oliver shouted, unable to control his rage.

"You don't understand!" Ely retorted.

"How can we understand? You don't tell us anything! We know nothing about our family and you've hidden anything that could tell us about them!" Oliver snapped.

"That's *enough*," Ely growled. "Go to your rooms. Both of you!"

"Ely if you'd just explain-" May begged, looking painfully uncomfortable with the confrontation.

"I said *enough*! Out. *Now*," Ely demanded, pointing towards the door.

Oliver threw the handful of paper to the floor in a shower of white pieces then stormed from the room, hurrying upstairs.

May followed Oliver closely and shut the door behind them as they entered his room.

"We need to call someone," Oliver said, turning sharply around to face his sister.

"You just threw away the evidence!" May said, sounding frantic.

Oliver swore loudly at his stupidity.

"You don't think straight when you're angry," May accused.

"I'm sorry, alright?" he snapped.

She rolled her eyes and marched out of the room, shutting the door firmly behind her.

Oliver threw himself down on the bed, balling his fists in the sheets as his mind rushed with questions.

5

A Dark Fate

Oliver had spent the rest of the day in his room, passing out finally at midnight to the sound of heavy rain which was destined to wash away the snow. He was haunted by strange dreams, making him toss and turn in a hot sweat.

He looked down to find the strange, heptagonal pendant in his hand. His name blazed on the back of it, glaringly bright.

"Oliver?" A familiar, female voice spoke.

He looked up and saw his mum. A hazy, golden light emitted from the pendant, illuminating her form but barely penetrating the darkness surrounding her.

"Mum? Where are you? Please come back."

She looked sad and lost then she vanished and the scene changed. His hand was still outstretched but the pendant was gone. Someone took hold of it and pulled him forward. He could see the back of a large figure, a man, dragging him toward a bright, blue sphere of light.

"No, stop," Oliver said, tugging his arm back as fear invaded his chest.

The man turned to him but his face was indistinct, hidden by shadow. "Come with me son."

"Dad?" Oliver said and a sense of hope grew inside him. "I thought you were dead."

"I am dead," he said and his face became clear. It was a bloodied skull but the eyes were intact, gazing at him out of boney sockets. Sinews dangled from the bone.

Oliver gasped and tried to tug his arm away once more but the skeleton dragged him on towards the light.

"No-"

A scream ripped through Oliver's dream and he awoke with a violent jerk. It sounded again and a chill engulfed him as he realised it was May.

In a panic, he ran flat-out to her room and flung the door open.

Oliver fumbled for the light switch, squinting into the darkness as he desperately tried to find it. He cursed as he gave up and hurried into the room, his eyes adjusting slightly and focusing on a solitary figure on the floor.

May was curled up in a ball, squirming and writhing. She let out another, shuddering scream and Oliver threw himself to her side, rolling her over to try and stop her body from spasming.

Panic set in and he shouted for Ely.

It seemed as though an age passed before Ely appeared in the doorway though Oliver knew it couldn't have been more than a minute.

"What's going on? I can't see a thing," Ely said, sounding frustrated.

The overhead light came on and the blood drained from Ely's face as he spotted May. He leapt to her side, suddenly a man in control. A look of concentration crossed his features as he examined her carefully.

May's eyes were open but they roamed unseeing, bloodshot and red. What scared Oliver more were the dark bruises that covered her body and the thick, black veins that slithered like snakes between them under her skin.

The marks weren't like anything Oliver had ever seen, they swirled and pulsed as if they were alive. Those that ran down her neck were larger and darker than the others and led towards the worst mark, sitting just above her heart.

"What's wrong with her?" Oliver asked frantically.

Ely shooed him away and continued examining his sister.

May gasped suddenly as the black veins reached up towards her temples.

"*Help her.*" Oliver clasped May's face as if he could stop the veins himself. He felt helpless and lost as he gazed at her, his world collapsing around him.

"I've never seen anything like this. I may be able to harness the curse temporarily..." Ely trailed off and continued to mutter to himself under his breath.

Oliver couldn't make out the words.

"Curse? What do you mean? She's sick. We need to get her to a hospital." Oliver stood up, meaning to find a phone, his brain finally clicking into gear.

Ely grasped his arm tightly and pulled him back to his knees.

"You need to listen sharp, Oliver. I'm only going say this once and it's going to sound all shades of crazy, but you better trust me because I'm the only chance she's got. Got it?"

Oliver nodded, stunned.

"There's no doctor in this world who can cure May from this-"

"But-" Oliver cut in.

"No buts. You listen to me. No doctor in *this* world can help her, Oliver. But there are other worlds. And that's where this curse can be healed. I know someone who might be able to help but we'll have to go through the Gateway."

Oliver pulled away from his grandfather, gazing at him in astonished horror. "You're mad. She needs a doctor. She could *die*." The word left a bitter taste in his mouth and he felt his shoulders begin to tremble as he pressed his palms into the carpet, readying to stand once more.

Ely grabbed his arm again, not letting him get up. "I know it sounds mad and I wouldn't tell you at all if it weren't a life or death situation. But I need to get her to Aleva."

The word rang a bell in Oliver's head but he couldn't place it.

May screamed again.

"Hold her still for me, Oliver," Ely said, firmly.

Oliver didn't move, the rhythmic beat of his pulse sounding in his ears like a war drum.

"*Now*," Ely commanded, his eyes blazing at him.

Oliver wordlessly did as he was told, staring wide-eyed at the man. Ely rolled up his sleeves and waved his hands slowly over her body. May struggled beneath Oliver's grip but he held her firm.

A light appeared, glowing orange and warm from Ely's palms. Oliver blinked to try and clear his eyes of the strange hallucination he was having but the vision didn't fade.

Incredibly, as Ely's hands hovered over May, the veins receded and flowed back into the black, pulsing patches dotted across her body. They paled and decreased in size before flowing like water towards the largest patch on her chest.

Ely pulled away, out of breath.

The remaining mark faded slightly and stopped pulsing, resembling a large bruise.

Oliver fell back, gasping and looked at Ely in shock. "H-how?" It was all he could manage to get out.

Ely pulled a half smile through his deep breaths then said, "I told you so."

May groaned and her eyes refocused as she looked up at Oliver.

"How do you feel?" he asked gently.

"I'm okay. What happened? Did I fall out of bed?"

Oliver smiled with relief and pulled her into a hug. "You're fine now, you lunatic."

"I'm not a lunatic," she said, her voice muffled by his t-shirt.

Oliver laughed. Relief swept through him in a wave, washing away the fear in an instant. Ely patted him on the shoulder and squeezed May's arm.

"I think you two had better come downstairs for some hot cocoa. We need to have a little chat."

Ely exited the room and Oliver pulled May to her feet. They followed their grandfather down to the kitchen where two steaming cups of cocoa were waiting for them. They took seats around the breakfast bar and waited for Ely to speak.

"We need to talk about that mark, May. But first it's best if I give you some information that will help you understand."

"What mark? What's going on? What happened?" May asked, her brow furrowing anxiously.

Oliver described how he had found her on the floor covered in the strange bruises and how Ely had somehow saved her. She looked just as unbelieving of the story as Oliver would have been if he hadn't witnessed it himself.

She looked down at her chest where the remaining bruise was peeking out above her top and touched the mark in shock.

"Am I going to die?" she breathed, sounding panicked.

Oliver squeezed her arm. "No chance."

"Of course not. I wouldn't let that happen. I have a friend, Grelda Grey, who's a specialist in curses. There isn't a curse she can't cure, trust me," Ely said confidently.

"Curse?" May said in confusion.

Ely nodded and ran his finger slowly around the rim of his mug, letting out a breath that sounded as though he were relieved. "There are other worlds. Seven in fact, including Earth."

"*What?*" May said.

She caught Oliver's eye and the expression on his face silenced her.

Ely watched May for a moment, running a hand up into his beard and scraping his fingernails down the skin.

When she said no more, he continued. "It's called an intraverse: a universe within a universe. It's been named Heptus. The worlds are connected to each other in what you can imagine as a spiralling string."

He waved his finger in the air and a glowing, blue spiral materialised in front of them which reflected on the ceiling in flickering strands of light as if they were underwater.

Oliver leant back in his chair and May gasped. He remembered the spiral diagrams they had found and realised what they were.

"One world is connected to the next and that one is connected to another, all via Gateways."

Coloured spheres representing each world appeared along the spiral and, as the names of the worlds materialised beside them, Oliver recalled the words from the diagram.

Ely paused before continuing. "There are also mages in our intraverse: people who possess magic. As you can see, I am one of them."

His eyes flicked between the two of them, gauging their reaction.

"This is crazy," May said, blinking hard as she looked to Oliver for support. "What is this? Some sort of hologram?"

Oliver didn't answer. He had seen it twice now and could come up with no better explanation for what it was.

"It's magic," Ely stated.

May snorted and glanced at Oliver once more but he stared back at her with nothing to offer.

Ely rubbed his fingers together and lightning appeared in his palm, crackling and sparking.

May jumped to her feet. "Oh my God," she said, eyeing the magic with fear.

Oliver felt his entire body tense as he gazed at the lightning. He wondered what else his grandfather was capable of and then, in a panic, what he himself might be capable of. He stared at his hands like they were about to combust.

"There's no chance I'm a, I mean, I'm not a-?" Oliver asked in a fluster, gesturing towards Ely's hands.

"No, you're not a mage. Magic inheritance is complicated." Ely tittered, extinguishing the sparks.

"You wish." May laughed halfheartedly, keeping her eyes on Ely's hands.

"Shut up," Oliver said, his cheeks warming.

"And now I can stop looking this old." Ely chuckled and ran a hand over his face, the lines decreasing and the grey in his hair disappearing.

Oliver narrowed his eyes as he took in Ely's appearance. "This is how you looked when we first met."

Ely nodded. "Mages age a little slower than other people. I was careless not to have aged myself before we were introduced, it completely slipped my mind."

May's eyes roamed over his face. "And do you not work? You never leave the house."

"The tree within Oakway Manor contains the Gateway to the next world, Aleva. I am its Keeper. I'm employed by the Council to regulate the challenge for those who wish to go through to Aleva."

"And that's why so many people are here all the time? They're from the other worlds?" May said slowly, clearly trying to understand.

"Yes, precisely," Ely said. "Your arrival coincided with the celebrations for those who had just won keys to Earth. Anyone coming through from Aleva for the first time has to be briefed about the rules here. I've also been telling anyone who came through the Gateway that you two were unaware of the other worlds so they didn't reveal the truth."

"Why don't we already know about these other worlds though?" Oliver interjected, confronting the notion.

"A King decided long ago that Earth wasn't to know the truth. It was at a time where Britain was undergoing great change; the Normans had just taken the throne and the new King, William the Conqueror, wanted the secret kept."

"How come?" May asked, tilting her head to one side.

"The King wanted to be the first to step through to the other worlds but he was unable to complete the challenge. So, in the meantime, he established a secret society to make sure word never got out, on pain of death. However, he never passed the test and instead told his son the truth about the other worlds.

"But as each King was succeeded the secret was passed down from son to son, none of them ever managing to complete the challenge. Today, the descendants of that society still uphold it, though it is unknown whether today's royal family are aware that it exists. You, yourselves have met a member of that society."

They looked at him with confused expressions.

"Hawking," Ely revealed.

"But why did he hide evidence of Mum's disappearance?" Oliver asked angrily.

Ely frowned. "There are very few people on Earth who know about the other worlds and the society has a list of every single one. Alison is, of course, on that list. So if anything mysterious happens to someone involved with the other worlds the society will step in to ensure that nothing compromises their secret. It would appear that Alison's room was destroyed by magic and, as she seems to have disappeared off the face of the Earth, they have concluded that she actually has."

"What? So Mum's in one of the other worlds?" May asked incredulously.

Ely nodded, looking grave. "All the evidence points in that direction."

"But doesn't that mean she would have had to come here to go through the Gateway?" Oliver asked.

Ely continued to nod and a sparkle of light caught in his eyes. "Yes," he breathed. "She would have passed right under my nose."

"Are you even allowed to tell us all this, about the other worlds?" May asked, looking around like Hawking might burst into the room at any moment.

"Yes, those permitted to know are the families that learn about them because of their ancestry, like mine. So I have every right to tell you. It's just..." Ely trailed off.

"Just what?" Oliver asked, frowning.

"Your mother didn't want either of you to know. That's why I never met you before. When the police tracked me down and asked me to take you in I couldn't say no, but I had to honour her wishes. That's why I've been so distant and why I hid my children's belongings. I'm sorry, I just didn't see any other way."

Oliver suddenly felt furious. Not only had his mum inexplicably disappeared, but now it turned out that she had lied to him his whole life and kept them from meeting their family.

A lump formed in his throat which he forced down before looking Ely in the eye.

"Why didn't she want us to know?" Oliver asked through gritted teeth.

"I'm sure she was just trying to protect you."

"Protect us from what?" May asked, a crease forming between her eyes.

"Perhaps." Ely hesitated a moment. "Perhaps she was protecting you from the truth about your father, Oliver."

"My father? He died when I was a baby." He felt the blood rising in his face, the heat of it burning his cheeks.

"Yes he died, but not in the way you've been told. And not when you were a baby."

"What do you mean?" Oliver asked, fighting to keep his voice level.

"Your father was an explorer from Aleva. He set out to gain the keys to all seven worlds."

"And what's wrong with that?" Oliver asked, his curiosity overriding his anger.

"Nothing, not the first six keys anyway. But the seventh world is Vale," Ely said, the tone of his voice darkening.

"Why's that bad?" May asked, her voice hushed.

"Only two people have ever entered the seventh world. The first returned just a shell of a man, he was weak and wasted. The second was never seen again. Vale isn't a human world, you see? These *creatures* live there, varks we call them, they're vicious and alien."

"Why would someone go there, then?" May asked.

"The first man didn't know what he'd find," Ely said. "He was an incredibly powerful mage and highly skilled scientist named Dorian Ganderfield. His experiments led to the discovery of the other worlds and, eventually, Ganderfield found a way to tear holes between them. It was only later that he realised he couldn't repair the rifts."

"Why did it matter?" May asked.

Ely shook his head gravely. "The worlds have evolved separately from each other for millions of years. Without restricting access between them, what is to stop one world from waging war on another? The more advanced worlds would conquer those that are weaker."

Oliver nodded.

"So Ganderfield created Gateways between the worlds and set up the Council of Heptus to maintain intraverse-wide laws. He planned to lock the Gateway to Vale so that no one would ever be tempted to go there. But, alas, it was impossible. The Gateways could only be restricted."

"Restricted how?" Oliver asked.

"Ganderfield designed challenges for those wishing to pass through them. He wanted to restrict the Gateway to Vale with a challenge that he hoped no one would ever *want* to complete, thereby, effectively locking it."

"What was the challenge?" Oliver asked, feeling the hairs on the back of his neck inexplicably creep up.

May leant forward in her seat.

"Vale's challenge is to sacrifice someone you love before the Gateway: a family member, a friend, a partner - anyone that you hold dear. Ganderfield believed that even the most coldhearted of people would never murder someone they loved."

Oliver nodded slowly and leant back in his seat. "But what's any of this got to do with my father?"

"Everything, Oliver." Ely let out a slow breath. "Because, your father was murdered by the second person to ever enter Vale: his closest friend, Isaac Rimori."

6

What Lies Within

The words seemed to bounce off of Oliver's ears, taking a moment for them to unfold in his mind until he understood the implications of what he'd been told.

May looked between Oliver and Ely, chewing at her lip.

"You're telling me my dad was *murdered*?" Oliver got up, unable to stay seated a moment longer.

"I'm sorry you had to hear it this way, but you need to know the facts before we go to Aleva. It's for the best that you find out from me and not someone else," Ely said softly.

"Why? Who else would tell me?" Oliver demanded.

"Your father is somewhat famous in the other worlds. He, Rimori and another man travelled to Vale's Gateway with the supposed intention of finding a way around the challenge. Rimori betrayed your father, murdered him and entered Vale alone. The other man fled to the Council and recounted what had happened. When the public found out, the story spread like wildfire."

Oliver nodded slowly and realised he was pacing. May reached out an arm to stop him and he met her eye, softening at her worried expression. He returned to his seat and dropped his head into his hands.

"But why did they want to enter Vale?" May asked.

"There's a cult in the other worlds that worship a god-like being called the Arc which resides in Vale. They call themselves the Arclites. Their ideology teaches that the Arc is the source of all power across the seven worlds and that it alone is responsible for bestowing magic upon the mages. "Arclites believe that the Arc will one day come to the other worlds in human form, gifting each of its followers with magic. The Arc would supposedly destroy the Gateways which would leave the rifts open for anyone to walk through then unite the seven worlds as a single empire under its one rule," Ely explained.

"So you're saying my dad was one of these *Arclites*? Oliver asked.

Ely nodded. "All of them were, he and his friends."

"Including Mum?" May asked with a concerned frown.

"I think perhaps she was, for a time," Ely said. "Though I'm certain that is far behind her now. Once she had you, Oliver, your mother's priorities changed."

Oliver nodded, feeling marginally comforted by the thought.

"Is that why they went to Vale then? To find the Arc?" May asked.

Ely nodded. "Though no doubt what awaited Isaac Rimori on the other side of Vale's Gateway was death."

Oliver couldn't help but feel a sense of satisfaction at his grandfather's words, knowing that the man had paid for murdering his father.

"Wait. You said my dad didn't die when I was a baby. How long ago *was* this?" Oliver asked.

"You were six," Ely breathed.

Oliver had grown up with an idyllic picture in his mind of the man he had never known. The person he had imagined was a lie, he knew nothing about the real William Knight. His father had been murdered for something that Oliver hadn't even known existed.

"You'll have to complete Aleva's challenge to get the key to the Gateway," Ely said.

"What's the challenge? Is it difficult?" May asked.

"I'm sure you'll both pass." Ely tutted to himself. "I've not been to Aleva in months, much too long. Follow me."

"Where to?" May gripped the table anxiously.

"You'll see." Ely chuckled to himself and headed off towards the staircase.

They stood and followed him out into the entrance hall. Oliver felt frustrated and hurt by his mother's lies but his gut also burned with curiosity at the possibility of other worlds truly existing.

Humphrey appeared from the staircase and wound his way around Ely's legs. May scooped the cat up and placed him on her shoulder where he nuzzled her neck and began purring loudly.

Ely entered the tree but, instead of going up, placed his palm on the inside of the trunk and pushed. A door swung open, revealing a staircase that spiralled down into the cellar. Oliver peered after Ely as he disappeared down it out of sight.

The door was left open, inviting them in to its mysterious depths. May moved inside and Oliver crept after her.

Dim lights cast an eerie, green glow in the darkness. The tree trunk gave way to mud walls filled with gigantic, tangled roots. As he descended, Oliver felt the wooden steps beneath his feet meld into soft earth.

The passage began to open up and they emerged in a large, underground chamber.

At one end of the room was an enormous, arching gateway created by roots hanging from the ceiling and winding up from the floor, weaving together as they met in mid-air. Thinner roots formed intricate patterns on the archway and, embedded within them, were twinkling jewels.

The Gateway looked onto nothing but the earthy wall behind it, no trace of a portal to be seen. Despite this, a low humming noise emitted from the structure and Oliver was overwhelmed by the sense that he was stood in the presence of something immeasurably powerful.

He raised his eyebrows in awe.

"Whoa," May whispered into the cool air, putting Humphrey on the ground.

"This." Ely pointed. "Is the Gateway to Aleva."

"It's incredible." May stepped forward to get a better look, tucking a strand of hair behind her ear.

"This Gateway was created almost a thousand years ago by Dorian Ganderfield himself. He also designed the challenge that you are about to attempt."

"What do we have to do?" May asked, scanning the surroundings for a clue.

"You'll find out momentarily. But first, I must send a message to my daughter." Ely knelt down and Humphrey trotted over.

He stroked the cat then held his hand beside the animal's head. Golden mist seeped from his palm, disappearing into the cat's pointed ears. Humphrey's eyes glinted gold momentarily then returned to their usual fiery orange. He mewed happily then trotted towards the Gateway.

Lightning flashed across the Gateway in ribbons of white and blue. Humphrey walked confidently into it and vanished instantly, the lightning dying as he disappeared. Oliver started and took an instinctive step backwards, suddenly fearing what lay beyond the portal.

Ely chuckled at the looks on Oliver and Mays' faces. "Right, follow me."

They hurried after Ely towards the darkest corner of the chamber, moving away from the Gateway as he started rubbing his hands together until a glow emitted from them. Oliver blinked his eyes as an orb of light gathered between his hands, growing stronger and brighter by the second.

Ely widened the gap between his palms and the light burst away from them towards the high ceiling that was formed from compacted earth and roots. It cast a warm, orange glow in the chamber and illuminated a single, wooden doorway embedded in the dirt wall.

Ely gazed at them seriously. "You will only be successful in this challenge if you can stay in it long enough."

"And how long is that?" Oliver asked.

"I don't know, it differs for everyone," Ely said.

"Why?" May asked, looking nervous.

"You will want to leave the challenge. Knowing how long you have would make the process easier to bear."

"What do you mean we'll *want* to leave?" Oliver asked, his mouth becoming dry.

"And *bear* what?" May said with wide eyes.

"You'll find out shortly. If you wish to exit the challenge at any time you need only ring one of the bells."

"Bells?" May questioned.

Ely nodded. "There will always be one close by."

"But what do we actually have to *do* in this challenge?" Oliver asked.

"Put simply, my boy, survive it," Ely said, his face darkening. "So, who's first?"

Before Oliver could consider volunteering May piped up.

"I'll go first," she said. "I'm the one who's caused all of this."

"May, it's not your fault," Oliver said earnestly.

"I know but, I'd feel better about it if I go first," she said, her gaze dropping to her feet.

Oliver chewed the inside of his cheek as he watched her turn away from him.

"Off you go then, May. Good luck," Ely said, gesturing for her to go through the door ahead of them.

"Good luck," Oliver mumbled, his pulse quickening as he watched her.

May opened the door and Oliver tried to catch a glimpse inside but it was pitch black. May stepped forward and Oliver saw her pale face and bright, green eyes glancing back at him as Ely shut the door.

"She'll be fine," Ely said, catching Oliver's eye. "You can go in in a minute."

Oliver nodded and his stomach fluttered.

The minutes stretched on. Oliver couldn't think of anything to say so kept silent. He gazed around at the chamber and eyed the twinkling gemstones that were inlaid in the thick, gnarled roots that formed the Gateway to another world. The magical light that Ely had cast above them barely penetrated the heavy darkness of the earthen room.

The air was cool and held a dankness to it that Oliver assumed was to do with being underground. He could smell the damp soil and was suddenly filled with the uneasy feeling of being in a grave. He shivered and was grateful when Ely finally addressed him.

"In you go, Oliver. Good luck," Ely said encouragingly.

Oliver swallowed to wet his increasingly dry mouth as he stepped across the threshold and Ely shut the door, plunging him into darkness. He reached out with splayed hands and found a solid wall in front of him which he trailed his fingers along, discovering he was in a narrow corridor.

He followed it, keeping contact with the wall as he went.

"*Oliver.*"

He froze. The voice was no more than a whisper, spoken too quietly for him to tell if it was male or female.

"Hello?" Oliver called.

He waited, moments stretching on into minutes but no one answered. Cautiously, he continued onwards and emerged high up on a ledge overlooking a large cavern. The colossal roof was tinted navy blue from minerals in the rock that twinkled like stars in the night sky.

Burning torches illuminated a stone maze that stretched out below him the size of a football pitch. Its towering walls were moist and green with algae. Somewhere nearby, water dripped in a continual stream with a rhythmic *splat, splat, splat* as it hit the wet floor.

Oliver spied a dark set of stairs winding down towards the maze, leading to a tall, rectangular entrance where firelight flickered and danced. He steeled himself and started to make his way down the steps, keeping an eye on the amber glow emitting from the maze.

He moved into the light and approached the gap, gazing up at the walls. They seemed monstrous now that he was on the ground, perhaps twenty feet in height.

Oliver eyed the entrance to the maze where a corridor ran forward several feet toward a burning torch, before turning sharply to the right. A wind picked up and howled as it travelled through the narrow corridors of the maze, making the flames flutter in a frenzy.

A gust rushed through the gap with the sound of a sighing beast, ruffling Oliver's hair as the icy breath swept over him. He shivered and crept hesitantly inside towards the fire.

A grinding of stone made him swing around to find the gap in the wall closing. He dove towards it, colliding with the stone just as it shut.

Oliver turned and leant back against the rock taking a deep, calming breath. He knew he was trapped. His mind conjured terrifying images of what lay ahead in the dim passages.

He spotted a large, brass bell attached half way up the wall with a rope dangling down from it and wondered what it would take to make him ring it.

He started forward, turning right down a long corridor as he carefully picked a route through the rabbit warren.

"*Oliver,*" a voice whispered near his ear.

He paused and a shiver fled down his spine.

Whispers began from all around, growing in a crescendo until his ears filled with a hiss of noise. Most of the words were barely distinguishable but he caught the odd, disjointed phrase.

"*...can't take care of your family...father would be ashamed...nothing but a disappointment...*"

Oliver shook his head and pressed his hands to his ears but the voices didn't dim. He started to jog through the maze, hoping he could outpace the whispers but they only grew louder as he moved.

He turned down identical corridors at random, becoming disorientated inside the labyrinth.

"...*never be strong enough...*"

He met a dead end and backtracked, sprinting back down the passage past another bell and taking an alternative route.

"...*just a boy...*"

He emerged in the centre of the maze, a towering square space with no other exit but the one he entered through.

Words were painted on the walls in what looked like blood, the wetness of the red liquid apparent by its sheen. Drips ran down the stone as if they had been written just moments ago.

The voices began to repeat the words that were on the wall in a torrent of noise.

"*Abandoned. Useless. Weak. Failure. Worthless. Unwanted. Powerless. Alone.*"

He was struggling to keep himself grounded in reality, feeling fear creep into his chest. It was as if the maze itself had seen his darkest thoughts and doubts, using them to make him feel vulnerable.

He glanced at the large bell that was hanging on one wall then pressed his knuckles into his eyes, gritting his teeth and grinding them against each other to force the anxiety away.

"It's just words," he said aloud and the whispers stopped dead.

Oliver opened his eyes and his breath caught in his throat. A circular well had appeared directly in front of him, so close that the tips of his shoes hung over the edge. He stumbled backwards and eyed the endless abyss that dropped away before him.

"Help!" a woman cried up from it.

"Mum?" Oliver called in alarm as he recognised her voice, leaning forward and swaying as gravity tugged at him.

"Oliver! Help me!" Her voice echoed up from the bottom.

"*You can't save her.*" The whispers returned.

Oliver gazed down into the darkness, balancing precariously on the edge of the void.

A shrill scream rang up from the depths of the black hole, making Oliver stiffen in fright. He shuffled around the rim, frantically searching for a way down. The walls of the well were perfectly smooth and he could see no foothold.

"Mum!" he shouted, though he knew it was pointless.

"*Too afraid, too cowardly,*" the whispers said, taunting him.

Oliver's pulse thumped loudly in his ears as he stared down into the black pit.

"*Useless.*"

He breathed out through his nose, focusing on slowing his accelerated heartbeat.

"*Worthless.*"

He wasn't afraid of heights but the thought of what he was about to do made his instincts scream at him to stop.

"*Coward.*"

Oliver jumped forward into the well.

Air rushed past his ears and he let out a shout of fear as he hurtled down. He reached out his hands, trying to grip the wall but they slipped and slid down the smooth stone. He gasped as a jagged protrusion sliced the skin on his palm.

He landed in a taught, rope net and flew back into the air as it flexed from his weight. On the second bounce the net vanished and he cried out, his arms flailing as he plummeted toward the ground.

Oliver hit the stone floor with a *smack.*

A shaky breath escaped his lips as he mentally assessed the damage; he was grateful to find that the net had slowed his descent just enough that he had only bruised a few bones.

He stood and blood dripped from the laceration on his palm; he sucked the wound until it stopped bleeding, feeling shaken.

He looked up, taking in the square room and, as he swung around, blinked in realisation. He was back in the centre of the maze and a new exit had appeared opposite the one he had entered through; the words on the walls had vanished. He hurried forward through the exit and heard a rumble of noise as it closed behind him.

The corridor stretched into the distance. It was a narrow alley of dark, dewy walls and a damp floor that was coloured a murky green. There was no fire lighting the space, only a milky glow of what Oliver would have assumed was moonlight if he hadn't known he were inside a cave.

He wondered how long he had been in the maze and panic flooded him as the possibility entered his mind that the challenge could last for days.

He rubbed the sweat from his brow and resolved to continue on. As he stepped forward, a strange noise sounded somewhere ahead: a long *scrape* followed by a *clack*.

It grew closer and Oliver shrank into the shadows to conceal himself, taking slow, shallow breaths. He spotted openings set along the corridor that were barely distinguishable in the gloom and, as he squinted, noticed each one was flanked by a bell.

The noise grew louder and a disturbing figure emerged out of a passage several feet away, swathed in darkness and moving in a slow hobble. The apparition dragged one of its legs, scraping it along the floor behind it. The other foot dropped to the ground with a *clack* as if it were made of wood. The figure limped across the alley disappearing back into the labyrinth through another opening.

Oliver's heartbeat quickened and sweat gathered in his palms, making the cut on his hand sting. He hurried forward and darted down a passage on the left away from the sound of the terrifying being.

He met a dead end and cursed, spinning around in a panic, desperately wanting to put as much distance between him and it as possible.

Oliver walked purposefully toward the exit then stopped dead as he heard the being approaching once more.

Scraaaape. Clack.

He cursed internally, backing up against the wall and pressing a hand to his mouth to silence his erratic breathing.

The sound grew closer and he watched the space intently, expecting a shadow to cross its path at any moment.

Scraaaape. Clack.

The noise set his teeth on edge as the scraping ended with a sound like a knife slipping across porcelain.

Oliver stopped breathing as the figure appeared in the exit and paused, lingering in the doorway as if searching for something.

He waited for it to move, the seconds stretching on until his lungs burned for air.

"Oliver," a raspy voice sounded, making a chill run through his body.

The shadow turned slowly, its leg dragging in a sweeping arc behind it, and tipped its chin upwards so the hood fell back off of its head.

Oliver was suddenly face to face with the vision of his father from his nightmares: a skeletal form that looked as though it were decomposing, its bloodshot eyes glaring at him from oozing sockets.

"You're not real," Oliver breathed, though his voice quavered as he spoke, fear inching into his body like needles.

It stepped toward him with a *clack* and Oliver spotted the bloody, footless stump of bone that hit the floor, making his stomach churn violently.

Oliver sidled along the wall in a panic, unable to take his eyes off of the corpse that was pursing him.

The slime on its bare bones and remains of tissue hanging from its face made bile rise in Oliver's throat and sweat stream down his back in rivulets.

"You're dead," Oliver whispered, clawing his fingers into the cracks of the wall as he moved along it.

His fingertips touched something coarse and he wrapped his hand around it, feeling the rough hairs of a rope.

A gurgling sounded from the deathly creature in front of him then words formed from its decaying mouth. "Couldn't save your mother...won't save your sister."

If he rang the bell he would never be able to help May. The thought filled him with a slither of courage, just enough to make his hand snap back towards him and release the rope.

He turned towards the figure, preparing to face it.

7

Beyond

$\mathbf{A}$ grinding of stone sounded and a warm glow split the darkness in half.

Oliver rushed towards it with a wave of relief that spread through his entire body as he left the apparition behind. He sighed heavily as he found himself back in the underground chamber with his sister and Ely.

"Congratulations. You've both successfully completed the challenge," Ely said, grinning broadly.

"That was horrible," May said, running her hands up her arms.

"What happened to you?" Oliver asked, glancing back at the door as if the grotesque figure of his father might still be lurking there.

May grimaced. "It was like everything I'm afraid of was living in this awful maze."

Oliver nodded, subtly stepping away from the door behind him. "What did you see?"

"When I went in the walls closed behind me and I thought the best thing to do was to stay put. But then this guy appeared, he was huge and his face was just this hollow, black space and I tried to run from him but he grabbed my wrist and dragged me through the maze."

Her voice shook as she spoke and Ely looked at her with pity in his eyes as she continued. "He took me to this podium in the centre of the maze and I was strung up in front all these people, all with the same indistinct faces but their eyes were visible and they were just *staring* at me, waiting for me to speak or do something and I felt so vulnerable. I wanted to ring the bell, I almost did-" she cut off, her breath catching in her throat.

Oliver stepped forwards and hugged her firmly then she buried her face in his shoulder.

"I'm sorry," Ely said. "This Gateway challenge is testing and quite cruel. But you both did so well, do you have any idea how many people ring a bell and fail this test?"

Oliver stepped away from May and nodded. "We had to get through it. Now we can visit your friend who can help May."

Ely smiled brightly. "Yes. Now, I've got something for you both." He rummaged inside his jacket and retrieved two familiar objects that Oliver recognised from the attic.

Oliver glanced at May in surprise as they each took the heptagonal pendant inscribed with their name.

"They're called Locks. I made them for you years ago. I know your mother never wanted you to know about the worlds but I hoped one day she might change her mind." He winked at them.

Ely strolled over to the Gateway and plucked four, sparkling gems from it before returning to them. Oliver placed the Lock around his neck and May imitated him.

"You can only gain access to each world by possessing a key," Ely said.

"Key?" Oliver asked curiously.

"The keys," Ely held up one of the twinkling jewels from the Gateway. "They're mined for by gem trolls in Glacio." He rubbed the tiny sphere between his fingers.

Oliver looked closer at the translucent key in Ely's hand and suddenly recognised it. He retrieved the ball he had carried in his pocket ever since discovering it in the attic. It was identical.

"Where did you get that?" Ely looked stern.

Oliver realised his mistake. "I found it in the attic," he admitted.

"Oh, so you went exploring, did you?" Ely asked, shaking his head. "You're just like your mother." He softened and broke into a smile. "Well here you are," he said, handing them two each. "The Locks are designed to hold them."

Oliver took the tiny spheres in his hand, cupping them in the crease of his palm where they sat, twinkling up at him.

"Can't I use the one I found?" he asked.

"I'm afraid not. The gems must be taken from the Gateways and encoded within a brief amount of time, otherwise they become useless."

"Why?" May asked.

"The gems feed off of the Gateway, it's where they acquire their magic. The Gateways are intricately linked with the challenges so that a person can only receive a key if the Gateway recognises that they have been successful."

"Couldn't a mage just make their own keys with magic? Bypass the challenges?" Oliver asked.

"No. Dorian Ganderfield's challenges are impregnable, enforced by complex spells of his own design. You cannot go through a Gateway without a key and you cannot get a key without succeeding in a challenge," Ely said.

"Why have you given us two keys each?" May asked curiously.

"One of them is a key to Aleva and the other is your key back to Earth. You are given the one to your world of origin as standard practise once you have completed your first challenge."

Oliver rolled the gems in his hand; they were cool and smooth and looked as though they held a minuscule galaxy of stars inside.

"Hold out a hand both of you," Ely directed.

Oliver and May complied and, in a flash of movement, Ely pricked their fingers with something extremely sharp causing globs of blood to seep from the punctures.

Oliver snatched his arm away. "Why'd you do that?"

May went to suck her finger but Ely stopped her.

"Place the blood on your keys," he demanded.

Oliver gently pressed his bloody finger onto each key whilst Ely raised a glimmering palm of silver above it. The keys absorbed the blood, swirling around in a miniature storm before pulsing momentarily and dispersing. The gems gradually changed colour until one was an earthy green and the other an ocean blue; they continued to sparkle but were no longer transparent.

"Which one's which?" May asked.

"Aleva's key is green and Earth's is blue. Each key is coloured to represent the different worlds. You can pop them in their respective holes on your Locks."

Oliver lifted his pendant in one hand and eyed the labels around the rim before pushing the keys into their places between fragile, metal clasps.

"No one can use these keys but you. The blood magically encodes them to your DNA. I inscribed your names on the back of your Locks so you'll know they're yours," Ely said proudly.

"Thank you," May said, moving to give him a hug.

"Yeah, thanks," Oliver said, deciding not to mention that they had already seen the Locks. He turned his over to reveal the words etched in the metal and ran his finger over the indentations. "So, what now?" he asked.

"Now, we pack a bag and get going. It's chilly this time of year in the part of Aleva we'll be visiting so bring something warm to wear. I sent a message to the Council whilst you were completing the challenge asking them to send a stand-in Keeper to look after the Gateway while we're gone. We should only be a few days with any luck. I need to return to my position here and you two will need to get back to school."

* * *

The two of them hurried upstairs and May gripped Oliver's elbow as he went to enter his room.

"What did you see in the challenge?" she asked, gazing at him intently.

Oliver felt his guard creep up. He never kept secrets from May but he hadn't ever wanted to voice the fears he had about his father, it was a part of him he buried and tried not to disturb. "I was in the maze, too. Mum was there and I was trying to save her then there was this corpse chasing me around."

"Oh." Frown lines formed around May's mouth. "Were you tempted to ring the bell?"

Oliver shrugged off her hand. "No. Course not."

He felt guilt trickle into his gut and turned away from his sister, giving her a casual smile. He entered his room and started packing a backpack with warm clothes.

He didn't want May to think he was tempted to leave the challenge, she might translate that into thinking he wasn't determined enough to go with her to the other worlds. Though part of him worried that, if he had spent another five minutes in the maze, he might have rung the bell. The thought was disquieting.

He pulled on a coat, shouldered his bag then exited his room and found May waiting for him in the corridor bundled up in warm layers.

"What do you think it'll be like?" May wondered aloud as they descended the spiral staircase.

"I don't know," Oliver said thoughtfully as he pushed open the door that led to the chamber beneath the house. He had been so wrapped up in everything since May had woken him in the night that he had hardly spared a thought for what lay beyond the portal.

Ely was waiting for them in front of the Gateway, dressed in a heavy suede coat with a backpack hanging from one shoulder.

"Are we going to meet Mum's twin?" May asked Ely, looking hopeful.

"Yes, we'll be staying with her in Aleva. Stand over there by the Gateway and take out your Locks," Ely said.

Oliver pulled the pendant from underneath his top and watched as the earthy green key to Aleva began to glow brighter and brighter.

"Hold on to them tightly and walk through the Gateway after me," Ely instructed.

May gripped Oliver's arm, the light from her key catching in her eyes as she gazed up at him with concern. He nodded to his grandfather and Ely raised his Lock towards the Gateway.

Ribbons of light ripped across the arch of roots as the portal opened. Oliver could hear it humming quietly and he drew back a little.

May tugged his arm, bringing him back to his senses.

Ely stepped through the Gateway; the light seemed to bend around him then he disappeared with a crackle of noise.

Oliver blinked in shock.

"Ready?" May asked quietly.

"I'm not exactly sure what to be ready for," Oliver said.

"I know, can we walk through together?" May asked.

He nodded then shared one last anxious look with his sister before stepping forward into the abyss.

Oliver felt his stomach drop as if he were falling. The sound of May screaming seemed to echo around him as they fell and he gripped her arm tighter.

The light from his key glowed so brightly that it was all he could see. He felt weightless for a moment then his feet collided with uneven ground and he fell backwards onto it. May toppled over and Oliver groaned as she landed on his legs. She scrambled to stand up and he followed suit, rubbing his knees.

Ely hurried towards them and clapped his hands together, looking pleased.

Oliver gazed around at his surroundings. He was standing at the foot of a tree that resembled the one back at Oakway Manor, minus the house.

A large, circular hole in its trunk marked the Gateway on this side of the portal and the leaves on its branches were a bright, lush-looking green. There was a crisp chill in the air and Oliver's breath came out as a puff of vapour.

They were standing on a ledge that jutted out over a steep valley, high up on the side of a mountain. For miles around rolling hills and towering mountains disappeared up into wispy, white clouds. Oliver crept towards the edge.

A city was nestled between the mountain they were stood upon and one that rose up opposite. The buildings looked like a model from this height; lights twinkled in the windows and Oliver realised that daylight was already fading in this world.

A train emerged from a tunnel in the mountain opposite, running along tracks that ran outside the city in a large circle, making its way through smaller tunnels in the hills.

A sudden gust of wind made Oliver draw back from the ledge.

"Beautiful, isn't it? I'll never forget the first time I saw this view. The city you can see is called Alevale," Ely said.

"Are we going down there?" May asked, peeping over the edge with a look of fascination.

"Yes, we'll take the- " Ely was distracted by a loud horn that sounded from the other mountain.

Oliver located the source of the noise where a bright fire was burning on an outcrop. A booming horn responded to it somewhere further down the valley. The sound carried on the wind and echoed off the rocks, the two notes calling out together in a mournful cry.

"Ahh, that's a sound I've missed," Ely said with a smile.

"What is it?" May asked.

"They sound the horns at dawn, midday and dusk. The citizens of Alevale used to rely on them to tell the time and structure their day but nowadays they have modern technology which can do that. But the tradition has stayed in place."

A stone pathway led away from the Gateway, heading down through the thick woodland. They were sheltered from the wind on the path but Oliver still did up his coat against the icy air. They dropped steeply down the side of the mountain then curved to the left in the direction of the city.

The three of them approached a watch-post where Oliver spotted a man who was smoking by a small fire. A long, thin, horn-like instrument jutted out over the precipice in front of him. It curved upwards and back towards the fire. The mouthpiece sat near to the man's head. He got to his feet and walked towards them through a cloud of smoke, revealing shoulder-length hair, a bristly beard and a pipe held in the corner of his mouth.

"Ah, Ely Fox, long time no see," the man said in a gruff voice, puffing away on his pipe.

"Good to see you again, Corwell. These are my grandchildren, Oliver and May. They just received their first keys," Ely said, standing up a little straighter.

"Congratulations," Corwell said. "Let's see those Locks then please, you two." He gestured to Oliver and May.

Oliver held his up and Corwell ran a palm over it. Red lightning reached out from his palm and touched his Lock. It turned green abruptly and Corwell dropped his hand. "Thank you, hold yours up please, May."

She did so and Corwell repeated the process.

"Great. You're all set," Corwell said, taking another puff on his pipe. "You're now registered here as key holders to Aleva, you can come and go through the Gateway between Aleva and Earth freely."

"Thanks," Oliver said, feeling enthused as he concealed the Lock beneath his clothes.

"Thank you, Corwell. We'll be going back through in a few days, no doubt," Ely said.

Corwell nodded and raised a hand in goodbye as they continued on down the pathway.

The wood descended into darkness as the sun set and tiny lights sprang to life along the edge of the path, illuminating the way.

"Does he live up here?" May asked, glancing back at the Gateway Keeper.

In answer, Ely grinned and pointed to the tree canopy above their heads. Oliver squinted up into the leaves, spying a wooden walkway strung from branch to branch. He turned his head, following the precarious trail amidst the boughs towards a large treehouse that was wedged between two enormous trunks.

The bridge creaked and wobbled as a creature hurried along it above them, heading down towards the end of the path where a woman was waiting.

Oliver had to double take; she was the image of his mum. Her long, blonde hair was only dissimilar to his mother's in how it curled rather than hung straight. She wore a red coat and her hands were tucked into the pockets.

A black shape dropped gracefully from the trees and trotted over to her, rubbing up against her legs. Oliver recognised Humphrey as they closed the space between them.

Ely rushed forward and pulled the woman into a hug. She was much taller than her father, his head barely reaching her chin. He released his daughter and tugged her towards the two of them.

"This is Laura. And Laura, these are Alison's children, Oliver and May."

She smiled warmly. "It's lovely to meet you. I'm so sorry to hear about your mum's disappearance. Have you had any news at all?" she asked, looking concerned.

Oliver shook his head, gazing into her blue eyes that were the exact shade of his mother's.

"No," May said quietly.

Laura lifted Humphrey into her arms and he purred loudly. Ely reached out a palm and sent the gold mist into his ears once more. Laura kissed the cat's head and returned him to the ground.

"Off you go," Ely instructed and Humphrey shot off towards the Gateway, his tail waving madly in the air as he ran.

"Did Humphrey tell you we were coming?" May asked in confusion.

Laura laughed. "Dad sent a message to me with him. He waited here with me, he's been playing in the trees."

"Aww," May said as she watched the cat go with adoring eyes.

"There'll be a train along in a minute, we'd better hurry," Laura said, turning back down the trail with a swish of her coat.

They followed her out onto a train platform made of white stone. The tracks, which sat several feet below the edge, were twice as wide as those on Earth and were an incandescent blue, bright enough to light the area.

The tracks veered sharply to the left around the mountainside in the direction of Alevale city. To the right, the tracks led away into a dark, circular tunnel that was cut into the mountain. The tunnel began to grow bright with two pinpoints of light, hovering above the ground and growing closer by the second.

The front of an immense train emerged and slowed to a stop in front of them in near silence. It was black as obsidian, towering two stories high and topped with vast storage containers.

The first floor was glazed with large windows that were bordered by red, velvet curtains; the floor below was busy with sofas and armchairs that were upholstered in blues and greens and arranged around small tables.

Laura walked to the front of the train where five, manned ticket booths were embedded in the side though only one was open. She returned a moment later and passed them tickets that were made of the same blue metal as the tracks, glowing brightly in the darkness.

"This is a Traverser train. They transport people from Alevale City to as far away as Crome," Laura said, her gaze flitting between Oliver and May.

"That's about two days away from here. It's where they hold the challenge for the key to Glacio," Ely explained.

"What's the challenge here?" May asked. "I'm not sure I'd want to do another one."

Laura grinned, revealing a perfect set of teeth. "They're not all as bad as Earth to Aleva's. To get a key to Glacio you have to compete in a race that's held every few months. I work at it as part of my job."

"What do you do?" Oliver asked curiously.

"I work for the government in the Gateway division. I regulate the importation of ambiculis gemstones from Glacio which are made into keys for the Gateways."

"That sounds interesting," May said.

"It isn't really. The best part is working at the Gateway challenge."

They had to scan their tickets at the train door to allow them access. Oliver held the rectangular piece of metal up to a blinking scanner and the doors hissed as they opened, allowing them access.

They made their way into one of the carriages on the bottom floor and occupied a couple of sofas by the window.

"How long 'til we get there?" Oliver asked.

"Not long, it only takes ten minutes from here," Laura replied.

The train pulled out of the station with a smooth grace. There was little sign that they were moving apart from a whirring noise and the feel of gliding.

Oliver rested his head against the window to look outside. He could just make out the towering shape of the mountain through the darkness as the train hugged its outline, veering left towards the city.

He caught Laura's eye. "When was the last time you saw Mum?" he asked.

"Oh, *years* ago. After it all came out about your father illegally marrying your mother, she was banned from seeing him and had to move to Earth-"

Oliver couldn't help cutting her off. "Wait. *Illegally* marrying her? What are you talking about?"

Laura threw an alarmed look at her father who gazed back with a guilty expression. "Don't you know any of this?" she asked, looking between Oliver and May.

"We literally found out about the other worlds earlier today. Mum kept *everything* from us," May said, sounding exasperated.

"Oh, wow. Well, where to begin?" Laura said in a daze.

"We'll begin after we've settled in. We're not discussing this right now," Ely said firmly.

"You're kidding, right?" Oliver said in disbelief. "We deserve the truth."

"And you'll have it. But I'd be much happier having this conversation in private where there aren't prying ears to hear us." He gestured to the other people on the Traverser who couldn't be paying them less attention if they tried. An old man woke himself up at the sound of his own snore then promptly fell back asleep.

Oliver huffed.

Laura nodded slowly in agreement. "Dad's right. This stuff should be heard in private."

"You can tell them what they need to hear," Ely said.

"We need to hear it all," Oliver insisted.

"Look, just, drop it for now will you?" Ely said, clearly frustrated.

Oliver pressed his cheek against the cool pane of glass, looking away from his grandfather. He had been sure Ely was done with keeping secrets from them but now realised he was wrong.

A bright mass of lights appeared in the distance, catching his eye. Some of them rose high up into the sky. The clouds parted above them and two moons were revealed: one small and one large, both were tinted a dusty yellow.

"Are you gonna be here for the race? The next one is in a couple of weeks," Laura asked Ely.

"We won't be here that long unfortunately, just a couple of days. I haven't watched one in years though, it's a shame."

"You never visit Aleva for more than a couple of days at a time, that's why. Is it because of Mum?" Laura asked, the corners of her mouth turning down.

"Of course not, it's nothing to do with that woman. You know I can't leave the Gateway for long periods of time. Do you see much of your mother?" Ely asked the question airily but Oliver sensed tension in his voice.

"Quite a bit. Larkin's just turned eighteen. He'll be competing in the coming race," Laura said.

"Hmm, wonderful," Ely said, sounding uninterested.

"Who's Larkin?" May asked.

"He's my half-brother," Laura said. "Mum had another kid after she remarried."

"So, he's like our half-uncle and he's only eighteen?" Oliver asked in surprise.

"Will we get to meet him?" May asked hopefully.

Laura smiled and opened her mouth to respond but Ely stepped in before she could.

"There won't be time," he said firmly.

May looked crestfallen. Oliver glared at Ely but he looked away, pretending to be occupied by the view outside the window as the train pulled into a station.

"Ready to go?" Ely asked as he stood up.

8

Forbidden

The station formed a glass tunnel around the train and a large sign greeted them as they moved through the crowd of people. Oliver cast his eyes over the words:

Welcome to Alevale, the City Between the Mountains.

The floor was made of white marble with twisted pillars that rose to the roof, holding it in place.

They let the crowd sweep them towards the exit and Oliver gazed up at the glass ceiling. The darkness outside caused the scene to be reflected on the pane and Oliver caught sight of himself as they moved.

The crowd was funnelled towards the exit, the walls growing closer together as they neared a marble arch. A booth sat in the centre of the arch stationed by two guards who were scanning tickets.

One by one, they shuffled up to the booth. Oliver stopped in front of a guard with a large moustache who held out a hand to take his ticket. Oliver passed it to him, watching as the man inserted the ticket into a handheld machine. Its blue glow died in an instant and the guard dropped the ticket through a slot in the desk in front of him.

The guard nodded at him and Oliver moved forward.

He took a deep breath of cold air as he exited the station, the fresh scent of nearby trees filling his nostrils. He looked around, wondering why he couldn't see a road or hear any traffic.

Laura gathered her red coat around her and ushered them towards a set of stairs. "This way," she said as she disappeared down them.

"Don't they have cars here?" Oliver asked.

"No, just wait and see," Ely replied and followed Laura out of sight.

Oliver shared a curious look with May before descending the staircase. They emerged in an area that reminded Oliver of an underground train station. In front of them was a raised bar on the floor that glowed blue, running the length of the station and disappearing at both ends through a tunnel. Intermittent, horizontal bars led away from the main track toward the crowd.

"Why do the tracks glow?" May asked as she gazed at them.

Laura looked amused as if she were enjoying explaining things. "It's Alevinum: a material that naturally holds electricity for years. It's used for all kinds of things but the tracks use it to power vehicles."

"Does a train run along these too?" May asked.

Before Laura could answer, a completely spherical, white object appeared on the track. Two people stepped forward and opened a circular door in the front of it before entering. There were porthole-like windows running around its edge that allowed Oliver a glimpse of the interior.

It held a circular seating area with a small, round table at its centre. He craned his neck to get a better look but the vehicle glided out of view before he had a chance to see more.

Several more of the vehicles appeared as the station became increasingly packed with people. The spheres varied in colours and sizes and, whilst some of the interiors looked luxurious, others were plain and basic.

Oliver turned to see Laura queuing for a panel on the wall close by. When she reached it, she pressed her palm flat to the screen until it read:

Laura Fox identified - payment confirmed

"My pod will be along in a moment," Laura said as she returned.

"Pod? Is that what they're called?" Oliver asked, excited about the prospect of riding in one.

"Yes, mine isn't the fanciest but it gets me around. Plus, it's cheaper to park a smaller pod," Laura muttered, wringing her hands.

May moved closer to the row of pods which were diverting off of the main track towards the crowd. "Which one's yours?"

A small pod, that was slightly more egg-shaped than the others, glided to a halt in front of them and Laura pointed at it.

"This one. What do you think?" She eyed Oliver and May, biting her lip.

Her expression reminded Oliver of his mother once more and he found himself studying her features, trying to spot the differences between her and her sister.

"I love it!" May said and Oliver nodded his agreement, jolted out of his reverie.

Laura moved forward, pressed her palm to the door and a blue ripple appeared in the shape of her handprint. The print disappeared and a brief, ethereal noise sounded before the door opened.

Oliver climbed inside after the others, discovering that there was room for four people on a circular, cream sofa around the rim. The walls and floor had a smooth, wood-effect apart from the door which remained white on the inside too.

"Where would you like to go, Laura?" The image of a young, blonde man popped into existence on the white of the door seemingly projected on an invisible screen embedded within it.

May jumped visibly and Oliver laughed.

"Take me home, please. And put on the heating in here would you?" Laura instructed the image.

"Going home and initiating heating. Enjoy your trip," the man said, grinning a lopsided smile at her before disappearing.

Laura glanced at Oliver and May. "You can choose different personalities for each pod, even celebrities. This one is a presenter named Truvian Gold."

May nodded, a glint entering her eye. "He's really hot."

"I know, right?" Laura knocked shoulders with her and they giggled.

Oliver shared an uncomfortable look with Ely as the pod took off down the dark tunnel.

* * *

The pod whizzed along at break-neck speed, turning sharp corners until it finally stopped in another station. This one had numbers from one through to twenty printed along the walls next to mirrored doors. Above them was a sign that read:

Chance Street

"This is us," Laura said brightly, climbing out of the pod onto the platform.

She shut the door and moved over to another panel on the wall, pressing her palm to it for a moment then the pod glided out of sight in response.

Ely stretched laboriously. "Can't wait for a cuppa," he said through a yawn.

Laura walked to the door marked with a black number three. She stood in front of the mirror and a tinkling bell sounded before the door slid to the side to allow them access.

They ascended a wooden staircase to an open-plan kitchenette and living room. Soft white armchairs and sofas faced a wall composed of floor-length windows covered by wooden shutters. The space was designed to be simple and bright with tones of white and grey broken up with small touches of green.

Laura moved to the kitchenette and began fussing around with various Alevinum metal devices. She returned with a tray of cups and a tall, pink pot that had a long, winding spout. Oliver could smell something sweet and earthy coming from the pot which made his stomach rumble.

"Try this. It's Glacian Tea, it'll warm you right up," Laura said.

She poured the liquid, which was white and creamy in colour. The tea tasted as good as it smelt and it warmed Oliver through to the bones in seconds.

"So, about my parents?" Oliver prompted, unable to contain his curiosity any longer.

Laura took a sip of tea and smiled. "Well, your parents went to university together here in Alevale. I went at the same time, but we were enrolled on different courses. They were interested in the Gateways but I was more into politics."

"Here in Aleva teenagers go to university at sixteen through 'til eighteen," Ely chipped in.

Oliver nodded, excited to know more.

Laura continued. "Your mum and dad got together in their first year. Your dad, William, had a friend called Isaac Rimori who he was completely inseparable from. They were both obsessed with the Gateways. And I mean *obsessed*. I couldn't stand hearing about it for more than five minutes." She rolled her eyes. "My brother Eugene-"

"I don't think they need to know about Eugene," Ely cut her off sharply.

Laura threw him an angry look. "Yes they do. They should know the whole truth."

"We want to know," Oliver insisted.

"Please?" May begged.

Ely looked as though he were about to protest further but Laura barrelled on. "Eugene went to university a year after me and Alison. He got to know your father through Alison and became like William and Isaac Rimori's puppy dog." She wrinkled her nose. "The four of them were really close by the end of their final year and your parents and Isaac were planning a trip to the other worlds to see how many keys they could win. Eugene was a year behind them so he was unable to go. He got so upset about it that he just dropped out of university so he could join them."

"Let's not go on about it too much," Ely said, looking hurt.

"Sorry Dad. Well basically, Isaac and William took part in Earth's challenge and they both won keys. Eugene and Alison already had keys because they grew up in Earth so the four of them went through the Gateway that day. From what I heard, William proposed to your mum and they ran off to get married straight away."

"And why was that illegal?" Oliver asked.

"Oh, of course, sorry I'm forgetting you actually don't know anything about anything." She laughed. "So, your dad was a mage-"

"Seriously?" Oliver blurted and May said "*What*?" at the same time.

"Yeah, but your mum isn't. She's a Dud like me," Laura said.

"Wait, wait, wait, now I'm confused. What's a *Dud*?" May asked, screwing her face up.

Laura looked at Ely who waved a hand for her to continue.

"I told you it was complicated," Ely said before she began.

"A Dud is the first child born to mage parents. Me and Alison are twins so we're both Duds. The second born child is termed a Renic mage and the third born child is a Lanic which is always the most powerful. You can't bear a magical child unless the parents are *both* mages. It's illegal for a mage to marry someone who isn't magical, including Duds."

"Psh, they *can* just not until they've *done their duty*. As long as they've married a mage and produced magical children they can petition for divorce and marry whoever they like once their kids are grown up," Ely grumbled.

Oliver guessed this was what had happened between him and Laura's mother who, he realised with a pang, was his grandmother. It was a strange feeling to have spent his life within a small family to suddenly discover he had a seemingly extensive one. He thirsted to know more about them.

"So, if mages don't have children together there won't be any more born?" May confirmed.

Laura nodded. "Exactly, it's thought that there used to be mages in Earth but they died out before Dorian Ganderfield went there because they rarely had children together. He positioned an Alevian mage at the Gateway in Earth and later the Council placed some amongst the King's society to aid them in keeping their secret.

"Mages are still fairly rare and a few worlds, including Aleva, revere those that remain. Some are even famous. The Council of Heptus passed the law to stop them becoming extinct because they're needed to maintain the Gateways, their magic is what keeps them intact."

"And this Council can create laws that apply across all of the worlds, can it?" Oliver asked.

"Yes, it's the law in all seven worlds that mages can't petition for divorce until they have brought up three children so there are always two mages to replace the two that produced them. It never used to be that way but mages started declining in numbers," Ely said.

"That's awful," May said.

"It can be. It makes sense but it takes away a basic freedom. Many are placed into arranged marriages by their families from a young age. They're usually paired according to their level of power so as to produce powerful children," Ely said.

"But why don't the Council just make mages have more children, why just three?" Oliver asked.

"Mage couples can't have more than three children. Only in very rare cases do they have four and that's usually a case of twins, as with me and Alison. No one really knows why."

"So when your dad married your mum they were defying the Council. But the Council didn't find out for three years. You were already born, Oliver, in Brinatin," Laura revealed.

"I wasn't even born on *Earth*?" Oliver asked in shock.

Ely shook his head.

"But how could I have gone through the Gateways without a key?" Oliver asked.

"Children can go through accompanied by a key-bearing adult up until they're sixteen years old. Then they are permitted to attempt the Gateway challenges in order to get their own keys," Ely explained.

Oliver nodded, not sure how he felt about knowing his true heritage. He swallowed in an attempt to wet his mouth but failed.

"So, what about my parents? What happened after they got married?" he asked.

Laura ran a finger around the rim of her mug as she spoke. "The High Mage, who's the head of the Council, banned them from seeing each other. He ordered your dad to marry the mage that he already had an arranged engagement with. That's when your mum took you to Earth."

"And you didn't see her again after that?" Oliver asked.

"I still visited her occasionally. It wasn't until your dad died six years later that she cut everyone off," Laura said.

"Did she see my dad in that time?" Oliver asked, wondering if he had ever spent time with the stranger that was his father.

"No, they couldn't. Not only were they banned by law but your father had gone into hiding." Laura glanced at Ely who shook his head slightly in response.

"What is it?" Oliver interjected, sure his grandfather was trying to hide more of the facts.

"Dad, he should know. It'd be worse if he hears it from someone else," Laura muttered out the corner of her mouth.

"What? Tell me," Oliver insisted, feeling his heartbeat quicken.

Laura's eyes shifted to his. "There was an *incident* involving your father's betrothed. William and Isaac were seen leaving her premises on the night she died, Rose Isla was her name. They were accused of her murder and William, Isaac and Eugene went on the run soon after.

"I doubt William could have gotten to Alison after that, the Gateways were being tightly monitored. No one heard anything from them until six years later when the news of William's murder came out," Laura said.

"But there wasn't any evidence to prove my dad killed her?" Oliver asked, feeling an inexplicable compulsion to defend him.

"Well, no," Laura said slowly. "But he was a mage. He could have destroyed the evidence."

"How did she die?" May asked, her pale skin somehow paling further.

"It appeared that she overdosed on some narcotic. Rose was very popular amongst the people, she was a high born mage who used to speak out on issues of human rights. When she died, the people of Aleva were in uproar and, when a witness came forward to say they had seen William and Isaac present at the scene of her death, the public wanted blood."

"But his friend, Rimori, it must have been *him*. He was the one who killed my dad. *He* was the murderer," Oliver argued, refusing to accept the accusations about his father.

"Perhaps you're right," Ely said but Oliver sensed it was only in an attempt to keep him calm.

"What happened to Eugene?" May asked and Oliver was aware that she was purposefully steering the subject away from his father.

He listened, but began to chew the inside of his cheeks anxiously.

Ely shifted in his seat. "My son was tried in court for conspiring against the Gateways and assisting Rimori in getting to Vale. He had also been on the run from his own arranged marriage like your father. They locked him up for almost ten years to make an example of him. He only got out a few months ago."

"But he didn't do anything wrong," May said sadly.

Oliver thought of the dusty bedroom back at Oakway manor, feeling a twinge of sadness at the thought of Ely packing up Eugene's things. He realised Ely must have sealed the boxes shut with magic.

Laura shook her head. "He did. It's one thing to believe the Gateways shouldn't be in place but to actively go against them is an act of terrorism against the Council." Her voice quavered slightly as she spoke.

"Did you visit Eugene in prison?" May asked.

Laura nodded. "Just once. He wasn't the same. Something about him wasn't my brother anymore. He said he was too ashamed to talk to me and didn't want me to visit again." Laura's eyes glistened with tears. "I know what he did was wrong but he was harmless. He would never hurt anybody."

"Will you visit him now he's out of prison?" May asked gently.

"Maybe, but he's living in Brinatin so I'd have to take a trip there. I was hoping he would contact me but so far I've heard nothing," Laura said, a sad look creeping into her eyes. "You haven't heard anything have you Dad?"

Ely shook his head firmly.

Quiet fell over them but Oliver's mind was a clamour of noise as he went through everything he had been told. The blood that ran in his veins could be that of a murderer's. He didn't want to believe it and it was going to take a lot more than speculation to convince him.

9

A Desolate Land

Ten Years Ago

Rimori fell through the Gateway to Vale and landed on his knees, splitting the skin on razor sharp rocks that lay beneath him. His right hand was shaking, his fingers still gripping the knife so tightly that it hurt. He eyed the blade which was covered in fresh blood and felt the full force of what he had done.

He suppressed a wave of emotion that threatened to overwhelm him and opened his eyes to take in the world before him. As far as the eye could see was black rock, swathes of it reaching ahead of him into the distance. He rose to his feet and gazed at the landscape of Vale in silent awe.

The Gateway was embedded in a blackened, charred tree that curved over like a withered hand. The baked-looking earth sat beneath a blood-red sky and the atmosphere was heavy and oppressive, making Rimori's lungs labour a little harder than usual.

A few feet ahead, the rough terrain dropped away into a massive canyon that disappeared into a shadowy abyss. Rimori crept towards the edge and gazed down into the impenetrable blackness where, far,

far below was an obsidian river only distinguishable because of its glossy, ink-like sheen.

He drew away from the ledge and gazed into the distance where enormous, dark mountains towered into the sky, their shapes irregular and curved. It was as if the rock had once been a chaotic, black ocean that had frozen in time.

Rimori wiped the blood from his knife and attached it at his hip, thinking through the movements carefully as he concentrated on remaining calm.

The ground shook in a sudden earthquake and Rimori ran towards the Gateway, clutching a branch tightly as he watched part of the canyon wall crumble away into the nothingness below.

The shaking ceased and he gathered his thoughts, considering the plan he and his friends had discussed over and over for the past few years.

He needed to find the shadow creatures that lived in Vale, the varks. He gazed around wondering where they might dwell within the desolate land. The varks were the main reason he had travelled to the seventh world and was certain that they would lead him to the truth behind the Arc.

The ground beneath his feet trembled again and he stumbled to his knees, still clinging to the Gateway tightly.

"Doriannn?" a voice hissed inside Rimori's mind and he threw a hand to his forehead in shock. "Doriannn?" it hissed again.

"Who's there?" he shouted, his voice shaking uncontrollably.

"You musssssst pay for whattt you didd," it said and Rimori crumpled to the floor as pain ripped through his body.

He screamed, feeling a slashing, ripping sensation as if a beast were clawing at his gut.

It stopped as abruptly as it had started and he looked down at himself, panicking as he expected to find his torso torn to shreds. He was astonished to discover himself whole, his entire body free from a single scratch.

"Stop, stop, *please*. I'm harmless," Rimori gasped, desperate not to be subjected to the pain again.

There was no one close by but he could feel a shadow pressing down on his body, somehow weighing a tonne yet there was no sensation of being physically touched.

"Doriannnn," it repeated.

"No, I'm not Dorian. My name's Rimori. Isaac Rimori," he said frantically, his mind finally registering what the voice was saying.

"Rimmorii?" it repeated in a deep, gravelly hiss.

Rimori squirmed on the floor against the vark's unwavering hold.

"Yes, Rimori. Not Dorian," he said through gasps, the air being squeezed from his lungs.

"Magee. Magicc. *Burningg.*" Its anger was increasing.

"No. I'm not a mage. I can't hurt you," Rimori wailed, willing the creature not to attack him again.

"Why havvve you come to my worllld?"

"I want to destroy the Gateways. I want to make an allegiance with your kind."

"Allegianccccce? Yessss, yesss," it hissed.

Rimori felt a twinge of hope. "*Yes,*" he groaned.

"No allegianccce with humansss."

Pain ripped through him again. His body convulsed violently and his eyes rolled up into his head.

"St-stop," he managed.

The pain ended abruptly and Rimori's breathing came in tiny pants as he struggled to draw air down into his lungs.

"Please. Give me a chance," he wheezed.

The vark didn't answer for a moment then said, "No chancessss."

Rimori braced for more pain, screwing his eyes up and clenching his fists.

"No mmagic. You havvve none," it said after a moment.

"Yes, I have no magic. I can't hurt you," he said in relief.

"You'll commme with me. Yess, yess. Follow closssssely or mmore painn."

Rimori felt the creature release him and he rolled onto his back, his chest rising and falling erratically as his breathing returned to normal.

"*Come,*" the vark ordered, the voice vibrating in his ears.

Rimori's hands shook as he pressed them to the ground and righted himself.

He could feel vibrations emitting from the vark a few feet away and a barely perceptible shadow signalled its position, almost as if a cloud had drifted over the sun. He discovered that its form became nearly visible in the periphery of his eye but, if he tried to look directly at it, the vark was indistinct once more.

"Thissss way," it hissed. Based on its voice alone, Rimori would have guessed the creature was male but he wasn't even sure that varks had genders.

Rimori stumbled after it, feeling his way using the vibrations it seemed to dispel.

The vark led him to a cave, the entrance to which lay at the bottom of a tall rock structure shaped like a giant, piercing thorn that jutted up into the sky. He descended deep into the dark cavern where the rocks resembled hot coals giving off a faint, red light which appeared to burn from inside them.

Rimori reached the main chamber, crossing to the heart of the chasm where he sat down on a plinth of stone. Exhaustion dragged at him. Even in the days before he entered Vale, he had eaten very little and barely slept a wink. Worry racked at him as he wondered where his next meal would come from.

"What's your name?" Rimori asked the vark in an attempt to make peace with it.

He felt it shift around him, making his body quiver.

"No namee. No need for namessss."

* * *

Rimori went four, excruciating days without a drop of water. Hunger was a burden he had hoped we would never experience again. It was ironic, he thought, that he would die the way his life had begun: starving and alone.

The creature visited him throughout each day and, although Rimori pleaded for nourishment, it offered none.

The familiar vibrations humming through the cave meant Rimori sensed the vark's presence well before it spoke.

"Rimmmmoriii?" it said in a snake-like hiss.

He was lying in a heap on the floor, his body curled up and foetal-like. He wondered if the vark was checking if he was still alive. He hadn't been well enough to speak with it for long periods of time because his head ached so badly that it felt as though his brain had shrivelled and was tugging on the inside of his skull.

"Mmm?" was all he could manage.

"Why youu lieee there like thatt?" it asked curiously.

"I'm dying," Rimori whispered through parched lips.

It was all worthless. He would be dead in another day, two at the most and all his planning and effort would come to nothing. He could have returned to Arideen but, even if he did so, the scorching desert stretched a four day walk to the nearest settlement. Besides, he couldn't return to the other worlds without having achieved his goals. He would rather die.

He would have cried if he had had enough moisture in his body to do so but instead he let out a pained noise which encompassed his grief.

"Dyingg? Can't diee."

"Maybe *you* can't, but I can. And I will. Perhaps today." If he was fated to die then he hoped it would end soon, rather than lingering on in agony.

"*No.*" It sounded angry.

"Yes. I need water."

He felt the vark's presence lift from the cave and doubted it would return to him again. He knew he would die there alone and his dreams would die with him. He closed his eyes, preferring to be asleep when it happened.

* * *

The sound of something large crashing to the cave floor stirred Rimori from his sleep. His lips were cracked and sore and his eyes were curtained by darkness, blurring his vision.

"Food. Eatt. Livee," the vark's voice said, drawing him back to consciousness.

"F-food?" Rimori blinked away the curtains and his eyes focused on the thing in front of him.

A hulk of meat lay on the floor, bloody and fresh. He pushed his body up and shakily crawled over to it, reaching for his hip and gripping the knife that still hung there. He ate the meat raw, savouring the sustenance, knowing he would survive.

Once he had fed, he wiped the blood from his chin and pulled himself further into the cave. His vision sharpened and the pain that had set into his body started to recede as his senses slowly returned.

"Thank you," he whispered, still feeling the vark's presence.

"Yess. You will livee now."

"Why did you save me?"

"For allegianccccce."

"You trust me?"

"Yesss, yesss."

"Will we bring the Gateways down together and unite the seven worlds?"

"Yesss."

Rimori lay down and rested a hand on his full stomach which ached and grumbled as it digested food for the first time in days. "Leave me a while. I must rest."

"Yess. I will let you ressst." The vark disappeared and Rimori closed his eyes once more.

He could barely believe his turn of fate, it was as if some higher power had gifted him with life. The thought gave him such faith in his coming plans that he felt overwhelmed with the feeling that he had somehow been chosen. It was *he* that would lead the seven worlds into the future, uniting them as one, great empire over which he would rule.

He vowed to never give up on life again. A creature of Vale had saved him; it was the most unlikely situation he could ever have imagined.

He had to focus on gaining some control over the vark. He needed to be in charge if they were going to succeed. The creature didn't seem overly intelligent and had left him when he asked it to. Perhaps he had a chance.

When it returned to him once more, he decided to try something that would begin the steps towards bonding with it: he was going to name it.

10

Whispers in the Night

Oliver awoke in the early hours of the morning to the sound of voices coming from the living room. He strained to listen and recognised Ely and Laura.

"-it was just on the news!" Laura exclaimed.

Oliver's ears pricked up at her anxious tone.

"Are you sure? It can't be possible. Not after all this time," Ely hissed.

"It is. They're *certain*," Laura said.

"But how can it be?" Ely asked in fearful voice.

Oliver couldn't hear a response from Laura.

"I don't want Oliver or May knowing about this," Ely said firmly.

Oliver frowned, hearing the soft pounding of footsteps as someone moved up and down the living room.

"But what if they hear it from someone else while they're here?" Laura said. "It's all everyone will be talking about."

Oliver sat up in bed as he strained to hear more.

"They won't find out. We're only going to see one person and then we're leaving," Ely said.

"And what if she can't help May?"

Oliver chewed the inside of his cheek. He remembered the dark veins encircling May's heart with a wave of panic; he had never considered that Ely's friend might not be able to help her.

Ely hesitated before replying. "I'll deal with that if and when I have to."

There was a pause before Laura spoke again. "Don't you think it's a coincidence that Alison went missing just before this happened?"

Oliver's pulse quickened at the mention of his mum.

"I don't know what you're insinuating but-" Ely started.

"You know *exactly* what I'm insinuating," Laura hissed.

"Her room was *destroyed*, Laura," Ely said dismissively. "She didn't leave by choice."

"She could have faked it. She turned her back on her whole family in the past. On me, her own *twin*," Laura's voice broke and Oliver thought he caught the sound of a sob.

"Shh," Ely said.

Their voices lowered and Oliver felt a pang of annoyance as he could no longer hear the conversation. He pushed the bed covers aside and placed his bare feet on the wooden floor. He moved slowly, keeping as quiet as possible as he tiptoed toward the door.

He reached it and pressed his ear against the wood, listening intently.

"-then we're all in danger," Laura whispered.

"Yes, unless-" Ely cut off as Oliver shifted his weight and a floorboard creaked loudly beneath him.

Oliver froze, his heart galloping in his chest. He heard footsteps heading toward the door and turned on his heel, hurrying back to the bed as quietly as possible. The doorknob turned just as he slipped under the covers, shutting his eyes and laying dead still.

"It's fine, he's asleep. But let's finish talking about this elsewhere," Ely whispered then the *click* of the door closing made Oliver relax.

Oliver's head reeled with questions. He couldn't believe that, after everything, Ely still wanted to keep things from him and May. He let out a slow breath to release his anger and resolved to find out what his grandfather was hiding.

* * *

Oliver barely slept after overhearing Ely and Laura. He slid out of bed in the morning, dressed then entered the living room. Laura was sat beside one of the windows with the shutter open, gazing outside in a daze.

"Take a seat Oliver, I made wiffles for breakfast," Ely said, as he dished a few onto a plate for him at the small dining table.

Oliver picked up one of the corkscrew-shaped wiffles and ate it whole. The outside was sweet, flaky pastry and the inside was soft, doughy and filled with hot, melted, chocolate. May appeared soon after and grinned as she swallowed a piece of the pastry. Oliver returned the smile half-heartedly, breaking another wiffle apart but feeling too distracted to eat it.

"Are you coming with us today, Laura?" May asked.

Laura roused from her stupor. Her eyes looked heavy with lack of sleep but she smiled warmly as she met May's gaze. "Sorry May, I've got to go to work. But I'll be here when you get home later."

May smiled. "Okay."

Laura stood and started putting on her red coat.

"We'd better get going," Ely said, clearing away the remainder of breakfast.

Oliver grunted in response and May frowned at him questioningly.

"You okay?" she mouthed to him.

Oliver nodded, glancing at Ely over her shoulder. "Later," he muttered.

"I need to take the pod to work but you can get a taxi, right?" Laura asked, crossing the room toward the exit.

"Yeah no problem. Have a good day," Ely said.

"You too, and, good luck." Laura gave May a meaningful look then she left.

Ely turned to face them. "All ready to go?" he asked cheerfully.

May looked nervous. "Yeah," she mumbled.

They went downstairs and headed out the door into the station. Ely walked over to the panel on the wall and Oliver took the opportunity to talk to May. "I overheard Ely and Laura talking about something that's happened. I couldn't tell what it was but it sounded bad. Ely said he doesn't want us knowing anything about it."

May frowned over at Ely. "What could it be?"

Oliver shrugged as Ely began walking back towards them.

"How are you feeling anyway?" Oliver asked.

"Alright, I'm just worried I'm gonna be told I've got some terminal illness or something," May said, her expression darkening.

"Ely knows what he's doing. Whoever he's taking you to must be able to help," Oliver said, wishing he could be certain his words were true.

May sighed heavily. "You're probably right," she said but there was a hint of doubt in her voice.

A white pod appeared along the track with the word *Taxi* emblazoned on top of it. Ely pressed a palm to the door and it slid smoothly aside with a light jingle.

They climbed in and found it had just the right amount of space for three people to sit comfortably around a small table. Oliver eyed a folded newspaper on top of it, his fingers itching to take hold of it.

"Take us to Thugfox Road," Ely instructed the pod.

"Heading to Thugfox Road. Enjoy your journey," answered a smart-looking woman as she appeared on the inside of the door and the pod pulled away into the tunnel.

Oliver leant forward to pick up the newspaper but Ely snatched it away.

"It's all trash in there. Nothing worth reading," he said and shoved it firmly under his seat.

Oliver shot him a look of anger and folded his arms.

The taxi pod slid to a halt in a busy station. The crowd were wrapped up in heavy coats, scarves and gloves against the chill.

They climbed the steps to the street above and Oliver caught his first glimpse of the city, nestled between the two mountains that towered high above them. The buildings were all built from a matt, grey stone and bordered by jutting ledges that were decorated with swirling, silver symbols.

The tallest buildings had twisting spires that reminded Oliver of a church, and smaller ones had domed roofs decorated with the same patterns as the ledges. The morning sun glinted off of them, making the silver sparkle.

A thought occurred to him. "Ely, is the sun the same here?"

His grandfather turned back to answer. "Yes. It's believed the sun is what drives the connection between the worlds. It exists in all seven of them."

"What about the stars? And the moon?" May asked curiously.

"The stars are the same, yes, but not the moon. Aleva has two moons: Sire and Avis. The stars are the same because we are, technically, in the same universe but the worlds are in different dimensions. The easiest way to imagine it is that you are, essentially, on a different planet when you walk through a Gateway."

Oliver's mind was alight with curiosity.

Ely veered to the left and Oliver and May followed him through the bustling street. It opened up into a huge square with a towering monument at its centre.

The monument portrayed a man standing in front of an archway. It reminded Oliver of the Gateway at Oakway Manor. It was carved from stone and looked like a large tree. It was bent over so far that the top of it returned to the ground.

The man was tall, lean and wore a long cape with a hood. His arms were raised towards the Gateway as if he were worshipping it. Carved symbols covered the arch and, embedded in the highest part of it, was an ornate clock.

Ely noticed them eyeing the statue. "That's Dorian Ganderfield; the mage that discovered the other worlds and created the Gateways between them. It was almost a thousand years ago but they're still proud of the fact he was born here in Alevale," he said, the morning sun catching the light in his eyes as he gazed up at the statue for a moment then continued across the square with Oliver and May just behind.

* * *

They stopped outside a large house after a winding walk through the grey and silver streets. A small porch was illuminated by dim light with a black door that curved in an arch at the top. The street was empty and all Oliver could hear was the rustling of leaves in the wind.

Ely stepped forwards and knocked.

A hatch opened in the centre of the door and two eyes peered out. "Ely?" the woman asked, her eyes widening.

"Hello Grelda," Ely said with a grim smile.

Grelda blinked and slammed the hatch shut with a *snap*. A series of bolts and locks *clicked* and *clunked* as she unlocked the door and threw it open.

The door swung wide to reveal a tall women in a floor-length, black dress. Silver hair cascaded over her shoulders, framing a face that was all sharp angles with eyes that were warm and welcoming.

"I can't believe it. Ely Fox here on my doorstep. It must have been ten years since I last saw you and you've not aged a day," Grelda said.

"Nor you, my dear. Do you mind if we come in?" Ely asked.

Grelda eyed Oliver and May over Ely's shoulder. "Of course, come right on in. Who are these delightful people you've brought with you?"

"These are my grandchildren, Oliver and May."

"Pleased to meet you, I'm Grelda."

They followed her into a large hallway. It was roughly circular and had a grand staircase that curved up around the room. It climbed two more flights above them with landings in between. A black dog yapped at them from its soft bed on one side of the hallway.

"Quiet, Pippit," Grelda snapped and the dog complied.

"How's business?" Ely asked.

"Very well, thank you. I no longer work for the government, though. I now take on private appointments here in my home, it's much more satisfying," Grelda said.

"Do you still deal with many curses that way?" Ely asked.

"Oh yes, you'd be surprised by some of the magic my clients get themselves involved in."

"Grelda's an expert in curse-breaking and magical correction," Ely said to Oliver and May. "There's not a curse in Aleva she hasn't seen."

A look of hope grew in May's eyes.

"Yes, yes. Well we mustn't stand pottering here in the hallway any longer. Follow me," Grelda said and started up the staircase with Pippit trotting after her.

They climbed to the highest floor and emerged in a room that was completely circular with a domed roof made entirely of glass. A set of embroidered furniture sat at its centre which they all took a seat upon. Oliver perched awkwardly on a chaise longue.

The walls of the room were decorated with paintings. In several of them was the image of a bright ball of light that had electricity extending from it in sparks. Scenes of war and bloody battles featured in many of them and one showed a man reaching his hand out towards a ball of light that hovered above him. Something about the paintings set Oliver on edge.

Grelda waved her palm and a tall bottle zoomed out of a cabinet across the room and landed on the coffee table followed by four glasses, pouring each of them a drink.

"Praise the Arc," she said, raising her glass.

They raised their own in response then sipped at the drink. It was strong and bitter and tasted a little of aniseed. Oliver returned his glass to the table, fighting to hide the grimace on his face from the unusual flavour.

"Now, to what do I owe the pleasure of this visit?" Grelda asked Ely.

"I'm afraid we've come because we require your expertise," Ely said gravely.

May smiled hopefully at the woman.

"I see, and what precisely is the problem?" Grelda asked.

"May seems to have had a curse put on her. I've not seen anything like it myself but I managed to bind the magic long enough that I could bring her here to you."

"Do you know who put the curse on you, May?" Grelda asked.

May shook her head. "Me and Olly only just found out the other worlds existed. I didn't even know there was such a thing as magic, let alone curses."

"Oh, my, my, my, how very puzzling." Grelda rubbed her hands together and blue sparks crackled between them.

"Yes, it is that," Ely said.

"Can you help her?" Oliver pressed.

"Well, now, let me see. Shall I take a look, May?" Grelda asked. May nodded.

Grelda got to her feet and her high heels *clacked* on the hard floor as she approached May. She knelt in front of her and May pulled her top aside to show the woman the mark on her chest.

"Hmm, very puzzling. Bruise-like but no sign of the purple discolouration you get with a Manic curse. And Manic curses are nearly always on the hands," she muttered to herself and lifted May's hands, checking them over carefully.

"Without the bind, the curse was very virulent. I imagine it may have killed her if I hadn't got to her in time," Ely said in a low voice.

May visibly swallowed.

"And it came on at random? No chance a mage could have got to her?"

"She was asleep in bed. Oliver ran in and found her on the floor after being awoken by her screams. There's no way a mage could have got into her room and out again without one of us bumping into them. And I get notified the second anyone comes through the Gateway," Ely said.

"Then perhaps the curse was lying dormant and something sparked it to act. I've seen one or two in my time that are triggered like that but nothing that leaves a mark like this." Grelda got up and went to a bookcase on one side of the room. She grabbed a book off the shelf and started rifling through it.

"Very odd. Hmm," Grelda said then snapped the book shut a few minutes later.

"Unfortunately, the only way I may be able to help is if I see the curse in action myself."

"What do you mean?" Oliver asked.

"I'll have to take the bind off of it to see how it behaves," Grelda said, talking clinically. Oliver felt she was observing May as one might do a science experiment and suppressed a spike of anger.

"But it could kill her," Oliver said, getting to his feet.

"I can put a bind back on once I've released it," Grelda said. "She would be at no risk."

"But-" Oliver went to object but May cut across him.

"I'll do it," she said, her jaw visibly clenching.

"Good girl. Now lie back on the chaise longue and let me have a look at you," Grelda said, shuffling Oliver aside.

May lay down and Grelda leant over her.

"I may need your help Ely. If the curse gets too strong," Grelda said.

Ely nodded and moved to her side.

"Oliver go and sit by her head," Ely said.

Oliver dragged a foot stool over and sat behind May. Pippit joined him a moment later, surveying his owner.

Grelda held her hands above May's chest. A soft, gold light emitted from them which proceeded to float and swirl towards the black mark. The light seemed to absorb the mark as the veins drifted back up towards Grelda's hand then violet fire burned the chain of black back to May's body.

When the fire reached her, May screamed and Oliver's spine straightened as the noise pierced through him.

Black veins burst from the mark on May's chest and slithered their way up towards her neck and face. They had already spread down her arms and were moving at an alarming rate. Her hands flung to her neck and she clawed at her skin, trying to stop them. Her eyes rolled back into her head and she gasped for breath, the veins choking her.

"Grab her hands, Oliver!" Grelda commanded.

He lunged forward and prised May's hands from her neck, leaving bloody scratches behind. The purple fire flew up her neck, following the veins. When the fire reached the end of one vein it receded, returning it to the original mark.

Grelda's face strained as the fire spread over May's body. Some of it stuttered and died, leaving a small puff of smoke behind, having no impact on the veins.

"*Now, Ely!*" Grelda gasped, her silver hair flying about.

Ely gripped Grelda's shoulder tightly and blue light glowed beneath his palm, emitting a low, humming noise. The fire from Grelda's hand burned brighter than before and regained control over all of the veins.

Those on May's neck finally receded and she gasped for breath. Oliver released her arms.

Grelda stood up and stumbled away from May in a daze. She threw a hand to her head and started pacing.

May opened her eyes hazily.

Grelda pointed at her with a trembling hand. "That girl. She is marked by the Arc." Her hand flew around to point wildly at the pictures on the walls.

"What? What are you talking about?" Oliver asked her, looking between May and the paintings.

"The mark. I wouldn't believe it if I hadn't witnessed it myself," Grelda breathed more to herself than anyone else.

"Calm down, Grelda. You're not talking sense," Ely implored.

"The marks on that girl are the same as those described in the scriptures," Grelda said in a panic. She began reciting words Oliver didn't recognise. "And she will come as light and dark marked upon her of the Arc."

"What's that supposed to mean?" Oliver asked, staring around at Ely for support.

"It is a belief of the Arclites that a girl who is marked with the symbol of the Arc will be the sign," Ely said.

"The sign of what?" Oliver asked, furrowing his brow in frustration.

"The sign of the coming of the Arc in human form to unite the seven worlds," Grelda said. "The Arc is coming." Her eyes lit with a manic glee.

"She is a teenager who needs your help," Ely said furiously.

"I can't help her," Grelda said, shaking her head.

"You *have* to!" Oliver snapped.

May was still in a daze and Oliver assisted her into a sitting position.

"I helped you bind the mark, Ely. But it won't be long before it is released once more," Grelda said. "She has months, perhaps, but I can't do any more to help her."

"What are you saying?" Oliver demanded.

"She's saying she can't break the curse," Ely said disbelievingly.

"I've put a strong bind on it. It'll buy her a little more time," Grelda said.

"Before what?" Oliver asked.

Grelda threw Ely a serious look.

"Until *what*?" Oliver repeated, grinding his teeth.

"Until her death," Grelda breathed.

May blinked several times to focus herself. "What's happening?"

"We're leaving," Oliver said, pulling her to her feet.

"I'm sorry. I'm so sorry there wasn't more I could do," Grelda said.

Oliver was already halfway to the door, gripping May's arm tightly. He stormed down the staircase and threw the front door open. A gust of cold wind brought water to his eyes as he marched down the street.

"Olly, stop," May said, yanking her arm out of his grip and Oliver turned to face her.

"What the hell's going on?" she asked, her eyes wide.

"That woman said she can't help you," he said, pointing back at the house.

"-silly superstitions," Ely snapped, finishing a sentence as he appeared in the doorway with Grelda.

"Take this," Grelda said, forcing a book into his hands.

"I'm not going to read the Arclite scriptures. I don't believe in this nonsense," Ely said, holding the book back out to Grelda.

"You don't have to read the whole thing just read about the embodiment of the Arc," Grelda insisted.

Ely shook his head and dropped his hand to his side, gripping the book in the other. He turned to leave, looking defeated.

"I'm sorry, Ely," Grelda called.

Ely didn't look back as he joined Oliver and May.

"You're neck's still bleeding," Ely said, as he spotted the scratch marks on May. He reached a hand out and bathed the wounds in pale, green light. The skin knitted back together then the faint lines faded to nothing.

"Thank you," May said, touching her neck with an awed expression.

"Come on, let's go," Ely growled as he glanced back at Grelda Grey who was still watching them from the doorway.

They followed Ely back down the winding streets and Oliver only broke the silence when his grandfather stopped to order a taxi in the pod station.

"What are we going to do?" he asked.

Ely sighed and turned back to them.

"I don't know," Ely said frankly, shaking his head.

"But there is *something* we can do, right?" May asked in a panic.

"Of course. Don't listen to what Grelda said. She's become much more of an Arclite extremist since I last saw her," Ely said, clearly disappointed.

The pod slid into the station and they climbed aboard.

"Take us to Chance Street," Ely instructed as he took his seat.

"Heading to Chance Street. Enjoy your journey," replied the female hologram in the pod as it set off down the tunnel.

"Do you know another mage who can help?" Oliver asked frantically.

"I do, yes. But there's a problem," Ely said, scratching his beard anxiously.

"What kind of problem?" May asked, frowning.

"He lives in Brinatin which is two worlds away," Ely stated.

"You're kidding? And he's the only person you know who can help?" Oliver asked.

Ely nodded. "Unless I took you to the Council and I won't do that unless I can't avoid it."

"Why?" May asked.

"The Council aren't going to help you without a price. And it's not money they're after," Ely said. "We'd have to go to Brinatin to meet with them even if that was the better option."

"Do you really think your friend in Brinatin can help? I mean, we don't want to waste any more time. How long is this bind gonna hold?" Oliver asked.

May gripped at where the mark was located on her chest, concealed beneath her clothes.

"Wallace will be able to help, trust me. He's one of the strongest mages in the seven worlds, he's descended from Dorian Ganderfield himself. The bind Grelda put on you should hold for a few more months."

May sighed and sat back in her seat. "That's plenty of time then."

"Well, it should be," Ely said quietly. "We'll have to get you signed up to the next race as soon as possible. They might not even accept your application this late but sometimes teams drop out so there could be a chance..."

"What do we need to do?" Oliver asked.

"You need a team of five to enter," Ely said.

"What kind of race is it?" May asked.

Oliver remembered the maze with a sick feeling.

"It takes place over two days. It's been made into a televised spectacle. Fifty teams are in the race and you have to place at least tenth amongst them to win a key," Ely said.

"Sounds difficult," May said, looking defeated.

"It is. And a lot of the teams train for it in advance," Ely said with a sigh. "It only runs four times a year so you have to compete in the next one, but it's taking place in just a couple of weeks time."

"Okay, but saying we do manage to get a team together and are somehow accepted, do we have a chance?" Oliver asked, grasping at straws.

"If you've got a place, you've got a chance," Ely said.

"Obstruction ahead. Please prepare for an unscheduled stop," the female hologram said as the pod braked to an abrupt halt.

11

Shadows

Oliver moved next to his grandfather and they peered out of the window into the dark tunnel which was lit marginally by the blue tracks.

"I can't see an obstruction," Ely mumbled to himself.

"There's nothing there," Oliver said, squinting into the gloom.

"Pod, what's going on?" Ely asked.

"There's an obstruction ahead. Please remain seated. A PNM crew is on their way." The woman's face smiled at them calmly.

"What's a PNM crew?" May asked.

"Pod Network Maintenance." Ely huffed and sat back in his seat. "Hopefully, this won't take long."

Oliver looked down the tunnel again. He thought he could see a figure in the distance so cupped a hand over his eyes to improve his vision.

"I think I can see someone down there," he said.

May climbed over next to him and looked outside. "I can see them, too."

"Should we go and get them? Maybe they don't know we're here?" Oliver suggested, raising his eyebrows at Ely.

Ely looked down the tunnel and nodded. "Don't go far, just call them over. Bloody layabouts."

Oliver unlocked the door.

"Please remain inside the pod," the hologram urged.

He ignored it and pushed the door open, pausing as he looked down at the glowing track below him. "I'm not going to get electrocuted am I?" Oliver asked, glancing back inside the pod.

"No. You can't get a shock off of that stuff," Ely reassured him.

Oliver jumped down next to the track and May landed beside him a second later. He peered towards the figure in the distance and waved his hand at them.

"Excuse me," he called, his voice echoing around the tunnel.

The figure didn't respond so he started walking towards them.

"We're down here. HELLO?" May shouted.

They were halfway between the pod and the person when, whoever it was, vanished from sight around a corner.

"Hello!" Oliver tried again, frustrated.

They rounded a corner so their pod was no longer visible behind them.

Oliver felt the hairs on the back of his neck creep up and he stopped walking, throwing out an arm to halt May. The tunnel suddenly seemed thick with shadow and there was no sign of anyone ahead.

She jumped to his side in a flurry of movement. "What was that?" she blurted.

"What was what?" Oliver frowned.

"I felt something," May said, running a hand down the back of her neck.

"Like wha-" Oliver stopped dead as a strange noise vibrated near his ear. Then something moved behind him. He flung around and what he saw sent his heart racing.

A shadowy creature darted left then right in front of him. Oliver could see the movement but couldn't distinguish what it was until it appeared directly ahead. Its body was foggy and indistinct apart from six sharp, silver blades on each of its legs and one on a scorpion-like tail.

Oliver shouted out in alarm, roughly grabbing May's wrist and turning to flee. From nowhere it appeared in front of them once more, blocking their path. It slashed a blade at May and she flinched out of reach with a scream of fright.

The creature reared up and all six of its legs slashed together, interlocking to form a jaw-like weapon. Where it should have a face was a vertical set of serrated teeth which grated against one another as a guttural noise sounded from its throat.

It lunged at them, clashing its legs together with a *twang* of metal on metal. They broke apart to avoid the lethal blow and Oliver instinctively ducked his head.

"Run!" Oliver shouted and they fled down the tunnel, away from the being but also from Ely.

Their footsteps thudded along in the dark tunnel. Oliver could sense the creature close by as if it were hovering just over his shoulder. Adrenaline pumped through his muscles as every part of him tensed for an attack.

Vibrations buzzed inside Oliver's skull, making his vision hazy so the pod tracks became a blue blur. He squinted to counter it and encouraged his legs onwards.

Wind rushed through Oliver's hair then the creature materialised before them and swooped towards May. He dug his heals in and swung to the side, colliding with May so they crashed to the ground in a tumble of limbs.

A blade tore into Oliver's shoulder, the metal sinking into his flesh with an unbearable, searing sensation.

The creature disappeared with a shriek and the icy blade beneath his skin went with it. Oliver cried out and collapsed, breathing heavily through gritted teeth as he screwed up his eyes against the pain.

Blood pumped so loudly in his ears that the sound of May screaming seemed distant.

Bright flashes of light filtered through his eyelids. He opened them and saw red lightning pummelling the creature, sending a torrent of sparks into the air. The being span into the darkness and disappeared with a hideous, screeching sound that echoed throughout the tunnel for what felt like an eternity.

Oliver looked around to see Ely standing there, his hands raised defensively. Although he was a small man, it did nothing to take away from the sense of power that emanated from him at that moment.

Oliver's breathing became shallow as he watched Ely drag May to her feet. She was visibly shaking but she wasn't injured.

"Ely help him!" May cried.

The blood was flowing thick and fast and Oliver suddenly felt overwhelmingly lightheaded. He lifted a hand, his muscles feeling void of energy as he touched his shoulder and his fingers slipped through the blood.

Ely knelt in front of Oliver. "Move your hand aside," he commanded.

Oliver did so, the loss of blood making his head spin. Ely ripped away the remnants of his torn sleeve and Oliver looked down to see the deep wound, his gut churning at the sight.

"Oh my God. Are you okay?" May gasped, sinking to the floor in front of him.

Ely held his palm over the wound and green light flowed toward it. A cool, trickling sensation seeped into the torn flesh then changed to a soothing heat. Oliver's skin tingled as the pain eased and the dizziness in his head began to recede. He looked down to find the wound healed, the remnants of blood already drying onto his skin and clothes.

Oliver sighed. "Thanks."

"Good grief. If I hadn't come any sooner- well, it doesn't bear thinking about," Ely said, sweat shining on his brow and collecting in his beard.

"What the hell was that thing?" May asked, terror returning to her eyes with the memory.

"Well, I mean, I hardly dare to say what I think it was. I don't believe it myself. There's only been a few recorded throughout history but I've studied the creatures myself. I've seen drawings, read descriptions, but *never* would I *ever* have thought in all my years I would actually *encounter* one," Ely said in a fluster.

"But what *was* it, Ely?" May pressed.

"A vark. A shadow creature from Vale," Ely said, his bottom lip quivering.

"It came from the seventh world? How's that possible? I thought you said you can only travel between worlds through the Gateways?" Oliver panted as he got to his feet. His head spun violently once more and he felt May grip his arm as he swayed.

"Humans do but those *things* seem to have a way of travelling to the other worlds without the Gateways, perhaps only by accident. There's been brief sightings of them throughout history. I would guess that they don't come here intentionally or, judging by their ferocity, we'd all be doomed."

"We better get back to the pod. What if it returns?" May whispered anxiously, glancing around the narrow tunnel.

"Don't worry, I'm sure it's gone. But I think you're right about getting back," Ely said and started off towards the pod.

Oliver felt much improved as he walked next to May, their footsteps echoing off the walls. They reached the pod and climbed back inside.

"Are you alright? You still look pretty pale." May asked him.

"I feel better, just a bit weak," Oliver said, resting his head against the seat.

"I'm sorry I've never been the best at healing. The wound is gone but you lost a lot of blood. It will take a little while longer for you to fully recover," Ely said.

"Thank you for your patience. We will now continue to our destination: Chance Street," said the hologram and they glided onward down the track.

Oliver glimpsed a group of maintenance workers looking at them with confused expressions as they passed them further down the tunnel. He felt a touch of amusement at seeing them look so bewildered which was probably due to his woozy state.

"Should we report that creature? The vark?" May asked Ely.

"Don't worry I'll deal with it," Ely muttered.

They climbed out of the pod and entered Laura's house through the station. They had to wait for her to let them in as the mirrored door refused to admit them. Ely explained how it worked as Laura buzzed them in.

"It recognises the home owner. It won't let anyone have access unless they've been encoded to the property," Ely said as they walked inside.

Laura was cooking in the kitchenette and a delicious smell filled Oliver's nostrils, making his stomach growl for attention.

Laura looked up. "How did it go?" Her face dropped as she spotted Oliver and he realised his clothes were caked in blood.

"What in Vale happened? Are you alright?" Laura rushed over to them.

"A vark attacked them," Ely said in a serious tone.

"A-*what*?" Laura said, looking between their faces for the sign of a joke. "You are kidding, right?"

"Here, take a seat Oliver," Ely said, ushering him to the sofa. He sunk into the seat and sighed gratefully.

"It was a pincer vark if my memory serves me," Ely said.

Laura perched on the arm of a chair shaking her head. "What are the chances of one turning up in Alevale?" she asked, trailing off.

May dropped into the seat next to Oliver and no one spoke for a moment.

"Is there any possibility this is linked to Rimori?" Laura blurted and Oliver was alert at once.

"Rimori?" Oliver questioned, burning with curiosity.

"*Laura*," Ely warned.

"No, it needs to be said, Dad," Laura said firmly.

"This has got nothing to do with Rimori," Ely snapped.

"He's returned from Vale," Laura revealed, pushing back her shoulders defiantly.

Oliver started, not having expected this to be the news Ely had kept quiet. An icy chill ran through him.

Ely began to object but Laura stopped him with a look. "They deserve to hear this."

Ely sighed but didn't say anything, rubbing his eyes wearily.

"He's returned?" May breathed, sitting forward.

"How? *Why*?" Oliver asked frantically.

"There is a massive man-hunt underway to find him. He'll be caught in no time," Ely said.

"Didn't he enter Vale like ten years ago?" May asked, looking almost angry.

"Yes, and the chances of him surviving even a few days in Vale is absurd. Dorian Ganderfield himself returned half dead and he was a mage," Laura said.

"So, the man who murdered my father is what, *on the run*?" Oliver asked, the blood heating up in his veins.

"He was spotted in Theald," Ely said, nodding. "It's believed he's being kept hidden there."

"Why?" May asked with a look of disgust. "He's a murderer."

Laura nodded. "Yes, but the people of Theald are renowned for their devout belief in the Arc. There's concern that Rimori will use this to his advantage, after all it is said that the Arc will come from Vale in the form of a man."

"But the point is, Rimori isn't linked to vark attacks," Ely said, reining in the conversation.

"It was just an idea. It seems a bit of a coincidence that one would show up where William Knight's son is. Especially considering that there hasn't been a sighting of one in Aleva for maybe a hundred years," Laura said, sounding exasperated.

"No one can control varks," Ely said stubbornly. "It *was* just a coincidence."

"Why would Rimori bother attacking me anyway?" Oliver asked. "I mean, it's not like I'm any sort of a threat to him."

"Precisely," Ely said. "You have nothing to fear from Rimori. He'll be caught and trialled accordingly."

"Hold on- how did it go with Grelda?" Laura asked suddenly.

Oliver frowned to show his disappointment.

"Unfortunately, she wasn't able to help May. She put a stronger bind on the curse but she can't identify it," Ely said.

"Well, she *could*," May said with a bitter laugh.

"What do you mean?" Laura asked.

Ely sighed, retrieving the book Grelda had given him from his coat and placed it on the table. "Grelda suggested that May's curse was the sign of the coming of the Arc."

Laura snorted. "You're kidding?"

"No, and she *genuinely* believed it," Ely said, rolling his eyes.

"I didn't realise she was so serious about that stuff," Laura said.

"Yeah, and if *she* is, imagine how many other people could be. Rimori is in a dangerously good position to start an uprising against the Council and the Gateways," Ely said.

"Hopefully it won't come to that," Laura said, looking anxious. "So, what are you gonna do now?"

"I'm going to take May to Brinatin to see Wallace Ganderfield," Ely said with a resigned expression.

"*Brinatin*? But you'll need keys, you'll have to go through *two* Gateways," Laura said in alarm. "The next race starts in a couple of weeks and you don't have a team together."

"We don't have a choice," Ely said.

"How many teams enter the race?" May asked with a frown.

"Fifty," Ely said quietly.

"*Fifty*?" Oliver gasped, meeting his sister's anxious gaze.

Ely nodded, looking a little apologetic.

Laura's brow furrowed as she sat in thoughtful silence for a moment. "Well I suppose I could head to Crome a bit earlier. I have to be there in a few days to join the Race Committee anyway. My influence might help get you a place if there's one available but I can't do anything unless you have a team together," she said, shaking her head.

"How are we going to find teammates?" May asked.

"We don't know anyone here," Oliver agreed.

"Let's just get to Crome then we can start looking. There'll be thousands of tourists there for the race. I'm sure we'll find people who want to enter," Ely said. "We'll leave in the morning."

* * *

Oliver awoke early. His stomach twisted in a tight knot as his mind reeled about entering the race. His brain conjured unwelcome memories of the maze and his skeletal father. The race would be different, he was sure, but for all he knew it could be worse.

He got up to distract himself from his thoughts and began packing his bag so he would be ready to leave for Crome. As he zipped up the backpack, an idea occurred to him. He dropped it onto the bed and went to the living room where he found Ely asleep in an armchair.

"Ely?"

His eyes flickered open and he wiped the drool away from his chin with the back of his hand. "Yesmaboy?" he slurred, as he struggled to regain full consciousness.

"You know this mage we're going to see in Brinatin? Why can't he come to us?"

"He won't come here," Ely stated.

"Even if it meant that she'd *die*?" Oliver said disbelievingly.

"It's not that. It's-" Ely hesitated and Oliver narrowed his eyes at him. "Now don't overreact. But, no one's seen him in almost nine years." Ely winced a little as if preparing for Oliver's reaction.

"WHAT?" Oliver couldn't contain himself. "How do you even know where to look for him then?"

"I know where he lives, but he doesn't leave his house. Ever."

"So how do you know he can help us?"

"He's one of the most powerful mages alive. If anyone can help her, he can."

"If no one's seen him for years, how do you know he's still there?" Oliver asked, infuriated.

"He is. He has an employee that brings him supplies."

Oliver took a breath to calm himself but couldn't stop his hands from shaking. He was still angry but what was truly upsetting him finally slipped out. "And how are we ever gonna place out of fifty teams? What does the race even involve?"

"You have a small chance. And on the train I will go over what you should expect in the race."

"Is it-" Oliver paused, not wanting to seem pathetic.

"Is it what?" Ely asked.

Oliver folded his arms and released a sharp breath through his nose. "Is it as bad as the last challenge?"

Ely's features softened. "Oliver, I don't know what you faced in the maze but you shouldn't be ashamed that you were frightened."

"I'm not ashamed, I just..." he trailed off, shaking his head in annoyance.

"The maze is designed to face you with your deepest fears. For some, that can be more traumatic than it is for others. Some people's fears are physical such as spiders or the dark whereas others are afraid of more intangible things. I hope it isn't overstepping the mark, my boy, by guessing that you yourself struggle with a fear of loss?"

Oliver dug his nails into his arm, unable to meet his grandfather's eye.

Ely continued. "You lost your father at a young age, now your mother is missing and your sister is ill. It isn't a giant leap from there to reach such a conclusion. But you need to know that it's nothing to be ashamed of."

Oliver met his eye and nodded, the knot in his stomach unravelling a little.

Ely smiled warmly. "Go get your things. We can leave when you and May are ready."

Oliver turned to leave but paused before exiting and glanced back at his grandfather. "Ely? What did you face in the maze?"

Ely cleared his throat and shifted in his seat. "Oh, well that was a very long time ago. I was just a lad like yourself."

Oliver waited for him to go on, raising his eyebrows expectantly.

"Well, as I'm sure you've noticed, I'm rather on the short side. As a teen I was often subject to bullying and, well, had a fear of being insignificant. For me, the maze was full of people none of whom would help me, but instead recited the words I had been called my entire life."

Oliver grimaced, angry that anyone would treat his grandfather that way. "But you made it through?"

"I did." Ely nodded and a smug smile tugged at one corner of his mouth. "Now, go on. Get your sister and we'll leave."

Oliver nodded and exited the room, feeling somehow lighter than he had before entering.

12

Blood Ties

The Traverser station was packed. At midday they queued towards one of the trains and Oliver noticed that, under the light of day, the black exterior shimmered like oil. Every now and then tall machines, with a large, clawed hand, would pluck containers off the top of the train and carry them out of the station.

Oliver shuffled forwards after Laura and May as passengers boarded the train ahead of them.

Ely appeared moments later, grinning broadly. The look of triumph on his face turned to horror as he tripped forward onto the ground in a heap, parting the crowd around him. Oliver rushed over and returned him to his feet as quickly as possible and Ely brushed his hands down his clothes, trying to regain composure.

A deep voice spoke that was thick with sarcasm. "I'm *so* sorry, sir. I didn't see you there."

The man emerged from the crowd behind Ely. He was extremely tall and broad with golden hair and bright, blue eyes that were set into a chiselled face.

"Ely Fox, is that you? Oh, how terrible." His voice was drenched with feigned apology.

"Chester Pipistrelle, how nice to see you," Ely said, his jaw clenching.

Oliver looked from one man to the other, feeling the tension that seemed to charge the air between them.

"Hi, Chester," Laura said, embracing the man.

"Ah, Laura, lovely to see you again," Chester said, flashing a perfect smile as he returned the hug with his muscular arms.

"Is Mum with you?" Laura asked, glancing over the man's shoulder.

With a jolt, Oliver realised he was about to meet his grandmother.

"Yes, Delphine's just buying the tickets with Larkin. I didn't know you were heading to Crome this early?" Chester inquired.

Oliver spotted Ely glancing around nervously like a horse that was ready to bolt.

"Yes, well this is Oliver and May, my sister's kids. They're hoping to enter the race, so I thought I'd go and put a good word in for them," Laura said with a smile.

"How kind. Our Larkin's entering this season. Shame there's no space for them on his team," Chester said, his tiny eyes roaming over Oliver and May.

A tall woman appeared next to Chester. Long, black hair cascaded over her slender figure and her bare legs protruded from a fitted dress. Chester slinked an arm around her waist.

A boy emerged next to them and it was as though Chester had stepped backwards in time thirty years. The only difference was his son was slightly shorter, around Oliver's height, and his blonde hair was darker with hazel running through it. Where his father stood, fully erect, with his chest puffed out like a bird of paradise, the boy was slack and casual. He flicked his hair as his eyes roamed over the girls amongst the crowd.

Laura rushed forward and hugged them both in turn. "Hi Mum. Larkin. How are you?"

Larkin shrugged. "Alright."

"Laura, darling, what in Vale are *you* doing here?" Delphine asked, flicking her dark hair in the same, vain way her son did.

"Well, Mum, this is actually quite strange..." Laura trailed off, turning back towards them. "This is Oliver and May. They're Alison's kids, your grandchildren."

Chester's eyes flicked to his wife and Larkin momentarily lost his cool in a look of astonishment, but it was nothing compared to the shocked expression planted on Delphine's face. Oliver felt a flush of self-consciousness and shifted his weight onto his other leg.

"Alison's? *What-*?" Delphine spluttered, staring at Oliver and May like they were alien creatures.

Oliver stepped forward. "Hi," he said, awkwardly holding out his hand.

Delphine took hold of it, the tips of her manicured nails pinching his skin. "Oh, Oliver! It's not your fault Alison kept you from me."

Oliver let go in an instant with a flare of loyalty towards his mum.

"Well, she had her reasons, I guess," May said, eyeing the woman suspiciously.

Delphine's grey-blue eyes roamed over May. "And what was your name again, dear?"

"May," she muttered.

Delphine smiled kindly but it didn't touch her eyes. "Well you're not blood of course, but that doesn't matter to me."

"Then why mention it?" Oliver asked, narrowing his gaze.

Delphine waved a hand to dismiss his comment and her eyes fell on Ely. "And how are you?" Her voice became stilted, her red lips barely moving as she addressed him.

"Very well, Delphine. We were just leaving. Excuse me," Ely said and walked towards the train, his body stiffened as he went.

"See you at the race?" Laura asked as she adjusted the bag on her shoulder.

Oliver felt that Laura was either completely unaware of the tension between her parents or, more likely, particularly well rehearsed at feigning her ignorance.

"Yes, see you then, darling." Delphine kissed the air and wiggled her fingers at Oliver.

Larkin followed his mother into the crowd then Chester nodded to them and hurried after his family.

The hum of the tracks filled Oliver's ears as he climbed the short staircase onto the train.

Ely passed back their tickets with a forced-looking smile on his face. "I almost forgot. I bumped into my old friend Norman who works in the ticket booths. He upgraded us to first class."

"Great," May said, grinning and Oliver was glad of something to relieve the tension.

They scanned their tickets and showed them to an attendant. She nodded and ushered them towards a spiral staircase. It was carpeted with red velvet and a wave of warm air hit Oliver as he emerged in the room above.

A man dressed in a smart, maroon-coloured uniform, stood in front of them. The word *Traverser* was emblazoned in gold on his breast pocket. They passed him their tickets as he held out a gloved hand.

"Good afternoon, and welcome to First Class on the Traverser. Please follow me and I'll show you to your rooms."

They turned left and moved through several lounges where people were sitting in velvet armchairs being waited on by staff. They walked down a wide corridor with numbered, wooden doors lining the walls. They stopped and the ticket attendant gestured to three of the rooms.

"Here you are. Your room numbers are on your tickets, just insert them into the door to gain access. Enjoy your stay on the Traverser." He bowed and walked away.

Oliver and May had the same room number. Oliver inserted his ticket and the door slid smoothly to the side then shut silently behind them as they entered. Inside was a small apartment with a living room, bathroom and two bedrooms all decorated in tones of browns, reds and golds. The main wall of the living room was fitted with a huge window that overlooked the platform.

"This is all ours?" May asked, taking in the luxurious room.

"Looks like it," Oliver said with an excited grin, moving over to the window to look down on the crowd.

A musical chime sounded outside in the station which seemed to signal that the Traverser was leaving. The train slid effortlessly forward out of the station and they were soon winding along the tracks past rolling hills covered in miles of green grass. The sun was hidden by a mist that clung to the hilltops though the light that filtered through it was bright and suggested the clouds would soon break.

He glanced over at May who was touching the place on her chest where the mark of the curse was concealed.

"May?" he said gently and she blinked as she was jolted out of a reverie. "Are you alright?" Concern nagged at him.

"Yeah," she said, breaking a smile though he could sense she wasn't happy.

"I know that you're not."

She nodded stiffly then dropped her gaze. "It's just easier not to talk about it."

He frowned. "Whatever this curse is, we'll figure it out. Ely knows what he's doing, this guy in Brinatin must have the answer."

"He thought Grelda had the answer." She bit her lip as if she wished she hadn't said it.

His chest tightened at her words. "Forget about Grelda. She was unhinged!"

A smile pulled at her mouth. "She was pretty weird."

"She was demented!" He raised his eyebrows so his eyes were wide and May laughed.

"I'm gonna go unpack," she said then headed off into one of the rooms.

Oliver decided to unpack too so carried his bag into the other bedroom and dropped it onto the soft, queen-sized bed.

When he returned to the lounge a while later he found May inspecting a panel by the door. He joined her just as she tapped her finger to it.

A man in the Traverser uniform was projected nearby and they turned to look at him as he began to speak. "Welcome aboard the Traverser. You now have access to our inbuilt control system. To get the most out of your stay onboard the Traverser we encourage you to use this panel," the man gestured to the panel he was projected from, "to navigate your way through a selection of applications, activities, menus, and help services. It will also serve as the main control for all devices found within your luxury cabin. Enjoy your stay on the Traverser; the number one train service in Lorence." The man disappeared and the panel went blank.

Oliver touched it and another hologram appeared in front of him that displayed a menu. He tapped the word *lights* and the room lit up. A series of options were displayed for dimming, colour and tone.

"Ooo," May cooed excitedly, testing a few of the colours.

Oliver returned to the main menu and tried a button he didn't recognise marked *survision*. He touched the air where a question mark hovered beside it.

A woman's voice spoke across the room, "Survision, or surface vision. This device allows you to watch a range of sense-provoking programmes, play the latest sense-engaging games, and use our onboard infoweb."

Oliver pressed the button and the question *wall or window* was displayed. May tapped the air where the word *window* was hovering.

The sound of gulls, a soft breeze against his neck and the smell of sea salt filled Oliver's nostrils. He span around and gazed out of the window where a sandy beach sloped away into a turquoise ocean that was lapping against it. Every sense told him he could walk out onto it.

He approached the window and reached out a hand. It was still in place, cool beneath his palm.

"This is amazing," May said, pressing her own hand against the window.

A tanned man appeared in a small pair of swimming trunks as he strolled along the sand narrating. Oliver recognised him as the presenter from Laura's pod. The programme seemed to be a documentary.

"Here, on one of Brinatin's most pristine islands, the Isle of Fay, I'm going to meet with Felix Rutt, a pygmisnout expert. He is known for raising orphan pygmisnouts by hand and has a rather novel way of training them to swim. I'm here today to give it a go."

Another man appeared, surrounded by a number of strange-looking creatures. They resembled elephants at first but their legs were splayed, causing their bellies to rub along the ground, and their feet were webbed.

They had thick, muscular tails about five feet in length that lay, swishing from side to side, leaving trails in the sand. Their trunks were almost three times longer than an elephant's and curled around in front of them on the beach.

"Great to meet you, Felix," the man said, shaking his hand.

"And you Truvian," Felix said as he stroked the trunk of a nearby pygmisnout.

A knock at the door distracted Oliver and May from the programme. Oliver walked over and opened it to find Laura standing there.

"Can I join you?" she asked, strolling into the room.

Oliver shrugged. "Sure, we're just watching some programme on pygmisnouts."

Laura looked at the survision. "Ooo, I love this show. Mainly because I like watching Truvian Gold," she said, throwing herself into an armchair and making May giggle.

"This is so much better than television," Oliver said, perching on the arm of her chair.

"Most of the other world's technology are based on each other these days. Aleva and Earth share a Gateway so a lot of their ideas come from each other. Brinatin and Theald have a similar relationship. There are the exceptions of course; the royal families across Glacio still insist on keeping their people living in the dark ages and Arideen, well, they're just too poor to fund any new technology."

Oliver folded his arms and looked back at the screen. Felix Rutt was now strapping Truvian Gold into a harness beside a pygmisnout that was wearing some sort of saddle. Felix Rutt clipped Truvian Gold onto the animal and his legs dangled over either side of its body. Oliver smiled, bemused by the odd sight.

Truvian gave the camera a thumbs up and Felix whistled then clapped his hands at the animal who immediately ran forward in an undulating fashion. Its tail whipped powerfully from side to side as it dove into the water and was soon swimming at top speed, cutting through waves that splashed Truvian full in the face.

The animal held its trunk above its head to breathe as it swam and most of its body became submerged so Truvian was half underwater. His screams could be heard as he disappeared into the distance and the camera switched to an airborne view that followed the creature out to sea.

Laura laughed, clearly revelling in the man's insanity. Oliver grinned at her and shook his head.

"How do you change the channel?" May asked, sitting down on the sofa.

Laura waved an arm in the air and a menu came up at the side of the screen. She waved her hand to select a channel. "It uses motion sensors. Look at this." She selected an option marked *maps.*

A list of the worlds came up and she chose Aleva. A globe not unlike Earth appeared, but with just four obvious divisions of land. She span it with her hand and clicked on a section, zooming in. "We're here, see? Aleva is divided into quarters then each quarter is divided by fractions, it's basically the same as continents and countries just with a different name. This is Fole Quarter and we're in Lorence Fraction. We have a president for each Quarter."

Oliver could see the land they were travelling across. There were mountains and lakes for miles around with only a few small settlements between Alevale and Crome. The blue tracks of the Traverser were visible, winding their way through the landscape in the direction of Crome. Laura zoomed in by parting her hands in front of her and Oliver spotted a red dot moving along the tracks, marking their train.

"The other maps aren't as detailed as this one but you could have a look through to get an idea of the other worlds if you're interested," Laura suggested, switching to the *wall* setting. The whole screen shifted from the window onto a wall in a smaller, rectangle shape.

The view outside the window was of a glistening lake with the sun setting beyond it, the orange tones in the sky reflecting in the water. Darkness draped over the mountains obscuring their tips from view.

A knock on the door brought Oliver's attention back to the room and May leapt up to open it.

Ely entered. "Dinner's at seven, I've booked us a table in the dining car," he said with a grin.

* * *

Just before seven o'clock they exited their room and waited for the others in the corridor. Oliver was feeling a little underdressed wearing jeans and a jumper, having not prepared for such an occasion on their trip. His sister, on the other hand, was over-prepared as usual, wearing a pretty blue dress given to her by their mum for her birthday last year.

Laura appeared out of her room in a pale pink dress with her usually curled hair now straight. She looked so painfully like Oliver's mum that he felt a sharp stabbing sensation in his chest as he was reminded of her absence.

Ely smiled as he emerged from his room in a smart navy suit and Oliver raised his eyebrows as he noticed his grandfather had shaved his beard and neatly styled his dark hair.

"Oh, you look handsome Daddy," Laura said, leaning down and planting a kiss on his cheek. "I've not seen you without a beard in years."

"Yes, well, let's not harp on about it," Ely said but a slight look of pride entered his eyes.

Laura grinned at Oliver and May. "You both look great," she said, casting her eyes over them.

Oliver frowned as he look down himself. "I didn't have anything better with me."

"You look *fine*," Ely said with a cheery smile. "Come on." He led the way towards the dining car where they were sat at a table for four by a large window that ran the length of the car.

The restaurant was at least four carriages in length and the tables were dressed with white silk tablecloths. In the centre of each sat crystal vases filled with unusual yellow flowers. They opened and closed slowly as if they were breathing, releasing a shimmering cloud of silver dust which evaporated before it touched the table.

"That's a little elaborate," Ely commented, eyeing the flowers.

"They're gorgeous," Laura said.

May reached forward to let the sparkles fall on her hand but they disappeared before they touched her. She tried again, waving her hand around, but the particles seemed to dissolve no matter which way she moved.

"They're nightbells. They only flower at night and let off this cloud to attract nocturnal insects. Once an insect touches it, the creature dies and fertilises the ground beneath it, making the plant grow faster. The most successful of them can reach ten feet," Laura said with a smile.

"Yes and they've become very rare since being used for this sort of display," Ely said disapprovingly.

"Why can't I touch the dust?" May asked.

"The plant reabsorbs it if it can't find an insect to kill, essentially recycling the substance so none is wasted. They're fascinating," Laura said, admiring the plant.

A waiter emerged with a set of menus. Oliver opened his to find a list of dishes he had never heard of.

"What's *snailweed*?" May asked, her face scrunching up in disgust.

"That's just a type of plant. They serve it as a side dish. It's a bit like cabbage but it tastes sweet," Ely explained.

Laura looked amused as May turned the page like it was contaminated. Oliver laughed and looked down to read through some of the dishes:

Flaming Fried Porgle with Chipper Egg Sauce
Textured Spattle with a portion of Lorence-Grown Grodnips
Baked Crawfingers topped with twice-rinsed Croddle Cheese
Sliced Abbicles in Mountain Sauce served with a side of Wittles
Durdled Horgin Fish with Tuttle and Tonns
Nectared Sombay sprinkled with Harp and Rid Seeds
Sizzled and Seasoned Beatichoke on a bed of River Leaves

"Can you recommend something? I don't know what any of this is," Oliver asked Ely and Laura.

"I'd recommend the Spattle with Grodnips. It's my personal favourite." Ely chuckled.

Oliver eyed the description of Ely's suggestion in the menu. "Maybe," he said, unsure.

"There's an interworld section at the back," Laura said.

May sighed with relief and turned to the back of the menu. "They do pizza? Amazing."

Oliver flipped to the back too and saw a list of options from Earth. Considering he was in a completely different world, there was no way he wasn't going to try something new.

"Try the Sombay. It's kind of like stew," Laura suggested.

"Okay, I'll get that," Oliver said decisively, throwing her a grateful smile.

They ordered and the food soon arrived. Oliver's meal was served in a deep bowl that gave of a yellowish steam which smelt rich and citrusy. He dipped his spoon into the creamy-looking broth that was thick with chopped, green vegetables and lifted a spoonful toward his mouth. It was salty and the vegetables added a delicious tang. He eyed the others' meals as he wolfed down several more mouthfuls.

Ely's Spattle with Grodnips turned out to look quite appetising. It was some sort of battered main with a side of potato-like vegetables that were shaped into triangles.

Ely had also ordered a portion of Snailweed for them to try. Oliver tentatively tasted a slither of the leaves that looked almost like cooked spinach. It was cold and tasted somehow both bitter and sweet; it wasn't half as unpleasant as Oliver expected though he wouldn't be tempted to order it in the future.

Oliver sat back in his seat and rested a hand on his full belly. His eyes fell on a familiar family as they entered the room. Chester towered over his wife and son with a hand on each of their shoulders. Oliver realised the waiter was directing them to the table next to theirs and Ely shifted uncomfortably as he spotted them.

"We just keep bumping into each other," Delphine said lightly as she sat next to her husband and Larkin sat opposite her.

"Hmm." Ely buried his head in the dessert menu.

Oliver smiled over at his grandmother, unsure what to say. Laura quickly filled the awkward silence with polite chit-chat. A young waitress served Delphine's table, taking orders. Ely waved her over when she was done.

The waitress had dark hair that curled and bounced about her shoulders; it framed her pretty face that was all petite features. She was small, perhaps slightly taller than May with pale skin and red lips. Oliver grinned at her stupidly.

"Could you bring us each a serving of Alevian trifle please?" Ely asked, clearly not wanting to be scared away by his ex-wife and her new family.

"Of course, would you like anything else with that?" the girl asked.

Oliver realised he was staring at her as she met his gaze and dropped his eyes to his empty bowl, embarrassed. She cleared their table and leant across Oliver to collect May's plate. Her dark hair brushed his cheek and he realised, too late, that he should have passed the plate to her. She frowned at him then walked away.

May raised her eyebrows at him.

"What?" Oliver challenged her.

"Nothing," she said in a sing-song tone and he turned away from her.

Oliver noticed Larkin's eyes following the waitress across the room and clenched his jaw.

Delphine was muttering to Chester and elbowing him in the ribs. Chester frowned angrily and leant back in his chair, making it creak loudly. He cleared his throat and turned to face their table. "So, Ely,

I suppose you've heard about the search for Rimori? What do you make about all that then?" he asked with forced politeness.

Ely stiffened. "I imagine they'll catch him pretty quick."

"Hmm, I doubt it, personally," Chester said as though he knew better.

"Some people don't want him to be arrested," Delphine chipped in.

"And are you one of those people?" Ely asked accusingly, his eyebrows reaching towards his hairline.

"*Dad*," Laura warned.

"I'm just asking," Ely said with exaggerated innocence. "I don't know much about your mother these days."

Oliver shared an awkward look with May.

"Well, as a matter of fact, I think Isaac Rimori has one or two views about the Council and the Gateways that I *would* agree with," Delphine said, jutting her chin upwards.

"Not much he didn't get right, I say," Chester said.

"Apart from murdering my father," Oliver blurted before he could stop himself.

Chester's small eyes slid down to meet his with a look that suggested a child had spoken out of turn. Oliver held his gaze stubbornly.

"Yes, apart from that," Chester said slowly.

"I dunno. One life for the chance to bring down the Gateways? I can see why someone might," Larkin said, folding his arms and gazing at Oliver with a sneer.

Oliver felt anger coursing through his body as he glared back at him.

"*Larkin*," Delphine snapped.

"Calm down, my dear, I'm sure all Lark meant was that sometimes sacrifice is necessary for the greater good," Chester said, throwing Larkin a wink.

"It's easy to say that when you don't know the person who was killed," Oliver said.

"I heard you *didn't* know your father," Larkin said with a smirk.

Oliver was about to answer when the waitress returned with the mains for Larkin's table. Larkin winked at her when his parents weren't looking and she rolled her eyes at him before hurrying away from the table. Oliver fought a laugh and Larkin glared at him.

"Ely, I was wondering if you've been to see Eugene since he was released? He was asking after you the last time I saw him," Delphine said.

Ely's face flushed red. "No I haven't," he said stiffly.

"You ought to," Delphine replied sternly. "He's been quite rattled by the whole experience."

"What I ought or oughtn't do is none of your concern," Ely said, avoiding her eye.

Delphine looked hurt for a moment then began to eat her meal. The waitress reappeared with their desserts, giving them an excuse not to talk to the other table for a while.

Oliver made a point of taking May's from the girl's hand and passed it over. She smiled at him and he shifted uncomfortably in his seat. He noticed Larkin watching them from the corner of his eye.

The individual trifles were served in tall glasses. Oliver tried what he expected to be cream at the top but was surprised to discover that it tasted almost like white chocolate. The middle was thick with blended fruits coloured red and orange; the bottom had a layer of almost luminous, yellow sauce that was slightly sour but complimented the sweet fruit perfectly.

By the time they were finished the room had almost emptied and the waiters were starting to strip the tables.

"I think we'll call it a night," Laura said as she sighed contentedly.

"I suppose you're right," Ely said, clearly relieved not to have made the decision himself.

Laura stood with a yawn.

May looked at Oliver. "Fancy staying up a bit longer?"

Oliver spied the waitress across the room clearing a table. "Sure." He nodded vaguely.

"Okay, see you in the morning," Ely said. "Good night," he said stiffly to Delphine and the others.

Laura smiled at them, pecked her mother on the cheek and followed her father out of the dining car.

"Let's go to the lounge," May said, getting up.

Oliver was torn between not wanting to be around Larkin and wanting an opportunity to talk to the waitress. He sidled out of his seat and May followed him.

"Good night," he said, mostly to Delphine. Chester and Larkin didn't look up at him.

"Night, darlings, we must have a proper catchup soon," Delphine said to them, her gaze lingering on Oliver as she smiled warmly.

They nodded and left the dining car. Oliver threw a final glance in the girl's direction but she wasn't looking his way.

He followed May down the corridor into a lounge where several people were sat around sipping drinks. He and May found a couple of armchairs in a corner and dropped into them. The room was warm and stuffy so Oliver took his jumper off to keep cool, revealing the black t-shirt beneath.

A waiter offered them Glacian tea which they accepted gratefully and Oliver sipped the sweet liquid, relaxing back into his seat.

"What do you think of the Pipistrelle's?" May asked, a smile itching at the corner of her mouth.

"I like them," Oliver said confidently, holding a straight face.

May's eyebrows reached upwards knowingly.

Oliver looked at her seriously and said, "I can see me and Larkin being lifelong friends."

May snorted with laughter. "I can't believe he's your half uncle."

"*Our* half uncle," Oliver corrected, raising a single eyebrow.

She shook her head. "Na-ar I'm pulling the adoption card on this one."

Oliver burst out laughing.

May almost spat out a mouthful of Glacian tea as she started giggling. An older couple across the room glared at her disapprovingly and Oliver felt his stomach muscles ache with laughter, unable to stop.

"Maybe Mum had the right idea about keeping them at arms' length," May said as she reigned in her laughter.

"Ha, yeah," Oliver said, regaining composure.

Oliver took another sip of tea just as he caught a word from the older couple that made his ears prick up.

"-Rimori?" the grey-haired man finished.

"I just hope they catch him before it's too late. If he gets enough support from the Arclites he could start some sort of uprising," his wife responded dramatically.

"Now, now. No one's starting an uprising, dear," her husband said, getting to his feet.

She stood and they linked arms as they walked past Oliver and May to exit the car.

Oliver frowned, thinking back to the night he had overheard Ely and Laura talking. He wanted to piece together what they had been saying.

"What?" May asked, eyeing his expression.

Oliver explained what he had heard and, with a pang, realised what Laura had been insinuating. "She reckons Rimori returning and Mum's disappearance are linked. She suggested Mum actually chose to go to him."

"The timing is pretty coincidental," May said thoughtfully. "But Mum wouldn't abandon us to go and meet up with some murderer, especially one that killed her husband. Plus, we saw her room, it didn't look like she left by choice."

Oliver pushed away the feeling of dread that stirred inside him."You're probably right," he said slowly then lowered his voice. "But what about that curse on you? What are the chances of all these events happening within a few weeks of each other?"

"I can't see the link though," May said with a frown, touching her chest where Oliver knew the mark was located beneath her dress.

"We don't know enough about all of it. I feel like there's a whole lifetime of information we've missed out on and now we have to try and catchup," Oliver said, exasperated.

May nodded slowly, sipping at her tea. Oliver finished the remains of his, mulling over his thoughts. The waitress flashed into his mind again and, with a burst of confidence that he was sure had more to do with the tea than himself, almost considered going to find her.

May yawned. "I think I'm done. I'm knackered."

Oliver nodded vaguely then they stood and returned to their room.

He shivered at the cool air that was being pumped into the room and fiddled with the panel on the wall until he figured out how to turn it off. "Oh, I left my jumper in the lounge," Oliver said in realisation.

"Okay, I'm going to bed," May said, yawning broadly.

"Night then," Oliver said, heading back out the door.

He grabbed the jumper from the chair in the lounge and made his way back to the room at a slow dawdle. As he entered the corridor he spotted Larkin standing in front of someone in the entrance to the dining car, blocking their way.

"Come on, let's have a drink," Larkin said.

"No thanks. Excuse me," a girl's voice answered.

Oliver found himself walking towards them.

"Just a drink, don't be boring," Larkin said, spreading his arms out to lean on the door frame.

The girl attempted to duck under his arm but he moved so she was pinned against the frame. Oliver recognised the pretty waitress from dinner.

"One kiss and I'll let you pass," Larkin said with a cheeky grin.

"No way," she said, folding her arms.

Larkin leant towards her.

"Oi!" Oliver barked.

Larkin span around and his eyes landed on Oliver, narrowing to thin lines. "What are *you* looking at?" he spat.

The girl took the distraction to duck under Larkin's arm.

"Looks like someone being rejected." The words were out of Oliver's mouth before he could consider how Larkin might react and he felt his heartbeat quicken.

"What did you say to me?" Larkin asked in a deadly tone, turning to square up to him.

The girl wandered over and stood next to Oliver. "He has a point," she said firmly.

"Give over, you were well into me before this loser showed up," Larkin said.

"Oh, please," she said, rolling her eyes.

"Didn't look that way from where I was standing," Oliver said, folding his arms.

Larkin looked as though he was going to retaliate then walked forward and barged Oliver with his shoulder as he passed, disappearing in the direction of the lounge.

Oliver was suddenly painfully aware that he was standing alone with the girl. He looked at her and all words seemed to desert his mind. Instead, he made a strained noise in his throat then coughed to cover it.

The girl looked at him with a furrowed brow. "Erm, thanks," she said with a half smile.

"No problem. I'm Oliver by the way." His voice was higher than usual and he felt a flush of embarrassment.

"Anna," she said. "That guy's a tool."

Oliver grinned. "Yeah I noticed," he said, glad his voice seemed to have returned to its usual tone.

"He told me I was the luckiest girl on the train because he'd chosen to have a drink with me. That was his opening line," Anna said with a laugh.

"Seriously?" Oliver grimaced.

Anna laughed. "Yeah."

A woman appeared from the dining car and raised her eyebrows at Anna. "Could you check the drinks cabinet is locked up in the lounge, please? Then you'll be finished for the night."

Anna nodded. "Sure, night Nadine."

The woman smiled and disappeared back into the dining car.

"Wanna come with me?" Anna asked Oliver, her dark brows raising up.

A warmth spread through his chest and he nodded. "Yeah, sure."

He followed her back to the lounge which was now empty. She pressed her hand to a scanner which opened a hatch in the wall. A cabinet of bottles were revealed behind it all suspended on wracks of silver.

She helped herself to one filled with amber liquid at the bottom of the cabinet and grabbed two glasses from a trolley. "Want some? This one's for staff," she said.

Oliver shrugged as she dropped into an armchair and he sat opposite as she poured him a glass.

"What is it?" Oliver asked, swirling the amber liquid around.

She frowned in confusion. "It's Jinu," she said as if it were obvious.

Oliver took a sip from the glass. It was fruity and sharp, fizzing pleasantly on his tongue and throat on the way down.

"This is great," Oliver said as she topped his glass up.

"Haven't you ever had it?" she asked, her brow furrowing.

"Nope," Oliver said, holding the glass up to the light. He could see a faint glow swirling inside it that reminded him of the Gateway keys. "Is it alcoholic?"

Anna smiled with amusement, shaking her head so her chestnut-coloured hair danced around her shoulders. "No. It's one of the most popular drinks in Aleva! Where are you from? You don't look Glacian. Brinatin?"

"No, Earth actually," Oliver said, feeling like an alien species.

Anna burst out laughing. "You're funny," she said.

Oliver frowned, not getting the joke. She spotted the look on his face and stopped laughing.

"You're serious? You're actually from Earth?" Her bronze eyes went wide.

"Yeah, why's that funny?" Oliver asked, shifting under her piercing gaze.

"It's not, I mean, it sort of is. It's just most of Earth don't even know the other worlds exist so only a few ever come through."

"Well, my dad was from Aleva," Oliver said then hesitated before continuing. "His name was William Knight."

She gasped, clutching the arm of the chair. "*The* William Knight?"

"So I've been told," Oliver said slowly, anticipating her reaction.

"Oh, I'm sorry," she said gently.

"For him being my dad?" Oliver asked, irrationally offended.

"Oh- *No*, I meant sorry because, well he's, he-"

"He's dead. Yeah. But I didn't know him. I mean, it's awful and all but I never met him. It's hard to know how to feel about it actually," Oliver said with an exhale of breath.

"I guess you can't help who you're related to," Anna said thoughtfully.

Oliver nodded.

She took a sip of her drink and watched him as if she were itching to say something.

"What?" Oliver asked, anxious at what she might be thinking about his parentage.

"I guess you heard about Rimori coming back from Vale?" she asked tentatively.

Oliver nodded. "Yeah."

"Does it bother you?" she whispered as if she wasn't sure she should ask.

Oliver considered his answer. When he had found out about his father's murder he had been glad to know Rimori was gone. "It does," he admitted. "I mean, I think he should pay for what he did."

"Yeah, me too," she said with a smile and the tightness in his gut unfurled.

"Sorry, I didn't mean to pry," Anna said.

"I don't mind." Oliver sipped at his drink and leant back in the chair. "So, are you entering the race?" he asked to change the subject.

"I wish, but I can't afford the entrance fees. Plus mum would never let me." She rolled her eyes. "*Not 'til you're eighteen*," she mimicked her mother in a high-pitched squawk.

"Oh, that sucks. How old are you?" Oliver asked.

"Sixteen, what about you?"

"Same. I could have offered you a place on my team," Oliver said, finding himself wishing she could join them.

"You're racing? And you have a *spare* space? That's so not fair."
Anna threw her head back with a groan. "I've been working on the
Traverser with my parents to save up for it."

"Maybe I could talk to my grandfather and see if he can help out?
It's kind of urgent that we get a key to Glacio," Oliver said with a
frown.

"How come?" She bit her lip immediately as if she hadn't meant
to probe again.

Oliver didn't want anyone to know about May's curse despite
Anna seeming trustworthy. "My sister and I are going to meet
someone in Brinatin," he said truthfully.

"Oh right. Well, it's a really tempting offer but I couldn't ask your
grandfather to pay for me, that's absurd." She smiled and finished the
contents of her glass, getting to her feet.

Oliver stood up too.

"I'll still talk to him," he said with a grin.

She smiled again, lighting up her dark eyes. "That's really kind of
you but I couldn't. Maybe I'll see you around?"

"Yeah, course," Oliver said weakly, watching as she left the
lounge with a sinking sensation in his stomach.

13

Accomplice

One Year Ago

Rimori slowly scraped his fingernails across the stone. He dragged them towards his knees, leaving trails in the thick layer of blood that covered the cavern floor. The metallic tang that hung in the air barely registered with him anymore.

His teeth were gritted, his long hair and beard were matted with blood and his eyes were squeezed shut in concentration. A cracking noise stirred him from his thoughts and he opened his eyes reluctantly. An animal carcass had slipped forward off of a rock.

He pushed his hands into the coagulated blood and stood. His naked chest was slender, nothing but lean muscle. He exercised each day and lived off the raw carcasses brought to him by the vark. He imagined the way his appearance must have changed since entering Vale and wondered what it would be like to see his reflection again one day.

His head suddenly filled with the familiar voice of the vark he had named Kogure. The creature had shown him more of Vale over the years. The world was barren. Miles of dark rock, mountains of it. Rivers of black shadow and precipices filled with burning embers.

He hadn't wanted to stay this long but his return to the human worlds had to be meticulously planned.

After Kogure saved him in those first few days he had grown to relish the time he spent with the creature. The voice in his head had initially frightened him but now it thrilled him. He could communicate with the practically formless vark. Its body, if you could call it that, was a hulking shadow that could become invisible at will.

Kogure could be ruthless. It could hurt him through his mind and possess his body. It was more powerful than the varks he had known of before, even those with bladed limbs.

He soon realised Kogure held power in this world. The other varks did as he bid them to but Rimori would soon exert his will over Kogure when they returned together to the human worlds.

For now, he relied on Kogure to bring him food. He had grown to savour the taste of raw meat, his face and hands constantly bloody.

"Tell me mmore about your planss. Tell me mmore," Kogure's rough voice purred in his ear, sending chills through Rimori's spine.

"I will share with you when you have shared with me. Have you spoken to my friend?" Rimori spoke aloud. He didn't need to, but using his voice occasionally broke the silence of the cave.

He had discovered that Kogure could travel to the human worlds, not fully, but enough to be able to speak with his friend on the other side. It had taken hundreds, perhaps thousands of attempts to locate him but eventually Kogure had made contact.

The vark could only spend mere minutes in the other worlds before he was seemingly dragged back to Vale. It took days for Kogure to recover between each visit, but the vark persisted in the hope of appeasing Rimori. In return, Rimori promised Kogure many things once they returned to the human worlds, namely blood.

"Yessss. Yesss," it hissed. Rimori could almost feel cold breath on his ear.

"And has it been organised?" Rimori spoke evenly.

"Yess. He sayss it's almossst time. Almossst ready." Kogure's voice was quickening with anticipation.

"We must be patient."

"We've waited longg *enough.*" Kogure snapped the last word with a sound like that of gnashing teeth.

Rimori didn't fear Kogure. The vark could inflict pain on him if he wanted to, maybe even kill him but Kogure could be pacified with words. He wasn't the most intelligent creature but his abilities were useful and Rimori couldn't risk damaging their precarious alliance.

"Hush Kogure. We must play this right. There's no room for error."

"I want to hurrtt themm. Take the other worlddss for ourselvesss. Start the warrr. The othersss grow restlesssss." He spoke slowly and Rimori could hear the desire in his voice.

"You'll get your chance."

"I WANT IT NOW!" Pain ripped through Rimori's body and he doubled over, his hands clawing at the blood-smothered floor.

"Enough!" Rimori forced him from his mind, a trick he had learned a few months after his arrival, earning the hesitant respect of the creature.

"You promised," Kogure hissed like spitting fire.

"And I will keep that promise but you must wait a little longer."

A pause followed these words and Rimori braced himself for another attack.

"I cannn do that," Kogure said, resigned.

Rimori relaxed. "Now, tell me what my friend had to say. Did he mention the girl? Is she safe?"

"She issss. She still knowsss nothing of the other worldssss."

"Good. What else did he say?"

"You're friend isss still hessssitant to talk with me. Can we trusst him?"

"I would trust him with my life."

"He ssstill fearssss me."

"Do you give him reason to?"

Kogure was silent.

"Do you?" Rimori insisted, his temper bubbling under the calm of his voice.

"He cann be impertinenttt. Sssometimes he musst be taught a lesssssson."

"He knows I would never send you to hurt him. You're causing him to mistrust you. It will be your own fault that you cannot return to the other worlds with me."

Rimori cracked his knuckles.

"Noo. Noo. You promisssed," Kogure hissed.

"I can't be blamed. It is your actions which threaten our chances of bringing down the Gateways together. Perhaps I should find another vark to assist me," Rimori said coolly.

"Noo you musn't. I'll try harderr. I won't hurt himm. I will perssuadee him to trusst me." The creature had become desperate, just as Rimori had hoped.

"I will consider it. Leave me now. I wish to be alone," Rimori said.

"Yesss. Forgive mee, forgive mee." Kogure drifted from his mind and Rimori felt his presence lift from the cavern.

Rimori stood, his bare feet squelching in the blood. He began to stretch slowly as he thought through his coming plans.

14

An Invitation

Oliver awoke to the smell of Glacian tea. He rolled over to find a steaming cup of the sweet mixture on his bedside table and slurped it down, giving him the kick he needed to get up.

He dressed and went through to the living room, feeling particularly chirpy. "Morning," he said brightly to May who was sat in an armchair, sipping on tea and nibbling biscuits.

She smiled at him then nodded to the window. "Look at the view."

Oliver turned. The view beyond it was breathtaking; the Traverser was gliding through a picturesque valley bordered by towering, snow-capped mountains. A lake glistened and shimmered in the hazy, morning light where deer-like animals bathed in the lapping water.

A knock on the door sounded and Oliver opened it to find Ely standing there.

"Good morning," he said brightly as he entered and took a seat. "Beautiful isn't it? We're entering Crome's outlands. This is the sort of landscape you'll be racing through. It looks stunning, but trust me, it's not easy to traverse. You'll be relying on your team every step of the way to get each other to the finish line," Ely said.

"What place did your team come when you raced?" May asked curiously.

"My team placed seventh. But that was many years ago, they've made the race more difficult these days because it's become so competitive. It's a more popular idea to travel to the other worlds than it used to be."

"Is there any way we can prepare for it?" Oliver asked anxiously.

"There's not much time to build yourselves up physically but, I suppose, I can give you one or two pointers to help prepare you mentally."

"Like what?" May asked, putting down her tea.

"Well, the first thing you need to remember is that you compete as a team for a reason, to test how cooperative you are. It sounds simple, but many contestants are out for themselves and that can be their downfall."

"That would be easier if we knew who our teammates were," Oliver said in frustration.

"Yes, and often the teams that do best in the race are made up of friends. You'll be at a disadvantage but you'll just have to work extra hard to cooperate with your teammates."

"Okay, cooperate, check. What else?" May asked, determination etched in her features.

"The race will also test your resilience and perseverance to win a key. This is what most contestants focus on. They try to make it through the race on strength and speed alone. It's tough. It'll push you to your physical limits, that's why most people train for it.

"You won't have time to gain an advantage that way but you can pace yourselves. Don't exhaust yourselves straight off the bat. Let the stronger teams go ahead of you and hope they knacker themselves out whilst you progress steadily through the course."

"What do you mean *course*?" May asked.

"The first race day consists of a series of challenges that you'll have to work through to reach the finish line. It's a much longer day than the second but this is where most of the competition will be knocked out. The second and final day is a simple, flat out race to the Gateway for the remaining teams," Ely said.

Oliver nodded slowly.

"So, what chance do we actually have here, considering we don't even have a team together yet?" May asked, slumping down in her chair.

"Don't worry about that until we get to Crome," Ely said.

"Actually, I might have found us a team member," Oliver said excitedly.

"Oh? Who would that be then?" Ely asked, raising an eyebrow.

"Yeah, who?" May asked curiously.

"Her name's Anna. She's a waitress on the train." Oliver felt his cheeks heating up as May eyed him.

"Oh? *Forgot* your jumper, did you?" May teased. "You just wanted an excuse to talk to her."

"Shut it. No I didn't," Oliver said, overly aware of Ely's presence.

"Sure," May said airily and Oliver shot her an angry look.

"Why hasn't she signed up to a team herself if she wants to race?" Ely asked, ignoring May's taunts.

"Well, that's the thing, she can't really afford to enter," Oliver said awkwardly.

"Ah, I see." Ely rubbed his chin. "Why don't you ask her over later and I can decide if she would make a suitable team member?" he suggested.

"But you'd have to-"

"Pay. I know, but we don't have a lot of options. We aren't going to find many people who want to race but can't. If we start signing up people we have to convince to join then they're not going to give it their best shot at winning, are they?"

"That makes sense, I guess. I'll see if I can find her later," Oliver said, his stomach swooping at the thought of seeing her again.

"Good," Ely said, getting to his feet. "I'll see you both later." He let himself out of the room.

Oliver felt restless. "Wanna go explore the train?" he suggested to May.

She sprang to her feet. "Sure. Maybe you'll *bump* into Anna."

Oliver rolled his eyes as he got up to exit the room. He lobbed a silk cushion at her before heading out the door.

They roamed the corridors, passing the empty dining car towards the head of the train. The next room they entered was a spa where several people were sat around having their hair and nails attended to with Alevinum devices.

Oliver spotted Delphine on the other side of the room and caught her eye.

"Oliver, May, come join me over here," Delphine called, beckoning them with a manicured finger.

The woman doing her hair finished and Delphine pressed her thumb to a panel beside the mirror to pay. "What do you think?" she asked, bouncing her curls at them.

"Looks great," May said vaguely, eyeing the woman with disdain.

Delphine twisted around to eye herself in the mirror, adjusting a curl with a flash of light from her palm. "I could do it myself with magic but it's nice to be pampered occasionally," she said.

A woman shied away with a look of awe on her face and Delphine winked at her.

"Will you come and join me for lunch in my room today?" Delphine asked, turning back to face them.

Oliver shared a brief look with May. He wanted to know more about his grandmother but hadn't appreciated her tone with May when they had first met. "Sure," he said hesitantly.

"I'm in the Bane suite. Go past the pool and you'll find it in the next corridor. You'll need this to get through security." She pressed a token into Oliver's palm and he read the words upon it.

Traverser

Restricted Access Pass

"Shall we meet at midday?" Delphine asked lightly.

"Okay, see you then," Oliver said with a smile.

She beamed at them as a beautician returned to her. "Charge my account for any treatment these two would like," she said to the woman, pressing her thumb against the panel again.

"Oh no, we couldn't," May said in surprise, shaking her head.

"I insist. You've both missed out on a lifetime worth of gifts from your grandmother, it's the least I can do," Delphine said warmly.

She shooed the beautician away and got to her feet, sauntering out of the room and wiggling her fingers at them as she left.

"Would you like to see a treatment menu?" a beautician asked.

May nodded eagerly. "Maybe she's not so bad."

Oliver laughed. "Now that she's buying you things?"

She shrugged, fighting a grin.

* * *

May's freshly styled hair bounced and swung about her as she walked beside Oliver. May had convinced him he needed a haircut. Admittedly, he did feel better for it but it had served to remind him of his mother's regular trims.

At lunchtime, they walked into a carriage filled with a large swimming pool and were hit with a wave of humid air. The ceiling and walls were constructed entirely of glass, revealing the vast and wild landscape rolling past outside.

Oliver showed the token to an attendant guarding a door at other end of the room. He let them pass with a bow and the door slid aside as he pressed his thumb to a scanner. They emerged in a large corridor with two doors.

Oliver knocked on the door labelled The Bane Suite and waited, tugging at the hem of his t-shirt.

Larkin answered, his face contorting into a grimace at the sight of him. "What do *you* want?"

"Delphine invited us," Oliver said with a frown, thrown by Larkin's presence.

Larkin looked as though he was about to slam the door in their face when Delphine appeared over his shoulder.

"Hello, darlings. Move aside Larkin," Delphine said, sending a wave of light from her palm into his hair as he passed. The magic smoothed it back flat and he immediately ran a hand through it to mess it up again.

"*Mum*," he said through gritted teeth, then disappeared around a corner.

Oliver suppressed a smile.

They emerged in a lounge with a roaring fire to one side and a water fountain at its centre surrounded by a leather suite of furniture. The midday sun was reflecting into the space as it bounced off a lake outside; the light made a crystal chandelier sparkle and cast jewels of light about the room. Beneath it was a dining table laden with tiny, blue dishes upon which were morsels of food.

"Chester's having lunch with a colleague so it will just be us," Delphine said brightly.

Oliver wondered if she was including Larkin in that scenario and felt a pang of disappointment as he remerged a moment later and sat at the table.

Delphine gestured for them to sit and Oliver moved to sit in the chair furthest from Larkin, using May as a barrier between them.

"So, Alison still hasn't appeared? That's really rather worrying," Delphine said, after a round of polite chit-chat.

Oliver helped himself to a minuscule pastry puff and nodded. "Yeah. We moved in with Ely after she went missing."

"I imagine you're rather curious about your grandfather and I?" Delphine asked, using a delicate knife and fork to slice a pastry in half before eating it, one tiny mouthful at a time.

"Do we have to talk about that?" Larkin asked, shooting her an angry look.

"Don't be rude, I'm sure Oliver and May are quite curious about their family. Imagine if you had never met any of your relatives," Delphine said.

"Sounds like bliss," Larkin muttered, folding his arms.

Delphine pretended not to hear him and continued on. "Ely and I had an arranged marriage. It was always the agreement between us that we would have three children as required then petition for divorce to live our lives how we wanted. Though, perhaps, he is a little bitter towards me now," Delphine said with a sad look.

"Is that what most mages do? Divorce after they've brought up their children?" Oliver asked.

"It used to be but, nowadays, the High Mage of the Council is tightening the law so petitioning for divorce is much more difficult," Delphine said sadly. "The poor dears get stuck in a loveless marriage their whole lives. It's not right."

"But some mages must grow to love each other?" May asked hopefully.

"Yes, but it's not quite the same as having the freedom to choose, is it?" Delphine said, with a sharp edge to her voice.

Oliver couldn't help but agree. "Why is the law on divorce being tightened though?"

"The Council recently carried out a survey on the upbringing of mage children. Apparently those whose parents never divorced have a higher success rate at university and in their later careers. I think it's absolute nonsense. My children turned out just fine."

Larkin snorted. "Yeah one went to prison and another married a mage illegally. Good job, Mum."

Delphine snapped her hand backwards through the air and Larkin flinched his arm away in pain as a flash of magic struck him.

"Argh," Larkin hissed.

"Watch your mouth," Delphine warned and Larkin's face darkened as he dropped her gaze.

A moment later, Delphine got up and disappeared into the bathroom.

May kicked Oliver under the table as the silence stretched on between the three of them. He strained for something to say and decided to try and dissolve some of the tension. "You're racing right, Larkin? Got any tips?"

"Why would I give my competition advice?" Larkin said, his face contorting. "Only a moron would do that. But, then again, you are from Earth."

"So? What does that matter?" May piped up.

"Just that *Earthies* have got a reputation," he said with a sneer.

Oliver could tell he was trying to insult them. He remembered the way Anna had laughed when she found out that he was from Earth. "Yeah, and what's that then?" Oliver challenged him, his anger rising.

"That you're a bunch of idiots. You live next door to six other worlds and you don't even know it. It's embarrassing," Larkin said, smirking.

Delphine reappeared and Oliver took a calming breath.

"So, where are you headed? You must want to race for a reason?" Delphine asked as she returned to her seat.

"We're going to Brinatin to see someone Ely knows," Oliver said.

"Ah, and who might that be?" she asked, drumming her long fingernails on the tablecloth.

He decided it was best to stay vague. "I'm not sure, we're just going along for the trip really."

"But it's urgent enough for you to enter the race a few weeks before it begins? When you are clearly unprepared?" Delphine questioned lightly but her voice held a confidence in it that set Oliver on edge.

"Well, he can't travel if we don't have keys and he can't leave us on our own at the manor," May tried to cover for them.

"He could have left you in someone's care," Delphine said, running a fingernail around in circles on the cloth.

Larkin listened eagerly, making Oliver even more uncomfortable.

"He didn't want to abandon us so soon after mum went missing," Oliver said, holding her gaze.

"Of course," Delphine said.

They ate quietly for a while longer until the silence became awkward.

"How are you coping with everything after your mother's disappearance?" Delphine asked, looking at them as if they were abandoned puppies.

"It must be difficult hearing such complicated things about your family," Larkin jibed. Delphine threw him an angry glance.

"We're coping just fine," Oliver said, looking to his sister.

She nodded, smiling brightly.

"Of course, you've only been given one side of the story. I can hardly bear to imagine the terrible things that you've been told about your father and Isaac Rimori. It's not all true you know. You should really be given the chance to make up your own mind," Delphine said, clearly trying to tempt them in.

Larkin narrowed his eyes at her curiously.

"I think knowing Rimori murdered my father is enough evidence for me that he wasn't a great person and it sounds like my father supported most of his ideas along the way," Oliver said firmly, determined not to be rattled.

"And your mother of course," Delphine said presumptuously.

"I know she was friends with them, yes, and Eugene," Oliver said. "She loved my father."

"She loved him, yes, but she was as much of an anti-Gateway rebel as they were," Delphine said dramatically.

"What's your point?" May asked coolly.

"My point is that she was onboard with all of their ideas, *including* entering Vale. They would have done anything to achieve it," Delphine said, her nails raking across the tablecloth.

"She wouldn't murder someone," Oliver stated.

"She might understand why they would though, might go to the man who did, the man who fulfilled the plans they had all so carefully forged together." Delphine's eyes lit with excitement.

"Mum, what are you talking about?" Larkin asked.

"I think Alison went to Rimori. My girl, she was brave like that, she wouldn't have feared going to him," Delphine said wildly. "You're going to meet them, aren't you?"

Oliver was stunned into silence.

"*Aren't you?*" she demanded, slamming her fist down onto the table.

Oliver got to his feet, his blood boiling. "My mum would *never* be friends with a murderer, let alone one who killed her husband," he snapped.

Larkin's eyes flew back and forth between his mother and Oliver.

May got up. "Thank you for lunch but I think I just lost my appetite." She threw her fork to the table and it clattered down on her plate.

"There's no need to overreact. This is a good thing. We can all go together," Delphine said, her voice returning to silk.

"No thanks," Oliver said and turned his back on her. May followed him to the door and he glanced back before leaving. "She'd be ashamed to call you her mother. I can see why she cut you out of her life." Oliver knew it was harsh but he didn't care. He slid the door sideways, stormed out of the room and marched down the corridor.

He was furious. His heart pounded against his chest as he stormed past the swimming pool in a rage.

"Who does she think she is?" Oliver blurted as May hurried to keep up. "As if Mum would ever go anywhere near that creep."

"I *knew* there was something off about that woman," May said and Oliver could hear the anger in her voice.

He huffed loudly, not paying attention to where his feet were taking him as they barrelled through the dining car.

"My dad was murdered by him for God's sake. What about *that* would Mum want any part in? I doubt either of them knew what Rimori was capable of," he snapped, turning back to look at May.

He stumbled as he collided with someone and a crash of plates smashed to the floor. Oliver spun around to see what he had done.

Anna was standing there covered in sauce, the plates scattered around her feet. Her arms were raised as if she were still holding them.

Oliver's mouth opened and shut like a fish out of water for a few seconds before he found his voice. "I'm so sorry."

Her mouth hung open for a second then she started laughing. "You clumsy idiot," she said, kneeling down to pick up the pieces.

May rushed to help.

"No don't. Let me do it," Oliver said, immediately impaling his hand on a sharp piece of china.

"What's going on here?" It was Ely's voice.

Oliver looked up at him guiltily and Laura appeared next to him grinning. "I knocked the plates," he said, gesturing to the floor pathetically.

"Get up," Ely said tutting.

They stood aside and Ely raised his hands. The glow from them spread across the floor and the plates pieced themselves back together. The food collected into a swirling ball which he sent careening into a bin. He finished and the people around the room applauded.

"A mage. An actual mage, Mummy," squealed a little girl nearby.

"Come with me," Ely said, steering Oliver and May towards the exit with Laura hurrying along beside them.

"Wait, Anna," Oliver said and turned back to her, his heart suddenly hammering.

"This is Anna?" Ely asked, his bushy eyebrows rising.

Oliver nodded.

"Hi," she said, beaming.

"Can you join us for a minute?" Ely asked, siphoning the sauce from her apron with a flash of light.

Her eyes widened a little at the magic and she nodded. "Erm, sure."

Oliver smiled at her and they followed the others from the room.

"Are you alright?" Anna asked Oliver as they stood in the corridor outside their rooms.

"Yeah, why?" he asked with a frown.

"You're bleeding," Laura said, pointing at his hand.

As soon as he was reminded of the wound it started hurting. "Oh, it's nothing," he said with a shrug, glancing at the thin laceration in his skin.

Ely held his palm out and Oliver lifted his hand to let him heal it.

"Why were you charging through the dining car like a rhino?" Laura asked, suppressing a grin.

"We went to see Delphine," May said, with a look that said *it didn't go well.*

Ely cleared his throat, clearly sounding his irritation.

"Why were *you* there?" Oliver asked.

"Dad and I were getting lunch." Laura smiled.

Ely unlocked his room and they filed inside.

"Anna take a seat, don't be shy," Ely said encouragingly as he settled himself into an armchair. "I'm Ely, Oliver's grandfather. I believe you would like the opportunity to race?"

Oliver sat on the sofa and Anna joined him.

"Well, yes, but I can't afford it right now and I know Oliver suggested you might offer to pay but I really couldn't accept," she said in a rush of words.

"Nonsense. Oliver and May need a team as a matter of urgency and I'd be more than willing to cover the cost of your entry," Ely said.

Oliver grinned at Anna as she glanced at him awkwardly.

"I really couldn't-" she began.

"You would be doing us a great favour," Ely said brightly.

"Really?" Anna said, looking unsure.

"Really," May said, smiling at her from across the room.

Anna gazed around at them for a moment then her face broke into a grin. "Well, I guess I can't refuse. Thank you so much Ely." She stood and reached for his hand.

He gripped it tightly and nodded. "You're very welcome. Perhaps we could meet up with you in Crome?"

"Yeah, of course. I'll be staying at The Ganderfield Hotel," Anna said, getting to her feet.

"Alright. We'll look you up when we get to Crome," Ely said with a smile.

"Great," Anna said brightly. "I'd better get back to work."

Oliver got to his feet and showed her to the door, noticing the soft curls that fell around her shoulders as he walked behind her.

"Thanks again," she called to Ely.

Oliver followed her into the corridor. "So, I guess I'll see you in Crome."

"Yeah," she said, tucking a strand of long, dark hair behind her ear. "Thanks for this, Oliver."

"No problem," he said then remembered her original refusal. "Your mum will let you race, won't she?"

"I'll talk her round," she said, giving him a crooked smile. "See you later." She walked back towards the dining car and Oliver returned to the room.

"I think I'll order some tea," Laura said brightly, moving to the panel beside the door and using it to order room service.

A while later a waiter arrived carrying a tray with the characteristic teapot for Glacian tea atop it. He poured them each a cup before exiting.

May was thumbing through a book in her lap and almost spat out a mouthful as she turned a page. "Is this what Grelda Grey was talking about? The mark of the Arc?"

She held the book up so Oliver could see the page and he realised it was the copy of the Arclite Scriptures that Grelda had given to Ely. An image on the page portrayed a body with dark, bruise-like markings spreading across it.

"I can see why Grelda thought it," Oliver said frankly, taking the book from her to get a closer look. "These are pretty similar to the ones on you."

A caption beneath the drawing read:

The Sign: the mark of the Arc will appear on the body of the sacred.

Their death will signal the coming of the embodiment of the Arc.

Ely ripped the book out of Oliver's hands and snapped it shut. "It's nonsense. Utter nonsense."

15

Descendant

Oliver and May sat watching the survision the following morning, their bags packed and waiting at the door.

May flicked the channel to a news station and Oliver sat bolt upright in his seat as he read the words scrolling along the bottom of the screen:

Isaac Rimori sighted in Theald, The Council of Heptus prepare to hold a conference before action is taken.

A female news reporter sat in the studio between a full-sized hologram of a woman and another of a man.

The reporter addressed the female hologram, "Tara Hanks joins me, as a speaker on behalf of the Gateway Protection Committee and Affal Warrington from the political charity Free Worlds. Tara, we'll start with you, what do you have to say to those who are supporting the ideals of Isaac Rimori?"

The hologram of Tara Hanks responded, "I think it's absolutely outrageous that such a vast number of people are getting behind a man who is a renowned murderer. But, much more importantly than that, those who are against the Gateways simply have no idea of the devastation that would be caused without them-"

"I just *have* to interrupt you madam," the male hologram cut in in a thick accent. "Without the Gateways our worlds could become united and the benefits for the human population would be far greater than they are now. There are people in Glacio and Arideen who are completely deprived of the opportunities that the other worlds provide. It's nonsense to say removing the Gateways would have a detrimental effect."

"So, you support Isaac Rimori do you?" Tara Hanks asked.

"I'm not saying I condone the man's actions but I believe his outlook aligns with my own and he did what he did to prove a point."

"And what was that point, Mr Warrington?" the news reporter asked.

"He was making a statement about the Gateways. That challenge was put on the Gateway to Vale with intention. The challenges themselves limit the type of people who can move from world to world. Who was Dorian Ganderfield to say what type of person can go through the Gateways and what they should have to do to achieve that? Many disabled people aren't able to compete in the Great Race of Aleva now are they?"

"You have picked up on an interesting point there and one which has been highly debated within the Council of Heptus. What do you have to say in response to that Miss Hanks?" the reporter asked.

"I'm not denying there aren't issues that need to be resolved with the Gateways but bringing them down all together is absolutely not an option," Tara said. "What you are doing, Mr Warrington, is rallying a mob against the Council. That's what this is really about."

"You have no right-" Mr Warrington pointed a finger at her.

"I have every right. I have absolutely every right. You, sir, are supporting a cause which, ultimately, could upset the balance that the Council of Heptus has protected for-"

"No. I won't hear it. I will *not* hear it. Your beloved Council has caused more grief, more poverty, more discrimination than any other governing body across the seven worlds."

"The Gateways protect the worlds from one another. Look what happened to Arideen when Theald attacked them. Their world was completely obliterated," Tara Hanks stated in exasperation. "And who's to say the Council even have the power to bring down the Gateways? No one knows if it's even possible!"

"Oh, the Council have the answer, alright. They have access to Dorian Ganderfield's original works." Mr Warrington struck his finger through the air as he spoke. "Bring the Gateways down so that everyone can walk through the portals unrestricted. Put it to a vote. Give the public the chance to voice their opinions. Then we'll see where we stand," he said.

"And it may come to just that after the eagerly awaited release of a statement from the High Mage, Horatious Thrake, following the conference in the coming weeks. Thank you for your time, now for the weather-" the new reporter's voice stopped as May switched off the survision.

"This is bigger than I thought," Oliver said, feeling overwhelmed.

"Yeah." May chewed her lip. "You don't think Mum's really with Rimori do you?"

Oliver frowned. "I really don't know," he said honestly. "Wherever she is, I'm sure she's fine. You know Mum, she can look after herself."

May looked down, fiddling with a strand of hair. "Yeah, I know," she said quietly.

* * *

That afternoon, the Traverser arrived in Crome. The station had room for five Traverser trains divided from each other by platforms. The towering walls joined a domed ceiling made from jagged, grey boulders.

They moved through the gargantuan room as the crowd swept them towards a vast exit. A guard took their tickets as they exited the station onto a busy street that was flanked by white, stone buildings.

Oliver was grateful for the air that was fresh and cool after queuing amongst the thick throng of people in the train station.

A two-way stream of pod traffic ran along outdoors, unlike the underground network back in Alevale. A complex grid of tracks diverted to either side of the road at intervals to allow pods to change direction or pull over.

Ely paid for a taxi and they waited in line to enter one. The taxi pods were pale blue and the hologram inside was a smart-looking, middle-aged male with grey hair. "Where would you like to go?" he asked as they sat down.

"The Ganderfield Hotel," Ely replied. "We might as well stay where Anna is."

"Are we far from the city?" May asked, staring out of the window excitedly.

"Not too far. The Traversers are too large to go directly into it so we're just on the outskirts," Ely said.

The pod glided forward and seamlessly joined the flow of traffic. On the table were magazines filled with stories about the race. Truvian Gold was on the front of one with a broad smile on his face. He was hanging from a rope, his body dangling in mid-air inside an enormous cave. A caption next to him read:

Heartthrob Truvian Gold explores the Hogtrout Caves, home to the Great Race of Aleva, like no one has before. Turn to page twelve to read more.

"Did you ever compete in the race Laura?" Oliver asked curiously.

She nodded. "I had to for work. I occasionally take business trips to Glacio to visit the ambiculis mines but I rarely go to Brinatin or Theald even though I have the keys."

"Where did you place?" May asked.

"My team came tenth. Only just though, and I was lucky because there were a couple of strong teams disqualified that season for breaking the rules," Laura said.

They rounded a corner and the city of Crome came into view on the horizon. It sat nestled between an enormous mountain and a lake that disappeared into a swirling mist. A high mountain range loomed beyond it far in the distance, its peaks coated with snow. The city looked almost out of place in the rugged landscape.

The buildings were constructed of blue and white stone, rising sharply upwards into spires and points. They were paned with large windows that glinted and winked as they caught the afternoon sun.

Their pod continued amongst the relentless flow of traffic down into the city. The pod network wound between the buildings, up and over bridges and down through dark tunnels. Eventually, they came to a halt outside an old building in a narrow road with black lettering inscribed across a wooden doorway:

The Ganderfield Hotel

They climbed out of the pod and a doorman greeted them with a bow, opening the door to reveal a lobby with a white, marble floor that had pillars rising up out of it. They moved through it, passing by a lounge to the left where a fire crackled in front of a leather suite of furniture.

"Can I help you?" The sharp-featured woman at the desk regarded Ely as if assessing his worth.

"Yes you can." Ely tiptoed and held his open hand under her upturned nose. A crackle of gold light formed a three dimensional symbol comprised of three circles, intersecting to form a sphere. Inside it was a hand, the palm lines on it illuminated by fire.

"*Oh*, how may I help you today, sir?" she asked as she eyed the symbol in his hand with a look of recognition.

"We'd like to book four rooms up until the day of the race," Ely said, extinguishing the magic.

"Of course. I'll book you our finest suites with complimentary breakfasts included. Would you like to pay now?"

"Yes, thank you," Ely said.

"With your mage discount that comes to three thousand Lokens."

"Three *thousand*? I'll pay for my room, Dad," Laura implored.

"Nonsense, it's my treat," Ely said, holding out his thumb and pressing it to a panel embedded in the desk.

"Step forward one at a time and look at this screen," the woman said, gesturing to what appeared to be a mirror beside her.

"What is it?" May asked.

"We use facial recognition technology here to open the rooms and allow guests access to the facilities in the hotel," the receptionist replied. "Your room number will be displayed when the scan is complete."

Oliver stepped forward and looked into the screen. A blue bar of light ran up and down the glass then beeped to signify it was done. The number *503* flashed up and he stepped away to allow the others access to the device.

"Thank you. If you have any problems please don't hesitate to approach a member of staff. Enjoy your stay at The Ganderfield Hotel," the receptionist said brightly.

As they walked towards the lift, Oliver heard the clerks behind the desk whispering excitedly, "I can't believe it. That's the third mage to check in here this week."

They took a lift to the top floor and stepped out into the corridor, moving towards their rooms.

"I'm gonna take a shower," May said, walking up to her room's door.

Oliver was distracted by a couple at one end of the corridor bickering in muttered words. The girl huffed and disappeared into a room.

Oliver turned back to the door and realised the others had already entered their rooms. He looked at the mirrored door marked *503* expectantly but nothing happened.

He shuffled a little to the left, his puzzled reflection mirrored back at him. He tried the handle but it wouldn't budge then glanced down the corridor and spotted the guy still standing there.

"Hey, err, don't suppose you know how these doors work do you?" Oliver asked him.

He glanced up, clearly stirred from his thoughts. "Oh, sure. I'll show you," he said, walking over.

As he approached, Oliver couldn't help but notice the guy looked as though he had just walked off the set of a film. He was tall, dark haired and tanned with a handsome, chiselled face. His muscles were accentuated by his overly tight t-shirt and even the way he walked suggested he expected people to be watching him.

"You have to stand back a bit further, you're too close," the guy said.

Oliver stepped back and looked at the mirror again. It flashed green and the door clicked as it opened.

"Oh, cheers. Thought I might have to sleep out in the corridor tonight," Oliver joked.

The boy grinned. "Don't sweat it. I'm Rogan." He looked at Oliver expectantly.

"Oliver," he said politely, anxious to get into his room and take a shower.

Rogan frowned as if that hadn't been the response he was expecting. "You don't know who I am do you?"

Oliver shrugged. "Sorry. Should I?"

Rogan shook his head. "No, don't worry," he said, trying to disguise a smile. "How long are you staying at the Ganderfield?"

"'Til the race starts. You?" Oliver asked as the mirror flashed red and he heard the door *click* locked. He cursed internally.

"Same," Rogan said, his eyes flitting to the door then back to Oliver.

"Well, cheers for helping me," Oliver said with a smile that he hoped said *I'm grateful but I want to go now*. He looked at the mirror and it flashed green to signify the door unlocking once more.

"Yeah, cool, no problem," Rogan said, walking down the corridor. He turned and called back, "Hey, do you wanna hang out later?"

Distracted, Oliver collided with the door as it flashed red once again and he huffed in frustration. "Maybe another day, yeah? I'm pretty tired." He ground his teeth as he fought to keep a polite expression on his face.

"Oh, okay, sure," Rogan said, looking disappointed.

Oliver felt a twinge of guilt as he nodded to the guy, waited for the door to flash green and disappeared into his room with a sigh of relief.

* * *

The room was another large apartment, it seemed Ely hadn't skimped on the price. It was decorated in neutral tones of browns and creams and was lit by hanging, glass orbs in every corner.

Oliver unpacked and showered then returned to the lounge. Just as he was about to sit down, a knock sounded at the door and Oliver moved across the apartment to answer it.

"I found you," Anna said, beaming.

Oliver felt his stomach lurch in surprise and ran a tentative hand through his hair, hoping it wasn't a complete mess.

"Yeah you did. How did you manage that?" Oliver asked, trying to sound relaxed.

"I bumped into your aunt in the lobby," Anna replied, casting her eyes over his shoulder curiously. "Are you busy?"

Oliver shook his head. "Nope."

"Wanna hang out? I know this place round the corner from here. Plus, I really need to escape my parents. Mum's driving me insane. We've been put up in a family room so we're practically living on top of each other," Anna said with a look of horror.

Oliver laughed. "Yeah, let's go."

He followed her into the corridor and the mirrored doors on the lift allowed them to call it. An inflated feeling grew in Oliver's chest at the thought of spending some time alone with Anna. The lift doors opened with a *ding* and they entered the empty cab.

Anna stood close to Oliver so their shoulders brushed slightly. His fingers accidentally touched her hand and a jolt of energy rushed through him.

"Hold the doors!" came a voice out in the corridor.

Oliver shoved his arm out to stop them closing then Rogan appeared and stepped inside the lift.

"Oh, hey it's you," Rogan said brightly.

"Hey, man," Oliver said, feeling slightly disgruntled at having his moment with Anna ruined.

"Oh, Rogan this is Anna, Anna this is-," Oliver was cut off by Anna.

"Rogan," Anna breathed.

Oliver turned to look at her. Her mouth was hanging open and her eyes were wide as she looked at Rogan. His stomach twisted as he looked between them.

"Ganderfield," Anna finished.

Oliver frowned in recognition of the name. "Ganderfield?" He looked at Rogan then everything clicked into place. He was famous. With a jolt, he realised that not only was Rogan the descendant of Dorian Ganderfield but must also be the son of Wallace Ganderfield who they were hoping could save May.

Rogan smiled at her. "Yeah, that's me."

"I'm Anna," she said, still gawping.

The lift opened in the lobby and they all exited.

"You up to much?" Rogan asked them.

"No," Oliver said tersely.

"Yes," Anna answered at the same time. "We're going to Sumi's."

"Cool, mind if I join?" Rogan asked confidently like no one had ever said no to him in his entire life.

"Course not," Anna said, looking a little flustered.

Oliver felt his jaw clench.

"I've just gotta pay off a bill at the desk first. Meet you outside in a minute?" Rogan said, walking over to the receptionist whose cheeks flushed scarlet as he approached.

They exited through the revolving doors and Oliver regretted not bringing a coat. The early evening air had brought a crisp wind with it and Anna wrapped her cardigan tightly around herself.

"You don't mind him coming along do you?" Anna asked.

"No, course not," Oliver said untruthfully.

She grinned form ear to ear. "I can't believe we're going for a drink with *Rogan Ganderfield*."

"Neither can I," Oliver muttered, more to himself then Anna. She didn't seem to hear as she walked to a panel beside the door and ordered a taxi pod.

Oliver realised he had no money. "Err, Anna. I don't actually have any way of paying for things here," he said, the blood heating up in his face.

"Oh, right. Come over here. Do you have an account in Earth?" she asked.

"Yeah, but I can't use that here, can I?" he asked.

"Aleva has technology which links all bank accounts across the worlds. You just have to register and it will automatically change the currency when you use it," she said.

Anna talked him through the steps so that his bank account was linked to one in Aleva then he registered his thumb print so he could pay. "That's brilliant. Thanks," he said.

He realised Anna was standing extremely close as they both leant in to look at the screen. She looked up at him with her bronze eyes, making his stomach feel like it was floating.

"Ready to go?" Rogan's voice chimed in his ear like a klaxon.

Oliver stepped away from Anna in an instant and they turned to join Rogan. Anna's cheeks were flushed as she looked at the celebrity, making Oliver's heart sink.

They took the taxi pod to Sumi's. The restaurant was located down a spiral of winding stairs that led underground. The floor looked as though it were made of ice and the bar was raised up on a stage surrounded by a moat of turquoise water. People were queuing to it over three metal bridges. The water from the moat cast patterns on the ceiling and walls, giving the feel of being underwater. Waiters in blue uniforms hurried around passing out food.

The tables and chairs were made entirely of glass. Rogan rushed over to one in a corner and sat down, facing the wall. Oliver and Anna joined him.

"Do you mind bringing me a drink over? I just don't want anyone to recognise me," Rogan said.

"Sure, what do you want?" Anna asked.

"Jinu, please. And get a Tab," he said with a smile that Oliver imagined would have sent any girl into a frenzy.

"I'll come with you," Oliver said to Anna hopefully.

"No, don't worry. Do you want the same?" Anna asked.

Oliver nodded, his gut sinking as he sat down with Rogan.

"She your girlfriend?" Rogan asked as Anna disappeared into the crowd.

"No. Why?" Oliver asked defensively, his spine straightening.

Rogan laughed. "Just curious that's all. Don't worry, I'm a mage. I've been engaged since I was sixteen. Where in Vale are you from?"

"Earth," Oliver said, the weight in his chest lifting as he tried to recall everything his grandfather had told him about mages.

"Earth? You messing with me?" Rogan asked, a smile playing at the corner of his mouth.

"Nope. All of this stuff is new to me. I didn't know any of it existed until recently," Oliver said.

"That's crazy. It was so weird meeting you earlier and you didn't recognise me. I don't remember the last time I had to introduce myself," he said with a grin.

"Was that your fiancé back in the hotel? I saw you guys talking before," Oliver said.

"Fighting you mean," Rogan said with a frown. "She drives me nuts sometimes. I'm glad to get out for a bit, I needed a break. Though I don't normally risk going out in public."

Oliver felt a flash of guilt at having rejected Rogan earlier. He was about to ask why they had been arguing when Anna returned with a tray of drinks.

She passed the Jinu out and placed an object on the table shaped like a trapezoid. It was black in colour and the flat surface on top of it held a screen that displayed the price of five Lokens. Oliver assumed it was what Rogan had referred to as a Tab.

Oliver sipped the Jinu and felt the cold leave his bones. He spotted a group of girls nearby sidling closer and leaning backwards to get a better look at Rogan.

"You've got a group of stalkers," Oliver said, nodding to the girls.

Anna looked up at them. "I don't think they know it's you yet."

Rogan brushed a hand through his hair. Oliver spotted an almost imperceptible light ignite between his fingers and his hair lengthened to cover one side of his face.

Oliver suppressed a laugh. "It suits you like that."

"Shut it," Rogan said through a smile.

"Can't you just change your appearance to look like someone else completely?" Oliver asked.

"I think that's basically impossible and definitely illegal," Rogan said with a laugh.

The girls were closing in. One of them was leaning back as far as she could to try and see Rogan's face. A large blonde girl with broad shoulders pouted then strutted over purposefully to Rogan.

"Heads up," Oliver muttered to him.

The girl tapped him on the shoulder and, with a quick flash of light, Rogan rubbed his hand over his chin and swung around. He now had a long, bushy beard.

"Can I help you?" Rogan asked the girl in a rough and croaky voice that wasn't his own.

She looked taken aback for a moment. "Oh, sorry. I thought you were someone else," she said with a sigh. She returned to her friends, shaking her head and Rogan turned back to the table, sipping his Jinu.

Oliver and Anna suppressed their laughter as the girls walked away.

"Are you here to watch the race?" Oliver asked Rogan after a moment.

"I'm entering it. Quinn, my fiancé, got us a space on a friend's team. Are you guys racing?" he asked, running a hand over his face, returning it to normal with a glow of magic.

"If we get two more team members we might be." Oliver's throat went dry at the thought of competing against mages.

"You haven't signed up yet? I dunno if there's any spaces left. When you get your team together let me know and I'll put a good word in for you with the Race Committee. It pays to be famous sometimes," Rogan said.

"Thanks," Oliver said, his eyebrows raising a little in surprise.

"Don't suppose you know anyone looking to sign up?" Anna asked hopefully.

"Sorry, everyone I know who wants to race is already on a team," Rogan said genuinely.

"Hey, I thought it was you," said a male voice.

Oliver looked up to see who had spoken and his jaw automatically clenched as he spotted Larkin. Rogan turned and smiled in recognition. He got up and clapped Larkin on the shoulder.

"You alright?" Rogan asked Larkin.

Oliver shared a look with Anna who's lip had curled back slightly.

"Good, yeah. Why don't you come join me and Arrow?" Larkin offered, gesturing to a table where a dark-skinned boy the size of a tank was sitting.

"Thanks, but I'm alright here," Rogan said, gesturing to Oliver and Anna.

Larkin's eyes slid to meet Oliver's gaze and his mouth curved into a sneer. He looked to Anna with a nod. "Hey babe, you can come join us too."

"I'd rather not thanks," Anna said, rolling her eyes.

"What are you doing sitting with this loser?" Larkin asked Rogan, gesturing to Oliver.

"What's your problem?" Rogan asked Larkin in an even tone.

Oliver fought a smile.

Larkin snorted. "You kidding me? Come on, ditch the Earthy."

"Why don't you go back to your own table? I think your boyfriend's waiting for you," Oliver said, gesturing to Larkin's friend.

Larkin looked to Rogan as if he expected him to do something. Instead, Rogan sunk back into his seat and took a sip of his drink.

"Pfft," Larkin spat then slunk back to his own table.

Silence hung in the air for a moment.

"So Larkin's a tool," Anna stated brightly.

Oliver couldn't help but laugh and Rogan joined in momentarily.

"We went to university together. We've always got on alright but yeah he can be a massive tool when he wants to be," Rogan said. "He's always been closer with Quinn."

Oliver sensed something bitter in the way he spoke.

Rogan sighed. "I don't want any tension with Larkin, I'm racing with him."

"Seriously? You're on *his* team?" Oliver asked, not being able to imagine anything worse.

"Yeah, he's not all bad," Rogan said with a laugh.

Oliver nodded and sipped at his drink, not wanting to offend him. "Well I have to cut him *some* slack seeing as he's kind of my uncle."

"*What*?" Rogan said, laughing as if Oliver were making an odd joke.

Anna spluttered as she took a sip of her drink.

"No seriously." Oliver laughed and proceeded to explain his link to Larkin.

"Poor you," Anna said, grinning at Oliver and patting his arm in mock sympathy.

"Yeah, that used to happen a lot when mages would divorce and have a new family. It's gonna be pretty much impossible soon though," Rogan said.

"How come?" Oliver asked.

"The High Mage wants to put a stop to it completely. He says it's damaging to a family unit," Rogan said.

"What do you think?" Anna asked, leaning toward him.

Rogan shrugged and Oliver sensed he didn't want to give an opinion on the subject.

Anna took a sip of her drink and turned to Oliver. "What's your sister up to tonight?"

"I dunno but she's gonna be mad I didn't invite her out," he said, not mentioning he had thought he would be spending the evening alone with Anna.

"Is she on your team?" Rogan asked.

"Yeah, just her and Anna so far," Oliver replied.

"How old is she?" Rogan asked.

"Sixteen. Weirdly, she doesn't exactly have a birthday," Oliver said with a slanted smile.

"What do you mean?" Anna asked, her eyes twinkling with curiosity.

"When I was six years old my mum found her in the middle of the road. Just lying there in the pouring rain. She adopted her eventually and gave her a birthday as the day she found her, October twelfth. She looked about my age so," he shrugged in explanation.

"That's crazy. So you have no idea where she came from?" Rogan asked incredulously.

"Nope, never found out," Oliver said.

"Wow," Anna said, looking amazed. "Doesn't that drive you crazy?"

Oliver laughed. "It used to when I was a kid. I don't really think about it much anymore, it's just one of those things."

"Why don't we all hang out tomorrow?" Rogan suggested.

"We need to keep looking for team members though," Anna said hesitantly.

"Well, we could do both?" Rogan pushed. "You could bring May along."

"Sure, you could bring Quinn, too," Oliver suggested.

Rogan frowned. "Maybe."

"Why don't we go to the Hogtrout Caves?" Anna suggested excitedly.

"Oh, yeah, let's do that," Rogan said with a grin.

"Why?" Oliver asked.

"It's where the first part of the race is held. There'll be loads of people there we can ask," Anna said.

Oliver nodded. "Okay, sure."

They paid by pressing their thumbs onto the Tab, splitting it three ways despite Rogan's insistence to pay and exited the restaurant.

* * *

They entered the hotel lobby which was quiet, the reception now left unattended.

A girl was standing just inside the door looking both incredibly beautiful and terrifyingly angry. She had long, dark hair that flowed over her shoulders around her petite figure. Her large, chocolate-coloured eyes were framed by long eyelashes and her skin looked sun-kissed and glowing as if she had just returned from a holiday.

"Where. In. Vale. Have you *been*?" she said, pouting her full lips at Rogan.

"Ah, give it a rest Quinn," Rogan said, rolling his eyes.

"I will *not* give it a rest. Thanks for abandoning me all evening," she snapped, flicking her hair over her shoulder.

"It wasn't like that. You'd gone to your room anyway," Rogan said.

Quinn took a deep breath and expelled it forcefully like a bull. "What do you want? An autograph?" she barked, noticing Oliver and Anna watching her.

Oliver now fully understood why Rogan had wanted some space from the girl.

"Sorry, should I know who you are?" Oliver asked.

Rogan suppressed a smile.

"Are you trying to be funny? I'm Quinn Thorn," she said, her face contorting in fury.

Anna threw Oliver a look of warning.

Oliver shrugged. "Doesn't ring a bell. Night Rogan, see you tomorrow," he said, taking Anna's arm and leading her towards the lift.

"Meet here at ten!" Rogan called to them.

Anna giggled as they disappeared into the lift. Oliver caught Rogan's eye as the doors closed and Quinn's screeching was cut off as they clunked into place.

"She's gonna hate you," Anna said, grinning.

Oliver laughed. "Well she shouldn't be so presumptuous about her status in the world."

He grinned at her and their gaze lingered, making the quiet in the lift suddenly awkward. He realised he was still gripping her arm.

The lift doors opened on Anna's floor. He instantly released her as he spotted an angry woman standing there, her hair a shaggy, brown frizz.

"And where do you think you've been young lady?" she snarled, her eyes lighting up dangerously.

"Out," Anna said firmly.

"And you didn't think to mention you were going out? Your father and I have been worried *sick*," she said, glaring daggers at Oliver.

"It was my fault, sorry," he said, rubbing the back of his neck.

Anna's mother eyed him. "Come on, Annabelle."

Anna gave him an apologetic look as she followed her mum down the corridor.

The lift doors closed and Oliver leant against the back of it with a sigh. The doors opened again a few moments later and he made his way to his room.

A note had been slid under the door.

He picked it up and read it, recognising his sister's neat handwriting.

Ely's wondering where you are. I covered for you. You owe me.

Oliver grinned. He could always rely on May.

16

Wings of Fire

Oliver was awoken by a loud thumping on the door. He jumped up and ran to open it, realising too late that he was only wearing shorts. It was Quinn. She folded her arms, casting her eyes over his body so he felt somehow more naked than he actually was.

"What do you want?" Oliver asked, rubbing the sleep from his eyes.

"I came to apologise," Quinn said, looking irritated.

"Did Rogan send you?" Oliver asked, suppressing a smile.

"He insisted," she said, visibly gritting her teeth.

"Well, I suppose I forgive you. Are you coming to the Hogtrout Caves today?" Oliver asked, deciding to make an effort with her.

"What do you think?" she snarled and walked off down the corridor.

Oliver shut the door more forcefully than he had intended. He went to move just as another knock sounded at the door and he opened it to find May standing there in her pyjamas.

"Hey," she said and walked inside.

"Hang on a sec," Oliver went to his room and put on some clothes before returning to the living area where May was slumped in a chair.

"So, do you wanna explain where you disappeared to last night? I can't *believe* you left me. Ely spent the evening talking about Alevian politics with Laura. Turns out, it's just as boring as politics back on Earth. I almost went insane."

"Sorry, Anna asked me to go out," Oliver said sheepishly.

"Oh, I guess I'll let you off then seeing as you were on a *date*," May said with a smirk.

"It wasn't a date. This guy ended up coming along with us anyway. Sort of invited himself actually," Oliver said, grinning at the memory.

"What guy?" May asked and Oliver explained about Rogan and Quinn.

"So, they're celebrities?" May asked incredulously.

"Yep, and we're all going out today. That includes you," Oliver said.

"Hmm, okay. But don't go ditching me again," May said, reaching her leg out to kick at him.

Oliver laughed. "I won't. Go get dressed, we're leaving at ten."

"Alright, but go see Ely first," May said, heading for the door.

Oliver saw her out then went and knocked on Ely's door.

Ely smiled warmly as he opened the door. "Ah, there you are. Did you have a good rest? May said you got an early one."

Oliver nodded. "Yeah, thanks."

"Laura's joining the Race Committee today and I'm thinking about going with her. We can find out if any of the teams have dropped out."

"Great, well I'm going with May and Anna to the Hogtrout Caves to try and find team members," Oliver said.

"Good idea," Ely said, scratching at the stubble on his chin which was starting to grow there. "We only have ten days 'til the race starts so we better get a team together as soon as possible. Come knock for me when you get back and let me know how it goes."

"Alright, see you later," Oliver said as he left.

* * *

Oliver and May took the lift down to the lobby just before ten o'clock. Anna was already waiting for them in the lounge wrapped up in a black coat and green scarf.

"Good morning," she said brightly.

"Morning, I hope your mum wasn't too mad last night," Oliver said with a worried look.

"Oh, don't mind her. She's always like that," Anna said, shaking her head. "I love your outfit, May."

Oliver eyed her sister and noticed that she did look particularly nice, her blonde hair cascading over the navy blue material of her coat.

"Thanks," May said, her cheeks flushing pink as she fiddled with a button.

Oliver hated how badly she took compliments.

Rogan and Quinn appeared from the lift looking immaculate. The clerks at the desk kept glancing up at them, trying not to stare for too long.

"Is that them?" May asked, stepping closer to Oliver.

"Yep, how could you tell?" Oliver muttered sarcastically.

"Hey," Rogan said as he approached.

Quinn nodded her acknowledgement, glancing around the lobby as if someone more important might appear to take her interest.

"This is my sister May," Oliver introduced her. "This is Rogan and Quinn," he said to May.

May looked shy, her face paling from pink to a ghostly white. "Hi."

"Shall we get going?" Rogan said, his eyes lingering on May. "Quinn and I are gonna have to disguise ourselves or we'll be mobbed."

"I don't see why we can't just get a private tour. Why do we have to go in disguise? It's so degrading," Quinn said, rolling her eyes.

"Oh don't be so boring. It'll be more fun this way," Rogan said.

"If I get recognised and have to start pandering to people, I'm blaming *you*," she snapped.

"This *is* gonna be fun," Oliver said, looking at Quinn with a smile.

She huffed but didn't say anything.

As they passed through the revolving door, Rogan's bushy beard reappeared and Quinn's hair became a short, blonde bob. She put on a large pair of sunglasses and Rogan retrieved a peaked hat from his pocket and put it on.

"It'll still be pretty obvious if we stand too close together," Rogan said. "People might recognise us as a couple."

"Haven't you gone out in public like this before?" Anna asked.

"Not often. And not in such a large crowd. This is kind of an experiment," Rogan said with a mischievous grin.

They took a pod out of the city into an underground system that passed partially through the mountain. The tunnel was narrow and cut roughly through the damp-looking stone, lit by dim lights every few hundred meters.

May discovered a tourist setting in the taxi pod and switched it on; the hologram of the grey-haired man began talking.

"You are passing through Thorn mountain, home to the Hogtrout Caves which became famous for their use in the Aleva to Glacio Gateway challenge: the Great Race of Aleva. The race was first held approximately nine hundred and fifty years ago after the construction of the Gateways by Dorian Ganderfield.

"The race involves contestants making their way through the caves to find their way out to Glacio Lake. This tradition has been upheld but the caves have since been modified to make the race more difficult so as to slow down the volume of people allowed to pass between the worlds.

"This season's race marks the tenth anniversary of an act of terrorism on the caves carried out by anti-Gateway rebels. The attack destroyed several of the cave rooms that had been designed for the race. This season, the final three of those rooms will reopen with never-before-seen obstacles."

"Why are people against the Gateways?" Oliver asked the pod.

Quinn sighed in exasperation and Rogan elbowed her in the ribs.

"Those against the Gateways believe the worlds could live as one united empire. This idea was condemned by the Council of Heptus and their role in enforcing the Gateways have kept the worlds living peacefully alongside one another for almost a thousand years."

"Ha, what about Theald and Arideen?" Anna asked.

The hologram didn't respond but continued to talk about the history of the race.

"What about them?" Oliver asked.

"They went to war a few years after Dorian Ganderfield created the Gateways," Anna explained. "The government in Theald managed to find a loophole in the challenge on their Gateway that meant anyone from Theald could get a key to Arideen."

Quinn looked pointedly out of the window, ignoring their discussion.

"What happened?" May asked Rogan, tucking a strand of hair behind her ear.

"A massive army stormed through into Arideen and completely obliterated them. The people of Arideen were much less advanced. Theald has trained mercenaries and highly advanced weapons that completely altered the landscape in Arideen and, even now, hardly anything can grow there," Rogan said with a grimace.

"Are there people there today?" Oliver asked.

"They have one major city near the Theald Gateway," Anna said.

"The Council of Heptus took away Theald's right to have a say in the challenge and altered it to remove the loophole," Rogan chipped in.

"We have arrived at your destination: The Hogtrout Caves," the hologram announced and they jumped out, emerging in a large cave.

Water dripped down the brownish walls in slow trickles, gathering at the bottom in small pools. They ascended a steep set of stairs that had been carved into the floor. It climbed up towards the cave mouth where daylight poured down towards them.

Several people were milling at the top but none seemed to recognise Rogan or Quinn as they passed by. Rogan retrieved the sunglasses hanging from his shirt and put them on.

"This is great," Rogan said with a grin.

"I don't like it," Quinn hissed.

"That's 'cause you love the attention." Rogan rushed forward and tickled her sides.

She squealed. "*Rogan.*"

"Shh," he said, suppressing his laughter.

A group of girls looked around curiously at the mention of his name. Rogan and Quinn rushed forward before the girls could work out who they were. Oliver glanced back at the others with amusement as they hurried after them.

They reached the top of the stairs and headed along a track that was a mixture of gravel and sand, catching up with Rogan and Quinn. They rounded to the left and Oliver gazed at the incredible sight unfolding in front of him.

The ground beneath them sloped down dramatically towards an enormous cave mouth that was pitch black and ominous. Large stalactites and stalagmites joined the cave from the top to the bottom with gaps in between, giving it the appearance of an enormous mouth.

Surrounding the cave were a colossal amount of grey stone seats sloping high up above it like an arena. There were smaller caves around the edges where families were having photos taken.

"Wow. Can we go inside?" May asked, shielding her eyes from the glaring sun as she gazed down into the valley.

"Yep. This is where the race starts. The crowd sit in those seats and watch the teams enter through the cave mouth," Anna said, excitement lighting her eyes.

"We can't go in that far though. They have the chambers blocked off before the race," Rogan said.

Oliver felt nervous as they walked down the slope. He imagined thousands of people watching him descend into the cave mouth as if he were about to be eaten alive by it for their entertainment.

The cave was even bigger than it had appeared from the top of the hill. Oliver craned his neck to look up at the ceiling as he passed through two of the cave's teeth. The ceiling was so high that it disappeared into darkness.

In front of him was a sudden drop which they had to walk around to descend further inside. Railings had been put up to stop people from falling.

Burning torches were set around the cavern so that they weren't in complete darkness and the sound of scratching and squeaking filled Oliver's ears from somewhere high above.

"What's that noise?" he asked.

"It's the firebats. Look, see?" Anna said, pointing upwards as they turned a corner, entering a large chamber lit by fire. It flickered on the ceiling and around the walls, moving and swaying like an animal.

Oliver darted to the side as a fireball whizzed past his ear.

Rogan and Anna laughed as May ducked one with a squeal. Quinn folded her arms and tutted at them.

"Don't worry. Just one on its own can't do you any harm," Anna said.

"But there's a million of them in here," May said, staring up in horror at the firebats and gathering her long hair into her hands to keep it safe.

"They won't be leaving the cave until nightfall. They wouldn't let people in here if it was dangerous," Rogan said reassuringly.

May didn't seem to relax.

"Come here," Rogan said.

May's eyes flicked to his then quickly dropped to her feet as she stepped toward him. Rogan subtly ran a wave of light over her hair so a faint, amber glow emitted around her for a second then disappeared.

"Now you're fireproof," he whispered with a grin.

May nodded, her cheeks flushing. "Thanks," she muttered.

Quinn narrowed her eyes at Rogan and pulled him over to her, looping an arm around his waist protectively.

"We shouldn't draw attention to ourselves," Rogan said, detaching himself.

"Oh, but you can cast magic in front of everyone?" she snapped.

"Shh," he said firmly.

Oliver looked around, making sure no one had noticed. Everyone was too busy looking up at the firebats, swaying as they slept on the high ceiling. Now he was over the shock of seeing them, Oliver realised how captivating they were as their bodies blurred into one great fireball high above him.

Oliver overheard a male tour guide talking to a group nearby. "This is the largest firebat colony in the whole of Aleva. Years ago, masses of them were exterminated because of the damage they caused after a particularly dry summer. The firebats set hundreds of fields ablaze all over Lorence fraction. They're now a protected species and this colony is one of the biggest attractions of the Hogtrout Caves, after the race that is."

Oliver felt the heat coming off them as they warmed the entire cave and a sleepy feeling washed over him.

"How are they alive? They're on fire," a young boy asked the guide.

"They have a thick layer of oil on their fur which allows an almost constant fire to burn. The oil runs out when they reach an old age and the fire consumes them," the guide answered.

The boy gasped, looking sympathetically up at the creatures.

"It's just how they've evolved. The fire protects them from predators and keeps them warm throughout the cold winters. When they're born, they're lit by their mother's fire and don't stop burning until they die," the guide said.

"This is as far as we can go. When we start the race we go through the exit over there." Rogan pointed.

Oliver followed the direction of his finger towards a cavern that led out to a narrow passageway. It was cordoned off with a guard stationed there.

"At the end of that corridor is the entrance to several rooms. We have to choose one at random and hope it works out," Anna explained excitedly.

Oliver couldn't help but feel a little excited despite the circumstances they would be racing under. The inflated feeling dispelled as he remembered that they didn't have a full team together yet.

"And what if it doesn't work out?" May asked.

"You can go back and try another room but you might end up wasting time. If you can't get through the caves in the allotted time, you'll be disqualified," Rogan answered, looking grim.

"How much time do we get?" May enquired.

"Two hours," Anna said excitedly.

"That's all?" Oliver asked in horror.

"Yep, it's gonna be tough," Rogan said, bouncing a little with anticipation. "I can't wait."

"I wish we were racing with you guys," May said thoughtfully.

"I don't blame you," Quinn muttered, placing a hand on her hip.

"Quinn, you're such a cow sometimes," Rogan said, nudging her. "I'd rather be racing with them. Larkin was such an idiot last night."

"I'm sure he was just joking," Quinn said. "Argh, I have to take these off. I can hardly see." She pushed the sunglasses up onto her head.

"Yeah, it's probably more suspicious to be walking around with sunglasses on in a dark room," Rogan agreed, laughing and pulling his own off.

A couple of teenage girls appeared behind them and Anna took the opportunity to talk to them. "Excuse me, are you competing in the race?"

"Yes, why?" one of them asked.

"We're just looking for team members," she said, cocking an eyebrow.

"Well you've left it rather late haven't you?" the girl said loftily and walked further inside the cave with her friend.

Anna made a face at them as they went.

"Okay, strike one," Oliver said, nudging her and she smiled.

"Let's split up, we'll cover more ground that way," May suggested.

They spent the next couple of hours approaching people. Oliver soon realised that anyone who was competing already had a team and those who didn't, didn't want to compete anyway. He spent fifteen minutes atrociously attempting to flirt with a girl before she bluntly rejected his request. After a few more failed attempts, he decided to take a break.

He found Anna and May looking equally disheartened.

"This is going to be more difficult than I thought." Oliver sighed, feeling the afternoon slipping away.

"I told one girl where I was from and she said she didn't want an *Earthy* on her team even if she did have a place for me. What's that supposed to mean?" May asked, indignantly.

"Don't take any notice. Some stupid people still have stereotypes about people from Earth," Anna said, throwing a knowing look at Oliver.

May pouted and glared across the room at a girl.

"Where's Rogan and Quinn?" Oliver asked, looking around for them. He spotted them a little way away talking to a group of teenagers.

They walked over and joined them.

"I swear I know you from somewhere," a buck-toothed boy was saying to Quinn.

"I don't think so, bunny boy," Quinn replied coolly.

Rogan frowned at her. "Don't be rude. Sorry about her," he said to the boy.

"I know you too," the boy said, narrowing his eyes at Rogan.

"You're mistaken," Rogan said, stating it as a fact.

The boy's friend, a pretty girl with black hair, looked closer at Rogan. She gasped suddenly, clapping her hands to her mouth.

"Time to go," Rogan said, attempting to pull Quinn away into the crowd. The girl gripped his arm.

"Rogan Ganderfield," she whispered. Then she screamed so loud it echoed around the entire cavern. "ROGAN GANDERFIELD'S HERE!"

17

Fragmented

The girl pointed and bounced up and down as if she was on a pogo stick. The rest of her friends shouted out and started pointing too.

One of them looked straight at Quinn. "And Quinn Thorn! Quinn Thorn's here too! Ahh!"

The crowd in the room swung around to face them. Within a second they were mobbed. Oliver reached for Anna nearby and gripped her arm so he didn't lose her. May was forced aside by a boy who stepped on Oliver's feet then tried shoving him.

"Get out of my way!" Oliver snapped, losing his patience.

The boy frowned but stopped standing on him. Oliver couldn't see May anywhere amongst the swarming crowd. He forced his way through to Rogan and Quinn, still gripping Anna's arm tightly. He elbowed a boy in the ribs who tried to actively rip Anna's arm out of his hand to get through.

A group of girls were practically climbing Rogan. Quinn signed pieces of paper that were being waved in her direction, looking delighted at seeing her fans. Oliver used the space around Quinn to get to Rogan.

"You alright?" he asked Quinn as he passed.

"Just peachy," she said with a glare that gave away her real feelings on the situation. "Help Rogan will you." She rolled her eyes at the girls climbing him.

"I can't exactly stop them," Oliver said, frowning at them.

"No, but we can," May said, appearing at Anna's side.

Anna agreed readily and the two of them forced their way over to Rogan, shoving the girls aside. They managed to create a space around him next to Quinn.

A girl lunged forward and Anna stopped her with a look. "Take one more step and I'll stop you myself," she said threateningly.

The girl frowned at her but didn't step any closer.

"CAVE'S CLOSING! Please make your way towards the exit unless you want your hair set on fire by the bats!" a guard shouted as he waved people towards the exit.

Oliver sighed with relief. The guard helped usher the crowd out of the cave. Their group held back so they could get some distance between them and the fans.

"You guys go ahead," Rogan said. "I'll see if we can persuade the guard to let me and Quinn out a different exit."

"Okay, see you back at the hotel?" Oliver said.

"Yeah, see you later," Rogan said, walking over to the guard with Quinn.

The firebats were getting restless on the ceiling and the bright fireball was growing as more of the creatures gathered in the centre. Oliver, May and Anna hurried towards the exit and up the hill. A group of guards cordoned off the entrance as the first of the firebats flitted out of it, up towards the sky.

They reached the top of the hill and turned to look back at the cave, the sky had dimmed to a pale pink as the sun began to set.

"How are people gonna watch us in the race if we're down in that cave?" May asked.

"With Survision cameras. They film the race so the crowd outside and people at home can watch the action. It'll be broadcast all over the world," Anna explained.

"It's kind of exciting," May said.

Oliver smiled at her. His mind was taken off the race completely as he looked back and saw the hot, red glow of fire growing brighter from inside the cave. The glow was accompanied by the screeching of bats that sounded like air rushing through burning wood.

The fireball of bats burst from the cave, warming Oliver's face with the heat of the swarm. The noise was deafening. They came in a stream of fire and, as they rose, the mass of bats swirled and cartwheeled in the sky, leaving sweeping trails of light behind them.

The stream began to thin until the final bats left the cave and joined the flowing river of red and orange in the sky until they disappeared into the distance.

Oliver exhaled slowly.

"Wow," May said, her eyes wide.

"I forgot how incredible it was to watch. I came here to see it with my mum and dad when I was little," Anna said, leading the way towards the pod station.

Night had completely fallen by the time they arrived at the Ganderfield Hotel. The yellowy light of Aleva's dusty-looking moons shone down over Crome and the stars glittered in the navy sky.

They walked through the revolving doors and the noise of arguing filled Oliver's ears as he emerged in the empty lobby. He looked over to see Rogan and Quinn bickering in the lounge, their hair now returned to normal.

"I can't believe you've done this," Quinn was saying to Rogan. "What are we going to do now?"

"Why can't you just talk to him. He's just doing it to make a point," Rogan reasoned.

"He's not. I already *tried* talking to him," Quinn snapped.

"Do you know what? I don't even care. I'm sick of that idiot," Rogan said angrily.

"He's our friend," Quinn said, sounding offended.

"He's *your* friend. I never liked the guy much," Rogan said.

Oliver glanced at Anna and May. "Maybe we should just go upstairs?" he suggested quietly.

The girls nodded and they hurried towards the lift.

"Hey, *you*. Oliver!" Quinn barked, making him cringe.

Oliver walked over to them with a resigned sigh and heard Anna and May following him.

"What's up?" he asked Quinn brightly and Rogan shook his head at him in warning.

Quinn jabbed Oliver in the shoulder with a sharp fingernail. "*You* have made Larkin ditch us from his team," she hissed.

"How's that *my* fault?" Oliver asked indignantly.

"Because he doesn't like you and Rogan decided it was a good idea to side with *you* over him," Quinn said.

"Again. How's that my fault?" Oliver asked, glaring at her. She was slightly shorter than him so he was glad of having the advantage of looking down at her.

Quinn huffed angrily. "Because you're a stupid Earthy," she responded wildly.

"Seriously?" Oliver said, cocking an eyebrow in amusement.

"Guys, can I join your team please?" Rogan asked them politely.

"Course you can," Oliver said, ignoring a look of venom from Quinn.

"Please tell me you're joking? I'd rather sacrifice myself to a hogtrout than compete with *them*," she said, scowling at Oliver, Anna and May.

"Who said anything about you? *I've* got a place on their team," Rogan said, walking around to stand beside May.

"*Excuse me?* You are not competing without me," Quinn demanded.

"Well, I seem to have a team right here, do you?" Rogan asked, folding his arms. "I'd love to meet them, are they around here somewhere?" He looked around Quinn with exaggerated curiosity.

Quinn's face turned red with fury. "YOU ARE NOT COMPETING WITH THEM!" she screeched so high pitched that Oliver only just caught the words.

"Yes. Yes, I am. And if you ask really nicely, they *might* let you join their team, too," Rogan said, raising an eyebrow at them.

Oliver shrugged and Anna seemed stumped for words.

"You can join us if you want, Quinn," May said and Oliver glanced at her, his anger with Quinn dissolving as he was reminded of how much his sister needed a team.

Quinn didn't even acknowledge her. She shoved Rogan out of the way, stormed past him with a noise like an angry tiger and disappeared into the lift.

"Don't worry, she'll come around," Rogan said.

Oliver shoved his hands in his pockets, hating how much they needed her.

Silence hung in the air for a moment then Anna said one word that brightened his mood by a mile.

"Sumi's?"

* * *

They arrived at Sumi's and took a seat in the corner. Rogan's bushy beard was firmly back in place, only partially concealing the moody frown on his face.

"You okay, man?" Oliver asked as the girls went off to order them some food.

Rogan grunted. "She is the most infuriating person I've ever known."

"Yeah, me too. And I've only known her for half a day," Oliver said with a laugh.

Rogan joined in, breaking his bad mood.

"So, did you meet Larkin on your way home then?" Oliver asked with a flare of annoyance on Rogan's behalf.

"Yeah, we got a pod pretty quick with the guard's help then bumped into Larkin outside the hotel. He'd come over especially to tell us that he'd replaced us with two of his mates. Git," he said, gritting his teeth.

"Are you sure you want to compete with us? I know we're not exactly the strongest contestants," Oliver said, hoping he wouldn't back out on them.

"No, seriously, this is so much better. You guys aren't weak anyway. Did you see the way those two handled themselves back in the cave?" Rogan said, nodding to Anna and May who were chatting together in the queue.

Oliver smiled. "Yeah, I guess."

"Yeah. And I doubt you'd let anything happen to those two in the race, either," Rogan said, raising an eyebrow at him. "Especially *Anna*," he goaded.

"Shut it," Oliver said, feeling the blood rise under his cheeks. "You've got the advantage with your magic anyway."

"Nope. Magic's banned in the race, it'd be an unfair advantage," Rogan said, leaning back in his chair so it balanced on two legs.

"Oh," Oliver said in surprise. "I guess that makes sense."

The girls returned with some drinks and sat down, placing them on the table. May sat beside Rogan, leaving a sizeable gap between them.

Rogan glanced at her with a crooked smile and she returned it shyly, her cheeks colouring ever so slightly.

"Do you think Quinn will really join our team?" Anna asked Rogan.

"Yeah, she hasn't really got a choice," Rogan said, sipping his drink.

"Do you think she'll be okay getting on with us? If we race together we'll have to work as a team to get through it or we won't stand a chance," Oliver said, remembering Ely's pointers about the race.

"Don't worry she'll be civil. She wants to get a key as much as the rest of us and she'll do what she has to to get one," Rogan said.

"So, we've got a full team?" May said slowly.

"Looks that way," Anna replied with a grin.

"Cheers to that," Oliver said, raising his glass.

* * *

The next morning a knock sounded at the door in Oliver's hotel room. May turned down the survision as Oliver answered it to find Ely and Laura there. He let them in and they sat down together in the living room.

"What happened to you two last night? Laura asked them with a smirk.

"Please don't just wander off without mentioning it," Ely implored. "I have quite enough to worry about."

"Sorry, we went out. But we have good news," Oliver said.

"What's that then?" Ely asked.

"We found our last two team members," May revealed excitedly.

"Really?" Laura asked in surprise.

"That's fantastic. Who are they?" Ely asked.

"Rogan Ganderfield and Quinn Thorn," Oliver announced.

Ely and Laura both laughed.

"Yeah, right," Laura said disbelievingly.

Oliver and May looked at them straight-faced.

"Wait, how do you even know who they are?" Laura asked with a look of confusion.

"We didn't 'til we met them. And now they're on our team," Oliver said frankly, enjoying watching the expressions on their faces.

"Yep," May said with a smug look.

"Please tell me you're being serious?" Ely asked, his round eyes bulging at them.

"Yeah, we are," Oliver said with a smile.

"That's fantastic news!" Ely said, looking at Laura in astonishment.

"Come on. They're not being serious, Dad," Laura said, shaking her head.

"How about they come here for lunch?" Ely challenged them.

"Okay, I'll ask them," Oliver said brightly.

"The only problem now is getting you a place," Ely said thoughtfully.

"Have none of the teams dropped out then?" May asked, looking panicked.

Ely shook his head. "Not to worry, there's time yet." But the looked he gave Laura left Oliver with a sick feeling in his stomach.

* * *

Oliver and May took the lift down to Anna's room, knocking on the door marked *303*. Anna's mum answered the door, looking curious at the sight of them. Oliver was glad that she was no longer angry as she seemed like a woman you didn't want to get on the wrong side of.

"Hi, is Anna around?" Oliver asked politely.

"Yes she's about, come on in."

They followed her inside to a room that, although cosy, was noticeably smaller than the rooms they were staying in. Doors led off to bedrooms from the living area.

"Would you like some tea?" she offered.

The Glacian tea tempted Oliver but before he could say yes Anna barrelled into him and dragged him towards the door.

"I'm going out. BYE!" she shouted as she pushed Oliver through the doorway and May backed out ahead of them.

"Annabelle, that's very rude-" her mum's voice was cut off as Anna slammed the door shut behind her.

"Thanks for saving me. I've been going mad in that room all morning. Mum and Dad have been arguing about me entering the race *non-stop*. They've decided to only let me race if I promise not to use my key until I'm eighteen if I win one." Anna expelled a breath loudly.

"That sucks," Oliver said, frowning.

"Maybe they'll change their mind?" May suggested with a sad look.

Anna shrugged. "I doubt it." She sighed. "Anyway, where are we going?"

"Erm, upstairs," Oliver said with a laugh.

"Good enough," she said, smiling back.

They returned to the top floor.

"We need to find out if Quinn's definitely joining us," May said as they exited the lift.

Oliver nodded and they walked down the corridor.

"I don't know what room they're in," Oliver said. "It's around here somewhere." He gestured to the doors further down the corridor.

"ROGAN?" Anna shouted and May giggled.

A door to their right opened a moment later. "You called?" Rogan stood there, leaning against the door frame, his muscular arms folded across his chest.

"Hey, man, you alright?" Oliver asked.

"Good, come on in," he said with a grin.

They followed him inside. His room was far grander than Oliver's; a large seating area surrounded a raised, spherical tank filled with exotic looking fish with two heads. Floor length windows led out to a balcony that overlooked the city, a hot tub sat to one side of it.

"Wow," Anna said, looking impressed.

"Bloody hell Rogan, do you and Quinn really need all this space?" Oliver asked, taking a seat in front of the elaborate fish tank.

"Actually, it's just me. Quinn's in a room across the hall," Rogan said.

"You guys don't share a room?" May asked, almost knocking over a delicate glass ornament as she passed it.

Rogan righted it with a flash of magic and they shared a grin that said *almost*. "No, I mean, we're engaged but...we won't really share a room 'til we're married..." he trailed off, running a hand down the back of his head.

"Oh, right," May said awkwardly as she ducked around him and took a seat on the sofa next to Anna.

"When's the big day?" Anna asked.

"We haven't set a date yet. We have to be married by the time we're twenty one so we've got almost three years to decide," Rogan said with a yawn.

"Did she agree to join our team?" Oliver asked anxiously, watching as two fish swam around each other in circles.

"Yep. I talked her round. She's not happy about it by a long shot but she's agreed," Rogan said, dropping into an armchair.

"That's more than I expected to be honest," Oliver said. "You must be more charming than I realised."

Rogan picked up a cushion off his chair and lobbed it at him. Oliver ducked it with a laugh.

"And I rang my agent to sort out the details. He was so mad when I told him me and Quinn had swapped teams," Rogan said, grinning at the memory.

"But it isn't a problem, is it?" May asked, creases forming on her brow.

"No way, it's sorted. Someone dropped out of the race and we got their place. Easy peasy," Rogan said.

Oliver glanced at May who frowned.

"Our grandfather said no one had dropped out," May said.

Rogan shrugged. "Apparently they did."

Anna made a noise of excitement in her throat. "I can't wait for the opening ceremony!"

"The what?" May questioned with a frown.

"It's just a way of building up hype for the race. They do a quick interview of all the teams and introduce this season's guest commentator. Nothing to worry about," Rogan said confidently.

"As long as we're racing, that's all that matters," Oliver said with a sigh of relief.

18

Fame and Misfortune

The day of the Opening Ceremony arrived a week before the race began. Oliver, May and Anna spent the day shopping for clothes in the city. They bought outfits for the ceremony that evening and Oliver and May purchased extra clothes for their extended trip.

Late in the afternoon, they returned to the hotel to get ready. Oliver showered and began dressing in his new clothes. Before he pulled on his shirt he glanced at the place on his arm where the vark's blade had sliced it open.

Though there was no scar to mark the wound, the memory of it made him shiver and he quickly pulled his top on. He checked his smart outfit in the bathroom mirror, pushing away the thought of the creature. He flattened his hair down, pulled on his jacket and went to the lounge.

A knock on the door sounded and May stepped into the room in a pretty, pink dress that dropped to the knee. Her hair was curled up into a delicate bun with loose strands that fell about her face and neck. She twirled one with her finger and looked at Oliver with raised eyebrows. "Do I look okay?"

"You look nice. You remind me of Mum in that colour," he said with a sideways grin.

Her face fell a little and she touched her hair self-consciously. "I don't look like her though."

He frowned. "What do you mean?"

"I'm not related to her, so I can't resemble her," she said a little sharply.

Oliver was taken aback. "Where did that come from?"

Her eyes went skyward and the whites of them sparkled. "It's the truth."

He stepped toward her. "Maybe, but so what? What difference does it make?"

"I dunno, Olly." She blinked as she met his gaze. "It's just- you've found out so much about your family since we've been here and I can't help but think I'm never gonna know anything about mine."

"Me and Mum are your family," Oliver said with a pang of annoyance.

"I *know*. That's not what I'm saying. It'd just be nice to know where I came from. All I remember is waking up in that hospital when I was six years old like nothing ever existed before that moment."

Oliver softened. "I know, I'm sorry."

Her shoulders dropped. "Finding out about these other worlds has made me question everything," she said, looking exasperated.

He nodded, waiting for her to go on.

"I used to think the only way I could have ended up in that road is if someone abandoned me there or if I was in some accident. But *now*...now I don't know what to think. What if I'm from one of these worlds? Maybe my parents were looking for me?" She touched her forehead with a grimace as if she was getting a headache and he reached for her, pulling her into a hug. He wasn't sure what else he could do.

She sighed and he sensed the tension go out of her body.

"Thanks," she said, stepping away.

"Maybe we can look into missing person reports here or something?" he suggested but she was already shaking her head.

"No, I'm just being silly. We don't have time to do anything like that." Her hand moved to her chest where the mark of the curse lay beneath her dress.

He nodded sadly. "Well, how about...when you're cured we'll look into it?"

She chewed her lip then nodded. "Okay." Her face brightened and he relaxed.

"Good." He grinned.

A knock on the door sounded and Oliver opened it to find Ely standing there looking surprisingly dapper in a navy suit.

"Shall we get going?" he asked, and they followed him down to the lobby.

"Where's Laura?" Oliver asked as the lift descended.

"She's already there. She'll be interviewed with the rest of the Race Committee so you might bump into her backstage," Ely replied.

The lift door opened to reveal Anna standing there in a peach dress with her hair pulled to one side. Oliver's mouth felt suddenly parched.

"I'll just go order a pod," Ely said and exited through the revolving door.

"Good evening," Anna said, beaming as she bounced on her toes with excitement.

"You look nice," Oliver told her a little stiffly.

"Thanks," she said quietly.

Rogan and Quinn appeared in the lift looking impeccable. Rogan was dressed in a smart suit with the shirt unbuttoned at the top and the sleeves of his jacket rolled back. Quinn wore a full-length, red dress that was cut so low and slit so high that Oliver wasn't sure where to look.

The clerks at reception swung around to stare at them as the couple joined their group, whispering to each other in low voices.

"Excited?" Rogan asked with a grin as he approached.

Oliver shrugged. "They're only gonna be interested in you and Quinn."

"That's true," Quinn said loftily. Her eyes scanned May's outfit and she raised her eyebrows. "I love your dress."

May glanced down at herself. "Oh, thanks."

Quinn shrugged lightly and led the way out of the hotel.

Ely was waiting for them by a large taxi pod. They climbed in and Oliver felt his heartbeat quicken as the pod glided forward along the street toward the unknown.

The opening ceremony was held in an enormous stadium on the outskirts of the city next to the lake. It was a seven-sided structure with a sharp spire on each corner, towering into the air. Atop the towers were lights painting patterns in the night sky.

Thousands of people were queuing in through a large gateway but their pod continued to circle the structure until they were far away from the crowd.

They exited the pod and a doorman checked off their names as they entered the stadium through a private entrance. "Upstairs and to the left," the man directed.

They followed his directions and entered a luxurious room with a wooden floor, gold satin draped along the walls and a buffet table to one side. Groups of people stood around chatting excitedly and five officials sat at the far end of the room, amongst whom, was Laura. She waved at them and Oliver led the way towards her.

"How are you feeling?" Laura asked, grinning at them. "Not too nervous I hope?"

"It's bigger than I expected," Oliver said honestly.

"Do we have to go out in front of all those people?" May asked, looking slightly pale.

"You'll be fine," Laura said, indirectly answering her question. She gestured for them to lean closer, her face scrunched up with excitement. "Wait 'til you see who the guest commentator is."

"Who?" May asked.

Laura mimed zipping her lips.

"What's our team name?" Rogan asked excitedly.

"You're Team Pandalin," a dark-haired woman next to Laura said, handing out metal badges with the name on.

Oliver took one and pinned it on to his lapel.

"You'll be interviewed last in the line up of fifty teams and will be called up to the stage accordingly. The interview will last approximately five minutes. When you're ready, please make your way down the corridor to your left and take your seats by the main stage."

"Good luck," a bald man at the table said, crossing out their names on a list.

"You'll be great," Laura whispered. "Dad, your seat will be in the V.I.P area through there." She pointed to a door behind the table.

Ely nodded and turned to Oliver and May. "You'll do great. I'll be watching." He winked at them and walked off through the door.

A loud roar went up from the crowd in the stadium, making Oliver's stomach lurch as they moved away from the table.

A large man appeared from across the room, heading in their direction. He wore a brown suit with elbow pads and had an enormous gut that wobbled as he approached.

He knocked back a drink as he reached out a hand to Oliver who received a large gust of hot breath from the man right in his face. A strong waft of potent alcohol filled his nostrils. The man wiped the back of his hand across his sweaty brow and moved on, offering it out to the others.

"I'm Abbicus Brown, the Race Host. Great to meet you." He bent down and kissed Quinn's hand. She smiled graciously but wiped it subtly on the back of her dress as he released her.

"The two of you are drawing heaps of attention to the race," Abbicus said smugly.

"Yes, well we're looking forward to competing," Rogan said, his tone professional.

"Wonderful, wonderful. I suppose there'll be a few cheeky bets put on your team to place. Might put a little on myself in fact," he said, taking Quinn's wrist and squeezing it as he eyed her greedily.

Quinn indulged the man, but Oliver sensed it was making her uncomfortable.

"I don't like to brag of course, but you have me to thank for your team getting a place." He winked, opening his mouth as he did so.

"Why's that?" Anna asked.

"Well, let's just say that there weren't any teams dropping out by *choice* to make room for yours." Abbicus laughed with a low *haw, haw, haw* noise.

"What?" Rogan frowned. "You *didn't*?"

Abbicus tapped his nose. "I couldn't have Rogan *Ganderfield* and Quinn *Thorn* dropping out of the race. What kind of fool do you take me for?" He smiled haughtily.

Rogan and Quinn shared a brief look and didn't answer. Oliver couldn't help but feel a swell of relief that they had the mages on their team, pushing away the guilt for those that had lost their place.

Abbicus clapped Rogan on the shoulder. "You're welcome." He wandered off, retrieving a hip flask from an inside pocket and poured it into his glass.

"*That's* the Race Host?" Oliver asked incredulously.

"He has a lot of money, he bid for the position years ago," Anna said with a tone of disapproval.

"He's vile," Quinn said, her lip curling upwards.

"Agreed," Oliver said and Quinn half smiled at him as he caught her eye.

A blonde woman in a floor-length, silver dress entered the room and made a beeline for a man surrounded by a group girls. She extracted him and Oliver suddenly recognised the man from the survision programme. He looked out of place in a smart suit and styled hair. The woman in silver spoke with him briefly then hurried off through a door.

Quinn gasped as she spotted him then hurried forward, pulling him into a warm embrace. She tugged him towards their group by his arm.

Rogan stepped forward. "Hey Truvian."

"Ah, Rogan how are you keeping?" Truvian said, pulling him into a one-armed hug.

"Not bad. Come meet my team." Rogan introduced them. "This is Truvian Gold."

Truvian oozed charm as he held out a hand and introduced himself, flashing a set of white teeth at each of them as he did so. He leant in and kissed the girls on the cheek and, to Oliver's surprise, both Anna and May flushed red as he did so. Oliver raised his eyebrows at them but they fell into quiet giggles.

"It's a pleasure to meet you all. You'll be seeing a lot more of me throughout the race. Abbicus Brown asked me to be the guest commentator this season. I was thrilled, of course, I even cancelled a date with Jenna Lilly to be here."

Quinn jumped in. "I'm sure you'll find another girl to take on a date." She batted her eyelashes at him.

Oliver raised his eyebrows at Rogan but he just rolled his eyes as if this was her usual behaviour.

"Yes, well I may have already found one. I'm going to ask Ray Falls out for a drink tonight."

"You mean the commentator?" Quinn asked curiously.

"Yes, stunning isn't she Rogan?"

"Yeah, pretty hot," Rogan said with a crooked grin.

A man with a clipboard hurried over. "You're needed in five Mr Gold."

Truvian nodded, running a hand through his dirty-blonde hair and flexing his bicep as he did so. "See you later. Enjoy the show." He winked and walked off through a door.

"All teams please now make your way to your seats," a man called out from the Race Committee.

They were one of the last groups to exit the room. Oliver followed the others out of the door and into a long corridor. They climbed a staircase and walked out into the stadium, emerging at the top of a sloping set of seats running down towards a stage. The vast arena opened out in front of them and the noise from the crowd was deafening.

Oliver's heart thumped against his chest as he focused on finding his seat. They found their places amongst the mass of contestants, marked by their team name on the back of the chairs. Oliver sat on the end of a row with May dropping into the seat beside him and the others along from her.

The stage below them was ringed by a group of photographers and journalists who were all looking up them intently. The stage itself held a table with five seats and Oliver felt his palms sweat at the thought of sitting there.

The lights in the stadium dimmed and dramatic music started with a boom of drums and clash of symbols, making the crowd go wild. Oliver was glad of the sudden darkness as he let out a slow breath to calm his nerves.

The black floor of the stadium began swirling faster and faster until the centre of it span up high into the air above the crowd, forming a twisting pillar of darkness. The pillar disintegrated in a shower of gold and the effigy of a man stood there, towering in height; his long beard and swirling robes glittered with magic.

His form turned gracefully in time to the music as he threw his hands into the air causing fire, lightning, and showers of gold and silver to cascade over the audience, highlighting their awed faces.

Oliver marvelled at the magic, momentarily forgetting his nerves.

The man shrunk down to half size and a tree grew from the swirling mass beneath him, higher and higher as he raised his hands in time with its growth.

Sparks of every colour flew around the stadium until the tree stopped growing. The music dropped to a tense, low hum and the crowd fell dead silent. The vision of the mage began to bend his hands and strings of glistening, icy tendrils burst from his palms, attaching to the top of the tree. The beat of drums thrummed in Oliver's ears as the tree began to bend under the pull of the mage.

The audience clapped in time with the music until the top of the tree reached the ground and planted itself there. The archway that was formed came to life with a thousand tiny explosions of silver and blue until an image appeared within it: a fairytale landscape of snow and ice.

The ground spun so the archway turned and the music came to a final, dramatic end. The scene in front of them collapsed into the ground in a shower of sparkles and darkness prevailed once more, leaving tiny spots of light floating before Oliver's eyes. The audience went wild and he clapped loudly along with the rest of his friends.

The centre of the floor swirled once more and reached silently into the sky, forming a platform concealed by a swirling ball of fire. The fire extinguished and Ray Falls appeared there in her silver dress, the flash of a thousand cameras catching it.

"Good evening ladies and gentlemen!" Ray Falls' voice echoed around the stadium. "Is everyone excited for the Great Race of Aleva?"

The crowd screamed out to her.

"Are you ready to meet this season's guest commentator?" she called out.

The crowd roared with excitement as another, swirling tower of darkness slowly reached up and a new platform appeared atop it, this one surrounded by a ball of frosty ice.

"I said: ARE. YOU. READY?" Ray Falls shouted with a deafening response from the crowd. "Three! Two! One!" The crowd joined in with her as the countdown lit up in magical fire above her, suspended in the air.

"Everybody please give a huge welcome to Mr Truvian Gold!"

The ice shattered into a thousand pieces and Truvian appeared, his arms raised into the air. His face was alight with excitement. The crowd was deafening and Oliver joined in as people stamped their feet, filling the room with a tumultuous roar of noise.

"Good evening everybody!" Truvian shouted. "Are you excited to meet our contestants?" He pointed dramatically to where they were seated and a spotlight blinded Oliver as the whole stand lit up. The crowd cheered and Oliver felt his heart hammer in his chest.

Music began again and the two platforms plummeted toward the ground, Truvian Gold and Ray Falls raised their arms in perfect coordination and, just before they hit the ground, disappeared. In a flash of light they reappeared together on the stage. Oliver gasped along with the rest of the crowd.

"Please welcome Team Thrake," Ray Falls said, gesturing to a team several rows below Oliver's.

The group made their way down to the table and took their seats, looking confident. Their team was comprised of three girls and two boys, all of whom looked as though they could have been athletes; one of the boys in particular had rippling muscles protruding from his tight shirt.

A ringed area sat beneath the stage where a group of journalists were stood waiting. The crowd quieted and the interview began.

"Do you feel prepared for the race, Trent Carter?" a smart-looking female journalist asked.

The most muscular boy lifted his left arm up and flexed his bicep. "Do I look prepared?" he gloated and the audience laughed before he continued. "We set ourselves a six month training plan consisting of two to three hour sessions several times a week."

May turned to Oliver with a concerned expression and his gut dropped. He hadn't realised the extent of how underprepared they were.

"And what did your schedule comprise of?" the journalist asked.

An auburn-haired girl answered. "We spent a lot of time working on our cardio and building up our stamina. Then we added weight training and took weekends away hiking in the mountains around Crome to get a feel for the landscape."

The journalists focused on the details of Team Thrake's training for the remainder of their interview and they exited the stage to cheers from the crowd.

Although it seemed brief, Oliver feared the agonising moment as their turn approached. After twenty five teams had been interviewed, however, the lights dimmed and music began again.

Hundreds of dancers took to the floor in clothes that glittered and glowed as they moved, leaving trails of colours in the air behind them.

Musicians joined them, marching out into the centre of the floor; the music they played was accompanied by flashes of light emitting from their instruments. The ground came to life again in the form of a colourful dance floor, lifting sections of the dancers and musicians into the air in time with the music. The piece ended to applause and the spotlight returned to the stage.

Larkin's team was next: Team Visikin. Oliver recognised the large boy, Arrow, from Sumi's amongst them. His teammates were all male apart from one short girl who wore her hair in pigtails and had the look of a vulnerable mouse, accentuated by her big eyes and tiny features. The other two boys were tall and brutish with almost the exact same pinched expression on their faces that suggested they were related.

"Kuti Carmen, how are you feeling about being the only girl on your team?" asked a journalist with a bushy moustache.

The small girl leant forward and giggled like a young child. "I feel great. I'm so lucky to have the boys, we'll all be looking out for each other in the race." She leant toward Arrow who placed a hand on her shoulder to show their solidarity.

The crowd applauded and Ray Falls hushed them by raising her hands as a young woman in a frilly dress stepped forward to ask the next question. "Larkin Pipistrelle, what inspired you to sign up for this season's race?"

Larkin casually propped himself up on one elbow, running a hand through his gold and hazel hair. "Apart from the girls?" he jested, making the crowd chuckle.

Oliver raised his eyebrows at May who suppressed a laugh at his expression.

"Yes, apart from them," the journalist said, grinning at him.

"Hmm." Larkin mimed thinking, placing his hands behind his head and interlocking his fingers so the muscles in his arms tensed. "I suppose the main reason I'm doing it is to help some friends out."

"Oh?" the journalist questioned.

"Yeah," Larkin said, dropping his arms and nodding modestly. "This lot wouldn't stand a chance at getting keys without me." His words rewarded him with a swift punch in the arm from one of the tall boys and the crowd laughed.

Their interview concluded and Team Visikin exited the stage to deafening applause. Larkin caught Oliver's eye as he climbed the stairs and smirked.

Oliver was distracted as their time grew closer, barely able to concentrate on the interviews taking place below him.

After what seemed an age, Ray Falls called their team to the stage. "Please give a warm welcome to our final team of the night, Team Pandalin!"

The applause was like thunder, drumming against Oliver's ears as he got to his feet. They filed out onto the stairs and Quinn took the lead followed by Rogan then Oliver, May and Anna.

The flash of cameras blinded him as he descended onto the stage and took a seat behind the long table; Truvian Gold patted them on the back encouragingly as they passed.

Oliver took in the large crowd that were jumping up and down and waving at them from all around the arena and realised their team had been kept until last for a reason.

The journalists ahead of them shuffled their notes, readying to ask questions. Oliver felt the glare of a million eyes on him, making his throat dry. He glanced back and spotted an enormous survision screen above the contestants' seating area, projecting their faces to the world twentyfold.

"We'll now take our first question," Ray said to the journalists.

The group of people raised their hands and Ray selected one at random. A woman with a perm of black hair spoke.

"Rogan Ganderfield, what are your hopes for this season's race? Do you see your team winning?" She threw a glance at Oliver, May and Anna.

Rogan leant forward to the microphone positioned in front of him. Before he could answer a group of girls in the audience screamed out. "WE LOVE YOU ROGAN!"

The audience laughed and Rogan grinned cheekily before continuing to answer the question. "My team and I will be giving our absolute all to place in the final ten so we can earn our right to receive a key." The crowd went crazy with excitement when he finished.

The woman continued, "I was surprised by your choice of teammates. Can you explain your and Quinn Thorn's decision to compete alongside someone like Oliver Knight and his friends?"

Oliver's ears rang at the sound of his name, unsure why the woman had singled him out.

Rogan and Quinn shared a look and Oliver heard Quinn mutter, "*Knight?*"

Oliver had never told them about his father. He was suddenly terrified, a lump rising in his throat. He looked at the reporter and could tell she knew who he was. He gripped the table tightly as he tried to keep his expression composed for the cameras and hoped they couldn't tell how much his face was burning.

Rogan leant forward again. "I'm not sure I understand what it is you're suggesting but, I can assure you, we will all make a fantastic team as we compete together in the race." He flashed a perfect smile, making the crowd cheer again.

"Another question, please," Ray Falls' voice rang out.

She selected a tall man with a thick moustache who stepped closer before he spoke. Oliver leant forward and tried to catch Rogan's eye. His friend glanced at him briefly with a furrowed brow but his attention was drawn back to the crowd.

"Quinn Thorn, I was particularly surprised by your decision to compete alongside Oliver Knight, considering your family's involvement in the trial of Eugene Fox ten years ago."

Quinn looked around in confusion. "I'm sorry, I don't understand the relevance of your question?" But a dangerous look in her eye confirmed to Oliver that she had guessed the truth.

The man's moustache twitched as his mouth stretched into a wide grin. "Why, didn't Mr Knight tell you?" he asked with an expression of exaggerated shock on his face.

The crowd had fallen silent and Oliver was painfully aware of his face being projected at twenty times its normal size on the survision screen behind him. The whole of Aleva was about to see his reaction and he was powerless to stop it.

"He is William Knight's son. The same William Knight who was accused of murdering his betrothed, and who plotted to bring down the Gateways alongside Isaac Rimori," the reporter said the words slowly and licked his lips as if he could taste the sweetness of them.

19

Exposed

The man's finger pointed at Oliver accusingly. He swallowed, trying to force down the feel of a golf ball in his throat. Everywhere he looked he met accusing, glaring eyes that made his heart race. The crowd had gone mad, boos filling his ears.

Oliver found he couldn't move; he sat perfectly still, frozen to his seat.

Ray Falls tried to calm the crowd down and stay professional. "Another question please." She picked out the young woman in her frilly, blue dress.

The woman directed her question at Oliver. "Are you proud to be William Knight's son?"

He could feel the stares of his friends on either side of him, which was somehow worse than those of the crowd. May leant forward to look at him encouragingly, meeting his eye. He blinked, relaxing marginally and suddenly found his voice. As long as he had her on his side he knew he could speak.

"I only found out recently," he said pathetically, his voice echoing agonisingly back at him from around the stadium.

"What do you mean?" the woman asked, her brow furrowed.

"I was brought up without any knowledge of the other worlds, on Earth," Oliver said, hoping this would win back some credibility.

The man with the moustache stepped forward again. "Of course you knew. You just didn't want anyone to find out. Thought you'd hide yourself behind a couple of famous mages to take the focus off of yourself. But you don't fool me."

Oliver shook his head. "You're wrong, I didn't-"

The man cut across him. "You knew. And you let everyone believe that you're harmless. Were you planning on going to find Rimori, perhaps help finish what he and your father started?"

Oliver stood up in a flash of anger. "Of course not." He felt his face flush as his blood burned hot.

Ely appeared at the side of the stage and whispered into Ray Falls' ear. She bent down and shook her head at him.

Truvian Gold leant forward and said, "Team Pandalin are going to take a ten minute break before returning to answer your questions."

Ray Falls looked at him with fury in her eyes. Truvian shrugged and waved the group off of the stage. Oliver was boundlessly grateful to him in that moment as he ascended the stairs.

Ely pulled him into the corridor beside the stage whilst the others remained on the steps, their eyes following him. Oliver's head was spinning as he leant against the wall. He heard music start up again in the arena.

"What's going on? Why are they accusing me of helping Rimori?" Oliver asked, the words tumbling on top of one another.

Ely rested a hand on his shoulder. "They're trying to get a rise out of you but you mustn't let them, it'll only add fuel to the fire. They're reporters, it's their job to get a story but you mustn't give them one."

"How could they find out?" Oliver asked, his mind in a daze.

"Your name. It's not hard to find out once they started looking into it. I would have liked to have entered you under a fake name but it's not possible. You had to register yourself as a key holder when you entered Aleva, you can't lie about who you are without them knowing."

Oliver leant his hands on his knees, feeling sick. "All of those people out there hate me," he groaned.

"I doubt it. They'll understand that you only just found out yourself. It's not your fault that he's your father. If you can face it, I say you go out there and answer their questions honestly then they won't have a bad word to say about you."

"But what can I say? I hardly know anything about my father."

"Then tell them that. Just be honest. If you run away now they're going to print something terrible about you and, if they do anyway, then at least you will have had a chance to defend yourself."

Oliver nodded, feeling slightly better. He knew the only thing that linked him to William Knight was DNA.

Ely squeezed Oliver's arm encouragingly before he returned to the stairs. He braced himself for the questions from Rogan and Quinn but they didn't come. They all looked at him, clearly unsure what to say, which he found somehow worse to bear.

The music stopped and they returned to the stage in silence, sitting back down to the sound of boos and hisses.

Ray Falls chose another woman to ask a question and Oliver braced himself.

"If we are to believe you had no knowledge of being William Knight's son, then what's your explanation for that?"

Oliver took a deep breath to steady his voice. "My mother brought me up with my adopted sister, May, on Earth without any knowledge of the other worlds." He wanted to make it clear that May wasn't related to William Knight, although it was clear the reporters had done their research anyway.

The crowd was quiet as they listened intently and the woman asked another question. "Is your mother here today to answer on your behalf?"

Oliver knew he had to be honest. "No, she disappeared a few months ago and we went to live with our grandfather, Ely Fox, in Oakway Manor. That's where I learnt about the existence of the other worlds."

"Ely Fox, as in Eugene Fox's father?" The moustached man piped up.

"Yes," Oliver said and the crowd booed him again.

"And where did your mother disappear to?" the woman asked without a shred of empathy.

"I don't know."

The crowd muttered amongst themselves and Oliver caught the words *guilty conscious* from a bald photographer.

"Next question please," Ray Falls said.

A tall man stepped forward. "I'd like to ask Miss Thorn and Mr Ganderfield if they still intend on competing alongside Mr Knight after this news coming to light?"

Oliver gripped the table. Every chance he had of getting May to Brinatin was pinned on their answer. He peeked a look at Rogan's face but couldn't tell what he was thinking.

Quinn was shaking her head and was about to lean forward to answer when Rogan said, "Yes, we do intend on competing with him. People should not be judged by who they're related to but by their own actions and Oliver has done nothing to deserve persecution. I'm sure we will be good friends as well as teammates."

The weight in Oliver's chest lifted and he looked at Rogan with thanks written across his face. Rogan smiled at him, clapping him on the back. The crowd cheered and camera flashes went off in their thousands. Quinn smiled brightly, taking Rogan's hand supportively. Oliver eyed her and sensed her reaction was all for show.

To Oliver's relief, the questions finally turned to focus on Rogan and Quinn.

The woman in the frilly dress stepped forward again. "Will you be setting a date for the wedding any time soon?'

"We will hopefully be getting married early next year in Brinatin but we haven't set a date just yet," Quinn answered and stroked Rogan's arm gently.

"Yes, we can't wait." Rogan leaned in and kissed Quinn on the lips.

The crowd cheered and applauded. Cameras flashed like mad, stinging Oliver's retinas.

The questions continued to be aimed at Rogan and Quinn but Oliver couldn't get over what had happened. He barely heard a word that was spoken around him as his mind raced.

Ray Falls eventually announced the end of the questions. Oliver felt numb. He could feel the eyes of the audience watching him as he exited the stage. He saw people pointing at him from the stands as they talked amongst their friends.

Oliver didn't want to listen. He didn't want to catch the words that carried to his ears from the crowd.

He pushed past the others and legged it upstairs into the corridor. He hurried along back to the room with the golden silk draped along the walls.

Ely appeared a moment later then May entered from the corridor.

Oliver sighed with relief. "Can we go?"

"Just a minute. I think you better talk to your teammates," Ely said softly.

Oliver knew he had to but every part of him just wanted to run away.

Abbicus Brown burst into the room. He no longer looked merry and tipsy, his face was stern and he had pulled himself up to what, Oliver now realised, was a surprising height.

"How *dare* you neglect to inform me of your parentage!" Abbicus roared at him.

"William Knight is connected to Oliver by nothing more than blood. Why should Oliver be punished for the crimes of his father?" Ely stepped in.

Oliver felt a burst of hope at Ely's words. He was glad he was there to defend him because, at that moment in time, he wasn't sure he could have managed it alone.

"That's not the point. He's made a laughing stock of me. How dare you let the public think I allowed the son of an anti-Gateway rebel to enter the race,"Abbicus barked at Oliver, his jowls wobbling as he shook his head in anger.

"No one should have known. It's irrelevant and you will keep your word on letting Oliver race or, so help me, I will turn you into a pile of soot," Ely snapped, emanating power as sparks crackled in his palms.

Abbicus backed away. "Don't you threaten me you, you old cretin." He tried to keep himself composed but couldn't stop his eyes from flicking between Ely's hands.

"What's going on?" It was Laura. The rest of the committee had re-entered the room and were talking in hushed whispers. Oliver tried to catch Laura's eye but couldn't.

"This man is threatening me." Abbicus pointed at Ely with a trembling finger.

Ely rolled his eyes.

"Oh, do calm down Abbicus," Laura said. "We need to discuss this rationally."

Abbicus Brown looked as though he were about to retaliate but bit his lip to stop himself.

"Oliver's just had more of a shock than we all have so let *him* speak," Laura commanded, and all eyes in the room turned to Oliver.

"Do you still want to compete?" Laura finally met his gaze. Her eyes were warm, encouraging and so like his mother's he couldn't help but relax.

From the corner of his eye Oliver spotted Rogan, Quinn and Anna enter the room. He took a deep breath and answered Laura. "Look, I don't know much about my father but he didn't raise me so I'll never have any attachment to him. I want to compete. Please don't stop me because of *him*." No one answered for a moment.

"I don't see any reason why he can't compete," Laura said firmly.

"It's not up to you," Abbicus snapped.

"No, but it's up to the Race Committee as a whole. You'll have to put it to a vote," Laura insisted.

"But what if the boy's helping Rimori like his father did? We can't risk letting him compete," Abbicus said, a wild glint in his eye.

"Nonsense, Abbicus. Why ever would Isaac Rimori recruit a teenager to help him?" Ely said, shaking his head at the man.

Abbicus eyed Oliver warily like he was an assassin about to pounce then helped himself to another drink from the table. "I have every right to question the boy," he said, puffing out his chest as he added alcohol to his glass from his hip-flask.

"Oliver found out about all this mere days ago," Ely insisted. "Do you *really* believe that Rimori has returned from Vale, approached a sixteen your old boy, and plotted the fall of the Gateways with him in that time?"

"Oho, so *that's* what he's plotting is it?" Abbicus said, sipping at his drink. "Maybe you're in on this, too, old man. It'd make sense. Your son was another friend of Rimori's wasn't he?"

"You've gone mad," Ely said furiously.

"And you, you're the boy's aunt. How can I trust *you*?" Abbicus rounded on Laura. "We have traitors in our midst!" he announced loudly to the room, swinging his drink around to gesture at Oliver, Ely and now Laura.

The bald committee member put his hands on his hips. "That's *enough*, Abbicus. It has to go to a vote."

Abbicus stormed over to the table and concocted himself yet another spiked drink, muttering into it as he sipped. "Fine," he grunted a moment later. "I vote no."

"I vote yes," Laura said loudly.

"Team Pandalin would need a fifth member to fill Mr Knight's spot if he is removed. It'd be awfully inconvenient at this late stage to try and find someone else," said a white-haired woman on the committee.

Oliver felt hope balloon in his chest at her words.

"They'd be queuing in the streets to fill that position," Abbicus said, dismissing her comment with a wave of his hand.

The balloon in Oliver's chest burst, and he frowned heavily.

The four other committee members gathered together at one side of the room and began to have a hushed discussion. Oliver spotted Rogan muttering quietly to Quinn and his gut twisted sharply.

"We won't compete," Rogan announced loudly to the room. "Unless Oliver's allowed to."

Oliver's breath caught.

Quinn looked angry but didn't argue with him.

"You can't do that," Abbicus hissed.

"We can. And we will. And you'll lose all the publicity you would have gotten from us competing," Rogan said, folding his arms.

The committee looked alarmed then slowly, one by one, they all voted yes.

"Fine," Abbicus snarled. "You can compete, but this better not come back to bite me in the arse." He stormed out of the room.

"It'd take a whale of a mouth to bite that arse," Quinn muttered.

* * *

They returned to the hotel. Oliver didn't say a word on the journey home. He still felt the strong urge to be as far away from people as possible. He was beyond grateful to Rogan for swaying Abbicus's decision but guilt wracked at him. He hadn't been honest and now he had put his friends in the firing line alongside himself.

They exited the pod and walked into the lobby. Oliver trailed behind the others. He walked forward, intending to take the lift straight up to his room but Rogan put an arm out to stop him. "Can I talk to you a sec?" He was smiling but Oliver could tell he didn't have a choice.

He shrugged and followed Rogan into the lounge. Oliver looked back to see Ely and Quinn heading towards the lift. Anna and May were watching them from the lobby. They hesitated, looked at each other uncertainly, then followed Oliver and Rogan into the lounge.

"Look, before you say anything I just want to say sorry. I should have been honest with you Rogan," Oliver said. "I told Anna. I should have told you too."

She nodded a little guiltily.

"I get why you didn't," Rogan said, his mouth turning down at one corner.

"Thank you for standing up for me. There's no way Abbicus was gonna let me compete," Oliver said.

"Don't worry about it," Rogan said earnestly.

"There's something else." Oliver hesitated. He wanted to be completely honest about everything. "May do you mind?" He looked at his sister who's green eyes blazed at him.

She wet her lips before she answered. "No, but I'll say it." She looked at Rogan and Anna then took a breath. "I'm cursed. I have to get to Brinatin as soon as I can or the curse is going to kill me." Determination spread across May's features and Oliver felt a swell of admiration for her.

Rogan and Anna were stunned into silence.

"And we're going to see your father to find out if he can help May," Oliver said, delivering the final secret to Rogan.

Rogan nodded slowly and, for a moment, Oliver thought he was going to storm out of the room never to be seen again. But, instead, he took two long strides over to May and pulled her into a hug. "Then we'd better get you a key," he said, setting his jaw.

20

Those Who Wait

Ten Days Ago

"Kogure?" Rimori addressed the vark, pacing the cave. His bare feet slipped in the thick grime on the floor. He could sense the creature's presence.

"Yess. I'm here," he answered.

"Is he ready for us? Is it time?" Rimori snapped anxiously, his heartbeat quickening with excitement.

"Yess, yessss. It's timee. He iss beyondd the Gatewayyy. Let usss go. He iss waiting," Kogure's voice was full of anticipation. Rimori knew it was the most dangerous time to be around him but there was nothing he could do to prevent it.

Rimori stopped pacing and relief flooded every inch of his body. He almost felt like weeping. He was returning to the human worlds at long last after ten years in Vale. He could take Kogure with him, he hardly believed it was true. The creature had power over an army of varks and they were his to command now.

"Yes, Kogure. It is time to go at last." He glanced at the remains of his discarded bag in one corner of the cave. He didn't need it anymore. He kept the knife at his waist as one of the only items that would return with him, along with the Lock that had hung at his neck for all these years.

His clothes were in tatters and it was so long since he had been clean he had forgotten what it was like. His thick beard itched; he had dreamed of the day he could take a razor to it and now that day was within reach.

"Noww? Are we going nowww?" Kogure hissed anxiously.

"Yes. But you remember our agreement? You will stay with me unless I tell you otherwise. You will do as I command until we have conquered the seven worlds. Then, and only then, will you be free."

"Yesss. Oh, master, yess, I agree."

"Good. Then we shall go. Lead me back to the Gateway, Kogure."

"Yess." His voice became distant and Rimori could feel the pull of him.

He followed the vibration out of the cave and across the desolate landscape.

They arrived at the Gateway: just a blackened, dead tree. A branch curved over to make the archway on one side of it.

Rimori's heart was beating at an alarming rate. He couldn't believe he was returning after so many years of living in the same cave with only the vark for company.

There were so many things he had forgotten. It all started to flood back: hot showers, fine food, the feel of the sun on his skin.

"Noww. Do it noww," Kogure said.

"Hush. You must learn to be patient. Once we go through, there'll be many things to do before we'll be able to bring down the Gateways."

"I undersssstand."

Rimori nodded. He held up his Lock and red light the colour of blood emitted from the key to Vale. He felt the creature inch closer and the archway filled with light.

It had taken him ten years to reach this moment. Ten years in Vale.

He had greatly underestimated what it would take for him to be able to return to the human worlds with the vark. He had waited whilst his friend set everything in order. He had had to convince him to trust Kogure over time. His friend had performed new magic on the vark, designed from his own experiments, that would allow Kogure to come through the Gateway into the human worlds in his full form.

He hadn't realised that the varks who visited the human worlds did so at a cost to themselves. They were damaged by the journey in the same way he would be by returning from Vale, although, they weren't susceptible to death like he was. But he would survive, he had taken precautions to be sure.

He felt nothing but pure joy as he stepped through the Gateway, any pain to come would be worth it.

A soft breeze was the first thing he experienced. Then the smell of dust and a wave of heat from the desert in Arideen. He fell to his knees, his body suddenly weak and exhausted. He couldn't see because of how watered his eyes had become.

He felt pain rip through him so sharp that he almost passed out then the strong arms of someone pulling him into an embrace.

The sound of a man laughing with elation and saying his name. Someone actually saying his name aloud. The noise was music to his ears.

"Isaac, you did it. You *actually* did it."

21

No Going Back

On the day of the race, Oliver awoke in the early hours of the morning in a cold sweat. He had dreamt that he was entering the Hogtrout caves alone to a chorus of boos then Truvian Gold appeared in his speedos and ordered him to be sent to Vale as punishment for being William Knight's son. He took a deep breath and smiled at the stupidity of the dream.

He showered and dressed before sitting in the living room with the survision on quietly. A news broadcaster was presenting a story about hundreds of people who had camped out by the Hogtrout caves to try and get last minute tickets to see the race. Oliver's stomach knotted tightly.

He switched the survision off, laid his head back against the chair and closed his eyes. He had just managed to calm his thoughts and was starting to doze off when a knock at the door roused him. He glanced at the clock: it was already eight.

He answered the door to find Ely there holding two packages.

"Ah, you're awake. I suppose you had a rough night, eh?" Ely said, walking into the room.

Oliver nodded and rubbed his eyes which were aching with tiredness.

"What's that?" Oliver asked, gesturing towards the packages.

"These are your team outfits."

Oliver reached out for one. "Can I see?"

"This one's yours and the other's May's. I better go and make sure she's up. Come to my room when you're dressed. Oh, and pack your things and bring them with you. I can check out for you if you qualify for tomorrow's race and take your bags," Ely said, handing him the package and taking his leave.

Oliver opened it and pulled out a navy blue jumpsuit with light blue accents and some boots. On the front of it was the word *Pandalin* and, on the back, the word was repeated with his own name beneath it.

Oliver went to the bathroom and changed into it. The material was soft and lined on the inside for warmth but lightweight and flexible for ease of movement. He looked in the mirror, glad he didn't look too ridiculous.

Satisfied, he packed his bag, put on the pair of boots and went to Ely's room.

May was already there in her suit. It was a more fitted version and she had longer boots pulled over the outside of the material, giving it a more feminine look. Her long, blonde hair was pulled up into a ponytail.

"Well, don't you both look the part? How are you feeling?" Ely asked, briskly rubbing his hands together.

May bit her lip and looked to Oliver. "Pretty nervous,' she said.

Oliver nodded in agreement, dropping his bag onto the sofa next to May's.

"No surprise there. You'll be fine. You just need to focus. Don't think about anything but getting through the race in time. You've got a good team together so there's no reason for you not to qualify for the second stage," Ely said but the words did nothing to ease Oliver's nerves.

Another knock on the door sounded and Ely opened it to find Anna there. She was wearing her jumpsuit with her dark hair tied up like May's. "Hi, can I come in?"

Ely stepped aside and she strode across the room, slumping onto the sofa.

"Anyone else freaking out?" she asked, looking around at Oliver and May who both nodded. "All my life I've wanted to compete in the race and now it's actually happening I'm terrified."

"You'll be fine. You all will be. I have every confidence that, by this evening, you'll all be celebrating your first successful day," Ely said cheerfully.

The evening suddenly seemed like a thousand years away. Oliver couldn't think beyond the dreaded moment of stepping into the caves in front of a booing crowd in a couple of hours' time. He sunk into a chair.

"You alright?" Anna asked with concern.

"Yeah, it's all this waiting around. I can't stand it," Oliver said, tapping his foot.

"It's torture," May agreed, taking a seat next to Anna.

Another knock on the door sounded and Rogan entered, followed closely by Quinn. They had both managed to make the jumpsuits look incredibly stylish. Rogan had the buttons undone slightly at the top and the suit somehow accentuated his broad shoulders and muscular frame.

Quinn had her long hair pulled into a side plait and the suit was much more fitted to her curves than Oliver thought it should have been. He wondered if they had altered the suits using their magic which didn't quite seem fair somehow. He noticed May tugging on her suit's sleeve self-consciously.

"How's everyone feeling?" Rogan clapped his hands together and grinned.

He was brimming with confidence and was clearly excited about the day ahead. Oliver couldn't help but feel resentful as his stomach cartwheeled for the hundredth time that morning, sending a wave of nausea through him.

"Not great. You don't seem too bothered though?" Anna said.

Rogan bounced across the room and sat in between May and Anna. He pulled Anna into a one-armed embrace.

"You'll be okay, Anna," he said, rubbing her shoulder.

Quinn threw him a filthy look.

"You alright, man?" Rogan said, eyeing Oliver with a worried look.

He hoped his face didn't look green. "Yeah, I think so," Oliver said with a slight smile.

"Don't worry. We're gonna smash this," he said, making Oliver feel a little better.

Rogan took his arm off of Anna and patted his knees as he bounced up and down in the chair. May laughed and he grinned at her, making her cheeks burn bright red. Rogan didn't seem to notice.

"How are you feeling, Quinn?" Ely asked.

"Just perfect," she said with a forced smile.

"Are we all ready to go, then?" Ely asked and they nodded. "Laura should be downstairs, she went to check out."

"Why? Where's she going?" Oliver asked.

"She'll be staying near to the race with the rest of the committee," Ely said.

They descended to the lobby and found Laura waiting with her suitcase at her feet. Her face broke into a huge smile as she spotted them and rushed forward to hug Oliver and May.

"How are you guys feeling?" she asked, looking concerned.

"Not bad," Oliver lied and May smiled.

"You're going to be great," she said and turned to the rest of the group. "I've got a pod waiting outside to take you to the Hogtrout caves. You're going to be dropped off nearby where the teams will be briefed for the race. There's some food and drink there as well, so make sure you eat something because you're going to need the energy." Laura grinned around at them all and walked through the door.

They followed her to the large pod that was waiting for them and climbed inside. The seats were topped with soft cushions and peaceful, classical music was playing through the speakers.

They whizzed along through the city, taking a route through a tunnel in Thorn Mountain towards the caves. The closer they got, the more Oliver's stomach clenched.

No one spoke much along the way and Oliver could have sworn the trip had been longer the first time. The pod stopped in a torch-lit passageway that led towards an immense cavern.

They exited the pod and Oliver gazed at the giant, shimmering stalactites that hung from the ceiling. The crowd of people in the room moved between colossal stalagmites protruding from the floor.

Mineral deposits sparkled as they caught the light of burning torches set in brackets along the walls. The immense crowd filling the cavern were dressed in the same jumpsuits with different colours distinguishing the teams.

"This is where I leave you, I'm afraid," Ely said and Laura nodded as she linked his arm.

"Okay," Oliver said, distracted by his surroundings.

"We'll be watching you every step of the way. See you at the finish line. You'll be fantastic," Ely said as he climbed back into the pod.

"Good luck," Laura said as she followed him.

Quinn had already disappeared into the cave but Rogan and Anna stayed and waved goodbye as the pod zoomed away down the track.

"Are your parents going to be watching?" May asked Anna.

"Yeah, they got time off work to stay for the race. How about your family, Rogan?" Anna asked.

"My mum and sister will be. My brother Alecs is working back in Alevale."

They joined the queue for the breakfast buffet. The thought of eating made Oliver feel ill but he knew it was important to get something down. He took some toast and butter with a hot cup of Glacian tea and followed the others to a table.

It looked like it had been chiselled out of the cave wall with small boulders around it for chairs. Quinn had decided to sit elsewhere, which Oliver was actually quite pleased about.

He spotted her across the room sitting with Larkin and his team. They were dressed in maroon-coloured jumpsuits with their team name *Visikin* emblazoned across their chests and backs in black. He noticed Rogan looking over at them as well.

"I can't *believe* she's sitting with Larkin," Anna said, shaking her head at her.

"Do you mind her doing that?" Oliver asked Rogan.

"She can do what she wants. I just think we should all be sitting as a team right now," he said, though his eyes continued to flit in her direction from time to time.

Oliver sipped at his Glacian tea. It helped his nerves recede and excitement itched at him instead. He took another large gulp. May was sipping on a cup of her own and looked more relaxed.

Oliver glanced around the room to read the different names on the jumpsuits as he nibbled on his toast. He read several before he got bored:

Thrake, Lost, Zhoulin, Gallit, Harvin, Koop, Nittle, Relic,
Krandle, Suddle, Loop, Squail, Sister, Justice, Ninagoon,
Ganderfield, Thorn, Visikin and Pippin.

He recognised many of the contestants from the opening ceremony a lot of whom cast glances at Rogan and Quinn. The odd person eyed Oliver with discontent but he avoided their gaze, forcing himself to ignore them.

"Has anyone ever got hurt racing?" May asked tentatively and Oliver zoned in on the conversation.

"Quite a few. Injuries are pretty common. A girl lost an arm a few season's back," Anna said, her face contorting.

"Yeah, 'cause she tried to stop a rotating blade with her elbow. Idiot," Rogan said, swigging his drink.

"A rotating blade?" Oliver asked with a spike of panic.

"Yeah, one of the challenges was to get through a room with these blades flying around but there was an obvious pattern to it. Anyone could have done it," Rogan said but Oliver felt his insides churn.

"I hope we don't get that room," May said, turning a paler shade of white.

"A boy drowned a couple of years ago in one of the water rooms," Anna said sadly.

"What? He *died*?" May asked in shock.

"Yep," Rogan said then spotted the look on May's face. "Don't worry it doesn't happen often. Especially if you're not a moron about the tasks."

"If we take our time we'll be fine," Anna said, nodding repeatedly as if to reassure herself.

"The worst season was the terrorist attack," Rogan said, grimacing.

Oliver remembered the tourist information in the pod mentioning the attack.

"Yeah, that was bad. After Rimori entered Vale there was a sudden surge of anti-Gateway rebels all grouping together. I guess they got overexcited 'cause a group of them entered the race and when they got into one of the challenge rooms they blew the whole place up, including themselves and about five rooms around them," Anna said in a dark tone.

"And the people in them," Rogan added with a grimace.

"Is there any chance of that happening this time, seeing as Rimori's come back?" May asked in a hushed voice.

"I doubt it. They've *seriously* upped security since then and no doubt they'll be even stricter this season," Anna said.

"Please would you all be seated," a man's voice boomed out over the crowd.

The remaining people standing found a seat and silence fell over the room. Oliver spotted the man raised up on a podium behind the breakfast buffet. It was Abbicus Brown.

"I'd like to welcome you all to this year's third season of the Great Race of Aleva. You are all blessed with the privilege of taking part in Aleva's famous challenge, in the hope that you might win a key to Glacio. Although I am sure you will all race valiantly, only the first ten teams to reach the Gateway on the second race day will be granted this highest honour. But don't be disheartened. You may, of course, reapply for entry the following season.

"I must remind you that by taking part, you are responsible for your own safety. This is a high risk activity and accidents occur every season. You can reduce these risks by following the rules and taking time to assess each challenge. To reduce the risk of injury further we do have mages on hand to assist you if needs be.

"The following rules must be adhered to to avoid disqualification. Number one: no team is allowed to directly inhibit the progression of another team through the course, number two: all teams must stay together at all times throughout each race and must cross the finish line together to qualify. And number three: mages are forbidden from using magic during the race and will be equipped with gauntlets to prevent cheating."

He paused before continuing. "In a moment, I would like you all to make an orderly queue towards the pod station where you will receive a pack containing supplies. You must then proceed to take a pod to the next station along. When you arrive you will walk, team by team, towards the start line where you will await the commencing of the race. Good luck to you all," Abbicus finished.

A smattering of applause came from around the room and Oliver noticed that most people looked nervous. He spotted Larkin with a pang of annoyance who was casually adjusting his hair as if he were having a relaxing day out.

Quinn appeared at their table and they got up to join her. Rogan led the way to the back of the queue and they shuffled towards the pod station. Oliver was glad Larkin's team was much further ahead than them, not wanting to be faced with snarky remarks at that moment in time.

They took a backpack from a line of people who had t-shirts labelling them as Race Assistants in bright letters. The woman that passed Oliver his pack glared at him but he was too nervous to care. He glanced into the bag and saw a bottle of water and some energy bars but had to throw it over his shoulder and move forward before he could look through it properly.

He climbed into a pod after Rogan and they shuffled up until they were all inside.

"Everyone okay?" Rogan asked, smiling again.

A mumbled response came from their group as they looked around anxiously. The pod headed off down the tunnel so the windows revealed only darkness beyond.

Quinn retrieved two gloves from her bag that looked like they were made of black silicon. She pulled them on and flexed her fingers, eyeing them as if checking to see how flattering they were. Rogan imitated her a moment later, pulling on his own.

"So you can't use magic with them on?" Oliver gestured to the gloves.

Rogan nodded. "Yeah. They were originally designed for prisons so mage criminals could be restrained. They started using them in the race after a mage was caught cheating her way through it by secretly healing herself of exhaustion."

They followed the Ninagoon team up the steep steps, their bright purple jumpsuits glaring back at them.

The sunshine poured down on them and a crisp wind blew their hair backwards. Oliver blinked as his eyes watered. They rounded to the left, following the curve of the mountain. A roaring cheer filled his ears as they turned and the valley dropped away towards an incredible sight.

The stands were packed with thousands of people all looking down upon the dark and ominous mouth of the cave. Gravity tugged at Oliver's feet as they descended and Anna gripped his sleeve for support.

All fifty teams walked separately at intervals and he spotted the dark red of Larkin's team far ahead. They were nearing the starting line which had been painted in gold in front of the cave.

The flat, towering wall above the cave was now used to project the survision. Close-up shots of each team were broadcast as their names were announced by Ray Falls. She stood next to Truvian Gold high up on a podium near the survision. The crowd screamed every time a team name was announced.

"The Koops," Ray said and the crowd went wild. "Followed by the Visikins." The crowd cheered again.

Oliver gulped, the thought of getting booed filled his head again. They were closing in on the crowd now and the hill dropped down into a gully that swept between the stands and into the cave. They had to crane their heads upwards to see anyone. The crowd noise was louder down in the crevice as it reverberated off of the walls.

"The Ninagoons."

A shot of their faces burst up on the screen as they waved and the crowd whooped and cheered.

"The Pandalins," Ray Falls finally said.

Oliver craned his neck back to see their faces being broadcast to the world. Oliver looked as nervous as he felt. He realised the others were waving and threw his arm in the air to join them. He listened for the boos but, if there were any, he couldn't hear them.

Relief flooded his chest. It was over in seconds and Ray Falls was announcing the next team. "The Thrakes."

Oliver felt a rush of adrenalin as they took their place along the huge, gold line that marked the beginning of the race. Rogan was at the front, followed by Quinn, him, then May and Anna. They had to stand one behind the other so there was enough room for each team along the line.

Two of the Ninagoon girls were whispering and glancing at Rogan whilst fluttering their eyelashes madly. Rogan smiled at them which sent them into fits of giggles. Quinn leant into him and planted a kiss on his cheek like she was marking her property.

The rest of the teams lined up along the start line and the crowd was hushed into silence by Truvian Gold.

"The race will be starting in precisely two minutes." He threw an arm dramatically towards the screen and a timer flashed up in the right hand corner as a sweeping shot of the teams was aired. Oliver realised he couldn't see a camera anywhere. "How are they filming us?" he asked and Quinn shot him a glance as if he were completely stupid.

He raised his eyebrows at her.

"It's nanocameras. You can't see them," she said and he almost smiled but frowned instead as she turned away muttering, "*Earthies.*"

He returned his attention to Truvian Gold's voice. "Good luck to all the teams. And remember to check those watches because you've got exactly two hours to reach the finish line to qualify for tomorrow's race."

Oliver noticed everyone around him looking at their wrists. He fumbled in his bag quickly to find his watch and strapped it on, catching sight of May rolling her eyes at him.

The clock read thirty seconds on the survision.

"On your mark," Ray Falls said.

The crowd was counting down from twenty. "Nineteen. Eighteen. Seventeen. Sixteen."

"Get set," Truvian Gold said.

Oliver glanced at Rogan who gave him a thumbs up then turned back to face the cave, readying himself. Oliver felt his legs shaking with the anticipation of running.

"Nine. Eight. Seven, Six. Five." The noise was deafening.

Rogan was bouncing from foot to foot.

Oliver braced himself, forcing himself to focus. They had to do this.

"THREE. TWO. ONE."

"GO!" Truvian Gold and Ray Falls screamed together.

22

Below

Oliver ran forward at full pelt. He shot between two of the massive pillars of rock in the cave mouth. The darkness overwhelmed him. He held his hand out to reach for Quinn in the darkness but couldn't find her.

He veered left and light finally filled his eyes as they entered the firebat cave. Teams were already darting down the exit on the other side of the room but Oliver slowed. May and Anna bumped into him.

"Rogan?" he called.

People were barging into them so they kept moving towards the exit. He saw Rogan a few feet ahead of them, gripping Quinn's arm tightly.

"Hold onto each other!" Rogan called to them and he felt May clasp the material at his back.

He forced his way through a team in front of him and joined Rogan and Quinn. Quinn looked relieved to see them for the first time ever.

Oliver gripped the material on Rogan's back and he did the same to Quinn. They wound their way like a snake through the teams that were spread out in a disarray. They had soon gained ground ahead of many of them and ran down the long tunnel at full throttle.

At the end was a fork and Quinn veered to the right as several teams headed to the left. They followed her onwards until they reached several large, wooden doors that had been carved roughly to fit the shape of the cave's natural passages.

"We have to choose one. Half of them are occupied already!" Quinn shouted.

Every door they passed said *Occupied* in bright, red letters on a panel by the handles. They followed the corridor to the end of the doors and finally found one that said *Vacant*. They didn't hesitate. They went straight through as a team behind them charged towards their door.

Anna slammed the door shut and twisted a knob on the other side to lock it.

The room in front of them was daunting. There was a large chasm between them and the exit, bordered by two sand-coloured walls that were peppered with blackened, sooty holes.

A six foot long platform jutted horizontally out of the wall to their left, suspended above the dark abyss. The platform was just wide enough for them to stand on side by side; they were separated from it by a short gap.

"It's a challenge. There'll be a clue here somewhere," Anna said.

"Here!" May called, pointing to a plaque beside the door. She read it aloud. "A platform for all. Then minus one. Three on third, then two, then one."

"What's it mean?" Oliver asked, looking at the others. His mind could barely process the words from the adrenalin running through his veins.

Rogan looked at the platform in front of them thoughtfully. Quinn walked over confidently and stepped straight onto it.

"NO!" Rogan shouted as a huge flame burst out of the round hole on the wall, the height of Quinn's head.

Rogan yanked her back off of it just in time. She fell onto her bum and screeched in shock. The rest of them rushed over.

"Are you alright?" Oliver asked, unable to help being concerned. Some of her hair was smoking so he patted it down with his sleeve.

Quinn swatted him away. "*I'm fine.*"

"You can't just go ploughing ahead without discussing it with us," Anna snapped furiously. "If you go and get your head fried then we all have to drop out of the race, too."

"I know. Alright. For Vale's sake. Help me up, Rog growled.

Rogan pulled her up. "At least we know you can't step o. thing." He stifled a laugh and she threw him daggers.

"No not *alone* but I bet we can all step on it together," May s. and they looked around at her. "The clue says *a platform for all* that's the only platform in here so it must be talking about that."

"I think you're right," said Rogan after a moments' thought. "We better all step on it at the same time then. Everyone agreed?"

They all nodded, Quinn included. They lined up in front of the platform, their toes hanging over the ledge.

"On my count, then," Rogan said.

"Wait. Maybe we should duck down as we step on. Just in case?" Oliver suggesting, eyeing the smoking hole in the wall.

"Good idea," Rogan said. They all bent over so that the hole would be just above them. "One, two, three."

They stepped forward in unison. Oliver squeezed his eyes shut as his feet landed on the platform.

Nothing happened.

They all sighed in relief and stood up straight. A grinding, grumbling noise sounded as another platform emerged from the wall to their right. They would have to jump to reach it and the chasm beneath them looked formidable. There was no fire hole above it which would, hopefully, make it easier.

"Okay, any suggestions?" Rogan asked. "What's the next bit of clue?"

"It says, a platform for all. Then minus one. Three on third, then two, then one. So, only four of us can stand on the next platform?" May suggested.

"But that would leave one of us on this platform to get burnt!" Anna said, looking alarmed.

"I'm not staying," Quinn said abruptly, shuffling to the end of the platform.

"Shut up, Quinn. No one's getting burnt," Rogan said.

"What's the rest of the clue?" Oliver asked.

"Three on third, then two, then one," May repeated.

"Okay, so assuming there are going to be five platforms total it goes: five, four, three, two, one as in the amount of people who can safely stand on each platform, right?" Oliver said.

They nodded and no one spoke for a minute as they tried to figure out how they would manage to get across.

"How about four of us go onto the next platform and the one that stays here ducks down whilst the fire blasts out?" Anna suggested.

"Then what?" Quinn said, shaking her head so her hair fluttered about.

"I haven't thought that far," Anna said, glancing at her sideways.

"There's no fire blaster on the next platform so why don't we all jump onto it?" May suggested.

"Something else might happen. We can't risk it," Rogan said.

"How about four of us jump onto that platform and we find out what happens? It's the only way," Oliver said impatiently.

"You're crazy," Quinn breathed.

"We have to move, one way or another," Rogan said. "But, who's going to stay here?"

"I don't mind staying," Oliver said, unsure how strongly he actually felt that way but was conscious of wasting time.

"Okay, you duck down and the rest of us get ready to move. On my count," Rogan said.

Oliver knelt down on the floor and shuffled to one side, giving the others more room to manoeuvre.

"Three, two, one," Rogan said and everyone but Oliver jumped to their right onto the next platform.

The fire burst out above Oliver and he tucked his head down instinctively. The scorching flames didn't let up. He shuffled to the far edge and peeked up to see how they were doing, sweat collecting on his brow.

A third platform was grinding its way forward from the wall on the left with a fire hole at both feet and head height. There was no chance the wrong amount of people could be on it without getting burnt.

"Oh, Vale," Oliver heard Anna say.

"We *have* to have three on that platform, no more and no less otherwise someone's dead," Rogan said.

"Okay, three of us jump forward and Oliver jumps onto this platform?" Anna suggested.

"That's what I was thinking. I think it's our only option," Rogan said. "You hear that, Oliver? Three of us are gonna jump then you need to get on this one, quick."

"Got it. The sooner the better," Oliver shouted, his back starting to heat up intensely.

"I'm gonna stay here. You three jump on my count and Oliver you jump towards me," Rogan said. No one argued. "Three, two, one."

Oliver jumped as best he could from a crouched position across to the platform. He got to his feet and saw Quinn, Anna and May on the next platform, ahead and to the left. They were now halfway across the chasm which stretched endlessly beneath them into the darkness.

Nothing happened for a moment. Rogan grinned at him triumphantly then the floor beneath their feet trembled. The grinding noise returned as their platform began to recede into the wall.

"Oh, no," Rogan said, shuffling up to the edge furthest from the wall.

Oliver followed, precariously balancing on the trembling stone.

"Just jump onto our one!" May shouted with a note of panic.

"No. The fire will be set off," Oliver said, fighting against his instincts to jump.

They had less and less space by the second. Oliver glanced down into the abyss beneath them and his stomach lurched. He looked up and saw that another platform had emerged across from the girls' and an idea struck him.

"I have a plan. Two of you need to jump to that next platform but at the *exact* same time we have to jump onto your one," he said.

"Okay, no time to argue, let's go," Rogan said, with only half a meter left between them and the wall; the gap between them and the next platform was getting further and further to jump.

"Three-two-one," Rogan said, much faster than he had previously, and they leapt into the air.

Oliver landed and balanced with his feet firmly in place, then Rogan collided with him and he went flying toward the ledge. His insides seemed to float inside him as he fell forward.

Rogan gripped the back of his collar and Anna grabbed his arm, pulling him back. His hands shook as he steadied himself and took a slow breath. He caught his friends' eyes and they laughed nervously.

Across the room, May and Quinn were gazing at him from the next platform with alarmed expressions.

"That was close," Rogan said.

A final platform had emerged across from Quinn and May which would allow them to jump to the exit.

"Now what?" Anna said, her forehead crinkling in concentration.

"If Quinn and May's platform is the same as the last one then it will start going back into the wall if the wrong amount of people are on it," Rogan said thoughtfully.

"So why doesn't May jump to the final platform, then we all join Quinn and go one by one to the final platform then the exit?" Oliver said.

"We'll have to go really fast," Anna said, chewing her bottom lip. "We better jump at the same time May does so we get the longest amount of time possible on the receding ledge."

"Okay, ready? Three, two, one," Rogan said and he, Oliver and Anna leapt forward.

At the same time, May jumped on to the final platform that had a fire hole at head and foot height.

As soon as Oliver's feet hit the ground the platform started receding, fast. Worse than this, all the platforms around them were receding, including the one May was standing on.

"GO!" Oliver roared.

May jumped to the exit and, simultaneously, Anna jumped to the final platform as May vacated it.

"Jump," Rogan said, shoving Quinn in the back.

Anna dove towards May who was safely off of the platforms by the exit. Quinn leapt to the last platform, landing roughly on her knees. She sprang to her feet, and jumped to the exit as Rogan shoved Oliver forward.

The platforms were already halfway back into the walls.

Oliver jumped. Every muscle in his body strained. His arms were outstretched. His stomach crashed into the side of the final ledge and he scrambled to pull himself up, his heart thudding in his ears.

Winded, he ran and jumped as hard as he could, crashing to the ground next to Quinn by the exit. He rolled over as Rogan landed ungracefully next to him.

They lay on the floor for a moment and Rogan started laughing. Oliver dropped his head back onto the stone and joined in as relief flooded his body.

23

Silence is Key

They got to their feet and panted for a moment before exiting through the door at the back of the room. They emerged in a corridor and teams of people rushed past them.

"How much time have we got left?" Oliver asked, too exhausted to look at his own watch.

"Just over an hour," Anna said, glancing at her own.

"Not bad. Let's get moving," Rogan said and jogged down the passage after the other teams.

The floor climbed up at an angle, becoming steeper and steeper. The ceiling got increasingly closer to the ground until Rogan, Oliver and Quinn had to duck as they slowed to a walk.

"You're lucky you're so short," Quinn said, looking at Anna and May, her neck craned to the side.

Oliver and Rogan were bent over even more awkwardly than she was and a shooting pain had started running up and down Oliver's spine.

Anna and May grinned at each other.

The corridor ended in a spiral staircase carved from the stone of the cave. They emerged out on a cliff ledge ending in a sheer drop that overlooked a valley filled with trees. Oliver poked his head out to see people shuffling along a tiny ledge towards an entrance back into the caves.

"Great. Come on. Let's get it over with." Quinn took the lead, pressing her back against the cliff and shuffling to the right.

Oliver was surprised by how high they had climbed as he looked out over the valley below. The Ninagoon team appeared behind them and one of the girls screamed in panic as she realised what they had to do. Oliver's hands shook but he clenched them and forced himself out onto the ledge after May, at the back of the line.

The ledge was so thin that the tips of his toes hung over it. He pressed his palms harder to the smooth, cold stone behind him and continued moving. He kept his eyes on the back of May's head as he progressed, focusing on her golden hair and nothing else. A cold wind swept around them and Oliver tried to ignore the way it seemed to tug at his body.

When he reached the end he let out a breath that he hadn't realised he'd been holding and headed back inside a cave.

They were in another corridor full of doors, more spread out than in the last one. Quinn found a vacant room that they followed her into, emerging in a cavern that was incredibly dark.

A glowing plaque on the wall read *Silence is Key*. The light from it just about illuminated the other's faces. Rogan pressed a finger to his lips and the rest of them nodded in understanding.

Oliver looked out into the gloom. They walked across the room slowly but, when they reached the other side, they couldn't find an exit. They split into two groups and walked around the cavern, one to the left and the other to the right, meeting back where they had started near the glowing plaque.

"Anything?" Anna whispered.

"Nothing," Rogan said quietly and looked at his watch which glowed in the dark. "We've wasted ten minutes in here already."

"Why do we have to be quiet? There's nothing in here," May whispered.

"It's probably best if we don't find out," Oliver said, and leant back against the wall.

Dong.

His head had hit something metal and the sound reverberated throughout the room. A rustling and squawking could be heard from somewhere high up above their heads.

"What was that?" Quinn hissed in a panic.

They all looked up into the gloom but it was impossible to see anything. Oliver turned and felt the thing he had hit his head on. He could just make out a metal step, then another, and another, raising high up towards the ceiling.

"There's a ladder here," Oliver whispered. "I think we have to go up it."

"After you," Quinn dared him.

Oliver gripped the ladder and stepped up.

Dong. His boot on the metal made too much noise. He stepped back off it, hearing the rustling coming from the ceiling again. The noise made his skin prickle uncomfortably.

"Shh," Anna said.

"We have to take our boots off. They make too much noise," Oliver whispered.

He could just distinguish the others removing their boots as he took off his own.

"Put them in your packs," Rogan whispered.

"Good idea," Anna said as they tucked their shoes away and returned the bags to their backs.

Oliver stepped up on to the ladder again, his socks making for a silent ascent. He could feel, more than hear, the presence of the others following him up the ladder. It seemed to go on forever and his arms were beginning to ache.

He looked down to try and see how far they had climbed and saw the tiny glow of the plaque far below them. His stomach flipped but he kept climbing and, finally, pulled himself up onto a metal platform.

He helped the others up next to him as they appeared then turned around and felt a rush of excitement. An exit on the far side of the room was illuminated by a faint, glowing rim. The glow from the door threw just enough light into the room to see what they had to traverse to reach it.

The platform they were on was supported by thick cables that attached it to the roof. About ten feet across from the first platform was another and then another further on from that. The gaps between them each had its own obstacle that would allow them to cross.

A swing hung in the middle of the first and second platforms, wide enough for one person to stand on. The light slightly illuminated the cavern ceiling and Oliver squinted up at it. It appeared to be moving.

"Those are wolverbats," Anna whispered to them frantically as they gathered closer together. She pointed up at the ceiling.

Oliver spied the whites of Rogan and Quinn's eyes as they gazed upwards then clapped their hands over their mouths, looking fearful.

"What are they?" Oliver whispered as quietly as he could.

"They hunt by sound. If they hear us they'll rip us to shreds," Anna whispered in a panic.

Oliver looked at May, wide-eyed. He nodded, not wanting to make any more noise than he had to. He pointed to the swing and tiptoed over to it, cringing at every slight noise he and the others made.

It hung, just out of reach, over the chasm. Oliver knelt on the edge and leant out as far as he could. His fingertips brushed the wood but he couldn't grasp it. He gestured for Rogan to come over, considering he had the longest arms of the group.

Rogan knelt down next to him and leant forward. He pushed the swing with his fingertips so it swung away and then swung back towards him. He grabbed it and pulled it over to the platform.

Rogan stood up and pointed at himself and then the swing. Oliver understood and gripped the bottom of the wood so Rogan could step onto it. Rogan gave Oliver a thumbs up and he pushed him out into the abyss.

He wondered how on earth Rogan would dismount the swing without making any noise but apparently he managed it because the swing came hurtling back towards him a moment later. He grabbed it and peered out towards the platform where he could just make out Rogan's figure.

They crossed, one by one, until just Oliver and May were left. Oliver helped May up onto it and she gripped the rope tightly. "I'm scared," she whispered.

"Don't worry, you'll be fine," he whispered back, squeezing her arm.

She nodded and shut her eyes as he pushed her out across the gap. He clenched his fists anxiously as she went. She let out a small squeak and Oliver threw his head back to look up at the bats. Their faces were obscured as they slept in groups, huddled under each other's wings. They shuffled about at the noise, becoming more restless, but they didn't wake.

Oliver almost missed the swing as it flew up at his face. He grabbed it then struggled to stand on the wood without the help of someone holding it steady.

He shuffled towards the edge, held the rope tightly, and swung himself as hard as he could, bending his legs to propel himself further. He almost cried out as he sailed through the air but clamped his mouth shut. It might have been fun if he hadn't been swinging beneath a swarm of flesh-eating bats.

Rogan's outstretched arms came into view and they clasped hands. Rogan held onto him tightly and Anna gripped the bottom of the swing so Oliver could step down quietly. Anna gently dropped the swing back over the edge so it moved silently back into the gap.

"What's next?" Oliver whispered.

"A bridge," Rogan whispered back, looking grim.

"I'm guessing there's more to it than that?" Oliver said.

"Take a look," he moved aside and Oliver tiptoed towards the edge.

There were six stepping stones held in place by criss-crossing cables with about a metre's gap separating each one. They formed a bridge between their platform and the next but, Oliver realised with a jolt, there was nothing to hold on to.

"After you," Anna whispered in his ear and he could sense the smile in her voice.

Oliver took a deep breath then stepped off the ledge, reaching with his leg until he found his footing and hopped out onto the first stepping stone. The wires trembled with his weight so that the whole bridge wobbled and creaked.

He crouched down and gripped the sides of the panel until the shaking stopped, feeling sweat gather in his palms. He slowly stood back up, his legs quivering with the tension in his muscles. He gazed across the gap to the next stepping stone, judging the distance.

He sucked in another breath as he moved onto it, repeating the crouch, then returning to his feet.

Every time the bridge shook a sickening, fluttering sensation arose in his chest.

He repeated the steps four more times until he reached the end and waited for the others to cross behind him with a slow exhale of breath.

A short set of monkey bars connected the platform they were on with the last. A small, metal ladder led up to the bars which ran along just a foot beneath the ceiling where the creatures were sleeping. Oliver cursed internally.

"Oh Vale," he heard Anna whisper nearby as she noticed the bars.

"May, are you gonna be okay?" Oliver whispered to her with a pang of concern.

"If you can do it, I can," she nudged him and he relaxed marginally.

"I'll go first if you like?" Quinn said quietly.

Oliver was surprised by her willingness but said nothing to contradict it.

"Go for it," Rogan whispered.

She climbed the ladder like a pro and swung out over the bars. She crossed them in a few seconds. Oliver gaped at her as she landed softly on the other side like a gymnast then moved towards the exit.

Rogan shook his head. "Show off. You alright to go, Anna?" he asked in a whisper.

She nodded and took her time getting up to the bars. She hesitated for a second before swinging out onto them then worked her way across as fast as she could, dropping to the platform on the other side on her tiptoes. Oliver realised he had been holding his breath as he watched her go and released it.

"You go. Then I'll follow May," Oliver whispered to Rogan.

Rogan nodded and swung over the bars two at a time, like an expert. He stayed on the ladder on the other side, ready to help if

May needed it. She shook her head at the boys and climbed up the ladder.

Oliver followed and swung out onto the first bar behind her. His shoulders yanked as he swung from one bar to the next. May was moving slowly but he had a good enough grip that it didn't matter.

An overwhelming urge to look down came upon him so he forced his head upwards instead and came face to face with the most frightening animal he had ever seen. Its extremely long snout ended in a large, piggy nose. Running down its snout were long, serrated teeth jutting out in all directions.

His hands became slippery as they began to sweat. In a heart-stopping moment, he lost his grip on the bar with one hand.

He frantically grabbed for the one ahead but misjudged it and his watch slammed against the metal, making a loud *CLANG* which echoed around the room.

The bat's eyes flickered open at the sound and the other wolverbats around it uncurled their necks so that a hundred red eyes were staring at him.

His breath came in strained pants as his free hand clamped down on the bar at last.

"Go, May," he hissed.

She swung as fast she could towards Rogan who was leaning out to pull her in. A few of the bats took flight with a *whoosh* of wings as they soared under the bars. They snapped at Oliver's ankles and he kicked out at them, his grip loosening once more.

The screeching of the animals and the fluttering of a thousand wings filled the air as the rest of the creatures took flight. The noise was deafening. Oliver swung out again and finally reached the ladder.

He jumped onto the platform with a *clunk* as his feet hit the metal and a bat collided with his arm, taking a chunk of skin with it. He shouted out in pain and more bats swarmed towards him, attracted by the noise.

Quinn held the door open as Anna and May ducked under her arm. Oliver was almost to the exit when Quinn started running towards him.

He turned and spotted Rogan on the ground being mauled by two bats. Oliver gasped and followed Quinn back toward him. He kicked out at the beasts, connecting with one of their jaws. It flew away with a loud *squawk* but the noise drew the other's attention.

Oliver and Quinn hauled Rogan to his feet and they ran as hard as they could towards the exit. With every footstep Oliver could hear the creatures grow closer, just inches behind them.

They slid out into the corridor as the swarm of bats dived at their heads. Anna slammed the door shut and Oliver heard the sickening *cracks* of the creatures colliding with it on the other side.

He collapsed into a heap with relief, his chest rapidly rising and falling.

"You idiot," Quinn snapped at Oliver, her voice filled with venom.

"I'm so sorry," Oliver breathed, furious at how clumsy he had been.

"It's okay. Any of us could have done it," Rogan said, panting.

Oliver eyed his friend's bloodied arms and guilt racked at him.

Quinn pulled bandages out of her bag and wrapped them tightly around Rogan's wounds. Anna quickly followed suit and bandaged Oliver's arm. He barely noticed the pain from the adrenalin pumping through his veins.

They pulled their boots back on and got to their feet. Oliver took a deep breath to calm his racing heart. "I'm so sorry, Rogan," he said again.

Rogan clapped him on the shoulder. "Seriously, man. It's fine. All part of the fun."

Quinn glared at Oliver unforgivingly.

24

Cascade

Quinn stormed off down the corridor as a team rushed past them, covered in mud and blood.

"We better get moving," Anna said.

They nodded and hurried after Quinn.

Oliver looked at his watch and his heart fluttered. "Oh, no. We've only got forty five minutes left."

They began to jog as fast as they could and found Quinn waiting for them in a large cavern. At one side, the cave opened out onto a ledge overlooking a lake and an vast crowd of people.

"Down there. That's the exit," Quinn said and they followed her out to the ledge. Their faces were projected on survision screens far below and they could hear Truvian Gold's voice echoing around the valley that ran down to a long beach. Oliver looked at where she was pointing and saw a track leading up from a smaller beach further along the lake.

"The Pandalins have made their appearance up on the balcony. With just forty minutes left to go, will they make it to the finish line in time?" Truvian Gold said dramatically.

The crowd roared with cheers. Oliver could see survision screens flicking between teams undergoing various challenges. The Visikins were squeezing through a narrow tunnel on their bellies, the

Ninagoons were swimming through a dark pool of water, and the Thrakes were sliding down a muddy descent.

Oliver didn't linger to see any more. They retreated from the ledge and searched the cavern for an exit.

The only way out of the cave was through a narrow hole in the floor. They dropped down, one by one, and crawled along the descending tunnel as fast as they could. Oliver realised this must have been where the Visikins were being filmed. They weren't much further ahead than them, which gave him hope.

They rounded a corner and the floor became soft and slippery so they had to continue more slowly. He was at the back of the group with Quinn's heels kicking mud up at him as he followed her.

The material at his heel snagged on something sharp as he crawled along, and he was tugged backwards. He stopped and awkwardly tried to reach his hand back to untangle himself but the tunnel was too narrow. He reversed a few paces so the material was released and continued forwards.

The tunnel veered out of sight and he could no longer see Quinn. He continued in the darkness and turned the corner. The passage dropped down again and he slid forward on his knees several feet. He dug his palms into the mud to slow himself down and continued at a snail's pace.

He could hear shouts up ahead and tried to speed up towards them.Quinn's barked something loudly back to him but it was too muffled to make out.

"What? I can't hear you!" Oliver shouted.

The tunnel opened up a bit and he picked up the pace again. The shouts grew louder and he heard Quinn's voice above them all but still couldn't make out any words. He grew frustrated as he continued on. The dark tunnel was making him feel claustrophobic and he longed to stand up.

The floor disappeared.

He was falling.

His heart jumped into his mouth. He was plummeting head-first into the abyss. A hand clasped his collar and he was yanked upwards giving him half a second to grab the ledge above his head and pull himself up to face his saviour. Quinn.

"I *said.* There's a great big hole in the floor, you moron." She helped guide him across the gap and he scrambled into the space next to her, his heart pounding.

"Thank you. You saved my life," Oliver said, astonished.

"Don't get soppy on me. I can't finish this race without you." She turned away and kicked mud up in his face as she continued through the tunnel.

Oliver didn't mind. His hands were still shaking as he followed her and the tunnel began descending rapidly. He was barely able to keep his grip in the soft mud. Quinn slid forward in front of him and she screamed as she plummeted downwards. Oliver clawed the walls to slow himself down as he followed.

They fell, with a splat, into a huge pile of mud out of a hole in the bottom of the tunnel. The others were already getting up, their jumpsuits now filthy.

"Ergh, disgusting," May said, wiping a great blob of mud off of her leg.

"You didn't fall down that hole then?" Rogan asked Oliver, grinning.

"No. Thanks to-" Quinn was throwing him a look of death so he finished, "-you guys. I heard you guys shouting." She clearly didn't want any credit for saving his neck though he considered whether the moment had been broadcast to the world or not. With fifty teams to survey he wondered how much of their progress was being shown on the survision anyway.

"Good," Rogan said. "Let's keep going."

The room led to another corridor of doors and they chose the only vacant one. Oliver shut the door behind them and the sound of rushing water filled his ears.

The chamber contained an enormous, dark pool with a high waterfall cascading into it at one side.

"Where's the exit?" May asked, gazing around.

"I don't know. Where's the clue?" Anna asked.

"Here," Rogan said, pointing to the ground.

Embedded in the floor was a glass bubble filled with words that floated inside it reading:

Pull me and you'll see.

"Pull what?" Oliver asked, glancing around the room.

"Look, the exit's up there," May said, pointing skywards.

Oliver looked up and saw the door high up on a ledge at the top of the waterfall. "How are we supposed to reach it?"

"There's a rope. Look," Rogan said, pointing to the centre of the room.

Its colour blended with the back wall at first but, when Oliver focused, he could just make it out, dangling above the water.

"Let's go pull it then," Quinn said, waiting for a nod of approval from Rogan before wading out into the water.

The others followed her. Oliver felt the icy water seep into his clothes and, after only a few feet, the floor disappeared beneath him. They swam to the centre of the room and all gripped the rope with one hand. Oliver shivered as he tread water to keep afloat.

"Pull?" Rogan suggested and they nodded.

They tugged hard and several things happened at once. First, the water began to swirl around them in a whirlpool and they clung tighter to the rope to keep from being swept away. Then the waterfall became a powerful torrent, pouring gallons of water into the pool. The water level began to rise and the rope ascended too, keeping them above the surface.

Oliver looked up and saw another rope a few feet away. The water poured in until the other rope was within grabbing distance then stopped.

They all released the rope and the water level instantly dropped with a gurgling noise as if it were being sucked down a giant plughole. Oliver splashed his way back toward the rope and took hold of it but the water didn't rise.

"Everyone get back to the rope!" he shouted and watched as his friends swam back towards him and reached for it.

As they grabbed hold, the water level rose once more and the whirlpool sped up, dragging at Oliver's body. He dug his fingernails into the course fibres to stop himself from losing grip.

The water level finally stopped rising so they were high enough to grab the second rope.

"I reckon just one of us needs to grab the next one!" Quinn shouted over the rush of water.

"I'll go," Anna said, and launched herself into the whirlpool. She swam hard against the current, gripped the rope firmly and tugged hard.

The waterfall exploded again so a froth of white foamy bubbles appeared where it met the pool. The whirlpool began to speed up around them as they rose and the next rope came into sight, further out than the last.

"The current's only gonna get stronger. We need to leave the best swimmers 'til last," Oliver said as the water stopped rising once more.

"Someone will have to remain holding onto this rope the whole time," May said.

"I can do that, I'm not much of a swimmer," Quinn admitted.

"May, you should go," Oliver suggested.

"I'm a good swimmer," she insisted, her wet hair plastered to her face.

"What are you like?" Oliver looked at Rogan.

"Pretty good. You?" Rogan asked, squinting as water splashed up in his face.

"I guess I'm alright." He looked at May anxiously but knew she had always been a better swimmer than him. "I'll go."

The rope was much further out this time and the whirlpool swirled around the three of them, making them twist in circles.

Oliver let go and forced his way towards the rope. The pressure of the water pushing against him was exhausting and his muscles burned as he battled against the whirlpool. He slipped backwards several times but eventually the rope came into view just above his head.

Oliver waved his hand up and his fingers brushed the end of it. He dunked under the water and kicked out hard. He desperately reached his arm up as he breached, felt it bash against his palm and gripped it with all his strength.

"WOO!" he shouted, his voice echoing around the cave as the others laughed.

Oliver tugged the rope and the water rushed in again. He looked up as the rope yanked him upwards to see that they were closing in on the exit.

Oliver could just make out Rogan, May and Quinn over the swirl of water splashing around them as they stopped rising once more. The three of them were spinning erratically at the centre of the whirlpool.

May let go, judging the spin just right so it gave her some propulsion into the water. The next rope was opposite Oliver's on the other side of the room.

Oliver felt the water pushing against him but his rope kept him in position. He glanced across the sloshing waves to see Anna fiercely clinging to her rope nearby. May reached her one and the water rushed in for a final time.

The whirlpool became so strong that Oliver was dunked under repeatedly as they rose. When they stopped they were just a few feet from the top of the waterfall, one more torrent of water away from the top.

Oliver looked over to see Rogan and Quinn spinning out of control. The rope was directly behind them at the back of the chamber but Oliver doubted Rogan could see which direction to swim.

Rogan let go, disappearing under the waves. He powered up to the surface and let the whirlpool spin him around so he could locate the rope.

"Go Rogan!" Oliver shouted then the rest of them joined in, whooping and cheering as Rogan waged war on the water with fierce determination written across his features.

Rogan reached it at last and whooped with joy as he tugged the rope. The water poured in and they rose the final few feet to where they could climb out onto the ledge that led to the exit.

The whirlpool became a twisting, sucking monster. Oliver clung to his rope and eyed the ledge, wondering how they would get there. Before he, or anyone else could come up with a plan the ropes released from the ceiling and they were all untethered, dropping under the icy water.

The whirlpool claimed Oliver immediately and he fought against the strong pull of the current. He kicked with all his might and somehow reached the surface, gasping and spluttering. He set his eyes on the ledge above the raging waves and started to swim with all his might.

He launched himself upwards and his hand slapped down on the wet ledge with a *smack.*

Oliver clambered out and turned to see his friends struggling in the water. The ropes floated on the surface, swirling in the pool. He reached a hand down into the water, gripped one and pulled it out.

Quinn was closest so Oliver threw her the rope. She caught it on the second try and he reeled her in, digging his heels into the stone to brace himself.

She grabbed the ledge and he dropped to his knees, hauling her out of the water. She panted as she righted herself then leant over the edge and retrieved another rope from the waves.

Between them they managed to quickly hoist the others to safety.

Dripping wet and exhausted, they exited through the door and the sound of their heavy panting turned to laughter as relief filled them.

25

Smoke and Flame

Water dripped off of them in the corridor as they took a brief moment to catch their breath.

"Time?" Oliver panted, too exhausted to check his own watch.

"Fifteen minutes to go," Anna said, holding her side to ease a stitch.

"We'd better hurry," Rogan said, setting off.

They followed him at a jog down the corridor and descended a winding staircase, dripping water everywhere.

Rogan stopped dead at the bottom and Anna walked straight into his back. "Hey, what do you think you're -?"

Rogan held up his arm to silence her and pointed into the room. The first thing Oliver saw was a massive exit to the cave. It was surrounded by large boulders that lead out to a small beach in front of a perfectly still lake.

Relief swept through Oliver at the sight of it. They had made it out of the caves. They could only be minutes away from the finish line.

One of the boulders stirred and rolled over, making him jump. They weren't boulders at all. The animals were enormous, some the size of elephants. They were coloured a mixture of dark greys and browns and were all sprawled out across the cavern floor.

"What are they?" he whispered to Anna.

"Hogtrouts," she breathed. "I've always wanted to see one but, er, they're pretty dangerous actually..." she trailed off, looking concerned.

"Rogan? What are you thinking?" Oliver asked in a hushed voice.

"Best bet is to sneak past them. If they wake up they're gonna get angry."

"Let's do it." Quinn crept ahead and wound her way through the sleeping mounds, heading towards the exit.

She stopped a few feet away and gestured for them to follow, a small puddle forming around her feet as water dripped from her clothes. They tiptoed after her.

Oliver got close to the first animal and it rolled over making a guttering, rumbling noise that emitted from deep inside its throat. The hogtrout's face came into view and a puff of smoke emerged from its pig-like nostrils.

The body was seal-like and smooth but its head and front legs were completely alien. Its head was enormous and covered in long, brown and grey, wiry hair. Its snout was short and ended in smoke-emitting nostrils that were filling the air with a cloudy haze.

It had two sharp horns between its ears and curling tusks protruded from the mouths of some of the larger creatures. They had thick front legs and strong, hand-like feet where sharp claws glinted. Oliver felt his mouth go dry as he eyed the dangerous-looking beasts.

They were making good progress past the animals and the fresh air blowing in from outside was calling to him.

"Psst," a voice said from up ahead.

Oliver looked out towards the exit and saw Larkin standing there with the rest of his team. He had a rock in his hand that he was tossing up and down. The only girl on their team, Kuti, kept glancing around them as if afraid someone might see her.

"What are you doing, Lark?" Quinn whispered with a grin.

Larkin pulled a false frown. "Oh, sorry babe." He winked at her, caught the rock he had thrown up in the air and threw it as hard as he could at the hogtrout in front of him. He ran away laughing loudly with his team, Arrow's thundering guffaw echoing back to them above the rest.

The beast awoke in a sudden fury, waking the creatures around it. Its front legs pulled it up to a terrifying height and it emitted a ferocious roar that sent fear shooting through Oliver's body. Fire burst from its nostrils, aiming at Quinn. Oliver knocked her to the floor out of the way, sprawling across the rough stone.

They crawled behind a rocky outcrop for protection. Oliver chanced a look over the top to check that the others had escaped the blaze. He spotted May and Rogan huddled behind a large rock but couldn't see Anna anywhere.

"What in Vale was he playing at?" Quinn spat. Oliver frowned at one side of her face that was badly grazed from where he had pushed her to the ground.

"He's trying to stop us qualifying for tomorrow's race." Oliver raised his voice over the roaring of the hogtrouts.

He glanced over the outcrop again to see them focussed on an alcove at the back of the cavern. His heart sank as a piercing scream echoed through the cave.

"ANNA?" he shouted and stood up fully to search for her.

The animals were sending clouds of smoke and huge balls of flame into the air in their rage.

"Help! Help me!" he heard Anna screaming.

Without a moments hesitation, he leapt out from behind the rock and ran across the cavern toward her. He grabbed a handful of pebbles from the ground and threw them as hard as he could towards the animals.

He clapped his hands and shouted until they turned their attention towards him. They dragged their enormous bodies with their muscular forearms and closed in on him as he ran towards the exit.

He ducked as a fireball came his way but kept running out onto the beach, his heart galloping in his chest. The animals emerged, around fifteen of them, rearing their huge heads and shaking them angrily.

Oliver waded out into the water, hoping it would offer some protection from the fire. The hogtrouts kept coming and became more agile as they slid on their bellies into the lake. Their streamlined bodies allowed them to move swiftly towards him. Oliver started to regret his move into the water.

Some of the creatures snapped their short, stubby teeth at him. Oliver began panting as he struggled to keep the distance between him and the animals. He kicked out at one that almost took his leg off as it swam by. His heart raced and he began to panic.

A keening noise cut through the air. It pierced his ears and Oliver clapped his hands to them to try and shut it out. The hogtrouts wailed and moaned, also affected by the sound. They started to dive under the water and disappear. Oliver watched as their hulking bodies swam out into the lake beyond him, into its depths. The final hogtrout dived under and the noise stopped.

He took his hands from his ears and turned to see a mage with a dark beard standing on the beach with his hands outstretched. "You'll a'right, there?" he asked in a strong accent.

"Yeah. Err- thanks," Oliver said, feeling exhausted. He waded out of the water onto the small beach, his clothes sopping again. The mage walked back up the hill that led away from the caves. The rest of Oliver's team rushed out of the cave mouth to join him.

"That was brilliant," May said, looking at him like she had never seen him before.

"Yeah, thanks, man," Rogan said.

"You saved me," Anna said, her eyes sparkling. A deep burn ran up her leg and she limped as she walked forwards.

"Thanks," Quinn muttered, looking miserable.

Oliver and Rogan linked arms underneath Anna's to help her move.

"We've only got two minutes to cross the finish line!" Anna exclaimed, looking at her watch.

They ran full pelt up the hill, Quinn taking the lead.

Anna was half-carried by Oliver and Rogan, her legs swinging wildly as they ran. They huffed and puffed as they rounded the top of the hill then began a downhill descent along a pebble beach, thronging with people.

The crowd went mad at the sight of them. Oliver saw a clock ticking down on a screen ahead with less than a minute to go. His legs ached with the effort of running and carrying Anna.

The finish line was marked in red on the beach, just a few feet away. His feet slipped and slid on the pebbles but somehow he kept his balance.

They crossed the line with only a couple of seconds to spare. The roar of the crowd hurt his ears. They were ushered into a first aid tent for medical attention before Oliver could even register that they had made it in time.

A medic sent him to a bed and he collapsed onto it, his chest heaving as he breathed in and out. He heard Rogan laughing from somewhere to his right and started to join in as he caught his breath.

"We did it," Rogan said, pounding a fist into the air from his bed. He winced from the wolverbat bite on his arm and returned it to his side in pain.

"That was only the first day and I'm knackered," Anna exclaimed, flinching as a medic attended the burn on her leg.

"We barely made it," May breathed, reaching a hand to her chest.

"Yeah, thanks to Larkin," Rogan said, looking disgusted. "We were making good time before he turned up."

"Won't he get his team disqualified?" Oliver asked hopefully.

"Yeah, should do actually," Rogan said with a smile on his face.

A medic came over and tended to Oliver's arm where the wolverbat had attacked him. She pulled away the tattered remains of the bandage Anna had strapped there.

The mage held her hand over his wound. "Wolverbat?" she asked with a friendly smile and Oliver nodded.

"Nasty little buggers," she muttered.

"Tell me about it," Oliver said, wincing as the mage touched the open wound.

A familiar, green light trickled from her hand down onto the wound and his skin knitted together, leaving no trace of the bite behind. The pain diminished and Oliver sighed with relief.

"Thank you," he said.

"You're welcome," she replied with a smile, walking over to tend a boy whose hand was red and swollen. Despite the injures, the boy was more occupied with gawping at Quinn.

"Let me through. Where are they?" Oliver heard Ely say from outside the tent.

"You're not allowed in yet, sir. You'll have to wait," a medic responded.

"What nonsense," Ely said. "I'm family."

Oliver got up off the bed and walked outside to greet his grandfather. He was drawn into a hug by the small man.

"You did it. I can't believe it. Of course, I never doubted you. But you actually *did it*," Ely said, grinning from ear to ear.

"I know. I can't believe it either," Oliver said, feeling elated. "What happens now?"

"We'll just wait to get you all patched up. Is everyone, alright? No major injuries? May's not hurt at all?" he asked, trying to peer into the tent.

The medic zipped down the tent door in his face.

"Yes, they're fine. Anna burnt her leg, Rogan has a few cuts and Quinn grazed her face, but apart from that, I think everyone's great." Oliver still couldn't believe they had made it through to the next race. His head seemed to be floating through the clouds. "How many teams qualified?"

"You were the last team over the finish line. There were twenty seven before you so you've practically halved the competition already. Although, everyone will be fighting tooth and nail tomorrow to place in the final ten. But don't worry about that now. You'll be taken to the team cabins by the lake where you'll stay until tomorrow morning."

"Where are you staying?"

"With Laura. You'll be debriefed soon and they'll tell you which teams made it through and if anyone's been disqualified."

"Larkin's team better be." Oliver looked grim.

"Why, what did they do?"

"Larkin threw a rock at one of those hogtrouts and the whole bunch of them attacked us," Oliver said, fury rising in him again.

"They didn't show that on the survision. All we saw were the animals chasing you out into the lake," Ely said.

"But they'll know what happened, won't they?" Oliver asked desperately.

"Oh, yes. They have a whole team of people watching all of the cameras so someone will have reported it," Ely said, patting him on the shoulder.

The crowd cheered as the last of the losing teams finished the race back on the beach.

"The final team has crossed the finish line. I need all teams to gather by the lake in fifteen minutes," Abbicus Brown's voice boomed out over a speaker a few moments later.

The losing teams stumbled past Oliver and Ely into the various first aid tents. He saw two boys from team Suddle limping into one. They had both sustained burns around their ankles reminding Oliver of the fire holes in their first challenge.

Oliver's team appeared through the tent flap. Anna was already putting weight on her leg, Rogan's cuts were reduced to faint red lines that were fading by the second, and Quinn's cheek was fully healed. Their team had emerged relatively unscathed from the race.

"How are you doing?" he asked Anna.

"Not too bad. It stings a bit but the mage who healed me said I'll be completely fixed in an hour or so. That hogtrout would have burnt me to a crisp if you hadn't distracted them," she said, pulling him into a hug. He held on to her for a little longer than was necessary but she was smiling when he released her.

"Yeah, cheers man. We'd all be toast if it wasn't for you," Rogan said, nudging Quinn.

She placed a hand on her hip and smiled at Oliver appreciatively.

"Shall we go down to the lake?" May suggested, tucking her wet hair behind her ears.

"Err, I think Quinn and I better meet you over there. We might get mobbed if we go through the crowd," Rogan said and they headed off behind the tents.

Oliver had almost forgotten about their fame. He found it strange to think of them as celebrities.

He wandered after May, with Anna and Ely in tow. They reached the pebble beach that ran around the edge of the lake and gathered there with the other teams.

Oliver could see bandages and patches covering a lot of the other contestants. Larkin's team was irritatingly unharmed. Oliver rubbed his arm where the wolverbat had caught him, the pain was gone but it itched a little as magic tingled beneath his skin, finishing the healing process.

Rogan and Quinn joined them a moment later, accompanied by an outburst of cheers from the crowd, a hundred or so meters away. A stage with an enormous survision screen sat at one end of the beach. Abbicus Brown stood at a podium accompanied by Ray Falls and Truvian Gold, who were chatting together animatedly at the side of the stage.

Abbicus Brown cleared his throat into the microphone. "Congratulations to all of you. Although you haven't all qualified for tomorrow's race, do not be disheartened. You have raced with courage and strength and you can come back another season to win another day."

A tumult of applause erupted from the crowd and teams. Abbicus paused to let it die down before continuing. "So, without further ado, I'd like to welcome your glorious commentators up to the podium to announce the teams who have qualified for tomorrow's race: please give a round of applause for the beautiful Ray Falls and the fabulous Truvian Gold."

He clapped as he backed away, allowing them to step up to the podium. They waited for the crowd to calm down and ominous music was played across the survision to build tension.

"The first group across the finish line, and qualifying for tomorrow's race is, Team Thrake," Ray Falls said, clapping along with the crowd.

"The following teams have qualified and will be announced in the order they crossed the finish line," said Truvian Gold, listing off team after team. Oliver hardly listened until the last of the names were called out. "Teams Loop, Ganderfield, Zhoulin, Koop, Lost, Visikin, and, by the skin of their teeth, Team Pandalin!"

The crowd applauded as each team was announced but when their team was called out the crowd went crazy. Oliver looked closely at them to see banners waving in the air saying things like *We love you Rogan* and *Quinn to Win.*

Oliver raised an eyebrow at Rogan who laughed and whooped with the rest of them. He broke into a laugh himself and joined in with all the teams who had qualified as they cheered wildly.

"Now for some not so good news," Ray Falls said, looking sad. "Unfortunately, our survision team recorded two acts of rule breaking in the race. The first reprimand goes to Larkin Pipistrelle of Team Visikin."

Oliver's heart leapt as he heard the Visikins boo and hiss at Ray Falls.

She glared at them and continued. "Mr Pipistrelle was recorded aggravating a hogtrout which, in turn, put another team in danger. Therefore, it has been decided that Larkin and his team will be reprimanded with a warning and a sixty second time penalty at the start of tomorrow's race."

Oliver's team were booing now and many of the crowd joined in with them.

"He broke the rules. He should be disqualified!" Rogan shouted.

"Quiet. The decision has been made," Truvian Gold stepped in.

"The second reprimand goes to Team Zhoulin who split up during their second task, so that half the team had continued on through the course, leaving the other half behind. However, their separation was brief and they did start the next part of the course as an entire team. Therefore, your team will also be given a warning and a sixty second time penalty. A second warning for either team will result in disqualification.

"So, well done to everyone taking part, please make your way to the pod station to be taken to your cabins where you will stay until tomorrow morning. A party will be held for the qualifying teams but don't stay up too late because you'll need your energy for tomorrow's race," Ray Falls said with a grin, stepping down to a round of applause.

The crowd started to dissipate and chat amongst themselves and Oliver let them sweep him and his friends towards the pod station, his head buzzing with excitement.

26

After Night has Fallen

Their cabin was divided into two bedrooms, one for each gender, with a small living area in between.

Oliver and Rogan were sprawled out on their beds after an afternoon of resting. Oliver's legs had practically given way underneath him as the excitement from the race finally deserted him, leaving his body aching and tired. Somehow a nap had made his body ache even more. He groaned as he got to his feet.

He heard a kettle whistling in the living area so went through in the hope of finding some Glacian tea. May was there. She handed him a steaming mug which he gulped down quickly before she topped it up again. The warmth spread through his body like liquid fire and soothed his aching muscles.

"That's better," he said, leaning back in the fur-covered armchair.

Oliver stared out of the window that overlooked the lake and let his eyes droop as he watched the dusky light of the sunset ripple and dance across the water. He made out the vague outline of huge mountains overshadowing the lake on the other side.

The island was somewhere out there, with the Gateway to Glacio hidden upon it. A strong wind picked up and broke the calm water into little waves. He pushed the thought of tomorrow away and sipped at his tea, enjoying the temporary peace of the evening and warmth of the cabin.

Anna emerged from the girl's room in a navy tracksuit with their team name written in swirling writing across the back. Oliver was already wearing the same in the masculine version.

"How's your leg?" he asked.

"Yeah great, thanks. The burns are all gone." She smiled.

Oliver hardly felt up to a party after the day they had had but couldn't help feeling excited about qualifying. Clothes had been provided for them in the colours of their team which they changed into as the evening drew in.

Despite Rogan wearing the same suit as Oliver he had, once again, managed to make himself look like a film star. Rogan ran a hand through his hair with a spark of light that made his hair sit perfectly, having now removed the gloves which blocked his magic.

They met the girls in the lounge where they found them wearing dresses in the same colours. Quinn's was much tighter and lower cut than the other girls' and Anna was eyeing her with a frown on her face.

"Don't you look stunning?" Rogan said to Quinn and she rolled her eyes. "What?"

"Can we just get going?" Quinn said, placing her hands on her hips.

"Alright, just gimme a kiss first," Rogan said with a cheeky grin.

Anna and May sidled away from them and out the front door, looking uncomfortable.

"Leave me alone, Rogan," Oliver heard Quinn say grumpily as he hurried to follow the girls outside.

Quinn walked ahead of them as they headed to the hall by the lake where the party was being held. Others were emerging from their cabins, all dressed in the colours of their teams.

The sun had fully set now and the dappled light that was shining through the dark clouds reflected on the lapping water of the lake.

Oliver stuffed his hands in his pockets as a cool breeze whipped up. They approached the hall and a welcome gust of warmth rushed over them as they entered the grand room that was thronging with people. It was dimly lit with a large dance floor at one end where coloured lights twisted and twirled on the currently empty space.

Tables were spread around labelled with each of their team names, dressed in linen cloths and laid with silver cutlery. They found theirs at one side near a large window, overlooking the lake that looked almost black beneath the night sky.

A long buffet table ran most of the length of one wall and Oliver's stomach rumbled at the thought of food. He and Rogan made it to the buffet first and queued along the table as they started piling their plates high. Oliver didn't recognise much so chose whatever Rogan did.

The girls joined them at the buffet then followed them back to the table a moment later.

Oliver and Rogan began to wolf down their food and Quinn watched Rogan in disgust as he ate.

"Do you *have* to eat like that?" she asked him.

"Yesh," he said through a mouthful of food.

"So, I suppose you're planning on eating like that at our wedding, are you?"

"Yep," he scooped another forkful into his mouth.

Oliver shared an awkward look with May and Anna then stilled as he spotted Larkin approaching their table.

"Great," Oliver mumbled.

"Hello, losers," he said, flicking his head so his hair moved out of his eyes.

Larkin reached out a hand to touch Quinn's arm and she slapped it away.

"Don't touch me." She got to her feet. "What in *Vale* were you thinking?"

"Calm down, babe, I was just having a laugh. You qualified anyway didn't you?" he said, raising his eyebrows.

His friend, Arrow, shuffled up behind him.

"You could have gotten us killed," Anna said, stabbing her food with a knife.

"If only," Arrow said with a sneer.

Anna scowled at him.

Larkin looked at her. "Cheer up babe, frowning doesn't suit you."

"Well being a complete arse suits *you* just fine," Anna snapped.

"Ooo, get you," Larkin said raising his hands in mock fear.

"Why do you even bother talking to us?" Oliver asked angrily.

"I wasn't talking to *you* I came over to talk to Quinn," Larkin said.

"And clearly she doesn't want to talk to you," Oliver said, his temper rising. "So you can leave now."

Arrow moved around the table closer to May. "This your sister?" he asked Oliver.

May frowned at him. "So what if I am?"

"You're adopted aren't you? At least you're not blood-" Arrow was cut off as Oliver was on his feet in a second and shoved him in the chest.

Arrow blinked in surprise then his features rearranged into a snarl. "You'll regret that."

Oliver was forced backwards into the table as Arrow collided with him. Rogan jumped up and used a wave of magic to force Arrow off of him.

Oliver righted himself and realised most of the room had stopped to watch them. As far as he could tell, there was no one in the hall to monitor them.

"You might wanna think real carefully about your next move," Rogan said to Arrow and Larkin, sparks flashing threateningly in his palm.

Larkin eyed him warily then looked at Quinn for support. She glowered at him.

"Oh, this really is pathetic. Are these your *friends* now, Quinn?" Larkin said.

"Yes, so? You think you're better than them?" Quinn challenged.

"I don't think I'm better than them. I know I am, babe," he said and Arrow smirked.

"Don't call me babe." Fire lit in Quinn's hand and Larkin took a step back.

He looked like he was about to say something then changed his mind. "Whatever. See you, losers," he said then slinked away with Arrow in tow, trying not to lose face.

Quinn's brown eyes glittered but she blinked furiously to stop the tears from falling then stormed off toward the toilet. Anna jumped up and followed her, leaving an awkward silence in the room.

Oliver returned to his seat and everyone began to chatter excitedly amongst themselves in hushed voices. Rogan sat down and stuffed food into his mouth angrily; May watched him in silence.

Truvian Gold entered through the door at the other end and some of the teams applauded. Ray Falls entered next followed closely by a few members of the Race Committee but Laura wasn't amongst them. They all sat together at a large table then music started up and the lights dimmed down. Some of the girls around the room jumped up with squeals and started dancing in the space at the end of the hall.

Oliver gazed down at his plate, no longer feeling hungry.

Quinn returned a while later with Anna. She slumped into her chair and stared out into the room as Anna took her seat next to Oliver and threw him an anxious look.

"Is she okay?" Oliver asked quietly.

"I can hear you," Quinn said, not looking at him.

"Well, *are* you?" Oliver said, louder.

"I'm just fine," she said airily.

"You don't seem fine," Rogan chipped in but it was a mistake.

"What do you care?" Quinn rounded on him. "You never ask how I am."

"What? Yes I do," Rogan said, looking shocked.

Quinn got to her feet. "Just leave me alone, okay?" She stormed across the room into the crowd.

"What did I do?" Rogan asked no one in particular.

"I don't know." Oliver was out of his depth.

"She's just upset about Larkin," Anna said.

"Who cares about that guy? He's a complete idiot," Rogan said.

"She knows that now. But she thought he was her friend," Anna explained.

"And now he's not. Good riddance," Rogan said, starting to eat once more.

Oliver agreed but didn't say so out loud. "Let's just forget about it," he said.

"Wanna go dance, Anna?" May asked, clearly trying to escape the tension.

"Yes." She nodded, got up and followed May to the dance floor.

"*Girls*," Rogan said, shaking his head.

Oliver laughed and Rogan broke a smile. "Quinn drives me crazy sometimes," he said.

"How long have you guys been engaged?" Oliver asked.

"Our families arranged our marriage when we were ten," he said casually.

"What? Seriously?" Oliver asked in shock.

"Oh, yeah, I forget you're from Earth sometimes. My family and Quinn's are two of the most powerful in Aleva so we were a good match. We're both Lanic mages, third borns."

Oliver remembered Ely explaining but it was hard to imagine them being paired up so young. "So, you were engaged to her when you were ten years old?"

"Sort of, we spent a lot of time together as we grew up and then we got officially engaged at sixteen."

"And you're okay with that?" Oliver couldn't help but ask.

"Yeah, I mean, most of the time," Rogan said with a half-smile.

Oliver raised his eyebrows at him.

"I guess, in an ideal world I'd have a choice in who I marry but it's not like that for mages."

"That doesn't seem fair," Oliver said with a frown.

"Maybe not, but it makes sense. There wouldn't be any mages left eventually if we married other people."

"I suppose. So, are you happy that Quinn's the girl you have to marry?" Oliver asked.

"Yeah, she's great." He smiled. "Now, let's have some fun." He got to his feet. "Wanna dance?" He held out his hand in an exaggerated gesture.

Oliver laughed and smacked his hand away. He knew he was a terrible dancer but wanted to enjoy the rest of the night. "Okay, let's do it."

They joined May and Anna on the dance floor which was packed with people. There was no sign of Quinn and Oliver noticed Rogan glancing around for her occasionally. A swarm of girls tried desperately to get Rogan's attention but he ignored them and Oliver and the others formed a circle to isolate themselves.

Oliver didn't know any of the songs but he had rarely known who sung the number one back on Earth so it made little difference to him. A slow song came on and Oliver panicked.

The people around him were pairing up in couples. A group of girls shuffled closer to Rogan but he continued to ignore them and reached for May.

Oliver half glanced at Anna, wanting to ask her. He gripped her arm in a bold move and she moved toward him, looping her arms around his neck. She was closer to him than she'd ever been before, their bodies pressed against one another. Oliver couldn't see anything outside of their own space.

She looked up at him, her dark eyes highlighted with a hint of makeup. He suddenly relaxed, his mouth no longer dry. It was the most natural thing in the world to be this close to her. His heart thumped slow and regular against his chest.

He pushed a strand of hair behind her ear and he felt her move into his touch. Her mouth tilted up at him suggestively as he bumped into someone.

Oliver stopped abruptly and turned to see Rogan standing there holding May close to him. But his eyes weren't on her, they were on something across the room. May stepped away from him, turning to follow his gaze and Oliver swivelled to do the same.

Across the room, Quinn was perched on Truvian Gold's lap giggling and stroking his hair.

Oliver swung around to look at Rogan in shock.

"I'm gonna go for a walk," he said tersely, and marched straight out of the hall into the darkness outside.

Oliver looked around at Anna for support, he was still holding her waist and released her in a flash. "What should we do?" he asked.

"I better get Quinn. She's making a fool of herself," Anna said, and walked off towards them.

"I'm gonna go and check if Rogan's okay," May said and exited the hall.

Oliver was left feeling useless. He went to the bathroom and, when he returned, glanced around the room looking for the others. Anna was still in an emotional-looking chat with Quinn which he preferred not to be involved in. Instead, he decided to go after May and Rogan.

Oliver went outside and the cold, night air whipped around him. He couldn't hear anything but the lapping of water on the beach and the muffled sound of music in the hall. Something about the atmosphere unnerved him.

He walked back towards the cabin and called out, "Rogan? May?" There was no answer.

He walked the length of the beach then turned back towards the hall, assuming they must have gone the other way.

By the time he got back, the party was ending and people were fanning out onto the pathway. Groups were running down the beach laughing and splashing their feet in the water. He waited outside the hall for Anna but she didn't appear. He decided to walk on, away from the cabins, to keep looking for Rogan and May.

Further along the beach was a pier that stretched out into the water, casting a dark shadow underneath it. His skin crawled as he squinted at the dark space but something drew him toward it. He walked across the beach, the pebbles rubbing against one another beneath his feet so anyone beneath the pier would hear him coming from a mile off. He paused, sure he had seen a figure move within the shadows.

"May?" he called out again but there was no reply.

As he approached, he could see that the figure was standing over something. Oliver glanced back up to the light that was streaming from the hallway then turned and walked towards the person.

"Rogan?" he called, more tentatively this time. If Rogan or May were there, they would have responded to him already.

The figure stiffened and turned towards him.

"Is that you?" Oliver asked doubtfully.

The person ran, the sound of their shoes clapping against the stones.

Oliver stopped dead and watched as they pelted down the beach, vanishing into the darkness.

"Hey!" he called after them in confusion.

Oliver walked over to the spot where they had been standing. There was something half submerged in the water, the waves lapping gently against it. He bent down and felt the object. It was a person.

"Olly?"

Panic flooded his body. "May? Oh my God! What happened?" He pulled her up to her feet. She was soaking wet, her skin icy to the touch.

"I don't know. I think someone hit me," she said in a daze, her breath coming out as a puff of vapour. She reached up and held the side of her head with a shaky hand. Oliver could just make out blood seeping between her fingers and took in a hiss of breath between his teeth.

She stumbled forwards and he lifted her into his arms, fleeing up the beach as adrenalin fueled his muscles.

Oliver cried out for help as he approached the hall. Most of the people at the party had now left but Anna was waiting for them. Quinn and Truvian stood behind her, whispering and giggling together in the doorway.

"What in Vale happened?" Anna rushed towards them to help support May.

"May's been attacked," Oliver panted, blinking away the water that had gathered in his eyes from the cold wind.

Quinn and Truvian looked up in alarm and Truvian rushed over, becoming professional all of a sudden. "What happened?" he asked, taking charge.

Oliver lay May on the ground and fell to the floor beside her, cradling her head.

"She needs help!" Oliver shouted, angry that no one was doing anything.

Quinn rushed forward and sunk to her knees. Oliver met her gaze and saw only concern there as she reached an arm over May's head and let healing, green light flow down towards her.

Anna hovered next to Truvian and he gripped her arm to steady her. "Who did this?" Truvian addressed Oliver.

"I don't know. I didn't see them," Oliver muttered, shaking his head.

May groaned and her eyes refocused. She pushed herself up into a sitting position and Truvian dropped to his knees beside her. Oliver dropped his head in relief, pushing away the fear that had invaded his body like poison.

"How are you feeling? Can you stand up?" Truvian asked, tilting her chin to the side to get a good look at the now healed wound.

She nodded and he pulled her to her feet.

"Who was it? Did you see?" Oliver asked her through gritted teeth.

"No, they came up from behind. I was looking for Rogan. I saw someone standing there and thought it was him. When I went over, whoever it was had disappeared. That's when they hit me," she said, tears filling her eyes.

"I'll have to report this," Truvian said. "I can't believe this has happened."

"No, don't report it. *Please*. What if they don't let me compete?" May said, looking pleadingly him. Oliver realised her point and looked at him.

"We need this chance at getting a key. Please don't tell anyone," Oliver said to him.

Anna gazed hopefully at the man.

Quinn gripped Truvian's arm. "Please, for me?" Her large eyes glimmered at him.

"Well, I suppose if it's really that important to you. I don't want to jeopardise that," he said, squeezing Quinn's arm. "You sure you feel up to it?" he asked May.

"Definitely. I'm completely fine," May said with a smile, although the paleness of her face didn't suggest she was entirely fighting fit.

"I'll walk you lot back to your cabin," Truvian said.

"That's not necessary. We'll be fine," Oliver said, looping an arm under May's.

"But if the attacker's still out here I should really be around to help," he said, glancing about like they might appear from the shadows.

"I think I've got that covered," Quinn said as a crackle of light sparked in her hand.

Truvian eyed the magic. "I guess you do."

"Good night then," Oliver said and Anna moved to his side.

Truvian walked away, glancing back at them as he headed in the opposite direction. Quinn led the way as they walked back to their cabin.

"Thank you, Quinn," May said quietly.

Quinn turned back and threw her a sympathetic smile. Oliver felt a swell of gratitude towards the girl.

"This doesn't seem right. Someone did this to you, May. They should pay for it," Anna said angrily.

Oliver clenched his fists, the fear he had felt replaced by a burning, vengeful anger.

"Do you think it was Larkin?" May asked, looking up at him.

"If it was, he's dead," Oliver snarled.

"Larkin could have killed us when he threw a rock at that hogtrout. Seems like he's capable," Anna said worriedly.

"It's true," May said.

"You just better be careful. Don't go anywhere on your own, again. Let's just get this race over with," Oliver said, gritting his teeth.

"Alright," May said firmly, determination etched in her features.

Oliver opened the door to the cabin and found Rogan waiting for them in the living room.

"Where've you-" he stopped mid-sentence as he spotted May's pale face and the blood drying into her hair. "Are you alright?" he asked in a panic.

"I'm fine," May said.

"What happened?" Rogan asked frantically, escorting her to a seat and practically taking her from Oliver's grip.

"Someone attacked her," Oliver informed him angrily.

"*What?*" he growled, fire igniting in his palms. "Who?" he demanded.

"I don't know. They ran off before I could see who it was," Oliver said.

"We suspect Larkin," Anna said.

Quinn shook her head but didn't say anything.

"I went looking for you when you left. Someone came up behind me and hit me on the head," May said with a frown.

"Oh no, May. I'm so sorry. You shouldn't have come after me," Rogan said, kneeling in front of her.

"Maybe you're right," she joked, rubbing her head.

He touched her wrist and a flash of light ran up May's arm, drying every inch of her clothes as it travelled. Within a few moments the lake water had completely dried and May's hair hung about her shoulders looking silky soft.

Quinn fidgeted awkwardly as Rogan glanced at her.

"Are you two ever gonna make up?" Anna asked, looking between the two of them.

Rogan got to his feet but didn't make a move and Quinn glared at him.

"Come on, we have to race together tomorrow," Oliver said imploringly.

Quinn sighed in resignation and gazed at Rogan, her hard exterior visibly melting. "I'm sorry, I acted like an idiot tonight."

Rogan reached out a hand to her. She took it and he pulled her into a hug as she reached up and pressed her lips to his.

"Hooray. I'm going to bed," Anna said with a yawn and disappeared into the girl's room.

They all followed suit. Oliver crashed into the soft bed and listened to Rogan's low snores as he tried to get to sleep. His mind was on overdrive from May's attack and an ominous, nagging feeling of dread kept him awake for hours before he finally got some rest.

27

Ripples on the Water

A bellowing horn sounded across the lake and echoed through the cabins. Oliver jumped out of bed and almost ran into Rogan who was standing there in a skin-tight wetsuit looking uncomfortable.

Oliver laughed. "What the hell is that?"

His face dropped as Rogan held out another wet suit. "For you," he said, grinning.

"You're kidding."

"Nope. Here." He shook the suit at him.

Oliver took it and stomped into the bathroom to put it on. He returned, tugging the tight material away from his chest. He released it and Rogan laughed as it snapped back against his skin.

"Let's go see the girls. Quinn's gonna love this," Rogan said.

Oliver followed him into the living room and saw Quinn checking herself out in a mirror, admiring the figure-hugging suit. She turned around and cast her eyes over the two boys.

"Hey gorgeous," she said rushing forward and kissing Rogan on the cheek.

May stood awkwardly in the middle of the room with her arms folded across her body.

"This is a complete joke!" Anna screeched from the girl's bedroom.

She appeared in the doorway in the wetsuit with a towel wrapped around her.

"Oh, stop your complaining. You look hot," Quinn said, applying lipgloss to her full lips.

"This is *not* what I signed up for," Anna said, blushing furiously.

"You wanted to compete," Quinn said in a sing-song voice.

"Yeah, but that was before I realised I had to wear *this*," she said, gesturing to the suit.

A second horn sounded outside.

"We've got an hour before the race starts. I'll go and get us some breakfast," Rogan said, clearly taking the opportunity to escape the girls.

"I'll come with you," Oliver said, chasing after him.

They took some fruit and energy bars for everyone from the breakfast buffet and walked slowly back towards the cabin. The weather was perfect for the race; the air was cool and the sun was shining on the calm water of the lake. Oliver took a deep breath, trying to suppress the fluttering feeling in his stomach.

"When I saw May last night-" Rogan cut off, at a loss for words.

Oliver nodded in understanding. "I know."

"I'm gonna do everything I can to make sure we win a key today. I've been thinking about that curse and I wanna go with you two to Brinatin. I might be able to help you get to my dad," Rogan said.

Oliver stopped walking and looked at his friend with a swell of gratitude. "Thank you. That would be brilliant."

Rogan turned back to him. "I have to tell Quinn about the curse, you know. She'll be coming with us."

Oliver had known he would and, after Quinn had saved May the night before, he wasn't sure he minded. "I know."

"You can trust her. She acts like an idiot sometimes but she's a good person deep down."

"Yeah I believe you."

They continued walking back, their shoes kicking stones that had migrated onto the path from the beach.

"You know your dad?" Oliver asked tentatively.

"Yeah?" Rogan asked, elongating the word.

"Ely told me that he hasn't been seen for years, so have you not seen him either?"

"Nope, not since I was nine. I remember the last time I saw him-" he gazed thoughtfully across the lake "-he came here to Aleva. Dad worked in Brinatin but he started to come home less and less, he said it was for his job. Mum took it personally but Dad said he was working on something big, something important.

"He turned up on my ninth birthday here in Aleva, I hadn't seen him in months. He gave me a letter saying he had to go away for a while and all that evening he and Mum fought while I sat on the stairs and listened. I never saw him again after that." Rogan continued to gaze across the lake. "He didn't say goodbye."

"I'm sorry, that sucks," Oliver said with a pang of sadness.

"Yeah," Rogan said vaguely.

A third horn sounded out across the complex making Oliver tense up as his nerves returned.

"Oh, Vale. We've only got thirty minutes. We better go get the girls," Rogan said, running back towards their cabin as Oliver hurried behind him.

After wolfing down their food, Rogan and Quinn donned their gauntlets and they all headed back out towards the hall where the teams were readying for the race.

Anna had finally discarded her towel and walked awkwardly next May, trying to keep herself covered.

"You've got nothing to worry about, Anna." Rogan turned back to her with a grin and Oliver nudged him automatically. Rogan gave him a wry smile as Oliver looked back at her.

She turned bright red and linked May's arm. "Thanks," she said quietly, smiling at them both.

They shuffled up behind the crowd of contestants in the hall and saw Abbicus Brown standing above them at the far end. Groups of Race Assistants were moving amongst the teams, handing out packs.

Abbicus cleared his throat. "Welcome to the second day of the Great Race of Aleva. Today, you will participate in a one mile race to the island at the centre of Glacio lake. Each team will be provided with a rowing boat. Once you have reached the island, you must make your way to the summit of Mount Laurell where you will find the Gateway to Glacio. You have three hours to finish the race. The first ten teams to either reach the Gateway or make it closest within the time limit will be granted keys. Are there any questions?"

The room was quiet. Determination was etched into the faces of the other contestants and Oliver started to doubt their own chances.

"Very well, please make your way out to the lake where the boats await you at the starting line," Abbicus said.

Oliver and his teammates were the first to leave the hall and hurried along the edge of the lake towards a large crowd of people standing on the pebbled beach. In front of them, was a long line of rowing boats ten yards or so from the water's edge.

Oliver looked out towards the lake. In the time since they had awoken, a heavy mist had blown down from the mountain, concealing the island at its centre. He cursed internally and his fists curled into tight balls.

As they approached the boats, the crowd cheered wildly. Oliver tried to place Ely amongst them but couldn't see him. They found the navy blue boat inscribed with their team name *Pandalin* and stood beside it in a row.

Rogan lowered his voice as he spoke. "May, you sit at the front and direct us. Oliver you sit next to me, behind May. Quinn, Anna sit next to each other at the back and take an oar each." He nodded to Oliver and Quinn. "You two get on the other side of the boat."

Oliver and Quinn rushed around and gripped the edge of it.

The Visikins took their place next to them and Larkin sneered as he spotted them. Quinn turned away, looking toward the stage beyond the row of boats. Larkin frowned for a moment then quickly adopted a casual expression before turning back to his teammates.

Oliver glared at the boy, wondering if he was truly responsible for hurting May.

Truvian Gold and Ray Falls were standing up on the side of the stage giggling with one another. Abbicus Brown gestured at them furiously from the side and they rushed over to their microphones.

"Good morning everybody!" Ray shouted to the massive crowd who cheered madly back at her.

They seemed more riled up today than the previous day, making Oliver's heart hammer in his chest.

"The race will begin in two minutes. Family members of the contestants are to make their way to the ferry for your complimentary ride to the island to meet your relatives at the finish line. Anyone else can buy a ticket for a ferry once the race has begun," Truvian said, gesturing to three small ferries lined up along the pier behind him.

"Team Zhoulin and Team Visikin will need to wait for their sixty second penalty after the race commences before they can begin," Ray said.

"One minute to go," Truvian announced and a clock began counting down on a huge survision screen above him.

The crowd roared, the noise echoing across the lake and bouncing off of mountains that were veiled by the mist. Oliver felt Quinn brace behind him and mimicked her.

The crowd counted down from ten. Oliver could barely hear them over the noise of his heart pounding in his ears. He glanced at May.

Her jaw was clenched. He focused and took one, deep, steadying breath.

"Three, two, one, GO!" Ray Falls' voice cut through the noise of the crowd and Oliver began running and hauling the boat towards the lake.

He became submersed in freezing water up to his waist in moments. May jumped in the front and the others climbed in after, facing away from her. Oliver could hear them shouting his name as he continued to push the boat in hopes of giving them a head start. The muscles in his arms burned as he gave the boat a final push before pulling himself up into it.

Rogan helped haul him inside and water splashed over Quinn and Anna as he swung over the edge. They barely blinked as they focused their efforts on rowing as hard as they could. Oliver grabbed his oar and quickly fell into rhythm with Rogan, then concentrated on synchronising with the girls as May called out the beat. He pulled back hard then pushed the oar into the water with as much energy as he could muster.

Oliver could just see back to the beach where Larkin's team and the Zhoulin's were pushing their boats into the water at last. The red hull of their boat sped towards them and he could see the muscles tensing in Larkin and Arrows' backs as they rowed to the fast beat of Kuti's shrill cries.

He spotted several teams struggling to organise themselves in their boats and knew they must be ahead of at least half the competition.

Oliver gritted his teeth and focused on keeping up their own pace, letting May's voice fill his mind to block everything else out.

May started screaming, "VEER LEFT! LEFT, LEFT!" Her shouts intensified as they all steered as hard as they could.

"NO, *MY* LEFT!" she roared and they all desperately steered in the opposite direction.

They passed by two rowing boats that were upside down in the water, missing them by mere inches. The two teams were shouting at each other and frantically trying to turn their boats over. Oliver let out a breath of relief at the close call.

The mist descended on them as they sailed away from the chaos and the noise of the crowd began to die away into the distance.

"Just keep heading straight," May said with a heavy sigh then started calling out the rhythm again.

No one spoke. They rowed until their arms were burning. Oliver could barely feel his hands from the tight grip he had on his oar and was sure they would be blistered and sore when he eventually released them.

He could no longer hear any of the other teams around them. The only noise to reach his ears was the splash of water as their oars sunk in and out again and May as she said, "Row. Row. Row," in a voice that had diminished to a monotonous drone as the excitement wore off.

"What do you see, May?" Rogan asked after several more minutes of quiet.

"Nothing. I can't see anything," she said.

Oliver couldn't see a thing back the way they had come either. The mist had thickened so their vision was restricted to just a few feet around the boat.

"Wait. Stop rowing," May hissed.

"What? We can't stop we'll fall behind!" Quinn said, sounding outraged.

"Just *stop!*" May commanded.

Reluctantly, they did so. Oliver turned around to look at her, panting from exertion. "What's going on?"

"Shh. Listen," she breathed, holding a hand up to stop him talking and they fell silent.

The water lapping against the boat was the only sound Oliver could hear. That was, until he heard a scream.

The noise ripped through the air like a knife. It sounded close by and far away at the same time. The girl's scream echoed off of the surrounding mountains then abruptly cut off.

"What's happening?" Anna asked in a panic.

"May, can you see anything?" Oliver asked, trying to lean around her.

"No, nothing," she said, craning forward over the edge of the boat so her ponytail flopped over one side of her face.

"We should keep going," Quinn said.

"Towards the screaming? Are you mad?" Anna said in alarm.

"That's the direction of the island. We're already wasting time!" Quinn insisted.

"But what if we bump into whatever the team ahead of us just did?" Anna said, rubbing her arms in the cold, damp air.

"What if they need our help?" Oliver said.

"There are mages around to help. We need to get on with the race," Quinn snapped, glaring at him.

Oliver frowned back.

"Okay, we should keep going. But let's change direction slightly. We can veer away from the direction of the screaming then turn back towards the island," Rogan said.

"We could completely lose our sense of direction if we go off course," May said, looking back at him with wide eyes.

"Hopefully this mist will clear up soon. What other choice do we have?" Rogan asked.

No one spoke.

Oliver agreed with him. "Let's get-" he was stopped mid-sentence by a violent jerk of the boat.

"What in Vale was that?" Anna shuffled closer to Quinn who steadied her.

"No one get up, we'll capsize," Quinn instructed in a hiss.

The boat jerked again. A great thump from underneath sent May lurching forward and Oliver lunged for her arm but it was too late. She fell, with a splash, face first into the water then resurfaced with a scream.

"Rogan, help me pull her out!" Oliver shouted, rushing forward and grabbing her arm. Rogan grabbed her other one and the boat rocked precariously.

"Get me out. Get me out!" May said in a panic, gripping their arms tightly.

Another huge jerk of the boat sent Oliver and Rogan flying out into the lake. The ice-cold water filled Oliver's mouth and nose. He couldn't breath. He kicked harder and harder until he finally reached the surface and took a deep gasp of air.

He had floated a few feet away from the boat which was now occupied by just Anna and Quinn. They were pulling May up with Rogan pushing her legs as he treaded water beneath her.

Oliver swam towards them feeling vulnerable in the open water. His foot connected with something hard below the surface and he kicked backwards away from it with a shout of surprise.

The others looked up at him and he spotted that May was back in the boat. "What's wrong?" she asked, her face pale as a ghost.

"I felt something," Oliver said, spitting water out of his mouth.

He started swimming forwards again and, whatever had been beneath him, was no longer there. His heartbeat kicked up a notch as his mind conjured terrifying images of creatures beneath the water.

"Get out of the lake!" Anna shouted, staring wildly around him as if she expected to see a monster. "Come on. *Swim*," she encouraged, leaning over the boat with her arms outstretched towards him.

Rogan clung on to the side and Oliver reached him in a few, short bursts of forward stroke."I'll boost you up," Rogan said.

Oliver nodded and reached up to the side of the boat. The girls gripped his arms and Rogan pushed him. He landed in the boat awkwardly, twisted around into a kneeling position and leant out to help pull Rogan in.

He gripped the back of Rogan's wetsuit and hauled him upwards. Rogan was almost out of the water when he cried out and began slipping through Oliver's grip as he was tugged back down.

"ROGAN!" Quinn screamed and gripped his arm as tightly as she could.

"PULL ME OUT!" Rogan roared, digging his nails into Oliver's shoulder. A long, greyish green tentacle was snaking up and around Rogan's body. It curled upwards and slithered around his throat.

"*No, no, no,*" Oliver said through gritted teeth, pulling harder so his arms wrenched in their sockets.

Another slimy tentacle launched out of the water and wrapped around Oliver's wrist, then another and another, all latching onto his arms. The tentacles stung and burned where they touched making him almost release Rogan.

Oliver forced himself to grip tighter and his face contorted from the pain.

Quinn let go of Rogan, sending Oliver lurching forward a foot. He was about to shout at her for letting go when he saw her ripping the tentacles away. He felt arms encircle his waist and tug at his shoulders as May and Anna helped to hold him in place.

Oliver yanked Rogan as hard as he possibly could, making a noise of exertion in his throat. The tugging stopped abruptly as Quinn snatched away the last tentacle. Rogan was hoisted up into the boat and fell on top of them in a heap.

"Let's get out of here. *Now*," Rogan said, forcing himself up on to the bench with the oar already in his hand.

They returned to their positions and started rowing as hard as they could. Oliver's vision became blurry and he wasn't sure whether it was from exhaustion or from the stings on his arms.

He blinked away the water that had gathered in his eyes and looked down at Rogan's legs. His wetsuit was ripped and his skin was blotted with raised, red patches. His own arms were covered with smaller versions of the same thing and they burned like a fire was licking at his skin.

"You alright?" Oliver asked through heavy panting.

Rogan nodded but his face was pale and he looked dizzy and weak.

"I see the island. Keep going straight ahead," May said with a sigh of relief.

They got within a stone's throw of the beach and Oliver and Quinn jumped out to pull the boat up to the shore, the pain in his arms beginning to dull. Oliver counted eleven other boats already on the beach.

"We're in twelfth place. We have to move!" Oliver said, starting forwards.

"Wait a second, will you?" Quinn said.

Oliver turned back to see Rogan hobbling forward onto the beach.

"Dammit, I could heal this if I was allowed to use magic," Rogan said, wincing in pain.

"What the hell *was* that thing?" May asked, staring at Rogan's red legs, revealed beneath his torn suit. She rushed forward to support him.

"Damn luggerfish," Rogan said, ripping away the rest of the material that was pressing on his legs as he sat down on the beach.

"What's a luggerfish?" Oliver asked.

"It's got a long body covered in a tough shell and tentacles. Seriously gross," Rogan said.

"Yeah I noticed the tentacles," Oliver said, rubbing the stings on his arms.

Anna rushed to him and ran her hand gently over the bumps. She looked up at him with concern burning in her eyes.

"I'm alright," Oliver said and felt a warmth spread through him.

"I would have been a gonner without you guys," Rogan said with a grin. "I think I'll be alright in a minute. They've got venom in their tentacles but it's already wearing off. How's yours Oliver?"

"Yeah the pain's pretty much gone now," he replied, running his fingers over the welts.

"Shall we go?" May suggested.

They nodded. Oliver turned back towards the tree line at the top of the beach and started walking.

"Wait!" Anna called to them and they looked back at her. "There are boxes here for each of the teams."

Oliver noticed them now, large wooden chests running along the beach with the team names inscribed upon them. Many of them had been opened and soaking wetsuits lay inside.

"It must be a change of clothes," May said, looking around for their box and pointing when she spotted it.

It was padlocked.

"We don't have a key," Oliver said, looking up at the others.

"Wait, check your packs," Anna said, starting to rifle through hers.

They all swung the packs around off their backs and looked inside. Oliver took a quick swig of water after finding nothing in his bag.

"Here, it's in mine," May said, running forward with her hand outstretched.

She dropped to her knees and unlocked the box. Outfits the same as the previous day's were inside. May quickly passed them out to everyone and Oliver was half way through changing when Anna shrieked, "We have to change in front of everyone? We're being filmed!"

"Here," Quinn said, fishing out a couple of towels from the bottom of the box and holding one up for her. May took the other and stood opposite Quinn so the towels formed a circle. Anna smiled with relief and the girls changed one by one between them.

Rogan and Oliver were ready first. Oliver was grateful for the warm, dry material against his cold skin and felt ready to carry on.

No more boats had appeared since they had landed at the beach which was encouraging. They headed up towards the thick woodland with a renewed determination. There were several routes heading up the mountain all splitting off through the trees.

"Which one?" Oliver asked, glancing back at his friends.

"We're behind so better choose the quickest route," Rogan said thoughtfully.

"And how do we know which one that is?" Anna asked.

"The steepest," May said, pointing at a path that climbed up at a sharper angle than the others.

Rogan raised his eyebrows at her as they marched forward

"Larkin's team are already ahead of us," Quinn said angrily, pointing back at the boat marked *Visikin.*

"Then we better catch them up," Rogan said with a confident grin.

28

Encounter

They climbed the steep incline through the forest, occasionally stopping to catch their breath or help each other up a particularly difficult ascent. Parts of the route were so steep that they had to crawl on their hands and knees, dragging themselves up with tree roots and rocks that jutted from the muddy ground. Despite this, they were making good time though they hadn't seen any sign of the other teams.

They finally reached a clearing in the woodland. It was bordered by trees at one edge and the other ended in a steep cliff that looked back out across the lake. They paused to rest a moment, taking a snack from their bags. Oliver devoured an energy bar that was overly sweet and chewy but immediately helped him recover from the climb.

May walked towards the edge of the cliff, stretching her back. "Woah," she said and the others followed her to have a look at the view.

The island was much larger than he had first thought. They were about two thirds of the way up the mountain now and he could see the small beach where they had left their boat, far below them.

He spied several more boats lined up next to their's, meaning more teams couldn't be far behind. He looked out at the lake to see a swirling mist located solely in between the shore and the island.

"It's magic," Quinn said in realisation.

"What about those Lugger things?" May asked.

"I don't know. I mean, I know they live in lakes but those things were after us," Anna said.

"Maybe not after you. I noticed you kept pretty dry," Oliver teased and she grinned at him.

"We need to keep going," May said.

Oliver nodded. "We still haven't passed any of the other teams. What if they've already finished?" Panic broke through him.

"Don't worry. They won't have finished yet. We've made good time up the mountain and they all took different routes anyway. We can still catch them," Rogan said, though Oliver detected concern in his voice.

A rustling in the trees made them turn and Larkin's sneering face appeared, surrounded by the rest of his team.

"Well, hello, fancy seeing you here," Larkin said to the sniggering of his friends.

"Shove off, Larkin," Rogan said, rolling his eyes. "Let's go," he said quietly to the others.

They started forward in an attempt to go around the Visikins but Larkin moved to block their way and placed a hand on Rogan's chest.

"Take your hand off of me," Rogan said calmly.

"What are you gonna do if I don't? Can't use magic, it's against the rules," Larkin said, squaring up to him.

"So is ambushing other teams," Anna snapped.

Larkin took his hand away and held both of them up as if to prove he wasn't doing anything wrong.

"No one's ambushing. I just heard you coming up behind us and thought I'd come say hello to my friend." He moved towards Quinn who stepped away from him.

Kuti rolled her eyes from behind him. "Larkin I actually want to win a key. Can we go?"

"In a minute," Larkin dismissed her. "What's the matter Quinny baby? Come give me a kiss." Quinn squirmed as the boy's on his team roared with laughter.

"Back off," Oliver said, stepping towards Larkin. "We need to get on with the race."

Larkin's eyes snapped to Oliver's with a look of pure venom as his friend Arrow sidled up beside him. "Shut it, Earthy."

"Or what? You touch any of us and you'll be disqualified," Oliver said, glaring at the boy.

Larkin was in his face in half a second. He was so close that Oliver could smell his hot breath but he didn't blink.

"Go on," Oliver said, daring him. "Or is just girls you like to attack?"

Larkin frowned.

Oliver felt Rogan's presence beside him and that of Larkin's team closing in. No one wanted to make a move in case they were penalised. A crack of thunder broke their attention and Larkin's eyes slid to the sky. Oliver could tell it took everything the boy had to pull himself away and turn his back on them.

"Come on, we can get them once we win. Once the cameras have stopped rolling," Arrow said, smirking at Oliver.

"You're right," Larkin said, starting back towards the tree line.

Larkin's team lingered a moment longer before following him back to the forest but Arrow remained, cracking his knuckles at Oliver. They held eye contact until the boy finally backed down, turned and disappeared into the trees. Oliver's heart was hammering and he let out a shuddering breath to help calm his anger.

He looked to his friends, ready to rant about how much he hated Larkin, when a clap of thunder sounded again and rain poured from the sky in torrents.

"Come on. Let's get going," Oliver spoke loudly over the clamour of raindrops.

"If we run I bet we can pass them," Rogan said with a glint in his eye.

Before he could answer, a vibration in the air sent a wave of ice through Oliver. It was a feeling he had only ever felt once in his life. And one he had hoped never to feel again. The presence of a vark.

29

Bloodthirsty

It looked completely different to the one Oliver had seen before but he knew it had to be a creature of Vale. The vark stood as tall as the trees behind it, rainwater running down its body in rivulets. Its head was shaped almost like a wolf's but its snout was turned up at the end into a pointed nose and numerous fangs hung out of its jaw in a constant snarl.

Its eyes were like shadows with a thin, red slit for pupils that flitted from side to side, taking in its surroundings. Its arms were overly long and hung down to the ground, dragging enormous, curved claws behind it.

Its stance made its chest jut out to show protruding ribs as if the creature was starving to death. Its bottom half reminded Oliver of a giant ape as it stepped forward slowly, trailing its forearms behind it.

The others shouted out in shock. They began backing away towards the cliff in fear. May ran to Oliver's side and the two of them took several steps backwards away from the creature. The vark hadn't seen them yet and was distracted by something behind it. Oliver realised, with a sick feeling, that Larkin and his teammates were screaming.

The creature swung its arms around at them. Its claws ripped trees fully out of the ground and threw them aside to try and reach them.

Their screams retreated further into the trees and the vark gave up trying to force its way through the dense foliage, twisting around to face Oliver and his friends instead.

It set its blood-red eyes on them and let out a guttural roar that reverberated through Oliver's ears. All of them stumbled backwards, closer to the cliff edge.

"Is this part of the challenge?" Anna shouted over the thundering wind and rain that whipped about them.

"No!" Oliver shouted at the same time Rogan did. Oliver met his eye and saw that his friend knew what the creature was.

Rogan nodded and hurried towards Quinn, talking close to her ear. Her eyes widened in fright then she nodded and a steely determination crossed her features.

"Keep behind us!" Quinn shouted, the rain making her hair cling to her face.

Oliver, Anna and May took a step back as Quinn and Rogan moved steadily toward the vark, peeling the gloves from their hands and discarding them on the ground.

Rogan raised his arms and fire poured from his hands, searing the vark's arm as it swung towards them. The flames lit the scene with red and orange as it pummelled the vark's body. The creature roared in outrage but the fire didn't seem to be damaging it.

As the vark stepped closer, its claws buried deep into the ground behind it, digging up a mountain of earth as it progressed. It left a trail of black fire in the great gouges it tore through the ground that burned relentlessly despite the rain.

The vark's arms swung forward abruptly and a ball of the black fire hurled through the air towards them. Oliver, May and Anna dove forward onto the ground and Oliver felt wind rush over him as the fireball missed them by inches.

When he looked up, he saw Rogan and Quinn sending a tumult of electricity at the vark, causing it to roar in fury. The vark slowed under the attack but continued to ready another ball of the black fire that was caged in its palm by colossal claws. It swung the fireball and Oliver shouted for everyone to move as he and May dove to the left and Anna went to the right, leaving a large gap between them.

Oliver saw Quinn crumple to the floor in the corner of his eye and began to panic. It was only a matter of time before the vark was on top of them. His heart thumped against his chest as if it were fighting to get out. He leapt to his feet in a mad fury and waved his arms at the creature, luring it away from his friends.

It swivelled its ugly head towards him and locked its dark eyes upon him. Its lips were quivering and drool was pouring out between pointed teeth. It stepped towards him, leaving massive footprints in the wet mud. Oliver's plan was working but he hadn't thought any further ahead and his mind wouldn't kick into gear.

He glanced at Rogan who was running toward them, blasting the vark's head with a stream of lightning that sparked and cracked with blue and silver light. Anna was cradling Quinn on the ground and Oliver thought he could see blood. He ran forward in an attempt to reach them but the vark's clawed foot slammed down between them, blocking his friends from view.

Time seemed to stand still as the creature turned back towards Rogan who had closed the distance between them.

"Wait-!" Oliver tried to warn Rogan as the vark's enormous arm swung backwards and struck Rogan in the chest, sending him flying through the air. He landed hard on his back, unmoving.

"NO!" Oliver roared and ran towards him.

The vark's arm hurtled towards Oliver and he fell to the ground to duck the blow, missing him by centimetres.

He glanced back at May who was at the cliff's edge and saw the soft mud beginning to slide away beneath her.

"WATCH OUT!" Oliver cried to her but the words were lost over the sound of a bellowing roar from the vark.

The rain soaked him to the bone and he watched helplessly as his world fell apart around him.

Instinct kicked in.

He jumped to his feet and dove towards his sister as the beast's claws ripped through the ground he had just vacated.

The vark flung an arm at Oliver, colliding with his chest. The force of it sent him flying through the air. He was unable to breathe until he smashed into the muddy ground.

He slid to the edge of the cliff next to May, her fingernails clawing at the soft ground as she tried to stop herself from falling over the edge that was just feet behind them. Oliver started drifting backwards and dug his nails in to stop himself.

Oliver let go with one hand and reached out desperately towards May as they continued to slide backwards towards the cliff edge. She lifted a hand and her fingers grazed the tips of his.

The vark leered over them and stamped a clawed foot down hard in front of them, just inches away. Oliver felt the earth beneath them slipping and sliding away. He lunged and gripped May's hand and they clambered upwards, fiercely fighting against the disintegrating cliff edge but it was too late.

Oliver gasped but couldn't draw air as the ground disappeared beneath him and in one swift, terrifying moment they tumbled over the cliff.

Oliver lost sight of May as he fell through the canopy of a tree. He shouted out in terror as he fell, the branches ripping at his clothes and tearing at his skin. He hit solid ground again but it was so steep that he couldn't stop falling. He tumbled, feeling rocks bash his body on the descent as he rolled over and over.

He dug his feet in and scrabbled frantically at the soil, clawing for purchase. The ground disappeared once more and he fell at an alarming rate towards the woodland beneath him. He saw flashes of green leaves below and grey clouds above, then his head collided with something hard and darkness swooped in and consumed him.

Oliver's eyes flickered open. He had been out cold but sensed that it hadn't been for more than a minute.

His body was twisted around a tree that was growing at an angle out of the sloping ground. His head felt bruised and his entire body ached. He swung himself around and slid the last few feet to the bottom of the cliff. His hands shook from shock and he spotted cuts and bruises all up his arms where the material from his jumpsuit had torn away.

He slowly took in his surroundings, finding himself submerged in a dense forest but he couldn't see May anywhere.

"MAY? WHERE ARE YOU?" he shouted desperately. He listened as hard as he could. Everything was silent. He no matter how hard he strained his ears, he couldn't hear any noise coming from up on the cliff.

He set his jaw. As soon as he found May he would get help for the others.

The rain was easing now and the *drip drip drip* of it falling through the canopy was the only sound he could hear. He got to his feet and pushed his way through the foliage where the trees were spread further apart.

"May? Are you here?" he tried again, his breathing ragged.

Nothing.

His clothes were soaked through and he shivered in the cold, his heart hammering uncontrollably in his chest.

Then he saw her: a crumpled heap hidden by overhanging leaves. He pulled her out into a clearing and rolled her on to her back.

"You're not dead," he said out loud to try and convince himself. "May?" He shook her gently, then again more firmly.

"Olly?" Her voice was faint but she was alive.

He hugged her to his chest, feeling relief flood him.

"You're okay, we fell over the cliff but you're okay. Can you stand?" Oliver got up and held out a hand to her.

She nodded and stood up on wobbly legs.

"The others. What happened? We have to get back to them," May said in a panic, craning her head to try and see up the cliff through the thick trees.

"I don't know. We need to get help. We can't climb back up, it's too steep," he said, his voice shaking.

"Okay, let's go around." May set off through the trees, stumbling a little as Oliver hurried after her.

They had only been walking for a minute or so before the trees opened up, making the ground easier to navigate. The forest was silent but for their squelching footsteps.

He felt a chill creep up his spine and gripped May's arm to stop her, sensing that something was wrong.

The quiet of the forest was pressing in on him. He heard the *crack* of a twig from behind and spun around to find a man standing there.

Oliver sighed in relief at the sight of Truvian Gold. "Oh thank God," he said, walking towards him. "Did you see what happened? Is everyone okay?"

"It's unlikely," Truvian said calmly.

Oliver frowned at the man's demeanour. "Well, can you show us the way out of here?"

"We need to get help!" May snapped and Truvian's eyes slid to hers.

"I came to see you," Truvian said, keeping his eyes trained on May.

"*What?*" she said, glancing at Oliver in frustration.

Truvian reached inside his leather jacket and retrieved a long, slender knife. Oliver recoiled at the sight of the blade and his instincts told him to run but instead he stepped closer to May.

The knife was unlike anything Oliver had ever seen. It appeared to be comprised of shadowy black and purple smoke, but at the same time looked incredibly sharp. The hilt allowed Truvian's fingers to pass through it for grip.

"W-What are you doing?" May stammered in fear, reaching for Oliver's wrist. Her cold fingers clasped his skin like a vice.

Truvian ran a fingertip along the blunt edge of the blade and gazed at May with an intense, animalistic stare that set Oliver's heart pounding.

"I'd like you to know that I don't *want* to do this. This is so much bigger than you both," Truvian said, his voice like ice.

"What do you mean? What are you going to do?" May asked as her fingernails dug into Oliver's skin.

"I've been sent to kill you, May," Truvian said, taking a step closer.

The words rung in Oliver's ears and his breath halted in his lungs. He and May stepped backwards at once, keeping the distance between Truvian and them. Oliver knew he needed to stall the man, he had to buy them some time to escape but his mind was solely focused on the sharp blade that was pointed in their direction.

"Who sent you?" Oliver blurted, tugging May backwards another few steps.

Truvian smiled, seemingly enjoying his position of power as he took another, slow step toward them. "You wouldn't believe me if I told you."

"Try me," Oliver snarled. Part of him expected to hear Rimori's name, he couldn't imagine anyone else that might have a vendetta against them but was thrown by Truvian's answer.

"Your father, William Knight," Truvian said, a smug smile tugging at the corner of his mouth.

Oliver was frozen rigid as May pulled him backwards once more. His foot caught on a root and his mind kicked into gear as he stumbled, righting himself in a heartbeat.

"He's trying to distract you," May muttered but Oliver was too curious to ignore Truvian's words.

"What do you mean? My father's dead," Oliver said, trying to keep his voice from shaking.

Truvian shook his head and moved closer once more, passing the knife from hand to hand as if deciding which one felt best for when he attacked. "I know him quite well. In fact, he's been helping me plan this little ambush for a while."

"Don't listen to him, he's *lying*," May hissed.

Oliver wanted to face his sister, to look into her eyes and know whether she truly believed her own words. But he couldn't remove his gaze from the blade in case it gave Truvian the opportunity to strike.

"You think I'm lying, of course," Truvian said, raising a single eyebrow.

"Of course you're lying!" May shouted furiously, dragging Oliver backwards another few steps.

Truvian advanced, the smile dropping from his face. He pointed the tip of the knife at May as he spoke. "Keep your mouth *shut*. This is the third time we've tried to kill you, girl. And this time I'm not going to fail."

"But you helped May last night after she was attacked!" Oliver burst out.

"I only helped because there were so many witnesses around. It was William who attacked her, you know? She'd be dead already if *you* hadn't shown up."

"But why do you want me dead?" May breathed.

"I'm following orders," Truvian said with a shrug.

"From my father?" Oliver snapped.

Truvian's mouth curved up in a knowing smirk, making Oliver's skin crawl. "Yes, but not just him. William's orders come from the top of the chain, from Isaac Rimori."

Oliver stepped backwards and felt his spine press up against a tree trunk. He glanced at May in a panic then realised his mistake as Truvian laughed a short, triumphant laugh then lunged toward them, slashing the blade through the air.

Oliver forced May out of the way and charged toward Truvian, glancing a blow from the man's shoulder and throwing Oliver off balance. Truvian shot past him and powered towards May with the knife held out in one hand.

"RUN!" Oliver yelled as he began hurtling after Truvian.

The adrenalin in his veins and the thought of losing May made his legs work harder than they had in his entire life. May was still ahead but Truvian was only a few feet behind her, darting through the trees so Oliver lost sight of them intermittently.

Truvian leapt, his arms fully outstretched, with the knife clamped in one hand. He dragged May to the ground. They slid forward and May's head collided with the trunk of a tree, knocking her unconscious.

Oliver was on Truvian in seconds, ripping him away from her before he had a chance to use the knife. He stamped on the man's hand so the blade came free. Oliver lunged for it but Truvian grabbed his leg and he fell, face first, onto the muddy ground.

Oliver kicked out and felt his foot connect with Truvian's face, making him shout out in pain. He rolled over and glanced around for the knife amongst the debris on the forest floor, hearing a scuffle of footsteps behind him.

A deep, cruel laugh rang in Oliver's ears. He twisted around and spotted the knife with a pang of fear; it was held up high above him in Truvian's hand. Truvian grimaced at him, his cheekbone swollen and dirty where Oliver's boot had connected with it. Oliver scrambled away as fast as he could, his fingers sinking into the soft earth behind him as he moved.

Truvian rushed forward and gripped the material at Oliver's chest, yanking him upwards so his face was just inches from his own and spoke through gritted teeth. "Your death isn't part of the plan. Just give up the girl."

"Never," Oliver spat back and kicked out again.

His foot connected with Truvian's shin, making him release Oliver so he collapsed back down to the ground. Oliver rolled onto his knees and tried to crawl away but Truvian grabbed his hair, forcing the side of his face down into the wet leaves and mud. Truvian's knee dug into his spine, pinning him to the ground.

The cold blade pressed against Oliver's throat and his whole body stilled. His breathing came in short bursts through clenched teeth. All he could think of was May nearby and how she would be next if he died.

Truvian leant over Oliver's ear and pressed his knee down, making him groan in pain. Oliver wriggled as hard as he could but couldn't find the strength to push Truvian away.

Truvian's voice hissed in his ears. "You have been the thorn in my side ever since Rimori sent me to kill the girl. He's waiting to hear from me. He sent that vark as a distraction to give me time alone with her as he did back in the pod tunnels. But here you are again, always standing between her and her fate."

Truvian pressed the blade harder to Oliver's throat and he felt it begin to pierce the skin. He could barely register any pain, his beating heart was pumping too much adrenalin through his veins.

Oliver heard May groan as she regained consciousness and was filled with a surge of determination, forcing himself upwards with all the energy he could muster. But he couldn't escape. He closed his eyes, sure he was about to die.

Truvian froze in a gasp of pain and the weight of him left Oliver's body in one, swift movement. Oliver rolled on to his back and saw Truvian lying in a heap a few feet away.

Rogan stood above him, a red flame burning like a beacon in his outstretched palm. It extinguished and he rushed forwards. Oliver spotted a shadow of movement in his periphery and cried out in alarm as he spotted Truvian staggering towards May, dragging her up in front of him. She screamed out as he forced the blade up to her neck.

Oliver scrambled to his feet in a panic.

"Don't you dare hurt her," Rogan growled.

There was a mad glint in Truvian's eye and he licked his lips.

Rogan raised his palms defensively.

"Ah, ah, ah. I wouldn't try anything, Rogan. You wouldn't want my hand to accidentally, *slip.*" He jabbed the knife at her neck and Oliver flinched, feeling fear flood every inch of his body.

May let out a small squeak. Truvian crouched slightly, pulling her head backwards towards him so his face was partially covered by her blonde hair, using her as a shield.

"What do you want?" Oliver practically shouted.

"I want the girl dead, of course. But if I kill her now, you'll kill me. And I can't have that." He tutted at them, shaking his head.

"Then you might as well let her go," Rogan tried, fire flaring in his hands once more.

"Ha," Truvian laughed sarcastically. "I don't think so." He backed away from them, dragging May along in front of him.

"Why would Rimori send you to kill my sister?" Oliver asked, trying to understand the connection.

"May's death is the key to Rimori's success," Truvian said. "He's going to change everything. He's going to unite the seven worlds under his commanding rule."

"And what does my sister dying have to do with that?" Oliver demanded, taking a tentative step towards them.

"Everything and nothing," Truvian said, clearly enjoying the power he held over them all. "She's a loose end I'm simply tying up."

A brief flash of movement caught Oliver's attention behind Truvian and his eyes flicked over his shoulder.

With a surge of hope, Oliver spotted Quinn standing there supported by Anna who had her arm looped around her shoulders. Quinn's face was pale and her body was covered in blood. She held up a shaking, bloody palm towards Truvian and Oliver forced his eyes back to his face, not wanting to give her away.

It was too late. Truvian spotted the glance and span around, pushing May away from him. Quinn released a powerful surge of magic but it missed its target, instead engulfing May in a flash of white light for an agonising moment, before she crumpled to the floor. Truvian bolted into the trees and Oliver ran as hard as he could after him.

Anger burned inside him like nothing he had ever experienced. He wanted Truvian dead, ripped apart. Branches whipped his face, and caught his clothes. The man was getting too far ahead of him and his legs burned with the effort.

"STOP!" Oliver roared his frustration, knowing it was pointless.

Truvian's victorious laughter floated back to him then it was abruptly cut off. He reached the spot where Truvian must have just been but he was gone, vanished as if into thin air. Oliver searched the area as thoroughly as he could but Truvian had somehow escaped.

Oliver ran back to his friends and fell to the floor by May who was pulled up into Rogan's lap. Quinn collapsed to the ground beside them, exhausted, pulling Anna down with her.

Rogan had a palm rested on May's forehead sending green light out of it to heal her, his face a picture of concentration. But it wasn't working.

"She won't wake up," Rogan hissed. "I'm drained from fighting the vark, I don't have enough energy."

"We need help. Someone get help!" Oliver cried, pulling May into his arms.

Rogan got to his feet and, without a word, charged off into the forest.

30

Hopeless

May and Quinn were suspended in the air on stretchers as they were carried back through the forest by a team of medics. Oliver walked next to May, gripping her lifeless hand. Blankets were wrapped tightly around her but her lips were turning blue. She looked so small and vulnerable it practically broke his heart.

Oliver was completely numb, his mind in a daze. He barely registered the brambles and thorns scraping at his body with every step, determined to stay next to May no matter how much more difficult the path was made for him.

Rogan and Anna walked together in between the two stretchers, talking in low murmurs. After an age, they emerged at the top of a hill that sloped away into a small village. The ground became even and widened into a well-worn path.

They took off at a fast pace and found a series of first aid tents on the outskirts of the village. May and Quinn were rushed straight into one and Oliver, Rogan and Anna followed.

A nurse tended the superficial wounds Oliver had received from the ordeal. By some miracle he had avoided serious injury when falling down the cliff but his ribs were badly bruised from the impact with the vark's arm. He winced as the nurse ran her fingers down his side but he didn't care about the pain, he just stared at May in horror.

After Anna had been tended to, she came and sat with him. Her presence was warm and comforting and she gripped his hand tightly. He couldn't say anything to her but the look she gave him told him he didn't have to.

Two mages were brought in to tend to May. The blast she had received from Quinn had sent her body into shock. They spent a long time running their hands over her body, again and again, projecting different coloured light up and down her until, finally, one of the mages broke away and approached Oliver.

Oliver gripped Anna's hand so tightly he was sure it was hurting but he couldn't let go.

The kindly-looking mage gazed at him with empathy as she spoke. "She's going to be alright. She should wake up soon." She patted his shoulder then walked away.

Oliver released a breath and let go of Anna's hand as he sunk his face into his palms, the tightness in his chest releasing. He felt Anna's arm slide over his back and he turned himself, pulling her into a tight embrace, resting his chin on her shoulder.

They got up a moment later and pulled chairs to the side of May's bed. Oliver gripped her hand and was comforted to find it warm at last.

He looked over to Quinn who was already upright in her bed. Rogan was sitting with her, holding her hand. She looked over and smiled at them then winced in pain.

"Is everything okay?" Oliver asked.

"It's where the fire from the vark hit her. It won't heal properly," Rogan said to them as a mage pressed his hand to Quinn's side again.

She lay back in her bed and looked over at them. "I'm so sorry Oliver. I was aiming for Truvian. It all happened so fast," Quinn said in a fluster, tears filling her eyes.

"It's not your fault. You were trying to help. He's the one who's to blame," Oliver said, hatred coursing through his body.

"Don't think about that now," Anna whispered to him and his anger ebbed away as he met her dark eyes.

"Let me through. *Right now*," Ely's voice sounded from outside the tent. He rushed in with Laura at his side and they flew over to May.

"Wh-what happened?" Ely asked in a shaky voice.

"Is she alright?" Laura asked, gripping May's arm.

Oliver explained about the vark and Truvian Gold and, when he was finished, Ely and Laura's faces were twisted into shocked expressions.

"What? What do you mean? A *vark*?" Laura asked frantically.

"That's not possible. And Truvian Gold? That celebrity fellow?" Ely questioned in a tumble of words.

Oliver's head started to pound. "Yes, a vark appeared at the top of the cliff and forced me and May over the edge of it. Truvian was waiting for us at the bottom. He attacked us." Oliver could barely keep his voice down, his breathing becoming erratic once more.

"Alright, calm down. Did anyone else see the vark but your team?" Ely asked.

"Yes, Larkin's team was there. They ran away," Oliver said.

"Wasn't it all filmed on the survision?" Anna asked.

"It will have been. They probably didn't want it broadcast to the worlds," Ely said thoughtfully.

"Did Larkin's team see Truvian, too?" Laura asked in a serious tone.

"No, that was just us. Truvian ran off. Maybe someone can still catch him?" Oliver suggested.

"Catch him? I only saw him a few minutes ago down in the village," Laura said with a confused expression.

Oliver's brow furrowed, trying to understand what she was telling him. "What? He can't have been. He ran off into the forest. He disappeared into thin air. Why would he still be here? *He attacked us!*"

A couple of the medics turned their attention to Oliver but he didn't care.

"I don't know but I think the sooner I go and talk to the Race Committee, the better," Laura said, getting to her feet. "I'll return here as soon as I've spoken to someone. The medics will give you something to eat if you ask them, you look like the undead."

Oliver nodded as she exited the tent. His brain was almost as exhausted as his body. He squeezed May's hand again and she groaned. Her eyelids fluttered open and Oliver's heart skipped a beat.

"You're awake. Are you okay? How are you feeling?" he asked anxiously.

"Like I got hit by a truck," May mumbled.

Oliver laughed with relief.

"What's a truck?" Anna asked with a frown and May grinned sleepily.

Rogan looked over, placing Quinn's hand gently down on the bed. He joined them and planted a kiss on May's forehead. "You scared the crap outta us," he said, his mouth hooking up at one corner.

"Aww," May said quietly as her eyelids drooped.

"You can rest as much as you need to," Ely said with a look that was full of emotion.

May's eyelids fluttered a few more times before they closed completely.

Oliver sighed and sat back in his chair. The crushing fear in his chest finally ebbed away and he felt like he could breathe again. Exhaustion gripped him and he sagged in his chair a little. Anna and Rogan looked as tired as he felt. Their eyes were puffy and dark circles hung beneath them.

"You need to get some rest too," Ely said softly. "Laura's staying in a cottage down in the village, you can all go there to get some sleep."

They stumbled their way through the village following Ely. Oliver felt his rage at Truvian Gold itching at the back of his mind. But he didn't want to think about what had happened and what it all meant just then. First, he needed to sleep.

He and Rogan finally crashed into beds made up on the floor for them in Laura's cottage. Oliver was so grateful to have a pillow beneath his head that he wanted to turn around and kiss it. Instead, he passed out into oblivion.

The final, fluttering, hopeless, terrifying thought that crossed through his mind was that they hadn't placed in the race and his only chance of getting May to Brinatin was gone.

31

Bittersweet

Oliver awoke and pushed himself up into a sitting position, gritting his teeth against the pain coursing through him. The mage had cured the wounds on the surface of his body but his muscles had grown stiff and sore overnight. He rolled over and his hand hit something soft.

"Ouch, watch it," Rogan groaned as he woke up.

"Oh, sorry," Oliver said.

A dim light lit the room which Oliver realised was coming from his friend's hand. Oliver could see a pair of net curtains concealing a window. It was still dark outside. He groaned as he rearranged and his muscles resisted the movement.

"You alright, man?" Rogan asked.

"Just stiff as hell," Oliver said with a sigh of relief as his head sank back into the pillow.

Rogan rolled over, reaching a hand towards him. Oliver frowned.

"Don't go getting the wrong idea. I know how irresistible I can be," Rogan said with a smirk.

Oliver rolled sideways and punched him despite the pain it caused. He laughed at Rogan's expression and ducked backwards as he launched a counter attack.

"You want me to heal you, or what?" Rogan asked with a laugh and green light ignited in his palm. He touched Oliver's arm, letting the light ebb out over his body. It felt like warm water was seeping through his skin and reaching into his muscles, making them relax. The pain ceased.

"You're a lifesaver," Oliver said, stretching his arms above his head, enjoying the restored flexibility.

"Yeah, I know," Rogan said through a yawn.

Oliver yawned heavily in response. The soft pillow was calling to him again but his head was beginning to buzz with unanswered questions.

"Do you reckon they've arrested Truvian by now?" Oliver asked.

"Yeah, must have," Rogan said.

"Laura said she saw him down in the village after we got back to the first aid tents. Why wouldn't he run for it?" Oliver wondered.

"Maybe he knew they'd catch him anyway?" Rogan suggested.

"Or he's hoping no one will believe us," Oliver said, concern creeping up on him.

"There's five of us and one of him, course they'll believe us," Rogan said.

His confidence calmed Oliver's anxiety. "Plus he has a bruise on his face where I kicked him," he said with some satisfaction.

"Yeah, he might have had a mage heal that up though. Anyway, we can go straight to Abbicus Brown in the morning," Rogan said, his voice becoming sleepy.

"Hey, err, Rogan?" Oliver said after a moment.

"Mmm?"

"Thanks for saving our lives and all, you know." He was terrible at thanking people.

"No problem, man."

Oliver lay awake thinking over the events of the previous day and, at some point, sleep took him again.

* * *

"Wake up, wake up!" Anna's voice called through the door.

Oliver opened his eyes to find light filtering in through the net curtains. He sat up next to Rogan who was squinting against the daylight.

"Just a sec," Rogan called as he got to his feet.

Oliver got up to put some clothes on and Anna burst through the door. "Oh, sorry," she said, shielding her eyes and backing out of the room. "Come outside when you're dressed."

"Imagine if we burst in on the girls like that?" Rogan said in mock outrage.

"It's not the same!" Anna called through the door in a sing-song voice.

"Oi, get out of here!" Oliver called back to her, grinning at the sound of her laughter disappearing down the corridor outside.

They dressed and exited the room, weaving through the narrow corridors in the tiny cottage. Oliver opened the front door and they ducked through the small frame, finding everyone gathered out in the small garden.

A few other houses were dotted around under the shadow of the rising mountain on the island. Oliver thought he could see the cliff where they had encountered the vark the day before; the memory seemed like a horrible nightmare that had never really happened.

Ely was there with Abbicus Brown and the girls were standing around them. He and Rogan joined the group and Oliver was pleased with how well May looked, if perhaps just a little pale. He touched her shoulder and she broke into a relieved smile at the sight of him.

Abbicus Brown stepped towards Oliver. "Ely's been telling me what happened and he's made some very serious accusations. We are fully aware of the vark's presence on the cliff. We caught most of its attack on camera but what's been said about a certain guest commentator is beyond my belief. Now, Mr Knight, Miss Knight I would like to talk to you both in private," Abbicus Brown said sternly, walking past them into the house.

Oliver and May followed him through to the small, country kitchen.

"Are you alright?" Oliver whispered to her.

She nodded as they took a seat opposite Abbicus at a wooden table.

"So, I'd like you to go through the *exact* events that transpired after you fell over the cliff," Abbicus instructed without any empathy.

"You mean when that *thing* forced us over the edge of it," May corrected.

"Yes, yes. Please be patient with me, Miss Knight, I've had an extremely long night with all of this."

Oliver noticed the bags under his eyes that had been badly disguised with a dab of powder.

"Sorry you're tired," May said sarcastically. "But there are worse things."

Oliver nodded, resting his elbows on the solid, greyish wood of the table.

"If you could just begin," Abbicus said, sounding exasperated.

Oliver took the lead and explained what had happened in as much detail as he remembered.

He couldn't read anything from Abbicus's expression. There was no hint of surprise at the mention of Truvian's name or that Rimori had sent the vark as a distraction. Oliver neglected to mention that Truvian had insisted his father was alive, unsure whether he believed it himself.

When he finished, Oliver could feel his anger rising but took a deep breath to keep a level head.

Abbicus shook his head making his jowls wobble. "Well, whilst that's a fascinating story, Mr Knight, I'm afraid to tell you that Mr Gold was commentating with Ray Falls at the time you say he was attacking you in the forest. We have a hundred cameras as well as a very large crowd of people to confirm that."

May blinked in surprise and Oliver slammed his fist down on the table. "That's not possible," he snapped, certain that Abbicus had got his facts wrong somehow.

"The way I see it, either you two have some unknown, personal vendetta against the man *or* you both imagined the whole thing."

Oliver was on his feet with a screech of wood as his chair slid backwards. "Firstly, our friends: Rogan, Quinn, and Anna *all* saw him and, secondly, why would we imagine the exact same thing? That's ridiculous."

"I'm sure your friends would go along with you if you asked them to. Otherwise, you could discredit your whole team," Abbicus said.

"And I suppose you think we planned the vark as well? To come and push us off a cliff?" May growled, also getting to her feet.

Abbicus tutted. "Of course not, that's impossible. The appearance of the vark was a very rare, very unfortunate event that couldn't be foreseen. *No one* can control them, not even Isaac Rimori. I can see you aren't going to be truthful about what really happened. Perhaps you are even truly convinced it did but, I warn you now, if you push this matter, you won't win. Truvian Gold is a highly respected man and, as I said, the whole world witnessed him standing up on that stage when he supposedly attacked you."

Oliver's head was reeling. He had imagined Truvian locked up and shamed for what he had done. He couldn't understand how he had managed it.

"What if one of them was an imposter?" Oliver blurted, convinced it was the only explanation.

"My boy, you really must stop it. You sound like a raving lunatic." Abbicus Brown got to his feet. "And if you're not willing to drop this-" he fixed Oliver's gaze, "-I have the power to withhold your team's keys from you."

Oliver's next words caught in his throat.

"We won keys?" May breathed in shock.

Abbicus's gaze roamed over them. "Yes, by some mad luck your team still placed tenth. The three hour time limit ran out during the vark's attack."

"And you'll give us our keys if we keep quiet?" May asked in shock.

"That's blackmail," Oliver spat.

"If you want to put it that way, yes," Abbicus said, looking back and forth between the two of them as he assessed their reaction.

"Can I talk to my sister alone?" Oliver asked, not bothering to do so politely.

"Of course. I'll wait outside." Abbicus walked around them and turned back before he left. "Just remember, I won't offer you this deal again," he said then exited the room.

"What do you think?" May asked.

"We have to take it. We don't have a choice. You have to get to Brinatin as soon as possible."

"I know," she said sadly. "It just seems so *wrong*. Truvian's gonna get away with what he did to us."

Oliver fell into a thoughtful silence which was broken by the emergence of his friends in the doorway.

"Sorry, we couldn't wait," Anna said anxiously. "What did he say?"

Oliver looked at their concerned faces. "Abbicus said he'll confiscate our keys unless we agree to keep quiet about Truvian."

"We won keys?" Anna asked in disbelief.

Oliver nodded.

They all gazed back at him in surprise then Rogan said, "Why would he want to cover it up?"

"He doesn't believe it even happened," May said furiously. "Truvian was commentating on stage at the same time he was attacking us so he has about a thousand witnesses to prove he didn't do it."

"How did he manage that?" Quinn asked, her voice was hoarse and her lips looked pale. Oliver wondered why her magic hadn't helped heal her yet.

"He must have a mage helping him," Anna said.

May nodded, pushing a strand of hair behind her ear. "I reckon the Truvian on stage was a fake."

"No, it's unheard of. A mage would have to be constantly using magic to keep themselves looking like someone else. It's impossible," Rogan said dismissively.

Quinn nodded her agreement.

"But how else do you explain it then?" Oliver asked.

Rogan shook his head. "I dunno. It just, can't be that."

"Did Truvian say anything, like why he wanted May dead?" Anna asked.

"Truvian said Rimori sent him," Oliver revealed. "But he didn't say why just that May's death was important somehow."

"Oh, Vale, do you think he was being serious?" Anna asked, looking frightened.

"Why would he lie?" Oliver asked rhetorically. "He also said Rimori sent that vark as a distraction."

"*How?*" Rogan asked in disbelief. "Varks can't be controlled."

"Maybe they can. It's not the first vark that's shown up since we've been in Aleva." Oliver proceeded to fill them in about the vark that had attacked them in the pod tunnel. "Truvian suggested Rimori had sent that one too."

"Varks are seriously rare. There's only been a handful recorded in the last century. What are the chances of two turning up where you two are, *twice?*" Anna asked, gesturing at Oliver and May.

"It's unheard of," Rogan said, running a hand through his hair.

"That one that attacked us," Quinn chipped in. "I think it was a hunting vark. Only a couple of drawings exist to record their appearances. I saw them at university."

"So, you reckon Truvian was telling the truth?" May asked the group.

"It's the most likely answer, which suggests he was telling the truth about everything else," Rogan said ominously.

Oliver attempted to swallow the lump that had formed in his throat as he decided to reveal the final piece of information. "He said my father's still alive."

"What?" Anna said, her eyebrows raising in alarm.

"You're kidding?" Rogan exclaimed.

"Nope. Do you reckon he was telling the truth about that too?" Oliver almost felt hopeful then a flood of guilt consumed the emotion. From what he knew about his father, he wasn't someone he wanted to associate with.

No one answered but Oliver could guess what they thought. "We better go tell Abbicus we accept his offer." He sighed and walked out of the room.

They returned to the garden where Ely and Abbicus were talking. "TICK TOCK!" Abbicus shouted at them across the lawn.

Ely walked over to join them. "That sorry excuse for a man just filled me in on his *deal*," he said angrily, huffing his frustration. "I'm sorry to say that I must insist that you take it." He looked at May. "We need to get to Brinatin as soon as we can."

"We're going to agree. It's just so, *wrong*," May said, throwing a look of distaste at Abbicus.

"I know, but we don't have a choice." Ely said with a sad look. He walked back towards Abbicus and they followed.

Rogan slid his arm around Quinn as they walked across the grass and green light emitted from his hand as he pressed it against her side. She stood up straighter, the pain having eased.

"We accept your offer." Oliver stepped toward Abbicus.

"Good. I look forward to seeing you all at the key presentation ceremony this afternoon, then. It'll be held up at the Gateway so if you want to go through to Glacio today you better bring your things." The large man turned on his heel, waddled out of the garden and headed off down the path.

Anna walked slowly after him. "I'm going to go see my parents. They're down in the village. I'll come back later," she said and waved goodbye to them.

Oliver sensed that she wasn't happy but didn't know why. He watched the back of her head as she disappeared down the lane.

"Where's Laura?" Oliver asked Ely, wanting to say goodbye to her.

"She's up at the Gateway. You'll see her this afternoon at the ceremony," Ely said.

"I think we better go down and see our families, too. Quinn's not feeling too good," Rogan said, squeezing her arm.

"Okay, do you wanna meet here later before we go up?" Oliver asked.

"Yeah, I'll be alright in a bit I just need a rest," Quinn said with another wince. Rogan supported her as they headed after Anna down into the village.

Oliver and May followed their grandfather inside and sat in armchairs in the tiny lounge. Ely made them each a huge mug of Glacian tea and Oliver accepted his gladly, resting his head back in the chair as he sipped at the sweet liquid, soothing his anxiety.

* * *

Ely had bought them a brand new backpack each filled with thick, fur-lined clothes for their time in Glacio. There was space inside for their other things which Ely had brought from The Ganderfield Hotel back in Crome.

"Thank you for the clothes. And, well, just everything you've done for us," Oliver said.

May nodded next to him and gave him a hug.

"Not a problem," Ely said cheerfully. "As you might have guessed by the clothes I bought you, Glacio is pretty darn cold. You can put your snow boots on when we go through, they won't be comfortable for walking up the mountain."

A knock on the door announced their friends' arrival. Oliver and May shouldered their packs, following suit with Ely, whose large bag was almost the size of him. The weight didn't seem to affect him somehow as he walked forward with ease. Oliver suspected he was using magic to assist him.

Rogan and Quinn were waiting at the door with their own packs on their shoulders. Quinn seemed brighter after a morning's rest and even pulled him and May into a hug.

They walked out into the garden and found Anna leaning on the gate, her eyes were red and puffy. "I can't go," she said. "My parents insisted I wait until I'm eighteen before I'm allowed to go to Glacio. That's almost *two* years."

"It's okay, Anna, we'll see you again soon," May said, drawing her into a hug. Rogan followed suit then Oliver felt suddenly awkward as the others looked at him expectantly. Anna didn't meet his eye.

Rogan cleared his throat. "We'll go ahead," he said with a meaningful look at May and Quinn. Ely locked up the door and

Rogan quickly engaged him in conversation as the group began walking up the incline towards the forest.

Anna looked up at Oliver finally and his heart skipped a beat. He never usually found it difficult to talk to her but his vocabulary was suddenly void of words. Thankfully, she spoke first.

"I'm so glad we got keys, for May's sake," she said.

He nodded and his words returned. "Me too," he said with a sigh, feeling relieved.

"Will you come back to Aleva? After you get May help in Brinatin?" Anna asked after a moment. She was still hovering by the fence, a few feet separating them.

"Yeah, course." Oliver took a step forward.

"You'd better," she said with a playful grin.

He couldn't help himself. He walked over to her and pulled her into a hug, resting his chin on her head. She pressed her face into his shoulder and he felt wet tears seep through his shirt. He pushed her back a little and she looked up at him.

"It's okay, we'll be back in no time," he said, wiping a tear away with his thumb.

She looked down. "I know. I'm just being silly."

"Come on, let's go up to the Gateway. We don't have to say goodbye just yet," Oliver said, stepping away from her and taking her hand in his. He led her up the mountain trail, walking slowly to enjoy their time alone.

He didn't let himself think about not being around her and suppressed the twisting, sinking feeling in his gut as he gripped Anna's hand tighter.

32

The Hard Way

They were huffing and puffing by the time they reached the top of the mountain. A clearing opened up where a large crowd had formed. Towering over them all, was the Gateway.

It was completely different to the one back at Oakway Manor. Oliver recognised it from the opening ceremony but it was much more impressive in real life. An enormous tree had grown out of the ground, bent back over and planted the top of itself into the earth. Moss covered it in parts and the glistening keys were embedded in its bark.

A stage had been erected in front of it and he saw Laura amongst the Race Committee who were sitting to one side of it on a row of chairs.

He spotted his friends waiting for them at the edge of the clearing. His and Anna's hands unclasped as they rejoined them and he instantly missed the closeness. Ely took their packs and disappeared into the crowd to find a seat.

The teams that had won the race the day before were sitting in rows of chairs beside the Gateway, facing the crowd. Team Visikin was amongst them and a row behind them were in place for Oliver's team. They moved through the crowd and took their seats behind Larkin and his teammates.

Oliver ended up sat behind Arrow and the creases of his bald head grimaced back at him. Larkin threw a glance at them over his shoulder but didn't say anything. Oliver spotted Larkin's parents, Chester and Delphine, in the crowd. Delphine wiggled her fingers at Larkin but he ignored her.

Rogan and Quinn waved at a group of people who were standing in a cordoned off area at to the side of the crowd. They sat in red velvet chairs, much more luxurious than those the majority of the crowd were sat in.

"Who's that?" Oliver asked Rogan.

"That's my mum and sister, Aliyah, with Quinn's parents," he said.

Before Oliver could ask more, Abbicus Brown appeared and took to the stage. "Welcome, ladies and gentlemen, to the key presentation ceremony. This season, the three teams in first, second and third place are: Teams Thrake, Zhoulin, and Thorn." He paused for a round of applause. "And I think you'll all agree that both teams Visikin and Pandalin deserve a special round of applause for coping with the dreadful and unforeseen circumstances with which they were faced."

The crowd cheered and clapped madly. Camera flashes went off in dozens as journalists focused their attention on their teams. Oliver blinked as lights swam before his eyes.

"So, without further ado, can I please have a huge round of applause for all ten winning teams of this season's Great Race of Aleva," he said, raising his ham-like hands into the air and smacking them together as the crowd applauded. "Now, please welcome to the stage, for the final time, the two people who have kept us on the edge of our seats throughout the race. They have brought you the highs and lows of our contestants' journeys and they are here this afternoon to present the keys to our winners." Oliver's heart dropped into his stomach. "Ray Falls and Truvian Gold everybody." Abbicus clapped as he backed off of the stage, allowing the two of them to step up.

May gripped Oliver's sleeve on one side of him and he felt Rogan's whole body tense on the other. Oliver hadn't even considered the possibility that Truvian would be at the ceremony. He felt his face heat up as the blood rose under his skin.

"Thank you, thank you. We have had a fantastic race this season. The teams have competed with incredible vigour and we have seen some really brilliant competition from all of this season's contestants," Ray Falls said.

"The unforeseen vark attack will be re-watched for years to come," Truvian Gold added, flashing a perfect set of teeth.

Oliver shuddered at the sight of him as the crowd cheered once more.

"Now, please welcome to the stage, this season's winners: Team Thrake," Ray Falls said, clapping along with the crowd.

Ray stood at one end of the stage and gave each team member a key whilst Truvian stood at the other end, shook their hands and placed a medal around their necks. The team descended from the stage and shook Abbicus's hand who was standing at the bottom of the steps next to the Race Committee.

The crowd continued to whoop and cheer as Team Zhoulin were called up, followed by Team Thorn. Once they had all been handed their respective medals, Gold, Silver, and Bronze, Truvian placed another set of medals on his arm that looked as though they were made of a lighter metal.

Oliver cursed inwardly, he had hoped Truvian wouldn't have to place a medal on them. He didn't want him touching May. Or him for that matter.

Ray Falls called the remaining teams up one by one until she reached the final two. "Team Viskin!"

They filed onto the stage and the crowd went wild as Larkin raised his medal up triumphantly and kissed it. Oliver realised that, no matter how much he disliked Larkin, it was nothing to how he felt about the man standing opposite him.

"Please welcome our final team tonight. With a special thanks to Quinn Thorn and Rogan Ganderfield who did a great job of fighting off the vark." The crowd cheered madly and Oliver stood up and followed Anna, Quinn then Rogan, up towards the stage.

His heart was beating so hard he could feel it thumping against his ribcage. He took the key from Ray Falls then walked slowly over to Truvian who was grinning broadly, though Oliver was sure he could sense a smugness behind it. Truvian leant forward and dropped the medal over Oliver's head.

Truvian paused next to his ear for a second and whispered, "I'm coming for her." He adjusted Oliver's shirt around the medal. "Your father sends his love." He beamed casually.

It took everything Oliver could muster not to punch the guy there and then. He wanted to shout out to the audience and tell them what a monster the man was. It pained him to bite his tongue and say nothing. Truvian was going to get away with everything he had done.

"I'm going to make you pay. You won't get within an inch of my sister," Oliver said through gritted teeth.

Truvian reached out and pulled May towards him by her arm. From behind, it must have looked like a friendly tug but he didn't break eye contact with Oliver as he did it, which made it all the more threatening. Oliver glowered at him as Truvian placed the medal around her neck. She recoiled from him with a disgusted look.

Oliver glanced towards Abbicus Brown who was chatting animatedly with someone in the crowd. No one was looking. No one noticed anything. Truvian released May and they descended the stairs. It was over.

Abbicus Brown shook their hands and Oliver pulled away from him as quickly as he could. The man furrowed his brow in confusion but didn't say anything. Oliver couldn't wait to be a whole world away from Truvian Gold.

Relief swelled in Oliver's chest as he joined his friends and Ely.

Abbicus made his way back to the stage and Truvian Gold and Ray Falls stepped aside. "Now, I'd like to thank you all for attending this season's race. Those of you who have received keys please line up to get them encoded by our Gateway Keeper, Rex Haven." He gestured to a thin, bald man who waved them over.

The teams lined up, allowing the mage to prick their finger and use magic to bind the keys to their respective owners. Oliver shuffled up to the man who was sat behind an ancient looking table that looked as though it had grown from the ground. Beyond him, Oliver noticed a cosy-looking cottage nestled amongst the trees which must have been the Keeper's home.

Oliver held out his hand as he approached him.

"Name?" Rex Haven asked.

"Oliver Knight."

The man jotted it down in a large, leather-bound book then took Oliver's hand. He repeated the process that Ely had used when he had been given his first keys. The blood from his finger turned the tiny, spherical key to the colour of ice. It shimmered in the light like sun on snow. He retrieved the Lock from around his neck and placed the key in the clasp marked *Glacio*.

"Next," Rex Haven called, and Oliver moved aside to allow May access.

Oliver returned to join Ely who had found Laura amongst the crowd.

"How are you feeling?" Laura asked him.

"Much better thanks." Oliver smiled at her.

"Are you ready to go?" Ely asked.

"Yeah. I just want to say goodbye to Anna," he said, glancing over at her as a knot tightened in his chest.

"Of course," Ely said, following his gaze.

"You'll see her again when all of this is over, you know?" Laura said with a smile. "And you better come visit me on your way back too." She folded her arms.

"Definitely," Oliver said, grinning at her then sighed. "We have to focus on getting May to Brinatin now."

"Yes, that's the main thing," Ely said.

"What's the challenge in Glacio like?" Oliver asked.

"It's relatively simple," he said vaguely. "It won't take long to complete so we should be passing into Brinatin within a couple of days. The challenge is held in the Palace of Galice. Just wait until you see it."

"Sounds great," Oliver said, distracted. "I'll meet you by the Gateway in a minute."

Oliver walked over to his friends who had gathered together in a circle. May was hugging Anna goodbye and Oliver smiled at her over his sister's shoulder.

"Take care of yourself May," Anna said, releasing her.

"I'll be fine. I've got my idiot brother looking out for me," she said, laughing.

Rogan and Quinn took it turns to hug Anna goodbye.

Quinn pouted as she stepped away from Anna. "I could talk to your parents if you want?" She raised an eyebrow and Anna laughed.

"I don't think even you could take on my mum," Anna said.

Quinn folded her arms but looked as though she were fighting a grin.

Rogan turned to Oliver and May. "We'll meet you at the Gateway in a sec. Just gonna say goodbye to our families," he said and walked off with Quinn.

May waved to Anna and went to join Ely.

Oliver opened his mouth to say something to Anna but, before he could, she rushed at him, pulling him into a tight hug. "You better look me up when you get back here."

Oliver laughed into her hair. "I will."

She pulled away, sliding her hands down his arms and taking hold of his wrists. She squeezed then let go and walked away, throwing a glance back at him as she joined her family.

Oliver walked towards the Gateway where his grandfather was standing with Laura, holding their bags out for them. Oliver shouldered his pack and tugged Laura into a one-armed hug. When he pulled away she waved her hands under her eyes, trying to dry the tears that had collected there.

"Are you alright?" May asked.

"It's just been so good to spend time with you at last," Laura said with a sniff.

"We'll be back in no time," Ely said brightly, pulling his daughter into a hug.

Laura bent over and kissed his cheek. "See you Dad," she said.

The equipment for the ceremony was being packed away around them and someone had already dismantled the stage, leaving a clear entrance to the Gateway.

Larkin stood talking to Chester and Delphine, seemingly saying their own goodbyes. Oliver felt a pang of annoyance that Larkin would be going to Glacio too. Arrow joined Larkin a moment later, waving to his family as they walked together towards the Gateway.

"Great," Oliver muttered to May.

"What?" she said, clearly breaking out of a daydream.

He nodded to the two boys. "They're going to Glacio too."

May frowned and looked at them. Larkin and Arrow held out their Locks and the centre of the Gateway came to life with a shimmering, milky light.

Larkin stepped forward. He was almost knocked over as a huge man stepped through from the other side. He was dressed in dark armour with a gun-like weapon holstered on his hip, a canister attached to it glistened red.

"Oi!" Larkin barked, stumbling backwards.

"This Gateway will be closed until further notice by order of the Queen of Galice," the soldier said.

"What do you mean?" Abbicus Brown appeared.

"The Queen's son, Prince Kile, has been kidnapped. And, until he is returned, no one is allowed in or out of Glacio."

"This is preposterous. You can't close the Gateway without giving notice," Abbicus snapped.

"Please step away, sir," the soldier said. "A guard will be positioned here for the foreseeable future. Any person to step through this Gateway will be arrested."

"But we must get through, it is a matter of urgency!" Ely rushed over in a panic.

Oliver's eyes darted back and forth between the soldier and Ely.

The tall soldier looked down his long nose at Oliver's tiny grandfather. "Step away from the Gateway, sir," he growled, baring teeth like a wild animal.

Oliver stepped forward. "We have to go through. Can't you make an exception?" he said angrily, unable to help himself.

The soldier glanced at him then folded his arms and took a step backwards so he was firmly planted in front of the Gateway. "No."

"But it's an emergency!" Oliver snapped, overly aware of Larkin and Arrow listening to him.

"You have to let us through," May pressed.

"Oh, I have to, do I?" the soldier snarled, touching the weapon at his hip threateningly.

"Come on. Come away," Ely said, gripping their arms.

Oliver grimaced at the solider but let Ely pull him away.

"We have to get through the Gateway, we have no choice," Ely whispered to them, looking hard at May.

"Maybe the bond on me will hold for longer than you thought?" May suggested hopefully.

"We can't risk it," Ely said, shaking his head. "We *have* to get through." A wild look entered his eyes.

The crowd was disappearing as they filed away down the pathway, chattering excitedly about the soldier. Only a few people were left in the clearing and Anna lingered amongst those remaining, her family heading down the path.

Rogan and Quinn joined Oliver and the others, frowning.

Ely flexed his hands. "When the way is clear, go through the Gateway."

"*What*?" Oliver asked in shock.

"Ely, *no*," Rogan warned.

"We don't have time to argue," Ely snapped. "You two can do what you like but we're going," he said to Rogan and Quinn.

Oliver glanced doubtfully at the soldier then back at his grandfather. "Ely-"

"Do you want to save your sister or not?" Ely hissed.

Oliver went quiet. He would do whatever it would take. He nodded.

May stayed silent, gazing at the Gateway as if it held all hope beyond it.

Anna came over. "What's going on?"

No one answered.

"We can't," Quinn whispered to Rogan. "Our reputation-"

"That's not more important than May's life for Vale's sake," Rogan hissed at her.

"I didn't mean that, it's just, we *can't*." Quinn looked at him desperately.

The clearing was empty but for their group, Larkin and Arrow.

Ely made his move. A force like wind appeared in his palm and he propelled it towards the soldier. The man cried out as the magic hit him, forcing him to the ground. The soldier reached for his gun, struggling against the force of the magic, and aimed it at them as they hurried towards the Gateway.

"ANNA. GO!" Oliver shouted, not wanting her to get caught up in their plan.

She hesitated, standing frozen between him and the soldier.

Larkin slipped behind Oliver, holding his Lock aloft. The Gateway came back to life and he and Arrow charged through it.

"HALT!" the soldier roared from the ground.

Ely stepped backwards and the soldier fired. Everyone ducked the red beam that emitted from it but Anna glanced a blow on her head. Oliver lunged forward and caught her as she crumpled, unconscious. He adjusted her up into his arms, unsure what else to do, and ducked as he narrowly avoided another blast from the gun.

"You are arrested by order of the Queen of Galice!" the soldier shouted as he got to his feet, battling the wind-like force of magic that Ely was still propelling at him.

Oliver turned and ran towards the Gateway. His friends and Ely were already tumbling through the portal, glancing back to make sure he was following.

The Gateway consumed him and Anna. They were falling and falling into the abyss, travelling to Glacio: an unknown world of snow and ice.

Oliver was momentarily suspended within the portal, clutching Anna tightly to his chest. His stomach swooped in a rush of adrenalin and, for that brief moment, they had escaped.

EPILOGUE

Long Lost

William Knight travelled from Aleva with the assistance of the vark. Being able to bypass the Gateways was the only thing he appreciated about the presence of the creature. Kogure terrified him. It mainly spoke with Isaac but when it muttered inside his own head, his whole body turned to ice. He simply couldn't get used to it.

William paused before entering Isaac's bedroom. He had failed in killing the girl and so had Truvian. Now he and Isaac would have to reassess everything.

Anger boiled under his skin. He took a deep breath to calm himself then entered the room. Isaac was laying on his bed and sat up slowly as William entered. Isaac's face was pale and taught. He hadn't touched his food. William could sense Kogure in the room already and he shuddered.

"Kogure, leave us for a while. But don't go far," Isaac commanded and William was grateful. Isaac knew just how much William disliked speaking in front of it. He felt Kogure leave and felt as though a heavy weight had lifted from the room.

"The girl is still alive, Isaac, I'm sorry," William said, sitting at the foot of the bed.

Isaac coughed and William spied blood on his hand but his friend quickly wiped it away.

"How hard is it to kill a little girl?" Isaac growled.

"It's my son. He has become very attached to the girl. He protects her at the risk of his own life," William said, unable to help the swell of pride that filled his chest.

"He has inherited the devotion of his father." Isaac smiled at him, but then his body convulsed and he retched over the side of the bed into a large bowl.

William rushed forward and rubbed his back. "There may be a temporary cure to your suffering. I have, at great efforts, retrieved the original works of Dorian Ganderfield. They describe spells he used to cure himself of the pain. His death was put off for almost two years by the use of these enchantments. It would give us plenty of time to plan our attack on the girl more carefully. You wouldn't be cured but the pain would be manageable, with my help."

"Do whatever you can." Isaac lay his head back on the pillow with an exhale of breath.

William could see blue veins beneath his skin which had become almost translucent since the day he had met him at the Gateway to Vale.

"I will need time to prepare and learn the spells but I can ease the pain for the time being." William held his hand on Isaac's forehead. The skin was clammy beneath his palm. He sent healing, green light out towards him and heard his friend sigh with relief. When he pulled away, a hint of colour had returned to Isaac's cheeks and lips.

"Much better. Thank you, Will," Isaac said.

William smiled sadly at him. "I hate to see you like this."

Isaac reached out a hand and gripped his arm. When he spoke, there was a strength and passion in his voice that William hadn't heard since before Isaac entered Vale. "We *will* get through this together. If you return my strength to me we can continue with our plans. We already have so many recruits." A light burned in his grey eyes.

William couldn't help but smile. "You're right. You're much more popular than I expected. And when we reveal to them that I am, in fact, alive more people than ever will flock to us."

Isaac nodded. "Yes, even more so when we tell them how." He smiled, emphasising his high cheekbones. "In the meantime, have you spoken to her? Has she acquired it?"

William was glad he had one piece of good news to give him at least. He grinned. "Yes, she has it."

Isaac smiled a broad, handsome grin. He almost looked his old self again. "That is fantastic news. When will it be time to collect it?"

"Soon," he said. "Now, rest a while. I'll come and check on you shortly."

Isaac nodded and sunk further into his pillow. William exited the room and closed the door behind him with a *click*. He rested his head back against it and expelled a long breath.

He went downstairs, unlocked the door to the cellar and descended under the house. His weight made the stairs creak and he heard movement in the room below. An empty tray of food sat on the bottom step which he pushed aside with the toe of his shoe.

"You can't keep me here forever, Will."

"This won't be for much longer. I'm sorry." He walked over and embraced his wife. She wrapped her arms around his neck and kissed him.

"You can trust me," Alison said.

IF YOU ENJOYED CREEPING SHADOW...

Please take a moment to leave a rating and/or review on Amazon.

Every single review makes the world of difference to a self-published author like myself.

Thank you for your support :)

- Caroline

COMING SOON...

THE RISE OF ISAAC

BOOK TWO

BLEEDING SNOW

CAROLINE PECKHAM

ABOUT THE AUTHOR

Caroline Peckham graduated from the University of
Reading with a BSc in Zoology and now lives in a small,
rural town in Kent, England.
Her debut novel *Creeping Shadow* is the first in *The Rise
of Isaac* series.

Find out more about Caroline at
http://www.carolinepeckham.com

Cage of Lies
Book One

CHAINED

Terrified of the contamination and the creatures it has created, humanity hides behind The Wall. No one knows what lies beyond the wasteland. Maya has never thought much about what might still be out there, lurking in the forgotten places. But when she's thrust into the unknown, she is forced to question everything she has ever been told. Not everyone outside died, some of them became something... else. As her heart is torn in two, every choice she makes is harder than the last. What she discovers will change her forever. She knows she will probably die, but Maya has seen enough of death and she won't let it have her without a fight.

Find out more at:

Http://www.susannevalenti.com

Made in the USA
Coppell, TX
13 October 2022

84603746R00252